Books by Stephen Minot

GHOST IMAGES 1979

CROSSINGS 1975

THREE GENRES 1965

CHILL OF DUSK 1964

Surviving the Flood

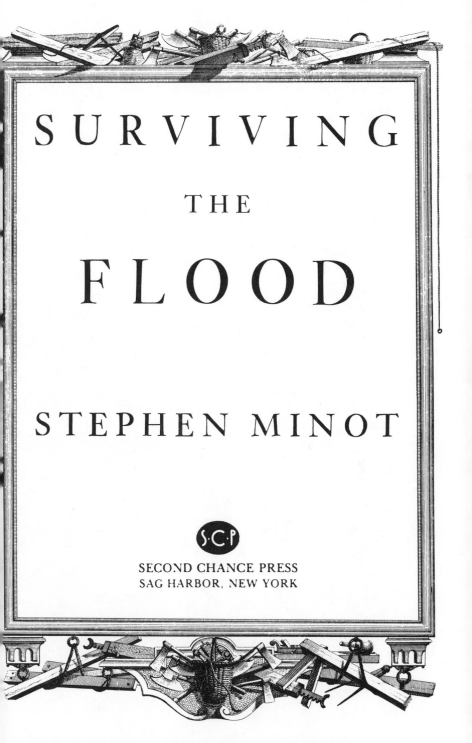

SURVIVING

THE

FLOOD

STEPHEN MINOT

S·C·P

SECOND CHANCE PRESS
SAG HARBOR, NEW YORK

Illustrations on pages 9, 119, 181, 231, and 241 are courtesy of The Bettmann Archive, and illustrations on pages 54, 261, 289, and 298 are courtesy of The New York Public Library.

Portions of this novel were published in *Ploughshares* (© 1979) and in *American Poetry Review.*

Library of Congress Cataloging in Publication Data

Minot, Stephen.
Surviving the flood.
1. Noah's ark—Fiction.   2. Deluge—Fiction.
I. Title.
PS3563.I475S9   1981   813.54   85·063551
ISBN 0·933256·62·0 (Cloth)   AACR2
0·933256·63·9 (Paper)

Originally published by Atheneum, 1981
First republication by Second Chance Press, 1986

For Ginny

Surviving the Flood

I

SWEEPING THE DECKS

ALREADY there are many who find our voyage hard to believe. Not surprising. We ourselves had little faith during the building. Imagine the sense of absurdity, laying down a keel as long as a temple out there in the dusty fields. Miles from the sea. Picture what it was like for a boy my age, eager to make friends, just beginning to notice the musk of girls, yet set to cutting planks all day in the heat of the sun, enduring the taunts of classmates.

I'd been uneasy from the start. I remember feeling a certain tension in the air the day our father announced that we would not work on the new temple with everyone else; no, we would work on a great wooden barge. The whole family. This during a drought, mind you, vineyards shriveling, the land turning to powder. I could tell then that we were in for some dark days.

Even my older brothers had their doubts as we got well into it. There was the night Shem and Japheth decided that the old man had lost possession of his mind, decided to finish walling up the sides of that crazy barge, roof it over, and then lock him in it, let him rave from there. Cage him like some wild leopard.

Toss meat in through the upper port. Protect the village; save the family name. We didn't have the nerve, of course; but just discussing it was dizzying. It was the kind of night a younger brother thinks he has come of age, has broken through into the stuff of adulthood. Not that I had. One never breaks through entirely, never leaves behind all trace of innocence. Even now, in my 900th year, I am still losing my virginity, grain by grain.

It got no easier when I was set to gathering the beasts and the birds and the rodents and all the rest, me and a gang of locals who helped for pay and for laughs. I'd had no proper training for it. Try putting camels, asses, wild dogs, geese, imported leopards, mice, pigs, serpents, vultures, desert weasels, and slugs in adjoining pens on the outskirts of town and figure out how to feed them, how to keep them from kicking out, gnawing out, climbing out, leaping out, flying out, slithering out, burrowing out; and then guarding against the town jokesters, wit brimming with wine, trying to loosen the cage doors, terrorizing the village with wild creatures—even at the time it was hard to believe.

For me though, the real start, the turning point, was later. It was when I had to sweep down the decks. I was the youngest son, not yet married despite what you may have read. I hadn't seen much of life. True, I'd been callused by the building and learned a thing or two about animal husbandry, but I had a long way to go before understanding the complexities of adulthood. That sweeping and scrubbing turned out to be a beginning for me—and for this account as well.

But first, an introduction. I am Ham, youngest brother of Shem and Japheth, youngest son of Noah—all dead now, each in his own way. Ham I am, youngest grandson of Lamech, youngest great-grandson of Methuselah. Youngest in my 900th year.

I swore I would never write my memoirs. I am no scholar. I rely on my reflective nature and an old man's memory. I have no causes to defend. I leave those to my sons and grandsons, those leaders of men, founders of cities and fortunes, shapers of history. Me, I have tended my vineyards in rocky lands and have kept to myself. Even now, returned of necessity to the city, cared for by descendants, I am concerned only with the events.

Simply a witness. Yes, I was there, I lived through it; but the whole flood affair is far behind us, an old and fading crisis drifting back into history along with its veterans, subject to doubt already and all the tired jokes of sceptics.

We were a year in the building, a dry time beyond memory. We used to dream of cooling rain. But it wasn't much better when the weather finally did turn. A few days of novelty, and then we came to detest that steady drizzle. Two months of it, slogging about in the wet, caught between relief and fear every time the sun broke through, imagining what it would be like if the skies cleared again for good, leaving our edifice as a world-renowned joke, our father forced to sell tickets to pay off the workers, conduct tours, wear a silly hat.

No, not until at last the waters rose in the streets, not until townspeople, our neighbors and friends, began piling possessions and their aging relatives on the roofs did we begin to breathe easy.

A terrible sight, of course—the water, dark and putrid, running through the town, chickens, lambs, and dogs swirling toward death. Alarming. But exhilarating. With that same swift current we felt respect for our father come flooding back.

You should have seen him that day—seized with a drunken energy without so much as a drop of wine, made young and lusty again for all his 600 years. We doing the brute work, of course, escorting the last of the beasts from the pens to the barge, trying to avoid the sullen stares of the villagers, violence poised in that dank and humid air; and all the while he was urging us on.

He was standing by the ramp, water swirling around the hem of his robe, hair and beard saturated, grinning and snorting like some great goat in rut. Shem led a donkey by and the old man's hand went *thwap!* on its rump. Japheth tugged at two baulking camels. *Thwap!* One beast kicked and the other nearly slid from the ramp. Our father whooped with glee.

And then proud Athaliah, Shem's wife, carrying a cage of finches, head high as if she were going to temple. *Thwap!* A puff of spray and a hand print on her rump. Down went the cage, a yelp from her. But he hardly noticed. He kicked at the roebucks, hollered at the fallow deer, pummeled the chamois, starting a stampede up the ramp, animals pounding the planks, squealing, defecating in panic, dividing left and right around Athaliah there on all fours, crouched over her up-turned cage of hysterical birds, her rear heavenward.

His attention swung to workmen struggling with a crate of snakes. She dragged herself up from the slimy planking and gestured toward his back, her palm out and five fingers spread, the obscene curse reserved for the crudest of men. Oh, I could see then it was going to be a lively cruise.

Luckily, our father missed the insolence. He saw nothing save his own success that day. There was no questioning that.

Those two months of drizzle were better for the townspeople than for us. For them it was a welcome relief to the drought, a confirmation of their decision to build a new temple; it was life as usual. No sign of danger. Lord did I tire of "Well, the fields need it," and "Wet enough for you?" No more of those now. It was a true deluge now. A true disaster. What a relief!

Whether it would ever be deep enough to float that great barge, I didn't know. It seemed doubtful to me. But not to the old man, our father. No, he knew it would float, knew the town would die. And nothing could have pleased him more. For a prophet of doom, only doom will suffice.

Perhaps the scoffers had goaded him more than we had realized. It had seemed for months that not a joke, not a taunt, not even the rebuff of the priests could reach his heart. Like the time when the Temple Elders barred him from the Sabbath Service, pointing to our great wooden edifice, suggesting that he had made *that* his temple. Not a word from our father. He merely turned, crossed the town square to our barge, climbed the ladders to the upper deck, and bellowed his prayers from there, his voice drifting across the town, a crosscurrent to the priest's own chanting. They didn't try that again.

And then the time the young wastrels lured him early one hot morning under the great cyprus which gives—gave—shade to our village square. They'd told him some story about having captured for him a wart hog and a mountain cat. A gesture of confidence, they said. But instead of live animals, they'd rigged

an ox-hide in the limbs of that great tree and filled it, bucket by bucket, with urine gathered over the course of weeks at our tavern. As soon as he stepped within range, down came the deluge, stinking and slimy, and the crowd screaming "Flood! Flood! Save us!" Then rolling in the dust, howling like gibbons in laughter.

Not a word of rage from our father—he who could curse the whole family for the length of a meal when an ant fell in his wine. No, not a word—though I expected at any moment to see arms, legs, and head fly in all directions from the pressure. But no, hold it in he did. And when the laughter died he said with deep solemnity, "Thank you, neighbors; you have given me the best portion of yourselves."

But now the rains were his, not theirs. The joke was his. Fair enough. No doubt it confirmed his sense of divine justice. In any case, his joy was unmistakable once the heavens made it clear that they meant business. Made it clear to *him*, that is. There was no question in his mind as soon as the waters had become knee-deep.

I, cursed by doubt from childhood, carried the last two boxes on, shaking my head, seeing that great barge not as a boat which would actually rise but more as a kind of fortress which would, at best, protect us against the rising waters from below, shelter us from the rage of heavens above. Oh, we'd seen floods from time to time; but never one deep enough to float a wooden palace.

I had the yoke across my back—the device with which we had carried buckets of pitch, two by two, for months. This time my cargo was two crates: on my right, a flock of spiders and on my left, a gaggle of filthy green slugs. Ungrateful and purpose-less creations, both. One could only imagine that the Great Yahweh had been practicing his creative talents, a rank begin-ner, turning out error after error before working toward his more meaningful creatures. And here I was, weighed down with two crates to house these errors—them and their food. Preserving them for what? To torment man for the rest of time? But tote I did, never really believing that the waters would rise beyond a height of one cubit at the most, doing my job as I had been ordered to, acting like some common servant as I, the youngest despite what some reports say, always had.

And could our father read thoughts? He cursed me as I plodded up the slippery gangplank, urging me on, chastising me for being late, for almost forgetting the two boxes, for almost leaving slugs and spiders to the rising waters. And was he cursing me also for my doubts?

"Run," he was saying. "Like the winds, boy. Quickly."

Quick, I thought, to save slugs and spiders?

A noise behind me—muffled in the rain, yet distinct—made me turn. Men and women stood there, dark waters up to their knees, some coughing, a child crying. They were speechless until I turned, but my motion, my hesitation sprung their minds, released them.

"And us?" one of them shouted.

"What right have you?"

"Why you?"

"We, your brothers."

First one by one, like drops, then a clutter of shouts, a deluge of protest. Arms raised. Fists clenched.

Me, standing there at the doorway, soaking wet, chilled, weighed down by my responsibility to slugs and spiders. What was I to say to questions like that? Somehow these issues had never been raised in our Sabbath classes.

Behind me, a great hand on my shoulder. "In or out?" my father roared in my ear. Not one for subtlety, he repeated himself, "In or out?"

I thought for a moment he was giving me a true choice, a moment of ethical awareness. Then I felt a tug—inward. I fell back, into the Ark and heard my brother shout, "Up the plank." In the confusion, I took this as an obscene oath—as he was wont to offer. But no, it was the gangplank he meant. Just as the crowd surged forward the winches whined, the chains ran taut, and the great walkway rose, groaning, spilling water and neighbors to left and right.

"Perfect," our father bellowed as the gangplank thundered into place, forming the door, wedged shut with cross planks and looking now like a continuation of the wall. "Look, look!" he commanded, peering up and down the crack, searching for a chink of light. Shem came down from the winch loft and slapped the door as if testing its strength, aping his father. "Workmanship. A perfect fit. Perfect!" He had to shout over what I first thought was rain beating against the outside hull but then realized was hands—hundreds of them.

The place smelled, of course. Little did we know what real stench could be like, but even then the wet fur, the unclean pens, the dung everywhere hit us hard. We fled up to the Main Deck, the one with the promenade, as if expecting the warm wash of sunlight.

Zillah, our father's mother, was there at the door with the rest of the family. She was shaking her head and muttering. I'd heard that she was once a beauty, the younger and more vivid of our late grandfather's two wives. She was known for her willfulness and her inclination to converse with spirits. Widowed now and bent with age, forced to lean on a staff like some ancient prophet, she had gone a bit strange—heard voices, saw fragments of past and future.

"It's a dark day," she said, her voice deep and throaty.

"Dark?" my father roared. "Dark, did you say? What do you expect with all this rain?"

"A dark day *for you*, I mean." She leaned on her staff and stared intently at her son. In such moments you could see the beauty she once was, see the past behind the ravages of the present. "They'll come back to you—all those faces out there. They'll come back to stay with you."

"No room."

"Plenty of room." She tapped her forehead. "Here."

"I'll not clutter my head the way you clutter yours, Mother."

"It'll all be there. The people. The town. Your old vineyards. Even their new temple."

We all shuddered. For over a year we had been careful not to mention the new temple. The very word set him off like an old war horse in need of exercise.

"Temple! *Temple* did you say? That pile of dung-bricks? Do you think that's what He wants? Do you?"

He seized his mother by the arm just as he had seized me. He was forever grabbing, clutching, grasping, shaking his listeners. Words were never enough. Finger to the chest, hand to the shoulder, a fist full of garment—the man argued the way lesser men rape.

Cries of protest. Even brother Shem put out his hand to restrain his father. He was brushed off like a cur. "Come. Look," our father said, dragging his mother out into the rain, that lean old crane of a woman slipping on the wet deck. "See that pile of brick and clay?"

Zillah nodded. What else could a captive do? We all looked. When our father said Look, you looked. You couldn't *not* look. And indeed, the waters were swirling in through the windows and out through the hole which was once the door. The altar must have been covered. Soon the clay would dissolve, the tile roof would collapse. For over a year they had been hard at it, starting when we had, way back before rains. It was the drought that had us worried then. The priests thought they could end it with a new temple and for a while it seemed as if they had the answer. Their faith was never higher than when those drizzly months began. But the wet never stopped. Now all their labors and their faith were sliding away into the waters, about to be lost even to history. It's a slippery business, guessing divine pleasure.

"Turning to slime. To slime," he roared. "While we are lifted.

Raised up. Who has answered the Holy Word? Who?" She must have been off on one of her reveries for she did not answer. "Who?" our father kept bellowing, "Who?"

"For God's-sake, *you*," I said.

"Right. Right!" So relieved was he to hear the answer to his question that he did not catch my profanity. On any other occasion it would have cost me a clout across the mouth.

My Uncle Tubal shouldered his way through the throng at the door and confronted his only brother in a way no one else could. He was a blacksmith and ironmonger, a man not gifted with subtleties, but strong on certain homey values.

"What's this, dragging Mother out here in the rain? Killing her too? It's not enough drowning the town, you have to kill your mother as well?"

He grabbed Zillah by the other arm and tried to wrench her from our father's grasp. She swung first one way and then the other like an old birch in a gale. I was sure she would snap.

Tubal's brute strength finally won and he dragged his mother to the doorway, a bear with his kill. But she was not one to remain passive. She twisted out of Tubal's grasp and turned to her other son, shouting over the winds, "Tried to kill me in your birth, you did; a beast in the womb and a beast in life. But I'll not let you treat me like one of your wretched animals. Not while I breathe. And breathe I will, come flood or a son gone wild."

Our father raised one arm to Heaven, bearing witness to the terrible injustice of his mother's charges, beating his chest with the other hand. "Lord, Lord, have you ever lived with the likes of that?"

"Impiety! Blasphemy!"—his mother at the door. "The Yahweh has no mother. Would that I had no son!"

"Must I save the vipers of this world as well?"

And from Heaven, fresh torrents and the crack of thunder, one more voice in the discussion.

The door slammed, leaving me and my father out there. We had all grown accustomed to the drizzle of two months, but this was something new: rains sweeping in on us in great gray curtains. You could hardly breathe. From where the two of us stood on that promenade deck, we could not see bow nor stern.

What on earth was I doing out there? Chance placed me there and it seemed unlikely that I could join the others until my father released me. They were probably toweling themselves down already, comparing notes. Strange that I should be the one stuck out there with him, we who had nothing in common but a kinship—and even that not exactly my choice.

He seemed to be having trouble letting go of his anger, still standing there, still gesturing, face to the heavens, still defending himself against his mother's accusations, protesting his fate, arms flailing as if the Great Yahweh was a reader of semaphore.

I stood there explaining to him under my breath that this was not the best time or place for a dialogue with the Deity when with horror I saw a hand appear on the railing. A white hand. A corpse, I thought. A spirit. From the Underworld. I tell you, that day anything could have happened.

A second hand. An arm. Then a terrible face. "Save us, it shouted. Perhaps not in words; perhaps just in the eyes. "Save us."

I stared, open-mouthed. Pointed. Our father turned just as the creature spoke.

"It's me, Asahel," it said, this time in words. "Your friend, Asahel."

"Off," my father bellowed.

"Your drinking friend, Asahel. It's me."

"No room for friends. I have no friends today."

"I'm of your line. Methuselah's lineage."

"No lineage. Not today."

"In the name of Yahweh."

"He put me here, you there."

Our father lunged for a locker on deck, for a tool to strike the intruder. I could hardly see him in the rains; but being close to the railing, I saw something else—more hands, more arms. Some big. More often small. A woman here, a child there. They were clinging to the railing, hanging there.

How? We were too high from the ground. They were appearing as they might in a dream. More every moment. I dashed to the side. There in the swirling water was a great multitude—chest deep now, shouting, swearing, pummeling our Ark with oaths. Close to the hull, some men had boosted their wives to their shoulders, a child to her shoulders, human columns, swaying. Only the third or fourth could maintain a tenuous hold on our gunwale. The planking was wet. They could get no further without help.

At the deep end, the bottom men stood in water up to their necks. They had to raise their heads to keep their noses above the filthy water. They had only minutes left. And in those remaining minutes, they were calling out to us. No doubt they would have lived longer if they had not chosen to boost the others up, but who was I to argue?

My instinct was to reach out, to grasp hands and arms, to pull them upward, saving them. My muscles ached, pulling toward them.

But which? Were we to take friends and not acquaintances? Were we to take the whole village but not the next? The whole world and sink our salvation?

My mind locked; my eyes shut like a mule pushed beyond its limit. Even with lids closed tight I could not erase the vision of those hands, those arms, those fingers clinging to the wet gunwale.

A great shudder. A rush of water from the rising river, we surmised later. At the time I knew only that the Ark had at last come to life. Awkward, ungainly, like a sleeping camel lurching to all fours, ass first, grunting, surly. No sense of grace. The craft lifted, caught, lifted again, swung in the currents. We were free. And free from the terrible entreaties as well. No more pleading voices, no tormented eyes. I thanked God for that.

More surprising still, my father's hands were on my shoulders —not shaking, not demanding. Merely speaking to me, holding my attention.

"Remember this day," he said, his face inches from mine. "I tell you this, but repeat it to no one: I too have known doubt. Even I. But all doubt has been washed from me today. We have followed the Word. We were right."

Doubt? Him? An incredible confession. A flood of filial love rose in me—a new sensation.

"Now get the broom and sweep down the deck." So we were back to business. A relief. I could not have stood such intimacy for long. "Sweep the deck clean and feed the leopards."

I nodded eagerly—enthusiasm in that gesture making up for my lack of speech. Nod, nod. My father turned, I stood there nodding foolishly to the winds.

"The broom," he said, bellowing over his shoulder, ". . . in the tool box." I nodded. Nod, nod.

Then the oddity of it hit me. Sweep? In this storm? Feed the leopards? With what?

His form was almost lost in the mists now, but I could see him pause at the tool locker by the door and return his axe. *Axe!*

With a second jolt—worse than that of the Ark's first shuddering motion—I looked down the deck. Then I knew what I was to sweep. And what morsels I was to feed to the leopards before they spoiled.

"In or out," he had said at the gangplank. A simple choice, it seemed. Survive the flood or not. No, not so simple. Now, sweeping, gathering the bloody joints in piles, I was beginning to discover just how much my passage would cost.

II

ESTABLISHING ORDER

O R D E R . System. These were his first concerns. It never would have occurred to me, not at my age, but somehow he knew that these were what you set up at the start of any voyage.

"A family conference first thing tomorrow morning," he said. "Establish rules, assign tasks, announce schedules."

"Of course," my brother Shem said. Of course? How did *he* know? He was as new to this as any of us.

It was the end of the second day. We had just finished our dinner, the first full meal we had been served, the whole clan of us including my two brothers and their wives and children, our three uncles—everyone. We were all feeling rather pleased with ourselves. After all, the waters had indeed been deep enough to float the ship just as our father had predicted ("Naturally," Shem had said), the vessel was steady enough to withstand whatever waves there were out there ("What did you expect?"), and we were safe and dry, which was more than anyone else in town could say. As a family, we'd done all right.

"Sooner the better," Japheth said, finishing off another mug of wine. "Why not a meeting right now?" Round-faced, round-bellied Japheth, middle son, always happy to prolong a meal.

"I said tomorrow morning," my father said.

"I just meant while we were all here. And in good spirits."

Athaliah, Shem's wife, said "Ptuh!" It was a word used only by her. It was not a happy sound. Translated it meant something like Your-mind-has-turned-to-slop or Your-mother-had-piglets. "A fine meeting we'd have, swilling wine."

"Sister," he said, meaning sister-by-marriage, "we may be here two or three days. Unbend a bit." He raised his mug of wine in friendly salutation, but she'd have none of it.

"If you unbend any more, you'll spend your life on your belly like a slug."

"And you could take pleasure in stepping on me."

"Ptuh!"

The two of them were like milchik and flayshig; it was never easy having them at the same table. And now we were going to have them together for the duration.

"Ptuh!" Japheth said in perfect imitation—except that in his version it came with a spray of wine. I laughed—then swallowed my laugh, pretending to cough, seeing my father's expression.

"*Enough!*" he said. "No more of that. Think about where you are."

"Safe," Japheth said, his smile like the morning sun. "That's where we are."

"At sea," Father said. "*That's* where we are. Alone on the sea. We're the only ones left. There's nothing out there. Just water. We're the sole survivors. The inheritors."

Pause. Sober reflection. I was moved. I hadn't thought about our isolation, about how we were the only object afloat out there on a limitless expanse of water.

As far as we knew we were indeed the sole inheritors, and when I pictured our craft alone on the waters it became a far smaller object than it had been on land. A chip, really, and we were motes on that chip.

Such isolation was diminishing for a family used to being the most visible, the most powerful in town. And being diminished is unsettling. We all must have felt it.

"Alone," he said, repeating for stress. "The chosen of chosen. Selected for our piety."

Piety? Was he serious? I expected guffaws but heard none. I looked around the circle: not a hint of a smile. Not even from Japheth. We all sat there, serious, waiting for him to wrap it up. Which he did, neatly, gruffly: "So don't act like a pack of animals."

Marvelous how he could mention animals without smiling. We were right on top of them, so to speak. But he didn't smile and naturally we didn't. Especially me, the youngest. Silence all around, him nodding, agreeing with himself.

Staring at him, I felt ashamed of myself. This was serious stuff. He certainly had the power to quell—black eyes, bushy brows, great mat of a beard that had never been cut. The power that had swept us into building that crazy barge was enough to convince me that maybe we'd been chosen on merit after all.

It was partly his look and partly the way he spoke that swayed us all. Surely the voice is half of authority. It's the voice which creates visions for the inner eye, creates landscapes for the spirit to inhabit. In the beginning of any enterprise there is nothing but words; the one who is master of them and gives them shape and power is master over logic, over reason.

This is, of course, a grown man's view. I've had a few years to reflect. At the time I knew only that he had quelled the dog fight, had put us back in our places the way he used to when we were children. It was time, I knew, for him to switch moods, to play the kindly father.

"Take some pride in what we've done," he said, words as soft as a hand caressing the heads of puppies. "Did you see how the great door closed? Not a sliver of a crack."

"Work fit for a palace," Shem said.

"Palace it is," our mother said. "Twice as big as we need. With more animals than we can possibly use. Half of them unfit for eating. But the work is good. It turned out better than I expected." She was an astonishingly short woman—chin barely to the table level. Solid. But her voice was deep and strong. We always listened. "Not bad for amateurs."

"Amateurs?" Japheth said. "Craftsmen, you mean. All this by

the sweat of our brows. All of us."

True, he did tend to sweat a lot, but I don't remember his working for long. Recollections vary. "That main loading door —what a job! You couldn't slip a finch feather through there. Two weeks we spent on that, tools wet, clothing wet . . ." They were off on an old game—mutual astonishment at their craftsmanship, their newfound skills.

But there was another side to tight doors, tight bulkheads. We had sealed the world out, all right; but we'd also sealed ourselves in. Every opening bolted shut. While they were boasting about conquering the *out*, I sat silent, thinking about the *in*, my eyes searching the shadowy corners of that great torchlit room, feeling just a bit like a caged tomcat.

It was not a new feeling for me. Long before we plunged into the boatbuilding business I had been stricken with the need to break out. Of what? No Ark then, certainly, and no thought of it. But something much the same. An invisible hull with *us* inside and *them* out there. Not to say that it was all bad. The tribe protects its own. And ours prided itself in its loyalty. Not friendship; loyalty. That's how we had survived all those generations. There were times, though, when I found myself hammering on walls I could not see, times when I was almost ready to throw myself into invisible waters. Or visible.

"Look at that rib," Japheth was saying. He had lurched from his seat, stumbled to the wall, was rubbing his palm down the cedar beam, wine mug swinging like some counterweight in the other hand. "Feel it. Cedar made smooth as marble. *I* worked on that. *My* labor. Sweat of my brow."

We all nodded. We weren't going to take that away from him. Except for wine-tasting (he did have a good palate in those days) and procreation (one daughter so far), fat Japheth had few enough accomplishments to boast about.

"Hey, boy!" Father had spotted me, his youngest son, the dark one—by which they meant moody—as if for the first time. "Why the long face? We're dry, son. And afloat. There's millions of men and women out there who aren't. So cheer up."

I shrugged, grinned, fought an inclination to crawl under the table. I mean, there was no denying that I should have been happy—grateful to the Yahweh for his kindness, his loving benevolence.

Yes, we were safe, secure, afloat, and dry. Yet for all that, I didn't like it. Somehow it wasn't what I had expected. During all those months of building I never realized it would be this closed in, this dark. Roofs and walls complete, solid; loading door bolted shut. Even the two promenade doors locked. Strict orders to leave them so. Not so much as a quick look at the rage outside. So we had to supply our own light—the flickering pitch torches along the walls and the oil lamps, turning days and nights into a steady twilight of our own making. And a perpetual haze of smoke. This was no ship, it was a palace under siege. But who was our enemy?

That didn't bother them. Things that bothered me never bothered them. For them, the practical matter at hand was establishing order. System. A family council.

Family? I looked around the table. Eleven of them there—my parents, my two brothers and their wives, my Uncle Tubalcain the smith, those two half-uncles, Jabal and Jubal, and my grandfather's two surviving widows, Adah and Zillah. All there but my great-grandfather Methuselah, who lived in his own chambers on the deck above us. All there, but one would hardly guess that we were grains from the same stalk. Even those two half-uncles, brothers to each other, delivered from the same womb, linked by parentage and by the very sound of their names, even these, Jabal and Jubal, were as far from each other as rain is from sun. Jabal, the elder, was a stern and simple sheepherder, a tent dweller, a stark man whose mouth never bent into a smile and barely opened when he spoke. Jubal, the younger, played both lyre and pipe, could move a crowd to tears or to laughter merely by notes. A gentle, melodious man, lazy but in his musical arts, he was fed and housed like a child in return for his harmonies. Who could imagine those two springing from the same root?

Yet in spite of appearances, there was a bond we could not see, heavy threads woven into our earliest training. Almost before I knew my own name I was aware of my lineage—back through Methuselah, the living patriarch, back through succes-

GENESIS Chapter VII. Verse 22.

The UNIVERSAL DELUGE.

G. Bunter sculp.

sive patriarchs, back to Seth and then Adam himself. We were the central trunk from which branches were right then being torn away. A major pruning.

If I had any doubts about our special status, they were being swept out to sea in the tides. Hadn't we been selected for survival? Here we were, diverse in appearance but still afloat, still dry. Even with meat and wine.

We were the chosen of chosen. That much was clear. But why us? Everyone else seemed satisfied with my father's claim to piety and this was not exactly the time to question it. Not out loud. But I felt as if I were back at Sabbath School: the questions which were the most interesting were the ones we weren't supposed to ask.

I would have pursued this further, but my eyes were following a servant girl, a foreigner named Sapphira. She belonged to Shem and Athaliah so I'd seen her around, but now they had her serving at meals. "A decorative addition," Shem had said.

Barefoot like all servant girls, she was taller than most, straight-backed, head high, and with large, round, solemn eyes. Never had I seen that face smile. I stopped worrying about the mysterious source of good fortune and tried instead to imagine what a wondrous sight it would be if this girl's face were lit up with a smile.

I watched the way she walked, the way she poured, the way she deftly dodged the hands and arms which seemed to gravitate in her direction as she passed. Then I saw my mother's eyes watching me, peering up at me from across the table. She was more observant than her husband, always taking care of details. Her glance was tipped with fire. I returned to the voices around me with exaggerated interest.

They were discussing who had the best cabins, complaining in subtle ways, wary of our father's wrath. A pointless exercise. None of us had a view anyway. And none of us would ever be able to persuade him to alter the room assignments. Not just the family, but every servant and every beast, bird, and crawling creature had its ordained place, its station. Our father had a mind for order.

We the family had all been assigned to a single deck. Well

above the waterline, it was the one surrounded by the promenade which I had cleaned up the day before. *Our Deck,* we came to call it, giving it a certain value. Above us there was only one small deck, the Top Deck, a well-appointed chamber reserved for the Ancient Methuselah, Patriarch of patriarchs, my paternal great-grandfather. He had turned 969 that spring and didn't come down for meals.

The only time I saw him was when he was carried to temple for feast days, attended by a silent old manservant who must have been almost as old. Methuselah seemed to me more like a ritual object than a human being. Still, his was the Top Deck, the highest chamber, first class.

We were under him and under us were the servants. The Servants' Deck contained their quarters, the kitchens, storage rooms, wine keep, carpenter's shop, and the rest. Through their wall had been cut the large loading door, but now it was closed, spiked, and swollen into place for the duration. Just above the waves, it was built strong as a fortress wall.

Below the servants were the two animal decks. First the clean beasts—the oxen, deer, sheep, roebucks, and our two leopards imported at great expense from foreign parts. No, there were no elephants. What a preposterous idea!

At the very bottom, dank with leakage, poorly lit, reeking, yet warm and somehow inviting in its musky isolation, was the deck of the unclean animals. Don't ask me how they won that unkind designation. I once asked in Sabbath School and they fell back on It-is-written. Those priests used to get my goat, but they weren't around any more. In any case, that was where we kept the two irascible camels, the hares, and the aviary filled with such inedibles as the vultures, eagles, ospreys, kites, hawks, storks, and seven ugly bats. And in the stern, the swine. We were supposed to have only two of them, the creatures being totally taboo for the likes of us, but the sow gave birth while we were waiting for the rains and I couldn't bring myself to break up the family.

"Space!" Athaliah was saying, her voice humming with pent-up indignation. "We'd have plenty of cabin space if it weren't for all those stinking casks. A floating winery, this is."

"Barely enough for survival," Japheth said.

"Survival! One jug for ritual use is all we need for survival. One small jug. But I watched them rolling on casks for half a day. And each was the weight of the wardrobe I was told to leave behind. 'Just essentials,' I was told. 'Just essentials.' So I left my wardrobe behind—all my pretty things snatched by looting villagers, worn by riffraff parading in the streets, dragged in the mud, while you were rolling on more kegs each of which weighed as much . . ."

". . . as a man," I said. Sudden silence. "Or two children," I added, my voice growing hesitant, confidence withering. They looked at me as if I had uttered some profanity, then turned back to the subject at hand.

"Leave wine for the fishes?" Japheth cried. "Our vintage barrels?"

"Wine and you too!"

"Curse the grape and you curse the family."

"May your grapes shrivel and fall off."

Japheth heaved himself to his feet. "May your children have snouts."

She flung herself at him, clutching his robe with one hand and pummeling his stomach with the other. "Wine-bellied sot." Shem jumped from his seat and gave his wife a husbandly clout, defending his brother. Our father was up with a roar, wrenched the arm off his chair, swung it hard left and right, treating them all like camels in rut. It was a wonder to see him take command.

III

EXPLORING THE LOWER DEPTHS

MIDST all this shouting, I spotted the girl, Sapphira, standing by the wall, wine flask in hand, mouth open in utter astonishment. No doubt she had never seen Noah's family exchanging views.

I left my seat just as the table overturned, spilling dishes and wine mugs with a roar, and went to her. But what to say? Oh I had done my share of spying on girls, had got a grip on one a couple of times in the back room after lessons, but I was not the master my brother Shem was. Indeed, beyond the close study of goats, I had no clear idea just what one was supposed to do after the giggling. Still, it seemed right to go to her and assure her that this was not at all unusual in our tribe and she'd better get used to it if she planned to stick around for the entire trip.

She backed off from me, but that was no problem. I'd spent the past month rounding up skittish deer and sheep and all, returning them to the pens when they'd been released by local jokesters. I just put out both arms straight, one on each side of her, and placed my palms against the wall behind her, caging her.

I grinned, feeling rather accomplished. But what to say? All that experience with beasts gave me no practice with words.

An awkward pause. Fortunately a jug hit the wall beside us, shattered, and gave me my opening. "Don't worry," I said, smiling with what I assumed was the look of confidence. "I'll protect you."

"They've gone mad," she said. She spoke with the lovely accent of southern tribes—non-believers.

"No, in our language we say they *are* mad, not gone mad."

"That's different?"

"Oh completely. When you *are* mad—angry—you don't have to be locked up. It passes."

"Why aren't *you* mad?"

That startled me. Why wasn't I? Once again the old feeling of being a member yet not a member—was this right or wrong? "Because I wanted to talk to you," I said, ducking the issue, recalling my brothers' descriptions of what men said to women. "I like you."

"Why?"

That wasn't fair. I didn't have a ready answer. So I went back a notch. "You wait," I said, "they'll be settling down in a moment. Once they catch their breath, they'll be talking about the vines just as if they weren't all under water by now. The vines and the good old days."

"Why did you want to talk with me?" she said. I was beginning to find out, but it was hardly something I could utter aloud. We were standing so close that I could smell the musk of her body. It wasn't like that of a goat or a sheep, I can tell you.

I was wrong about the family quieting down. Instead of a lull, the storm suddenly redoubled—a deafening turmoil.

"Pig!" someone shouted, almost a squeal.

"Swine!"

This was no longer a simple family dispute. Those were terrible oaths. I'd only heard them uttered aloud a couple of times in my life—most recently at that unpleasant moment of closing the hatchway against the villagers. Clearly things were out of hand. Were my brothers at last at the point of fratricide? The blood of Cain surfacing?

I turned, pressing Sapphira behind me, instinctively protecting her against the impending slaughter. And then I saw it—a *real pig!*

A piglet, really. No bigger than a plump puppy. And fast—running right at Athaliah, dodging her kick, skuttling around the upturned table, darting out the other side, slamming into the wall, bouncing, heading for our mother, lunged at from all sides, disappearing in a forest of legs. The air was filled with shouting and shrieking, a flock of outraged birds.

"The girl," Shem was shouting. "Get the girl." He meant Sapphira. "Don't kill it!" He meant the pig.

This, the most unclean of all forbidden meats, we could not even touch when dead. Except Sapphira, being a foreigner; she could violate our ancient customs. Even deal with swine. "The girl," Shem kept shouting, though she was right there. Then to her, "Catch it. Quick now."

The creature spun about the room, lively as a white mouse, then shot out the door. Sapphira after it. And me after her. Down the dark corridor. Skidding to a stop at the end. Up the stairway—no other route. Hop, hop, hop. A fat furless rabbit with no ears. The two of us right up after it, she with her eye on the beast, me eyeing the flash of her calf, the curve of her ham. Shouts from below—"Quick now. Hurry!" Shouting to her, I suppose, urging her to make the capture before we woke the ancient Methuselah; but at the time I took their shouts a different way, as urging *me* on in a different quest.

Up there in the forbidden corridor, top deck, rain louder on the roof above us, wind moaning—a sudden stop. At the end, a door open. Silhouette of a thin, bent and bearded figure, the Ancient himself.

"Stop," he said, raising a staff. Yes, this was my father's grandfather himself, awesome in his 969 years. Even his rasping whisper was authority enough to stop stampeding camels. Our legs locked, all of us, pig as well. The little creature thrust all four feet out, skidding half the length of that hallway, then turned and for a moment scampered stationary, little feet treading like a desperate swimmer, scatch-scatch-scatch, until he picked up traction, then shot right between our legs like an arrow. The two of us, heavier by far, continued skidding on the polished planks, colliding with the Ancient himself, collapsing in a tangle of age and youth, the old one rasping hoarse insults so terrible we scarcely could interpret—"Raven-eaters, bat-lovers!" In the jumble of arms, feet, thighs, I pressed my hands over her ears, saving her innocence from what I knew by the tone would turn us to toads. She, on her part, pressed her mouth to mine, doubtless saving me from some manly retort, some defense, valiantly tangling her tongue with mine to prevent speech, the three of us writhing like snakes in a wine keg.

Then up, still grappling in the dusky light. I grabbed her arm —"Come," I shouted. But it was the old man's shoulder I was tugging at and I realized he was no heavier than a sheaf of wheat. We could have shaken him apart without knowing. I stood him up, dusted him off, stammered apologies. But he would have none of it. He backed off under his own power, leaning on his staff and the wall, and tottered toward his room muttering and wheezing.

All this time the girl remained on her knees, arms around my buttocks, covering her ears in the folds of my tunic, burying her face in my groin to avoid, I assumed, the vile curses from the old man.

"Come," I said again, pulling her up, tugging on the fabric of her bodice which, being servantswear, tore. My hands struggled to fit the pieces together, touched flesh, fumbled. But we could not linger; the chase was still on.

Down we went—corridor, stairway, across the next deck, curses fading behind us. The family was there, pointing.

"Down, down," they kept saying. So the creature had plunged down the stairway to the Servants' Deck. We were to pursue. It was all right with me. I was warming to the chase.

Down the stairway to the kitchens. Beautiful smells of breads, stews, spices. Sapphira leaping over benches and crocks, fleet as a fallow deer, nimble as a chamois, holding the fabric of her blouse together with the left hand as best she could—not too perfectly. A rush of warmth hit my cheeks—the ovens still heated so long after the meal? Around the kitchen table, cooks and servants joining us, some with staves, some with cleavers. "No killing," I shouted. There was something grand about all this running—a counter to our confinement, perhaps.

Quick as a darting kite, it plunged into the storage corridor and for a moment we almost had it, thrashing in a flour locker, a white ghost of a creature, the two of us throwing ourselves in the powder, sneezing, lunging for whatever bit of flesh we could see, clutching blindly at what turned out to be a thigh, a hip, a floured breast.

"Out here, out here," they were shouting as if the piglet were our main concern. Out we plunged, two specters, following a white path down the corridor, turning right through the servant girls' dormitory, a great flurry of shrieks as if we had broken into an aviary. Then down the stairway to the Clean-beast Deck, leaving human voices behind us. Here the pens, row on row, with the sound of hoof against plank, an occasional low and snort, the smell of mammals and burning pitch from the torches along the walls. Warm and humid.

Even here the white trail was clear—into the ox stall, out again, over the slats to the wild goats, out again—the poor creature was looking for his own level, his own pen, following his snout. He was not the enemy, we were not the hunters; we were all searchers for the right spot. Into the grain vault and out, under the straw pile and out again right under our feet, and down the final stairway down to where he had come from, down to the Unclean Deck.

Darker, warmer, steadier—for here we were well below the waters, below the pitch and rock of the upper decks. The musk was overpowering at first. Sensation of drowning. Air thick as pollen. We paused at the bottom step, panting, learning to breathe at these lower depths.

In the twilight here she let go the rent in her dress. It fell to where it was gathered at the waist. No doubt she assumed I could not see, though it wasn't *that* dark. Not a word from me —careful not to embarrass such a simple creature.

"Come," she said suddenly, and we ran down the length of that long, moist passageway, following the little creature, the two of us holding hands so as not to trip on bales of hay and piles of dung.

There in the stern, at the lowest level—intentionally so—the swine. Senseless, I had once thought, to build pens for tabooed creatures. If they were truly the misfits of creation, why had the Great Yahweh included them among the survivors?

We stopped, arms around each other, watching the piglet in his frantic joy, squealing at the scent and sounds of his own kind, hopping, hopping to pass over the gate, to enter the pen. The leap to safety was too great after so long a chase. A hysteria of squealing. You'd think he was about to drown.

Together we reached down and boosted him over the railing. He dashed to his siblings, rolling over with them, wriggling up to the great belly of his mother, nuzzling, trembling. A celebration, a tangle of love, and we were in the pen, down on our knees, romping with them, tickling, caressing, fingering, down in the musky straw, squealing and grunting at each other, bare as piglets, and then locked together, me on top and—the wonder of it—in her, tiny snouts tickling on all sides, wriggling bodies and running feet on my back.

"Oh Ham," she cried and looking down I saw, brighter than any pitch torch, the radiance of her smile and the two of us— ablaze—lit the lower depths.

N.° 5   STALLS for CATTLE.   N.° 6.

SECTION. N.° 4.

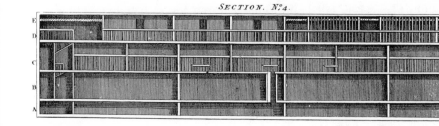

ELEVATION. N.° 3.

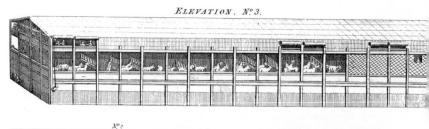

N.° 2

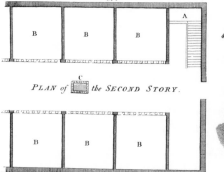

PLAN of the SECOND STORY.

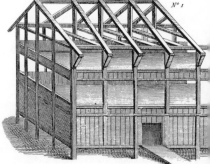

N.° 1

I V

TESTING THE RULES

BY the third day, we'd all begun our assigned tasks. I'd been paired with my brother Japheth, toting the buckets. Lord, how those rawhide handles cut our palms.

Japheth had the temerity to ask our father why this was necessary, since we were fortunate enough to have survived with our servants. The answer was terse: We were privileged to be alive and we would show our gratitude with good works. We were not to go slack. Such a policy may seem harsh these days, but it is not uncommon whenever there is a shared emergency.

Fond as I was of Japheth, I would not have chosen him as a work-mate. Normal motion was a challenge for him. Supporting that stomach was like carrying a dead calf for the length of the day. It hardly seemed fair to ask him to take his share of the bucket suspended between us. His side dragged along the floor leaving a wet trail.

The bucket was heavy even empty. Made of cedar—denser even than oak or gopher wood. Filled with water, it was the weight of a man. And filled it was—this and the next and the next.

The plain fact of the matter was that we were leaking. None of us expected it. We'd been blinded by our father's confidence. But I do recall hearing one of the shipwrights say to another that it took at least a week for a ship to swell, to tighten, and that any fool would have included some manner of pump as standard equipment. But he never passed this on to his employer. Perhaps even then he suspected that the workers would not be invited to share the fruits of their labors. They were receiving top pay, of course; but as the clouds gathered, some must have wondered if an employer's benevolence can be measured entirely by the wages he offers. In any case, that shipwright kept his mouth shut and so did I. Can you imagine advising a man whose blueprints have been drawn by the Creator Himself?

So leak we did—like any vessel built by mortals. That part's as clear in my memory as the more publicized details. It gives me no special satisfaction to counter what has been recorded. For centuries I kept quiet about the whole voyage. There was too much debate, too much conjecture, rumor, and dispute without my adding fuel. Besides, I had moved away, had planted my own vineyards, launched my own tribe. They did not invite me back to testify. An oversight, perhaps. Or perhaps not.

But now I hear I'm the last surviving witness. The rest have all departed, one by one. And judging by the street sounds outside our palace walls, my turn may come up next. Currents swirl and tides rise and fall even where there are no seas.

So I find myself writing as if one of my grandsons—Nimrod, for example—had said, How was it, Old Man? What was it really like? As wet as they say?

Not that he or anyone would actually ask. To do so would be to cast doubt on the Official Report, and God knows how sacred *that's* becoming. Even among freethinkers. No one wants to question the painstaking work of historical commissions, inquests, review boards, men who have done wonders to integrate the contradictory testimony of my famous father, my two brothers, my uncles, and a delegation of servants—whose very existence was then deleted.

So the Report has stood these years without benefit of my contribution. But whenever it is read there are whispered queries, muttered doubts, silent pauses in which the minds of the pious take great risks. Unuttered questions drop and disappear like spatters of rain in the hot sand—no one saying "Is that rain?" for fear that in the asking the answers will come too fast—first a squall, then a flood sweeping all before it.

Still, the questions are asked. Plunk, plunk. How is it that in one line the Deluge lasted but 40 days—long enough, I can assure you—but in others it is 150 days? A third verse raises it to seven months. No slight slip of the quill there. And how is it that the waters are described as a mere 15 cubits deep—the height of four men—and that this, they say, was enough to cover the mountains? The same report describes our barge as 30 cubits high. With such measurements we never would have been afloat. Even 15 cubits over the mountains (giving the Scribes the widest benefit), we would have snagged on a temple roof. How is it that I, proudly the third son, am listed only once as the youngest and the rest of the time as the middle son? Why refer to me as already married as if I were a grown and settled family man, an echo of my older brothers? More surprising, why did they delete the presence of my great-grandfather, Methuselah? He was, after all, our patriarch, and anyone who studies the given dates will see that he was aboard. And in the aftermath, how could this single family repopulate the world without violating our sacred prohibition against marrying first cousins?

No, that report will never do. Not for careful readers. This is not to underestimate the effort. All those commissions and review boards. They had their share of literary minds well trained in the demands of narrative form—the balance of scenes, consistency of character, the logical sequence of events, plausibility for its own sake. Lord knows they did their best.

But behind them were other forces—conceptions of how it should have been. "Men struggle," the ancient Methuselah whispered to me once, "no harder to control the future than they do to control the past."

Back then, though, right in the middle of it, our thoughts were not on literature. Our minds and bodies were fixed on bilge. Up it came from the lowest deck, part waters from the outside and part liquid from the inside. The leak we could have predicted if we had consulted the experts, but who could have guessed that animals would produce such a flood from their collective bladders? On land, dirt floors sop it up. But in a floating stable it gathers at the lowest level, contaminating the bilge. Bucket by bucket the stinking stuff had to be hauled up the stairs. It was hardly our fault, not anticipating all this; after all, we were novices, self-taught in the art of survival.

We worked blindly, our minds weighed down by the effort. The servants too. In fact, they must have taken the brunt of it. I heard no complaints, though. Perhaps a certain sense of gratitude sweetened their labors. Still, it couldn't have been easy. Those buckets had to be lugged up from the so-called Unclean Deck to the Clean-beasts Deck, then to the Servants' Deck, through the kitchens and up to our own level. Here the job was turned over to us.

They were to deposit each full bucket at the head of the stairs; Japheth and I were to carry it halfway down the corridor. Then, oddly, our father himself lifted it without help and carried it to the unlocked doorway out to the promenade, where he dumped it over the side.

He was a great one for systems, hierarchies of labor. We were used to that. But this particular arrangement placed the mule's share of the work on him. We weren't used to that. Surely there was no special skill to dumping buckets over the side. No skill and plenty of effort. It must have been a strain for a man just turned 600.

We got to mumbling about this, Japheth and I, keeping our voices low enough to be private.

"Why not the shafts?" I asked. "Why not use them?"

The shafts were where we relieved ourselves—two little squat-holes for men and an adjoining room for women. Another pair of rooms for the servants on the deck below.

"Too slow," Japheth said. "It would take forever to trickle these buckets down the shafts. Besides, this way he gets to breathe deep right there in the fresh air."

"He could do that any time," I said. "He's the one with the key."

"Doesn't want to be caught taking private privileges."

"Never worried him much before."

This made Japheth laugh, made him release what little weight he had, made the water slop down my leg. I wished I'd kept quiet.

The next time our father came for the full bucket he noticed the slops and cursed me, assuming as always that the fault lay with the youngest present. No doubt Japheth got his share when he was with his older brother.

"You want to sink us?" the old man bellowed.

I thought about that but he never gave me time to answer. He hoisted the bucket as if it were empty and shuffled down the corridor.

"Did you smell that last bucket?" Japheth asked when we were alone.

"How could I miss it?"

"There isn't any rainwater in that. There's got to be something else leaking in."

"Like what?"

"Here's what: God held back since creating Eve. Bashful. Didn't want to be watched by a woman. But at last even He has to let go. After ten generations. That's not rain out there, it's God's torrential piss."

Japheth's mind worked in wondrous ways.

"Piss or not," I said, "the breathing out there must be better than in here."

"Better than wine." Some confession for Japheth, but remember that we'd been at sea three days and the stink of animals hung in the air thick as fog. To read the Official Report, you'd think they all employed intestinal restraint. I can assure you that this is not the way in the animal kingdom. Aside from their contribution to the bilge, there was that which required shoveling. No sign of restraint on their part, no sense of gratitude, no recognition of the fact that they were a part of a divine scheme. Strange that we, acting on holy orders, should as a part of our task be faced with such an astonishing variety of dung, droppings, pellets, crap, turds, excrement, flaps, chips, and moist manure—as many shapes, colors and textures as there are creatures, all melding in so awe-inspiring a heap as to make one wonder what we living creatures are made of. With all that bodily activity, what sign is there of the spirit?

The same odd rule which kept us from going on deck to empty the buckets kept us from dumping the solids. And since there was far too much for the shafts or even for our father to cast into the seas, we merely heaped it up at either end of each animal deck, a total of four increasingly impressive mounds.

Oh for the incense which the priests in former days employed to punctuate our religious ritual and adorn our spiritual life. We should have appropriated it at the first sign of rain. After all, we voyagers had a greater need for it now than did they.

More than incense, we needed air. Remember that in addition to the stink of animals and men, there was the smoke from the torches. To what avail would it be if we survived the wet only to be preserved like a crate of smoked herring? I was sure that our greatest danger was not drowning but smothering to death.

"It's not good," Japheth said. "This business of being closed in."

"Not good for the lungs."

"More than that. Things happen."

"Things?"

"People do things they wouldn't otherwise."

"From being closed in?"

"They see too much of each other. Too close."

"Who?"

"Never mind who." Pause. "People you wouldn't suspect."

"Like who?"

"Maybe even Ophir."

He was serious but I couldn't help smiling. His round and gentle wife was not that type. As boys we had become expert on the type of wife who would do such a thing. She had to be tall, well shaped, restless, and full-lipped. We knew the type. Ophir was not one of them.

"That's a stupid joke," I said.

"I hope so."

"You've seen . . . ?"

". . . Seen? Watched? I'd never do any such thing. But she hints. She lets me know she's desired. By someone else, I mean.

And within these walls, we're all too close. We practically touch as we sleep. I can't stay awake to guard. And during the day . . ."

"She takes care of your daughter."

"The hired girl does that. Ophir's got more free time than she knows what to do with. I can't spend the day trailing her about."

I decided that the bad air must be affecting his mind. It was the only explanation. "It's in your head," I said. "A dream. As soon as he opens the windows, it will be like waking up. You won't remember all this. He'll be opening up the windows as soon as the rain stops. We'll get some air in here."

Japheth shook his head. "The only air is for those with rank. Just for our father and the Ancient." He gestured upward with his head, up to the deck above, where Methuselah lived. "He has his own vent, remember? In the roof."

"I remember it well. I worked on it." I remembered too some mixed feelings. The space, the elegant cabinets, and especially the view—all appropriate privileges for a patriarch. But I confess I had twinges of jealousy. I couldn't help imagining what it would be like to look out from that uppermost chamber, to gaze down on the whole world whatever its condition. Better than an eagle's view since the owner of that room would have the human wisdom to make something of the scene, to put it in perspective.

"That's rank for you," Japheth said. "Fresh air and no buckets to haul." But there was no real bitterness in his voice. With an easy shrug he pulled a hunk of dried beef from his robe, smelled it, smiled, licked it, started chewing. His face took on a look of deep, spiritual peace. "There are compensations for the likes of us," he said.

Food, like wine, had a strange effect on Japheth's perception of the world. He lost sight of man's darker side, saw instead a world directed by logic and compassion, a peaceable kingdom. With the first taste of that beef he let go his suspicions about Ophir and lost all caution as well.

"Why are we waiting here? If it's a good whiff of sea air we want, we should just ask him. Simple as that."

"He's not likely to—"

"Not here, of course. We'll go down there now before he closes the door and say, 'Let us help you with that bucket' or 'Say, what's the weather like?' and then before he's had time to consider an answer we can take two or three deep breaths. What can we lose?"

I shook my head but he hardly noticed. He was off, acting on impulse as always, lurching a bit in his wine though it was mid-morning as close as I could figure. No point in reminding him that we were under orders, that we had been warned, that the old man never did enjoy having his procedures amended. No point either in reminding my brother that his timing was off, that the old man must have already done the dumping, had taken his two or three deep breaths, was heading back with the empty bucket. With Japheth's weight, his wine nose, his sunlit smile, you'd never know he was his father's son; but in willfulness, he was the old man's mirror image. We all were. His gift to us.

I waited there by the stairway for the next bucket to be brought, my head against the oak beam, breathing deeply, waiting also for what I knew would come from down the corridor, like seeing blue-black clouds building and hearing the winds rise, knowing for sure that lightning is on its way.

It struck: a bellow like a gored bull, a flood of oaths—Lord how he cowed us with his curses. Then the familiar *thunk!* —fist against fat stomach or jaw or shoulder, whatever suited him. Then, yes, yelps like a puppy in pain. Yip, yip, yip—my brother, a married man, father to his own offspring, yelping like a whelp.

He appeared again, crouched over, hands pressed to his lower belly.

"I wouldn't advise," he said, "asking questions."

V

RAISING QUESTIONS

FOR as long as I could remember, my father had a special reverence for work. Back in the sunny days of my youth, it was the vineyards. No matter how many servants there were, members of the family had to put in their time. Then out of a clear blue sky came all that carpentry business. Saw, trim, and hammer until the smell of pitch seeped into our dreams. And now this strange yoking of animal husbandry and what I took to be a seaman's life. We worked to keep the place clean and dry six days a week and we worked at worship on the seventh. He expressed no regrets about having left the priests behind, but he did carry on their sense of moral rigor. He wouldn't let go of his determination to keep us from going slack.

I respected this partly because it was all I had ever known and partly because dutiful cooperation seemed preferable to a clout in the face. There was, of course, an obligation to obey the Great Yahweh and, more directly, the laws of the tribe; but none of that had quite the moral force of seeing my brother doubled up and gasping for air.

So we kept at it. But not unrelentingly. Those who live

under stern taskmasters learn to reshape their tasks in subtle ways. I'd put in seven days as water boy with Japheth when, just as was predicted, the planks began to tighten. Before I could be reassigned to something worse, I volunteered to care for the unclean animals on the lowest deck. It was a job I might have drawn in any case, but I was commended for my selfless gesture.

After a prudent lapse of time, I reminded my father and Shem of the special problem with the pigs: if one should die, I would have no way of disposing of the tabooed body. If only—my straight-faced plea—we had a foreigner to help.

"It's a rotten job at best," Shem said. "Give him the pig girl." My father agreed with a shrug.

Success! True, I had not been altogether honest, but I convinced myself that I had awakened in them a sense of fairness, a respect for the equal distribution of labor. "Let her do the dirty work," my father said. "The stench would kill the likes of us." His sympathy, it seemed, was somewhat limited by tribal loyalty.

In any case, the pig girl of foreign faith, my beautiful Sapphira, was ordered down to the lower depths to work, as they put it, under me.

With good fortune like that, one tends not to ponder at length about Who planned the flood, what His motive could possibly be, why some were chosen to float and others sink, and what might be in store for mankind. It seemed natural at the time to ride with the current.

Remember too that my father's rigid code was only one model on that ship; the lower orders on those lower decks had another. And it was down there among the simple creatures that I had begun to find my place, to feel at home. It was a pleasure to see the hares burrow tunnels in the straw as they once did on the arid plain and the storks building nests as if on some familiar rooftop rather than below the surface of the sea. In this same spirit I set about making my own little den. True, the rest of mankind had drowned, been swept away like so many ants in the stream, but all that was on too grand a scale for me. I was no more able to grasp its moral implication than were storks or hares. If nature is a worthy model, it was natural and right for me to spend my time burrowing between the legs of my sweet Sapphira.

And what a marvelous, musty world that was! I had never imagined. What I had heard from my older brothers and their friends gave no hint of its wonder and pleasure. They tended to talk about women in hunting terms. "Now there's a little doe ready for the arrow," they would say, pointing at the prey, nudging each other. Or they would compare past victories: "Skinned her royally," they would say or "Felled the heifer right there in the wheat field."

Those with a poetic talent used figures of speech containing spikes, planks, spears, timbers, and ramrods. I heard how the older boys spent the night plowing, frying, roasting, nailing, pounding, and reaming some obliging lady friend. "Killed her proper" was a superlative used by the more mature. Since the girls and women under discussion appeared alive and apparently undamaged the next morning, I concluded this must be some kind of word play which I would eventually master.

When I came of age I was advised to get my start, as half the village had, with an herb-practitioner whose aperture was reported to be as wide as her reputation. I was assured that it would be "easy as dropping a bull down a well."

Headfirst? And then what?

None of that prepared me for my Sapphira. For us there were melodies played on the pipe, feasts in the dell, the smell of crushed ferns, soaring, gliding, and special occasions on which we simply dissolved in a shower of sparks. Hardly the kind of experiences you discuss with fellow males.

Not that it was all so dramatic. During those next two weeks there were also quiet times in which our voices and hands and mouths took turns gently touching each other. Even now—perhaps especially now at my age—I report it with reverence.

I was learning a wondrous amount about anatomy and the subtleties of sensation. It did not seem at all the right time to discuss philosophical issues or the behavior of my clan. Yet these concerned her. She kept asking questions which I found distracting.

Her insistence surprised me. I had assumed that those from foreign parts who worshiped strange gods would be somewhat limited in the disciplines of abstract thought and speculation. I mean, here was a girl who'd never even been taught about the fall of man.

Yet speculate she did. Not as an evasion or retreat from our post-climactic fondling, but in conjunction. She had a way of raising questions in random fashion just as our fingers wandered into strange and marvelous areas, as if hands and mind were equally curious, equally probing, each in a different manner.

"Why do they hide the Ancient up there?" she asked as we writhed leisurely in the aviary, entwined and featherless in the straw, ignoring the somber stares of the owls, cuckoos, kites, lapwings, nighthawks. "What's wrong with him?"

"Nothing. It's just that he's old."

"He's disliked for that?" She adjusted my massaging hand, muttering "Ah, yes." And then, "Age is not revered by your tribe?"

"More than anything."

"More than *this?*" She had her finger on the point she meant.

"Age *and* that."

"Then why hide him?"

"Same reason we hide that."

She considered that for a moment, those big eyes round with thought. "It doesn't make sense," she said.

"We don't show off our finest treasures."

"Why not?"

"We might lose them."

She shrugged and rolled back from me, legs parted in a way that suggested she wasn't deeply afraid of losing anything. We tussled a bit. Then serious again, "A strange family, this."

"Which?"

"Yours. All of you. The whole clan."

"No different than most."

"No? How is it that you are afloat and the others sank? There's one big difference."

"What's that got to do with—"

"Everything. I look at what you do—all of you—and how

44

you talk and how you dress and I ask myself, What is it that makes them so special? How is it that they are saved?"

"And you."

"Me? I'm like *them*. . . ." She nodded in the direction of two sleek cormorants staring at us, listening to every word. "You know, part of the livestock. I was chosen by your brother. He has his reasons. But you were chosen by . . ." Her sentence trailed off, her mouth occupied in other ways.

"By the Yahweh," I said.

She raised her head and I braced myself for her defense of her own gods. But no, she seemed unconcerned with that. She took a different position altogether. Astride me now, impaled but not in agony, in constant undulation like some slender butterfly preening on her prize poppy: "And the others who used to pray with you, raised their voices to the same God, sang the same hymns, did all those holy things and believed them— what do *they* think of their Yahweh's choice? I mean, what *did* they during those last moments before He drowned them?"

"But they were sinners."

"Oh." She continued to rise and fall, gently massaging our point of contact, letting my words sink in. Then, "What do you suppose they did to make them sinners?"

"The usual, I guess. Thievery, sloth, fornication."

"It must be all right to do two out of three, though. Like right now."

"Sapphira, must we talk?"

"I want you to teach me. I mean, there must be answers and you must know them. All that schooling. All those hours with learned men. If you don't know, Ham, who does?"

"Some other time."

"Well, just tell me this. What about the little babes? The ones just born. Still suckling. How do you suppose they managed to sin while lying in their mothers' arms?"

I tried to concentrate on her form—the length of her neck, the firmness of those breasts, the astonishing shades of skin pigments; but what came before me like a dark cloud was the vision of gray faces over the gunwale, those former schoolmates, jokemates, working partners, kindly elders. And babes. All going under. If not then, soon. Toddlers. Perhaps even now, their grip slipping from some uprooted tree, the whole scene made dreamlike from my haunted imagination; all this while I lay here in the straw, dry amongst birds, lovingly massaged. . . .

I looked up to her who had asked the question, past her to the upper decks where I had heard explanations of no value, no value at all; and were there answers above that? What could they possibly be?

Pondering, I wilted.

V I

THE CALL

"WHY me?" I asked.

"That's what they're wondering," Japheth said.

"Who?"

"Our father, Shem, everyone. 'Why Ham?' they're asking."

"It's a real honor," Ophir said, "being invited to talk with the Patriarch. Strange, but a real honor."

Only minutes before I'd been summoned from my downstairs pleasures by a shout from Japheth. I was sure I was going to be chastised by our father for being immoderate in my joy. I had the impression from my Sabbath School days that bliss was by nature a tainted state.

But this was not their concern. By the time I had prepared myself and climbed up from the Unclean Deck three flights to our deck, Japheth had about given up and was being shaved by his wife. It was a delicate operation at best, made into a dance with death by his drinking and gesturing, oblivious to that lethal blade at his throat. It was marvelous to see what trust he had in his wife.

But my own attention was focused on my good fortune. I

was not about to be reprimanded. Indeed, I had been honored by a call to see Methuselah himself. I felt a mix of relief and puzzled apprehension.

"It makes no sense," I said.

"No one said Methuselah made sense," Japheth said.

"Hush now," Ophir said. "Your own great-grandfather. And at his age. Of course he makes sense. It's we who have trouble interpreting his words."

"Ha!" Japheth lunged forward with a snort of a laugh and sprayed wine; the blade leapt clear of his throat, quick as a startled thrush. "A mouth full of tongues, he has."

"He *has?*"

"No, stupid, not flesh and blood; but that's the way his ideas come out, all cockeyed and upended. Not the phrases, just his notions. That's what I hear. And you have to stand close to hear —close enough to smell death on him. He's on the very edge."

"Don't wish him to the grave. You want that on your conscience?"

She was a simple woman and gentle, pious enough to believe in the powers of a curse—even an inadvertent one.

"It's not me that keeps him alive," Japheth said. "It's just that the Great Yahweh has forgotten to claim him."

"Forgotten?"

"Preoccupied, you might say; relieving himself for weeks on the likes of us. *Yeow!*" The blade had just drawn a drop of blood.

No way then to imagine what it would be like past 900. Except for that one brief audience I'd shared with Sapphira, I'd never seen more than the husk of the man, a relic carried to temple for what I assumed was some obscure symbolic reason.

No one really knew him. Not one could remember him middle-aged. There was a rumor in the village that as a child he had touched the hand of the aging Adam. It seemed unlikely, but who could deny it for sure? In any case, it was clear that he was the sole surviving witness to a great portion of our history. If he had told us that he had once wrestled with angels, we would have believed him.

Sore afraid as I was to appear before him, I hoped that he

would give me some answers. At least I could find out why he had singled me out. That much I could ask him directly. Did I dare try the larger question? Could he give me any idea why we as a clan had been singled out, had been saved while the others were left to drown? Surely a man who has touched the hand of the aging Adam would have some insights. *Adam?* Perhaps even *Cain!* Was that possible?

We were interrupted by a flurry of sounds from the adjoining room, a shrill, chicken-yard argument. Their daughter, Leah, came storming in, followed by Zilpah, the hired girl.

Leah stopped short, seeing me. Fuming with some complaint, she held it in as soon as she discovered that her parents were not alone. She was a healthy, fat little girl with an unfortunate squint which grew worse when she was angry. Right now her eyes were two dark slits cut in the soft dough of that round face.

"She won't let me brush her hair," Zilpah said. "Won't wear the clothes I laid out. Won't do her lessons. She's a won't-won't girl this morning."

"I'm *not*," Leah said, her eyes disappearing.

"Ah, my sunshine girl," Japheth said, sweeping her into his arms, smearing her face with his shaving soap. She pulled back, struggling as if she'd been seized by a shaggy ape, but he hung on to her. "My sunshine girl," he said, laughing, squeezing her, "how lucky you are. Here with your parents and Zilpah. Dry and safe."

"I hate it."

"Of course you don't. You're safe."

"I do too hate it. It's smelly and dark and creaky. I just hate it."

"But you can't, sunshine girl. You just can't hate it. Think of all the other little girls, face down and bobbing in the sea." Zilpah raised her hands and moaned, started chanting a prayer for the dead.

"I *can* hate it," Leah said, raising her voice over the wailing, still struggling to escape her father's grip. "I *can* and I *do*."

"You can't, dear sunshine girl, because you chose to come along. Think of all the other little girls who didn't have a choice—all your friends and classmates. All dead now, every one of them." Fresh wailing from Zilpah. "What would *they* think if they knew you hated it just because it's smelly and dark?"

"They can't think anything because they're all *dead!*"

Japheth shrugged and released the girl. "What's become of simple gratitude?" he asked the rest of us. And then to Zilpah, "Do stop your wailing. Can't you see the girl's upset?"

But Leah had apparently decided her nurse was the better of two evils. She went to the woman and the two of them left. At the door Leah paused, aiming those two slits at her father.

"I didn't choose to come anyhow. I was *brung*. So there."

"*Brought*," Ophir said sweetly. "The word is *brought*." But the door was already closed.

Ophir began lathering her husband again, replacing the suds which had been wiped off on their daughter. Japheth grinned in embarrassment. "A good girl, really. But given to dark moods."

"*Brung*," Ophir said, shaking her head, smiling. "Where does she pick up language like that?"

There was no time for speculation. I had to report to my mother and be prepared for my audience with the Patriarch. Indeed, I was already late. The moment I entered her room she told me that. Then she told me that for this appearance I must be dressed as if for a feast day. What feast?

She was no higher than my chest, remember, but solid; almost my weight. She had the face of a frog. This was not my imagination. I had heard my older brothers referring to her as The Frog. Just like that. Yet she had authority—not just as her husband's organizer and interpreter, but power of her own. When she lowered her lids down halfway over those amphibian eyes, we jumped as if struck. When she told me to dress, I dressed.

I did point out in an offhand manner that it was not, in fact, a feast day; my mother handed me the proper clothes. I asked for the reason; she told me to hurry. I asked when this audience would take place and she told me to scrub my face; I asked how long he would want to see me and she complained that my hair was filled with straw and turds and how could that be? She began brushing it fiercely, reaching up there with difficulty. I had to bend my knees and hang my head for her to manage the crown—me who had just entered manhood!

"But what am I supposed to say to him?"

"Your neck's filthy too."

She spun me around, spit on a rag, and began rubbing my neck as if it were stained with the brand of Cain. I had to take it, staring at the wall, my eyes fixed on that family tapestry hanging there. Its details were woven into my earliest memory. A lineage it was, starting at the top with Adam alone, up there close to the Yahweh Himself, then slightly below him his wife and his sons—Cain a broken strand—and the grandchildren on down, each familiar to me. The tapestry record ran from Adam down to Seth and then Enosh, Kenan, Mahalalel, Jared, to Enoch, father of Methuselah. It was Enoch who had walked with the Yahweh, shown here as something like a column of smoke or, to me at least, an enormous turnip stalk. Strange indeed that the Patriarch's father should have befriended a walking turnip—but who was I to question?

"Filthy," my mother said. I was sure she had overheard my thoughts. But even if she had caught me out in my doubts, I would never find a direct answer to my question. On the one hand, it seemed unlikely that the Creator would deign to come among us disguised as a feathery turnip stalk; yet the tapestry was Truth and the figure woven there was more turnip than anything else and who was there to ask without risking a slap?

Such questioning was not healthy. If they ever suspected how much I indulged in it, they might not add me to that family record. Perhaps they wouldn't anyway, me being a third son and considered a little odd and a slow learner from the start. Still, there must have been a secret portion of me which wanted to be included in the next panel, wanted my threads added to that field of green, wanted to become a part of the whole fabric.

My father suddenly appeared. He filled the room with himself and his discontent, complaining to my mother. Not a word to me. I could have been a coat hanging on the wall.

"For eleven days the Ancient has been up there and has not called on me, me his savior. . . ."

"He's not the sort to grovel."

"Grovel? Who's talking about grovel? I'm saying after all

this time he asks to see not me but this . . . this . . ." He gestured toward me with both hands, the room vibrating with the sound of an enraged man groping for an ugly word. "This . . . *Ham*. What idiocy is this? Some mistake."

"No mistake. That's who he called for."

"If he wants a grandchild, why not my eldest son? You suppose he's got them mixed up? What's the old nighthawk want to say anyway? What's the boy supposed to do? Just stand there? He's supposed to make conversation? Since when has the old bat put three sentences together? What makes him hang on the way he does anyway? What good is he in his condition? An ailing old she-ape. Addlebrained. What good is a man at his age? I never expected him to last until flood time. Still he lingers, taking up the best space. By what right? No more life to him than a slug but still he hangs on to life. For what? What's he done for any of us for the past hundred years? Well? Well?"

She paused, hands on those solid hips, looking up at him, the silence giving her a certain edge. Then, slowly, deliberately: "If this family had a cow flop for every one of your foolish questions, it would have built itself a mountain instead of this leaking casket."

With a roar he seized the pitch torch from the wall, gestured with it as if struck dumb in his fury, threatening to plunge it into her solid midriff, his expression blind rage; then his eyes opened wide in pain. Flaming pitch had spilled, splattering his hands. He bellowed like a gored bull; the torch went flying.

It is the nature of pitch torches to scatter fire when dropped, and this was no exception. What began as just another exchange between husband and wife, a private matter, leapt to instant crisis.

Shouts to me, to anyone within hearing; a dashing about for sandbuckets; a flurry of cries from others down the hall; a sudden rush of people stumbling and pushing each other, spilling sand where it ought not, slapping flames, cursing, yelping, bellowing orders and counterorders.

The torch itself was ablaze from crown to base, oozing hot pitch, popping and hissing. The crowd—family and servants from everywhere—attacked it as if it were a venomous snake, kicking it, beating it with brooms, stomping on it. But flames thrive on motion. Air gives life. And flaming pitch scatters, then sticks like burrs.

Slammed against the wall it let loose a shower of stars which flew against the tapestry. Howls of alarm, horror. A whole family threatened. Spreading red circles on the green fields, smoke enveloping Kenan, Mahalalel, and Jared. A red line advancing, the enemy: Surely it must be stopped before it reached the sacred turnip.

"The turnip," I shouted, words meaning nothing in the din. I flung myself against the fabric of our family, against the lineage, that great grid linking us with the primal patriarch, against the sacred turnip, beating them all with my hands, out-doing the fury of the flames, acting half as savior and half as attacker, beyond reason, taking on a certain madness; and in the process taking on the flames as well, my own robes billowing smoke, myself a torch.

"One side, one side!" Shem's voice. Authority of the eldest. The crowd parted, all motionless for that instant except for me since I was burning. Aflame, I was slapping my own robes now, leaping and dancing like a showman's monkey on a chain, hardly noticing my brother approaching with two wooden buckets of liquid which obviously would do better than sand. The first went on the tapestry, a deluge which saved it from destruction. The second went straight in my face.

After the first shock, my nose told me that he had not found drinking water. Keen-witted as always, he had turned to the nearest source, the slop jars from the neighboring bedrooms. If there is any stink on earth stronger than a filled slop jar, it is slop added to burning fabric.

I stood there, scorched, soaked, and putrified when in came Uncle Tubal-cain. "A message from Methuselah," he said. "The boy is to be sent up without delay."

þoe prime. þþa hine nengðro heht. hynðe þam hal
gan. heðþon cyninge ongan. oþoyt lice þ hoe þyrean
tnicle mihe cuhte. magun ragðe. þþaþ þnhulic hing
þþoþum to þhano. neðe þice hie. neþohron þær ge
ræh þ a ymb pincha þopn. þær þarþe micoð. gihþon
huþa mærþ. ghino hluþigihan. iwagn yuþun ðonðan
lime. geþarþoð þiþ þloðe. þopmoh. ly þelhctun
lic gynðniþ cynn. Symle bið þy þ ftuðna þehic hnloh
þicþc. rþhnce ræt rþhtumar. rþiðon hihnuð.

VII

THE ANCIENT

THERE was no time for proper preparations, no time for another change of clothes. Wiped clean as possible as quickly as possible, sprayed with lemon water but still smelling like a wart hog, I was escorted up to the revered Top Deck, aimed down the corridor, and given a little shove. Launched.

No, they would not go to the door with me, would not make a formal introduction. I knew this was due to their sense of awe—though a stranger might have thought their actions tinged with revulsion and fear. I was presented as an offering, a lamb for the beast in his lair.

Would he remember that I was the one who knocked him down during the pig chase? Or would that all be unraveled in his tattered memory? If fragments remained, he might well hold hostile feelings toward me.

Still, what could he possibly do? What strengths could re-main? Even in those days, 969 was more than just elderly. Who could be afraid of a man poised at the very rim of the grave? Grave! An unfortunate reminder. A man of his age might not be a physical threat, but he could have special powers. There were, after all, weird spirits about who lingered among us by drinking the blood of the young. Particularly the idle and lascivious.

I stood there in the twilight of the outer room, a kind of antechamber. Was this where he slept? It had all been so light and airy before we roofed it in. Now it was dark as some ancient prophet's cave. I had no sense of the outside world except for the muffled sound of the wind and the hiss of the rain on the roof. Ah, the rain. Somehow I had forgotten about that. I was closer to the Heaven here, but also closer to elements which were far from heavenly.

As my eyes widened catlike in the darkness I made out a figure standing there. The Patriarch himself? No, it was the man-servant, Nahum, the Ancient's ancient.

Voiceless as long as anyone could remember, expressionless, he was supposed to serve the Patriarch. But he was far too frail for any real service. He was retained as an aging watchdog who's long since lost his bark.

He stared at me. Then almost imperceptibly shook his head saying wordlessly, You are beyond belief, coming to see the Patriarch in this condition.

He reached out, starting to clean me up a bit perhaps, but thought better of it and withdrew his hand before it was contaminated. Instead, he pointed toward the inner door and gestured in pantomime for me to knock. He would not deign to usher me in.

I crossed the room, wishing I was anywhere but there, and rapped hesitantly—far too lightly even for a young man to hear. Of course I made no contact. Must I try the latch without being bidden to do so? There was no retreat. I opened the door and winced at the sound the hinges made, a sound only I could have heard.

"Ham."

Nothing but a rough whisper, but I jumped as if it had been shouted. It is one thing to be addressed by someone you can see; it is quite another to have your name come from darkness.

"Ham," it said again.

VII   The Ancient

This time I placed the sound. There against one wall was a
kind of crib or open casket—four sides of dark oak. As my eyes
began to pick out details, I could see that within this, propped
up on pillows at one end, was a human.

"Ham," it said, "come here."

If given a choice, I would have headed down to lower decks,
to where I felt at home. But I had no choice. I could not refuse.
How could there be such authority in so frail a voice? It made
no sense at the time. I knew only that there was a force there.
Later I saw that it had little to do with the man himself. Even
now when young ones who are such braggarts and cock-
crowers among themselves are led reluctantly into my own
chambers, they hush their voices until I can hardly hear them. It
is not I as a person who fills them with awe, shocks them into
solemnity. It is I as their history. I am the parchment, the
tapestry through which they can touch their past—a link which
they both need and loathe. My muscles have no strength these
days, my commands no weight; but I hold the young as if I had
shared that last free meal with Adam.

In the same way, I obeyed Methuselah with fear and trembling. Unnerving as death, he was not to be denied.

I approached, my eyes widening to the dim, strange scene.
I began to see that the room was carefully furnished—far more
complete than those below. In addition to the bed, there were
tables, wardrobes, chests, shelves of herbal medicines. A special
cabinet had been built to hold a multitude of scrolls. The room
was faintly lit not with a simple torch but an oil lamp of the
sort we used to have at home. And beneath my feet there was a
thick rug. It was a relief to discover that despite my father's
momentary resentment, he had a deep concern for his aging
grandfather. Why else would he have designed such splendid
quarters?

I had never seen this chamber in its final stages. When the
master carpenters and cabinetmakers began to add the refine-
ments, I was reassigned far below, troweling black, gummy
bitumen to the bottom of the hull for days on end. There was
an up and a down even then.

What to say? None of the phrases which we are taught to use when silence threatens seemed appropriate. Good to see him? Too blatant a lie. A simple Good Morning? Inappropriate with the weather continuing the way it was. How are you? Hardly a casual question for a man his age!

I considered apologizing for knocking him down. But there was a chance he had not seen us clearly or had mislaid the memory. No, I dared not risk reminding him. There was nothing left. It would have been easier for me to deal with a dead body. At least a corpse would not call for an exchange of pleasantries.

If trivia was out, should I try something of substance? Something informative? But what could be news to him? Here was a man who heard my father's infant howls, knew my uncles when they sucked at their mothers' breasts, was present at my late grandfather's conception. Here was a man who could see within every adult face an adolescent, a child, a wriggling infant; could detect in our gestures, our expressions, echoes of our parents and grandparents. What view, what opinion, what piece of information was there which he did not already know?

"Hello. I'm Ham," I whispered and wished at once I could suck back the words. It was hardly news to him who I was.

He raised his finger to his mouth. I was not to talk. A relief! Saving his voice perhaps. Looking at that raised finger, at that face now beginning to come clear in the twilight, I saw that he was essentially skeletal. Parchment skin was stretched over cheeks. Beard was no more than white strands, wisps. Lips practically gone. Only a narrow, crooked nose saved this head from being a skull.

I stared, hoping that he would misread my revulsion as a kind of reverence. I had never seen a living creature so close to decay before having the grace to die. He stared back. Was he as fascinated by youth? It did not occur to me then; it does now.

With great effort he hoisted himself up on his pillows. To talk? See me better? No, he was raising a bone of an arm with difficulty. Pointing now, arm and leathered finger, over the wooden side of his crib to a bucket on the floor. He wanted to be sick? Wanted a drink? I bent down and discovered a washrag hung over the side. It was warm. The water too was warm. Good

God, did he want me to wash him? *Touch* him? Yes, I was to take old Nahum's place. I had no choice. Thus it began:

I hold my breath, ring out the rag, and wipe his brow. He seems to be nodding. Enough? Is that all? I pause there, aching for release. The bony hand slithers out from the darkness and catches my wrist. It is the wizened grip of a monkey. There is no escape.

My hand is directed from face to throat. I begin cautious washing. He nods. Where will it stop?

On to the chest: worn leather stretched so tight over bone that it is about to rip. If it does, there will be no flesh there, no blood, only a dry, dark powder like last year's mushroom.

I slide the cloth over the surface with more fear than reverence —the slightest pressure will tear the pelt or crack ribs. There! May I stop?

Two simian hands tug at the folds of bedding and robes; exposed chest becomes a sunken stomach, a gray hollow. Scrub, scrub. I hear myself breathing. That and the old ship creaking. Sink. Let me sink. Let me drown with the others.

But why? This is not my doing. *He's* doing this to *me*. All right then, Old One, we'll go the whole way. You started this. I'll go right through with it, inch by inch.

Into a new stage, a new determination. Disliking it, disliking him, but determined. No worse, surely, than scraping scabs from an ailing camel, and I'm considered good at that. Even expert. No fear here of being kicked. So down we go, the length of you laid bare. No modesty for either of us. There, your old glory exposed—and less wizened than I expected. A wonder, really: sack large for one so thin, not drawn up in fear or shame, but waiting there for the wash-man's gentle touch. Such trust!

Then down those skin-covered sticks. Are these the supports we knocked out from under you in our pig chase? Why didn't they snap? More astonishing, are these the same limbs which lifetimes ago ran for you, jumped for you, climbed trees?

I pass over the knobs where one section is joined so imperfectly to the next; the dampened rag snags on the angles. In all our carpentry we never made a fitting so ugly, so careless in design. More nobs where ankles should be. And blackened toes.

Once pink and chubby? Wrapped in swaddling clothes by a mother whose name and face are remembered by no one? I have no way of knowing; there is no one alive to ask. How little true history I have for all those hours in class. All those bits and pieces held in my mind: who begat whom, who was blessed and who cursed. All that but no way to touch those people as people—not even those whose familiar names are woven for all time into the tapestry. And this one? Is there a real man under my hands? It feels more like another yellowed scroll, the record of a man long since gone.

Enough of that. I have a job to do. No choice but to push through to the end. And from the stink, it is the end which needs the work. No need to worry about my own sweet scent. I roll him over with breath held—not for the weight of it, but for the fear of having it break in two.

And what have you done with the body?

It just fell in half—head one way, chest the other; legs snapped like winter reeds. All in pieces. I'm very sorry. Not my fault. How was I to know?

The back—wash and massage. Down the length of it, smooth and dark as walnut. Each knob of the spine polished. And flesh-less butt. Much need of work here. Pause, hold breath. A quick temptation to run. No, this is only a self-stained, aging goat. The stink of life. Familiar. Scrub, catch breath, scrub again.

Then back over. Gently now. Don't break apart on me. Not now,

No, he did not break, did not crumble. Washed, powdered, re-robed, boosted up on those pillows, he looked regal. I smiled. I actually smiled.

"What's funny?" A gravely whisper, faint yet demanding. It could have silenced a crowd.

"What?"

"What's funny?"

"Nothing's funny."

"Of course there is. You were smiling."

"I'm sorry. I . . ." Words dried in my throat.

Those parchment eyelids shut. Exhaustion? More likely exasperation. My neck prickled in embarrassment. Old people were supposed to ask how old you were, how tall you were, whose son you were. Nothing in my training prepared me for saying anything honest to the aged and never had they in their turn asked anything meaningful of me. It was hardly fair of him.

His eyes opened, focused directly on me.

"Can't think of what's funny? Not a thing? At your age?" Pause. I shook my head. "Well, I'll tell you some . . ." Another pause. A wheeze for air. "Some funny things. *Should* make you smile. . . ." Pause again. I realized that it was not easy for him to take a deep breath. He rasped his phrases in short bursts. "Your father's notion to save all these animals . . . that's funny. Don't you think?" My face reddened. An incredible impiety! "This floating castle. A boat would have done . . . as well. Ah yes, the way . . . the way your father's turned himself into his own priest. After all he said about those he left to drown . . . a joke there. The way you and that girl almost killed me. Rutting . . . the two of you in rut. More blind than me, you were. . . . At your age. Funny. . . . But, I know, you weren't smiling at any of those. . . ." Pause. Air sucked in. Eyes shut with the effort. Eyes open again. "Not any of those. Not old enough. Not old enough yet. You've got to be strong to laugh at stuff like that. Strong like me."

He stopped, the mouth locked open, muscles tensed, fists clenched. Little shudders passed through his body. Convulsions? A fit? Then I realized he was laughing.

He caught hold of himself, sucked air into his lungs, steadied. "No, none of those," he said. "Not now. Good jokes, but leave them be for now. Here's what made you smile. . . . You managed to get through all that washing without . . . throwing up."

I started to deny it—the simple reflex of one carefully trained to lie when talking with the elderly. But I had been through too much with him to be on good behavior. I nodded and smiled again.

"Of course," he said. Then, "There's an old tradition—in all civilized tribes—washing the dead. You know about washing the dead?"

"I've heard."

"Unpleasant work. Pointless. The ground doesn't care. It consumes the washed and unwashed. . . . And the dead don't notice. No more vanity. So it must be for the living. . . . Know what it does for the living?"

I shook my head.

"Drains the mystery out of death. Cleanses the living. Makes the strange seem ordinary. I'm no corpse. Not yet. But close enough . . . I can't have you treating me like a spirit."

"I won't."

"I know you won't. Not after what you've seen. The whole reeking mess. You think it's any better for me? This wretched house I inhabit?" He stared, furious, caught his breath. "It leaks, it festers, it stinks. . . . It freezes me, leaves me quaking when others are warm; roasts me with fever when others are cool. . . . The worst is how it offends the eyes of others. Women, I mean. Wives have come and gone. . . . Wives and others. Some were beauties. But that's all over now. Gone. I wouldn't have one now even if she were offered on pillows. Couldn't stand the look on her face. Agh!" The disgust came up from the back of his throat and with it phlegm. He hardly noticed. I wiped his chin with the rag. Earlier that day I would have hesitated to touch his skin; now I did it without a thought.

"Why me?" I asked.

"You?"

"Why did you ask to see me?"

"Why not? Why are you surprised?"

"I mean, well, I'm not my father."

"That's one reason."

"If not him, then why not Shem?"

"You're the youngest of the three."

"Yes."

"I wasn't asking. I was telling. You're the youngest. . . . Still hope with the youngest. Third sons are special. If there's time, I can teach you. Still hope. Are we . . . ?" Pause.

"Are we what?"

"Really afloat?"

I nodded, too astonished to use my voice. He didn't even know? This was the man who was going to reveal Truth for me?

He gestured for me to pull his covers up. I did so. He was

nothing more than an old, sick man. He asked for some herbal concoction. I gave it to him, spooning it out of the jar, wiping his chin again.

He shook his head, and at first I thought he was rejecting his medicine. But no, he took another sip and muttered to himself. His mind had turned inward.

"Adrift," he murmured. "Who would have thought . . . ?" He turned to me with a surge of energy: "Your father and I don't like each other. We're not woven from the same thread. The man's a bull. Thickheaded like his father. But there's this: he *does* things. He charges ahead and *does* them." Then softer, almost to himself, "Really afloat, eh? Who would have imagined?"

There was a long pause. I looked at him, wondering whether this was real praise. But there was no way to ask. He was off on a new tack. "Tell me," he said, looking at me intensely. "Tell me, did you hesitate . . . ? Did you have a hard time?"

"Hard time?"

"Deciding. I mean deciding to come on board?"

"To come on board?" I stalled, astonished at the question. How had he known? It was hardly a subject I had shared with members of the family. And if my father had even noticed, he would never have mentioned it. Mixed feelings never concerned him. Besides, he hadn't even visited the Patriarch. I decided that I must be in the presence of a wizard.

"I asked you a question," he said, his voice gruff now. "Did you?"

"Yes."

"Yes what? Speak up."

"Yes, I wondered about coming up that gangplank. 'In or out?' my father was asking me and I was uncertain. But I came."

"So I see. And one day there will be another question."

"Like that?"

"Whether you'll leave."

"Leave?" Stupidly I looked around at that dim, viewless room, thought about the miles of water about us, the limitless sea covering the face of the earth. Had he forgotten? "Leave?"

I looked down and those lids had closed again. No sign of exasperation this time. In . . . death? No, there was a slight motion of the rib cage under the covers. As I lingered there, leaning close, I heard a faint wheezing and whistling, sounds like a covey of doves settling down for the night. It seemed to me as if it were a language, but how was I to learn it in time?

VIII

FAMILY CONCERN

I had gone up to that pinnacle cabin with fear and dread; I came down perplexed. What had I learned? *I* had to tell *him* we were launched.

A sad, baffling old man. Half here and half in the Afterworld already. How strange that the family should treat him like a high priest. What awed them so? His age, perhaps. But there had been others in our lineage almost as old. Adam made it to 930 in spite of setbacks early in his career. Enoch—the one who walked with the Great Yahweh and no doubt talked Him into special privileges for the rest of us—he made it to 962. So Methuselah the Ancient at 969 was a record-breaker but no immortal. Was there some special quality there I'd missed?

Already his wandering conversation had begun to blur. Somehow it was the washing that stuck in my memory and would not make room for anything else. The washing. A first for me. You never quite know what age is until you wash it. In the space of days I had learned much about women—their bodies, their smells, their preferences—and in a parallel way about ancient men. An opening of horizons on the high seas.

But I never asked him the questions I had planned. Why did they have him walled off up there? Sapphira's question. It had clung like a burr. Not a hint of an answer. Not from him. And wasn't I going to ask him why we were to travel with doors and windows barred? I had that in mind, but the question had flown from me like a raven as soon as he set me to washing. That took concentration, just sticking to it. It was one of those menial tasks which sweeps everything else out of your mind. It's no wonder servants don't dwell on the subtleties of life.

At the foot of the stairway I almost stumbled into Shem.

"Torch needs replacing," he said, removing the dead cone from its bracket. I hadn't remembered that being one of his assigned tasks. It didn't occur to me at the time that he might have been waiting for me. "Been to see the Ancient?"

I nodded.

"And how is he?"

"Very old."

"I asked, how is he?" Shem had hold of my arm as we walked and was applying pressure, adding emphasis to his question or perhaps suggesting in his subtle way that I was not to joke on this subject.

"Hard to tell. I've never seen him close up before."

We had passed down the darkened corridor toward the common room where we ate and spent our idle time. He gripped my arm with one hand and the burned-out torch in the other, one object as spent as the other.

There in the main room the whole family happened to be gathered. Even Grandfather's two aging widows, Adah and Zillah; and my two uncles, Jabal and Jubal. All of them. An unusual coincidence.

There was considerable clearing of throats and shifting of chairs as I entered, but no one actually noticed me. No one even glanced at me. They looked everywhere but at me, eyes studying the workmanship in the walls, the splendid ceiling beams, the floor planking, motes in the air.

Jubal was talking, but as usual no one was listening. His lyre lay at his side, unused, so he must have been told, as he often was, to leave it alone. It can't be easy to have artistic talents in a family which has no taste for it.

When he couldn't play, he told stories. Any stranger would have thought him a master at this. And we ourselves did as children. Repetition was a pleasure then and his voice was rich as good earth. But the older we grew the more tiresome his stock of stories became. No harm in familiar plots; his error was not adding variations, new twists, fresh insights.

"I was a young one then," he was saying, "not yet tested at sea. I tell you, when the waves rose to the height of the masts, I almost dropped the steering oar and ran forward—almost. Something told me it would be a disaster to do so."

We'd soon get to the part about the captain's whiskers. As children we had loved this one. Now I began to wonder whether he had ever been at sea.

"It was a seaman's instinct that kept me at the helm," he said. "I knew instinctively that if I left I'd get a thrashing." He let out a whinny of a laugh. No one even smiled. "Well sir, when we were down in the trough between those waves, the sails hung limp as sheeting on a calm day. Then we'd rise up the other side and the scream of the winds was enough to put out your ears. And our captain—a fierce bearded one—made a point of standing up right in the front, glowering into the storm. And would you believe it, by the end of that day the wind had wrenched the whiskers right off his face and left it smooth as a baby's butt."

Another whinny from the storyteller. His listeners somehow missed the humor of it. Shem let out a camel's yawn, Athaliah polished her bracelets on the hem of her robe, Uncle Tubal-cain picked at a callus, Japheth scratched his crotch.

Only Jubal's aging mother, Adah, laughed belatedly and shook her head in wonder. "Hard to believe," she said.

"Certainly is," Athaliah said, her voice dry as a serpent's skin.

"Ah, the adventures you've been through," Adah said. "A blessing to have you still with us." She raised her eyes in tribute as one does in prayers of thanksgiving. Shem raised his too—though not in reverence.

"There's Ham," my father said, discovering me. "Where have you been?"

Where had I been? Were they all in their wine? Not an hour

before they were cleaning me up, preparing me for the call.

"Nowhere special," I said with a shrug. Shem's grip closed down like iron. Some kind of correction was called for. "To see the Ancient," I said. "I was called to see the Ancient. Remember?"

"Remember? Remember? Of course I remember. You think I've gone addle-headed? I'm your father; it's my job to remember everything that goes on here."

"But you asked—"

"I asked *why* he wanted to see you. Why *you* of all people."

"Rather than Shem," our mother said by way of explanation.

"I don't know."

"Don't know? Don't know? You've been with him all this time and you don't know? What did he say to you?"

"I can hardly remember."

"Hardly remember? Hardly remember! Surely he talked with you. Said things. You didn't just stand there. Come on, boy, you can't expect us to believe that you stood there all that time waiting for him to talk. It's that half-dead Nahum who can't talk. Methuselah still has his voice." A knowing look at the others; nods. "He'll talk as long as he breathes. A born talker. Has more theories than a priest has lice. He must have spoken to you. So what did he say?"

Astonishing, this deep concern. A ring of faces, all on me. A third son is not used to such attention.

Athaliah came up to me with a gentle smile. I found it unnerving. Her harsh smiles I was used to—smiles of derision. Fall from a ladder and bloody your nose and she'd give you one of her lemon smiles—sour but not unnerving. Just good, familiar malice. But the semblance of kindness on that face put one on guard.

"We're just curious," she said, voice of clover honey. "The Ancient hasn't spoken to any of us for so long; we're wondering how he is. And what's on his mind."

"He wanted me to bathe him."

Consternation. It was woman's work, generally—or something for an aging husk of a servant like Nahum. Certainly nothing for someone like me—even at my age.

"How did you get out of that?" my father asked.

"I didn't."

"You bathed him? Bathed the old man? What do you know of bathing old men?"

"I learned as I went along."

A look of astonishment passed between my father and Shem; I had done something beyond belief. Washing an old man. It apparently had given me a special status, a privileged link with the Patriarch, with the source of our clan. But I had the uneasy feeling that it was not going to endear me to the family.

"All of him?" my father asked.

"All of him. Head to toes."

"Saying nothing?"

"Nothing during the washing."

"But afterward? Surely he said *something*."

Of course he had. But which of all those pieces were they looking for? Which had value? At the time, I heard only ramblings. Now they turned out to be treasures.

They came back to me only as phrases, fragments which formed no whole. I could hear that raw-edged voice muttering about the way our father had "turned into his own priest." And how what we had built was a "floating castle." Yes, and something disparaging about our father's efforts to save all those animals. It didn't seem wise to report much of that.

There was also something serious about third sons. How they were special. But my arm still ached from Shem's grip. No, that would never do. And the strange business at the end—the question of whether I would leave. Actually thinking that I might leave. They'd take that as sure proof of senility. Hardly fair.

They were looking for something. Like hounds on the scent. And I was supposed to help them. Yet I began to have the feeling that giving them information would in some way betray the Patriarch. How could that be? Weren't we all one family?

Athaliah again: "Surely, Ham, there must have been some suggestion—just a hint—as to why he wanted *you* there."

Difficult to resist that smile. A sweetness and an honesty there which was too often hidden. I had to respond.

"He said I was the youngest."

"Youngest?" my father bellowed. "You think we don't know that?" It did seem ridiculous at the time, yet later at the inquest he would deny it, would set me down as the middle son. Right then it was a simple fact. "But *why* was he singling you out? He must have said why. So tell us why."

I wished I could. It wasn't wise to leave his questions unanswered. I blurted out what little I knew just to fill the silence.

"He said there was still hope; he could teach me; I'd be his student. Something like that."

"Ah!" from my father. Just like that. "Ah! *Teach* you. I should have guessed."

He looked at my mother and they raised their eyes in exasperation. Shem slapped his thighs like a man who knew it all along. Athaliah withdrew that inviting smile quick as a lizard's tongue and said "Ptuh!" Whatever advantage I'd held for that short time had just dissolved. We were back to normal.

"Enough of this," my father said and ordered everyone back to work, telling them to hurry, telling me to stay a moment. I stayed.

I stood there, waiting for the others to shuffle out, trying to put pieces together. Nothing quite fit. What had I said? What had I revealed? In all the confusion, I had discovered only one new fact: Methuselah was not a mere husk as I had once thought. He was the very heart of the family.

Which is more than one might gather from the Official Report. Indeed, a careless reader might assume that Methuselah had long since died. "Noah went in . . . and his sons, and his wife, and his sons' wives with him into the Ark," it says, "because of the waters of the flood." And then references to clean beasts and beasts that are not clean and fowls and "every thing that creepeth upon the earth." All those fleas and ticks and slugs and spiders—but no clear word about Noah's own father and his grandfather, the Ancient himself!

A careful reading of dates, however, will reveal that Lamech died five years before the flood. More remarkable, those same figures confirm my version, show conclusively that Methuselah was indeed among us.

The authors hadn't intended such a revelation. But they had a fondness for dates. They included too many. Look closely at the document.

Methuselah, it states, was 187 when he had Lamech. (Or, as my dear Sapphira was wont to say, his *wife* had Lamech.) And Lamech was 182 when he (as we say) had Noah. By that time Methuselah must have been 369. Clear so far?

The rains came when Noah was 600. If we add those 600 years to Methuselah's age at Noah's birth, we see that the Patriarch was exactly 969 the year of the Flood. And how old was he when he died? Here is where they gave it all away! ". . . the days of Methuselah were nine hundred and sixty-nine years." Those are the very words they used in the Final Draft. It is available for anyone who has the talent to buy a copy.

For those who bother to add these figures, it is clear that Methuselah was alive and present at the time of the Flood. Whether he was left to the rising waters or taken on board is never mentioned. Extraordinary treatment for the senior member of the family and grand Patriarch!

Waiting there for my father to speak to me I somehow convinced myself that he was about to reveal to me everything about my great-grandfather, talking honestly, one grown man to another.

As soon as the others were gone he snapped his fingers for me to approach him. It was a signal he used for dogs and servants. It should have told me something.

He sat me down at the table and took another chair. I thought it a good sign that he was willing to speak to me on my own level.

"Ever see an olive tree gone beyond bearing, all hollow at the center?" I nodded. "Well, that's the way the Ancient is. Rotted out at the center. Still living but gone beyond his time. Mind rotted out."

"He talks."

"Of course he talks. I didn't say he was dead. Not yet. But sometimes his talk is crazed."

"Seemed sensible to me."

"*Crazed*, I said. Warped, twisted, kinked. You know, *crazed*. I'm not asking you, I'm telling you. You hear? I'm telling you not to go up there any more. If he calls for you, we'll tell him something. But you're not to go up there. Understand?"

I nodded. I understood what he was saying, all right. He'd made himself clear as always. But in the other sense I understood nothing.

"Even if he wants to see me?"

My father snorted. "Listen to this: He wanted to take Shem on as his student years ago. Then Japheth. Now you. It's an old man's hold on the living. Like a drowning man clinging to branches. Wants to fill your mind like a stallion fills a mare. Own you that way. Understand?" Then, more to himself than to me: "After all he's had—the wives, the women, the sons, the grand- and great-grandsons beyond count. After all that . . . All that and more . . ." His fist clenched. "After all that, he still can't keep his hands off *my* things!" Suddenly remembering me, he lowered his voice. "So just stay clear of him. Stay out of reach."

"But . . ." I hesitated, voice fading, then plunged on, spurred by the attention I'd been getting. "But I *want* to see him. I *like* him."

His hand came up for the strike, but I was gone before it fell.

IX

CAMELS AND SERVANTS

I NTO the fourth week and still not a whiff of unused air. Every breath had been used by man or beast. All of us locked in there like cattle during a siege. For our own good, he told us. It stretched our credulity.

We put up with it. What choice did we have? And we couldn't forget the fact that we were afloat while others were not. All the wild things he'd been saying over the past year had come true. A man earns credit that way.

But it was more than that. For all our individuality, we'd been trained as a family to follow orders during a crisis. My earliest memories were of him laying down the law and the rest of us grumbling but obeying without having the slightest understanding.

There was a time I barely recall when a young goatherd in our village had turned blotchy red, had been seized with convulsions and died. Our father called us in from the fields without explanation, had us stack grain in the hallways and drive sheep into the servants' quarters. Then he barred the doors and windows, spiking them shut. A hot day too!

IX Camels and Servants

We thought for sure that the heat had curdled his brain until we heard from neighbors through the door that the goatherd's sister had gone the same way and then the miller and a farmer's wife. That's the last we heard from the outside for the next month except for the sick and the frightened who occasionally scratched to be let in, whimpering for protection and food. When we came out, half the town was underground. There was hardly a family untouched except ours. Our father seemed to take a certain tight-lipped satisfaction in that.

Grandfather Lamech was much the same. Maybe harsher. A loud, fiery man, he was the last of our clan to have two wives. He died, you remember, five years before the rains, so my memory is fragmentary. But who could forget someone who boasted about having killed a man for striking him and another just for a harsh word? Some word!

He was also the only member of the family who spoke warmly of Cain. "If Cain shall be avenged sevenfold," he used to say, "truly Lamech seventy and sevenfold." Avenged for what? You didn't ask questions of a man like that.

He was a raw, unshaped version of my father. I always had the feeling that living with him had left those two wives, Adah and Zillah, dazed and a little addled like those who have served in battle too long.

He was remembered the most for events long before I was born. The town had been threatened by wandering tribes from Ur. They had no land, no law, no culture, and were unwashed. Grandfather Lamech learned that they were about to attack and were superior in numbers and in arms. Also in courage. In the black of the night, if the story can be believed, he secretly abandoned the village, moving his family, his cattle, his camels, and many servants up into the mountains where the oleander and the cedars grow.

At dawn the raiders swept across the valley, laid waste the town, looted everything in sight. They drank our best wine and our worst too, and then spent the night raping and stealing in the tradition of barbarians. It took them five days for their heads to clear.

Once sober again they could see that there was nothing left to take. They had burned most of the houses and trampled on the vineyards, but they had neither the talent nor the patience for reconstruction. For all their ferocity, they lacked staying power.

So on the fifth day they packed up their loot and a bunch of the younger women and left. And Lamech returned. It may well be that he was not welcomed with cheers and with song, but he had preserved his clan, his cattle, his camels, and many servants.

We were raised to believe that survival was one of the holy virtues, but there seemed to be a reluctance to record Lamech as a model. Perhaps it was his style that bothered them.

Obedience was also a virtue and there was no reluctance to dwell on that directly and repeatedly. The priests described it in divine terms, slave owners in legal terms, and parents parentally. They all sounded much the same to me. Obedience was the mortar which held any group together; without it, our society would be rubble, we would be rabble with no past and no future. So no matter how we grumbled and complained, we tended to do what we were told.

As for me, my volunteer work on the lower level had such dazzling compensations that I began to look at the servant's lot in poetic terms. Work and play slid together, lubricated with bodily fluids and smelling to me as sweet as crushed grapes.

Looking back over lo these many years I am astonished at how completely mood, not fact, determines our reaction to anything. The *fact* of a camel, for example, gives little promise of pleasure. The camel has none of the virtues of the pig. It is lacking in affection and has no humor. You don't nestle or romp with a camel. It is by nature a surly beast, given to balking, biting, spitting, and farting.

It is true that a camel will survive for weeks without water or food, but not happily. Given a choice, it eats and drinks enormous quantities; and what goes in one end comes out the other. Its naturally sour temperament turns rancid if its stall is not kept clean, and for spite it breaks out in rashes and boils.

Yet what a pleasure I took in my charges down there on the

Unclean Deck. Having worked with them all my life, I could boast to Sapphira about my talents, display for her my knowledge of the cruder arts. I knew how to treat them and took pleasure in showing Sapphira. You have to use the stick a good deal. Kicking helps. They have thick hides and feel little. You can't really hurt them. Once they learn that you are the master and always will be, a shout or a slap will do. But it takes regular shouting and slapping to remind them.

Down there Sapphira and I were fellow workers, equals. I thoroughly enjoyed my lowly state. I could almost forget that I was the son of a leader and the great-grandson of a patriarch. I became convinced that servants enjoyed a kind of freedom which was not available to those with higher responsibilities.

But there came a day when the scales fell from my eyes. We had been shoveling and were taking a little break, tickling each other with tufts of straw. Whoever laughed first had to perform exotic favors for the other. It was a game of infinite variations.

Right in the middle of it, a shadow crossed her face. What had been repressed merriment a moment before simply went dead. The mouth straightened, the muscles went slack. She dropped the straw and took up the wooden shovel, making dull, routine motions of work, head down, face turned to her work, to the dung.

The transformation astonished me. I wondered if it might be something physical—one of those mysterious ailments assigned to women by the Yahweh because of Eve's independence, a spell I knew very little about. Or had some wizard found a lock of her hair and placed her under his power?

No, it was neither of these. It was the sudden presence of my father.

"What are *you* doing down here?" he asked, seeing only me.

"My job," I said. "I volunteered. Remember?"

"Air's not fit for a human being."

A perfect moment to suggest he open the doors and windows up there, let the breezes circulate. Yet I did not. Could not.

"It's not bad once your eyes stop running."

"Not fit for the likes of us." He looked around, face contorted, mouth open like a great fish gulping air. "Leave it to them."

He gestured in Sapphira's direction with his head. She was turned away from him, making some halfhearted effort to load dung on her shovel, the pace of an old woman. I hardly knew her.

"This is Sapphira," I said.

"Which one?" He was looking at the camels.

"No, the girl."

"This?"

She would not look up at him so he reached out and grabbed hold of her chin, raised her face. I thought for a moment he was going to count her teeth, make a bid.

"Sapphira?" he said, not letting go. "Foreign name. Where'd she come from? Ah, Shem's. The pig girl." He laughed, expecting me to, all the time holding her face up.

"You're hurting her," I said. It was as far as I could go. I wanted to lunge at him, but what dog can bite his master?

"Hurt?" he said, still holding her. "You can't hurt a camel or a servant girl."

"Sapphira is a . . ."

Is a what? *Friend*, I wanted to say. Or maybe *person*. My pause was worse than not speaking at all. He looked at her as if in a fresh light and let out a bray of a laugh.

"So that's it." He let go of her. "Good, good. Just don't do your rutting about up there." She went back to work, turned away from us, looking like just another servant. He grinned, shook his head. "Ripe little melon," he said.

"Sapphira is a . . ."

"Good, good." He nodded, but he was looking over the camels. "Doesn't seem to affect them," he said. "This rotten air."

"She . . ."

"And these damn things." He had wandered down to the coney cages, me at his side. "They all alive?"

I nodded without any real assurance. They had burrowed into the straw and there was no way to take a census without disrupting their homelife. I wasn't about to do that.

"Good thing, your having a little sport down here." He started to put his arm around me but then seemed to think better of it. "Keeps things simple." He moved us on and I thought perhaps it was some flicker of respect for Sapphira. "Things aren't so simple up there."

As his voice lowered I realized that we were into some family matter. It wasn't concern for Sapphira's feelings; it was an instinctive inclination to keep secrets from leaking to the staff. It was always that way. Whenever mealtime conversations fell to a hush it was a sign that the family had begun to talk about something the servants should not know. I learned later that this was a shared ritual of some importance—the clan pretending that its private activities and secrets remained invisible to servants, and servants performing their part by never revealing the fact that they knew everything.

"It seems," my father said in a low, confidential voice, "that

Japheth suspects his wife. He's asked you about it? Mentioned it?"

"About Ophir? But he has no proof."

"Of course. Still, I warned him about her on his wedding day. She's got passion on her breath. You can always tell from a woman's breath."

"But without evidence—"

"I warned him. 'Watch out,' I said. 'She's round and placid on the outside, but she's got the musk of a lynx. A sure sign,' I told him. 'Keep the gate locked,' I told him. But he didn't listen. So now he has a problem."

"He *thinks* he has a problem."

"That's what I said. Lucky for you you've got your little lynx down here. Keeps your record clean. I want no bad blood within the family. None." He stopped, measuring his words, staring at a couple of coneys nuzzling each other in the straw. "Now that you're of age . . ." Pause. Suspense. "It's time you learned about propriety. You know that word?" I nodded. "No you don't. Propriety means you don't do your fishing within the clan. Understand?" Nod, nod. "Propriety means that if you're tired of this little lynx, there's plenty of kitchen girls." Nod, nod. "And if it's variety you want, your Uncle Jubal will tell you what to do down in the sheep pens. I don't recommend it, but it's all a part of growing up. Don't let anyone say I stood in your way."

Was I to nod at that again or shake my head? Luckily he had turned to other matters. He had loosened his robe and was releasing a great stream right into the coney cage.

"So," he said, jiggling the last drops off and gathering his robes, "stick with the little lynx. You'll get into no trouble down here, right?" His moist forefinger struck my chest like a ram's horn. "The old seed of Noah—spread it far and wide. We've got a world to populate!"

He let out an explosive laugh and in a surge of affection he struck my right shoulder, knocking me right into the coney pen.

As I struggled to my feet, wondering if I had crushed any of the little creatures, I saw him heading up the stairs. He was chuckling, muttering, ". . . the old seed of Noah . . ."

When he had disappeared, I looked for Sapphira. She was gone. "Sapphira!" I called. "Sapphira!" The only answer was the scuffling, scratching, and breathing of a thousand dumb and captive animals.

X

SPICING THE SOUP

I T was not like her to sneak off without a word. Normally she shared each thought with me, each emotion as it came to her, open and cheerful. Indeed, because of her I had decided that the moodiness, the irascibility of my own family was due to excessive schooling. I had come to depend on Sapphira's good nature, her words springing forth as naturally and melodically as birdsong.

So this was something new for her: walking off in some kind of sulk without as much as a touch of the hand or a syllable of explanation. What had come over her?

Was she upset because I hadn't included her in the conversation? Surely she saw I had no choice. Had she resented our being interrupted? He was my father, after all.

I concluded that it could not be irritation. It must be a game. She was hiding somewhere. I was to come after her. That was the Sapphira I knew.

Finding her shouldn't be so difficult. She was limited to the confines of the ship. She had no vineyard in which to hide, no hollow olive trees, no cedar forests. We were bounded securely by the walls of our fortress.

X *Spicing the Soup*

But there was a greater expanse within those walls than I had realized. As I began to search through the maze of passageways I realized that in many respects this was less of a ship than it was a domain. As I recall, that was how we thought of it most of the time. We were scarcely aware even of being afloat. After all, we never saw the outside and there was little to remind us that it existed. Only occasionally—as if in a dream—we felt a rise and a fall, a shudder or some vague turning. Perhaps even this was in our minds. No way to be certain. We had no sails, no chart, no course, no way of judging our movement. We were drifting with currents we knew nothing about. In spite of our education, our reverence for knowledge, our mastery of the written word, all we knew for sure was where we had come from.

So there I was, seeking a lost girl while I and all my clan were equally lost in a grander sense. Lost? Even the irony was lost on me.

My thoughts were fixed not on the grander scheme but on the immediate problem: finding her. I started out with what the two of us called "our area," the Unclean Deck. She had always felt at home in the aviary. I went down the rows of small cages, calling her name, stared at by ravens, nighthawks, cuckoos. No human form there. Just a hundred little red eyes, questioning as if I had the answers.

Then through the double doors and into the collective cage, the aviary proper, where the larger birds were kept in enforced concord—the vultures, the eagles, the storks, and those sad sea creatures who could no doubt smell the waters about them without enjoying them—the cormorants, pelicans, gulls. A great flapping of wings, a flurry of feathers, then a settling down again. To them, I was a familiar though strangely featherless and plodding biped. Perhaps they were envious of my freedom to enter and leave that airy prison of woven reeds—an illusory freedom at best.

I felt a certain kinship with these outlawed creatures even then. They had been condemned, ostracized, yet at the same time they were protected for life, strangely valued. Like Cain. It was a great satisfaction to have gained their trust, to be able to approach them. The vultures, for example, would accept strips of dried meat from my hand, and one of the cormorants would allow me to smooth his disordered feathers. Would that I could do the same for Sapphira!

"Sapphira!" I called. There was only a clearing of bird-throats, a nervous shifting from one foot to the other.

They looked knowing. I half-believed that they were about to give me some message. "She's just gone to relieve her bladder," from the pelican or "She'll be waiting for you in the grain bin." How marvelous if the bats had started tittering and the lapwings had begun to call out, "Waiting in the hay loft; look now; hurry now."

But they didn't. In the scuttling, scratching silence I lost my confidence. Perhaps she was not playing some girlish game; perhaps she was really avoiding me.

I left quickly, running past the pig pens and the rabbit cages, past the wart hog (we could only find one—what good was that?) and the grain bins. No Sapphira.

Up to the Clean-beast Deck. Along the rows, cleaner here, better lit (as if they deserved something a half-step closer to heaven)—past the spacious stalls for the roebucks, the wild goats, the pygarg, the chamois, the wild oxen. And, too, those creatures

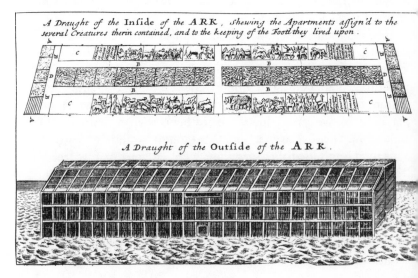

A Draught of the Inside of the ARK, shewing the Apartments assign'd to the several Creatures therin contained, and to the keeping of the Food they lived upon.

A Draught of the Outside of the ARK.

which were not forbidden but which for obvious reasons of good taste—or perhaps I should say decorum—we would never roast and eat: the mountain cat, the cheetahs, and the fearsome leopards. Imported from foreign parts, they were probably not even included in our dietary customs; still, you couldn't put them down with swine. So here they were, edible but spared by our chef.

From there through the poultry room. Smell worse than pigs, I can tell you. Only the word of priests from the time of Adam (the first priest?) could convince me that these molting, fighting, stinking creatures were fit for food. The fumes brought tears to your eyes. Still, they gave up their eggs, which were good enough once one washed off the layers of crud; and when they were done with laying, they gave up their bodies for our meals, leaving offspring to continue the cycle. The chicken's life of selfless service was often used by priests and our elders as an analogy to explain and justify the holding of unpaid servants down through the generations.

It did occur to me that we might have avoided this dependence if we were to grow grains and vegetables out there on the rain-slicked decks. I knew of holy men who never ate flesh and were as healthy as the rest of us. Why should one species draw strength from the enslavement of another? But that was as far as my social consciousness would stretch.

In any case, she was not there. I should have realized. The stink alone would have kept her out. She was no slop-jar girl. Besides, it was one large room like a dusky hen yard; there was no hiding place. She was not free to wander about openly as I was. Had she been caught in an area so far from her assignment, she would have received a thrashing from one of the family or a fellow servant. I was only beginning to understand how those who rule successfully manage to turn their subjects into lesser tyrants. The underlings learn to spy, report, and punish as handily as their betters.

On up to the Servants' Deck. There at least she could wander without being reprimanded. I had no idea what hours she was supposed to serve and who kept tabs on her; all I knew was that this was her assigned level—above the animals and below us.

Which is not to say I thought of our own position as lofty. After all, above us was Methuselah and above him, above layers of storm clouds, the Great Yahweh. In absolute terms, we were about half-way between the fishes of the deep and the divine. *We* knew that and we liked to think it kept us humble, but if those in the kitchen thought of us as far closer to Heaven, I'm sure no one on Our Deck said anything to dissuade them.

The kitchen—a marvelous great room. Warmer, nosier, more populated than our own deck, it served as common room for the servants. The stone ovens in the center; two work tables on either side, one for preparing foods and the other for serving meals to all of them. Remember that they outnumbered us by more than three to one. Just as the animals, naturally, outnumbered them. (I still recall from my first days in Sabbath School how this proved the singularity of the Supreme Being: Since the hierarchy of living creatures so closely resembled a pyramid, surely there must be a single peak.)

"She run out on you?" This from hefty Hephzibah, our master cook. "You've come after her?" She was chopping up chicken carcasses—heads in one bucket, backs in another, wings and cleaved breasts in a third. They had been slaughtered in the correct manner, of course, wind-pipe slit and blood thoroughly drained, guts checked for blemishes by our father himself. What she had there was religiously clean, but to me the great pile of carcasses looked more like a battle's carnage. "Would you be giving her a thrashing?"

"Me? Sapphira?"

"Well, I thought not." She turned and gave me a grin wide and warm as her heart. There was no one in my family as jolly as this—or as untutored. "Well, she wants to work the kitchens for a while. That's what she told me. 'Give me a job in the kitchens,' she said. So I threw the stones for her." These were an unattractive set of gall stones taken, she claimed, from a dead holy man. They foretold the future by the way they fell. "And she was ready for a change. That's what they showed. So I said to her, 'I'll find you a place for today. Then ask your master.' She'll have to go to your brother, you know. She's his property. But for now, I've given her a place."

"Working here? Where?"

"Now I don't know what *kind* of change. The stones didn't say. And there's only one throw for each rise of the sun. So maybe this isn't the change they meant. But change she gets. That's not me saying that, it's the stones."

"Where *is* she?"

"If she were younger, I'd say it was a different kind of change."

"Where?"

"But she's past that milestone. As I expect you know. Well past. Ripe, you might say. And ready for some new stage. You can't miss those change-signs. Like when I threw for the whole family back before the rains. Back during the dry times. Never saw the likes of it—every day for seven days. I knew we were in for it. I told your father, but he'd picked up signs of his own. There's strange forces in him too. Got them from his mother. But never mind that—I was saying I threw for the girl. She's in for something new. Some shift in—"

"Hephzibah, *where is she?*"

"Who?"

"Sapphira. Sapphira!"

"There's a ring to the way you say that. Well, you might look in the soup pantry. You just might look there." Again the laugh.

The soup pantry was kept separate because of the heat. It had its own stove. The fire was allowed to die each evening but the soup remained warm until it was reheated the next noon. The stove was fueled with wood and camel chips, a smoldering sort of heat for a simmering sort of soup.

The cauldron was big enough to bathe in. Above it were hung ladles and a variety of iron pots. One could dip in with a bowl or a bucket without depleting the supply. This extraordinary soup stock was always there, always warm, forever being augmented and drawn from, forever varying in texture and taste.

There also was Sapphira. She was stirring slowly with a wooden ladle the length of your leg. The soup didn't have to be stirred all the time, but now it was being reheated. New vegetable and meat stock had been added along with fresh herbs and spices. For an hour or so someone had to stir. It was not considered a skilled task.

"Found you!" I said. I half expected her to turn, laugh, fling her arms around me. Or perhaps it was only a desperate hope. In either case, I misjudged her mood. She would not even look at me. "Are you angry?" Slight shake of the head—just the suggestion of a no. "Something I said? Look, I tried to introduce you . . ."

I put my arms around her waist. Still she stirred her soup, remained rigid, would not turn; but she didn't object to my hands about her waist either. "What was it? Tell me."

I was slowly rubbing her stomach—same measured tempo as her stirring the soup. The heat of the place was getting to me, moist and heavy. And beautiful smells. The soup would not be brought to a boil until just before the evening meal, but it was growing warm. The air was so filled with vapors and herbal scents that we seemed to be floating in it. Sweat trickled down my face, down my neck, across my chest. Hands gently working—they too were moist from the very atmosphere as they massaged the flat of her stomach. Somehow they had found their way under her fabric on their own, following some blind, digital instinct.

"Is it because I talked with him so much?" She shook her head. "He is my father, you know." She nodded. "What then?"

In the silence I thought I detected the tremor of her crying, but all I could hear was the slosh of the soup. Then, almost inaudible, "Never mind. You can't hurt a camel or a servant girl."

That? Of all the slights, that was the one which had cut her? I was astonished. Such overreaction. There was no way I could comprehend it. Not back then. After all, the phrase was only a saying. I'd heard it a thousand times. He meant nothing by it.

"It's only a saying." She stiffened. "It's not that he doesn't like you. It's just that no one in my family really thinks of servants as human."

I could tell by the tightening of her muscles that this was somehow the wrong approach. I wondered how it could be that someone who had endured so much education could do so badly with words. I decided to keep quiet and leave persuasion to my hands. They seemed to be saying things the right way.

While the left hand lingered with the left breast, keeping that sweet nipple perked, the other inched its way downward across the stomach, wordless and gentle as an orchard snake, down into the dell. Surprise: In spite of past bitterness, the moss was moistly welcome. Never mind words, I said to myself.

I let my longest finger descend into the heart of the matter. Cautious at first, then deeper. The warming soup gurgled as her ladle gently undulated, liquid slurping.

There was too much fabric between us. Risking rebuff, I slid open my own raiment and raised hers, allowing her to continue her assigned task. With a slight bending of my knees, I found the proper height and rediscovered the familiar marshland from the rear. All fabric slipped to the floor. I too had a ladle and it had a way of its own, finding its route. So for a while we both stirred, rising and falling, steaming, dripping, eyes clouded in the vapors, tempo rising, heat increasing. At the very brink, my feet slipped on the wet tile and we toppled forward, face first into the soup. A mad scramble at first, but the liquid was no warmer than a bath. It enveloped us, invited us to stay, to complete what we had begun. Face to face we warmed again, joined again, this time sloshing and splashing like slippery dolphins in tropic seas, lubricated from without as well as from within. A gasping for air, a surge of strength, a rising tempest, the cry of sea lions.

Then a perfect calm.

We turned and lay back beside each other, heads resting on the rim, immersed to our waists, spent and limp as two plucked songbirds flung into the mix. Strength regained, we coiled into each other's arms, licking our lunch from chest and breast, receiving our nutriment naturally and gently from the other and, in return, adding our bodily spices to the family stock.

X I

REPAIRING THE
DAMAGE

A vision," Grandmother Zillah was saying, gesturing with a sweep of her hand. "I had this vision, clear as a waking moment."

"Now, now," Adah said, barely looking up from her sewing.

"A great ship lands and the doors open and creatures pour out, but they are all melded—no way to tell the men from beasts. Just a shuffling, stumbling, indistinguishable horde, and I stand there saying, 'Why save them? Why on earth save them?'"

"It's the herbs you take," Adah said, studying her work. "They create tempests in your head just before you sleep. There's no sense to doing that. No sense whatever."

Adah's voice flowed smooth as oil. I never heard her ruffled. A good thing, since the two of them, unnaturally yoked in marriage to the same man for much of their lives, now lived together like mismatched sisters in widowhood.

They were mending the lineage tapestry which had been burned by my father and desecrated by my brother during the torch episode. It had been dismantled and cleaned. Adah and

X 1   Repairing the Damage

Zillah now had the lower panel—the recent times—which had been most badly damaged. Flying pitch had burned small holes, spaces, blurring the family record. But the repair work was, as always, skillful.

I had been assigned to them as needle-threader. I was not pleased at being the temporary servant of these two old women, but someone had to keep threading the bone needles as the sewers shifted from one color to the next. The theory was that they were short-sighted, but it seemed to me as I worked with them that their eyes might be sharper than anyone suspected.

"It's not herbs and you know it," Zillah said. And to me, "The light blue, please. Sky blue. Sky? I can hardly remember it. No, it's not the herbs, Adah, it's being slowly roasted in this floating oven. Every day it gets hotter. I can't imagine why."

"It's the animals," I said. "They give off heat, and also the torches. It's much worse down there."

"Couldn't be," Zillah said and asked for another thread.

There was no arguing with her, but she was wrong nonetheless. For several days I had been assisting in the kitchen, working for that overweight and even-tempered mistress of the nether world, Hephzibah. My motive was simple: to convince Sapphira that I would do anything to be close to her. And perhaps too there was the thought that by serving time there I could disassociate myself from my family and convince her that I was a person in my own right, a person worthy of her affection.

I longed to tell Grandmother Zillah what it was like down there—the heat which rested on you like a great hand pressing down, doubling your weight, halving your strength; the sweat which poured down your face, stinging the eyes with salt, dripping into the food. There were no words which would help her to feel all that. And not Grandmother's fault, either. As the youngest wife, the beautiful one, the favorite, she had never experienced what it was like to be in a kitchen even under the best of conditions. As far as I know, she had never even consulted with the staff or planned meals. That had always been Adah's job.

"The boy's right," Adah said. "We're more fortunate than

those down there." I wasn't sure whether she meant the servants on the lower deck, the animals below them, or our friends and neighbors still further down. "We should give thanks for our blessings."

"Thanks? To a captain who won't give us a breath of sea air, much less a view? Thanks for keeping us from even looking at the outside world?"

"I don't imagine we'd enjoy it—all wet and windy."

"I'd rather drown in the deep than be slow-baked in this smokehouse." And then to me in a different tone: "Someone's standing behind that door listening to us."

Her mind was often plagued by dark visions, but they were not the type we could ignore. I went to the door expecting to see a servant with his ear to the crack. But it was only Leah, Japheth's pudgy little girl.

"Good," I said. "They sent you to thread needles?"

"No."

"It's not hard. Come look at all the colors." And to the

sewers, "I think maybe she's supposed to thread needles."

"They didn't send me," Leah said, squinting at us.

"Then why are you here?"

The girl was studying the threads and then the tapestry and pretended not to hear—a trick common to children and servants.

"You watch," I said to her. "If you study carefully you could make a fine threader."

We worked in silence, Leah watching solemnly. The two women were concentrating on the portion of the tapestry which contained the image of Lamech, the husband they had once shared in enforced concord. Though I had known Grandfather Lamech before his death, I never would have recognized the dark and brooding figure sewn in thread even as it was before the damage. Indeed, I had forgotten how forbidding he had been.

As for Methuselah, the figure just above, could this be the same as the poor old wasted husk of a man I had washed with such care? Here was the image of a young man no one alive could recall. Who could verify its accuracy?

The panels above that one had been detached and were being worked on by my mother and her daughters-in-law. They had the task of repairing Enoch, the one who walked with Yahweh. Above him were Jared, Mahalalel, Kenan, Enosh, and Seth who as everyone knows was the third son of Adam. The names roll in my head like an old prayer.

And of course Eve. Yes, she was there. The only woman shown in the entire genealogy. You'd think the men had done their begatting all by themselves with scarcely a grunt. I wondered how my grandmother Zillah with all her willful ways felt about patching the history of our clan which did not include her own image. Truly, not since Eve had a single woman been included. Who were they all? Didn't Grandmother care? Perhaps like the rest of us she had lived with that tapestry so long she could not think of it as just or unjust. It simply *was*, eternal as constellations.

Lord only knew which generation had begun it; the tapestry was reputed to be old when Methuselah was a boy. We were all brought up with it. You don't question anything that close to you. Not unless the world rips apart for you as it did for me. But that was later.

"Marvelous thing," Adah said, raising her eyes reverently toward the nearest torch, "his creating daylight from the blackness."

"No marvel if it chokes us all," Zillah said.

"We'll get used to it."

"I'll never get used to not breathing. If he doesn't smother us to death, he'll burn us to ash. Imagine, a grown man throwing torches around, risking everything. Turn this box into a flaming coffin, he will. End of the clan. End of the race. End of all these precious beasts and birds and every creeping and crawling thing. Turn the world into a great desolate waste. All his fault, him and his fire play. What would he have to say then?"

"I don't suppose," Adah said, smiling pleasantly, drawing the thread up from underneath the fabric, "he'd be in a position to say very much, now would he?"

They were interrupted by my mother, who entered at a trot. Small as she was, she carried several panels of the fabric in her two short arms without complaint.

"Through with Lamech?"

"You should talk with that husband of yours," Zillah said. "He won't listen to me. Keeping us inside like this . . ."

"No time for that," Mother said. "Our job is to get these panels back together. It's not right having it in pieces."

"Not right at all," Adah said.

Mother laid out the sections she had been working on. True, they were less damaged, but she had finished far more than the two old women.

It was not new to any of them, this repairing. It was a recurring task. And they were all wonders at it. Quick as a moth did damage, all the women would cluster about, discussing just how it had looked and how it might best be repaired. When the fabric began to fade or give way with age, woof parting from warp, they were at it again, taking no advice from the men, brightening the colors, sharpening the features until no one but the Great Yahweh Himself could tell for sure what was original

94

and what was replacement.

But not even my industrious mother could resist comparing their handicraft.

"Ah," she said, spotting for the first time the repaired Lamech. "Black cloak, I see."

"He's always had a black cloak," Adah said sweetly.

"Of course. And his foot on . . . On a *baby's face?*"

"No indeed, that's a lion. Lamech the conquerer."

"Ah yes," my mother said. "Of course. Foot on a baby lion."

Then it was her turn to show the renewed Enoch, the one who walked with the Yahweh. Yes, there was the giant turnip stalk, just as He always was, unchanged. Eternal. But had Enoch himself been the same height? He was significantly taller than his son, Methuselah, on the next level. I remarked on that.

"Naturally," my mother said. "Any man who walked with the Yahweh has to be a head taller than his son."

There was a certain logic to that. Coming from my mother, it had to be true. I blamed my own memory for the confusion.

"Time to attach the panels again," my mother said. It made her uneasy to have our history in pieces. Indeed, all three worked with a special urgency, as if we as a family remained vulnerable until the past was reconstructed.

"Our work would have gone faster if I had had both daughters-in-law. Ophir had to care for that daughter of hers."

"Leah?" Adah asked. "She wasn't with Leah."

"Of course she was. That's why she couldn't help me."

"The girl's right here."

"Leah?"

At first it appeared that the girl had left. But then we found her under the table sucking her thumb.

"You're too old to be doing that," Zillah said.

"But I *am* doing it," Leah said.

"Never mind that," my mother said. "Aren't you supposed to be with your mother?"

"No."

"Where *are* you supposed to be?" My mother had as strong a sense of order as my father—everything in its place.

"She told me to go down and look at the animals."

"No place for children," Grandmother Zillah said. "Filthy creatures. And dangerous. You should be in your room."

"No I'm not. That's where my mother is and the door is barred."

"She's *in* there?" my mother said. "All alone?"

"Not all alone."

"Leah dear, who's she with?"

Silence.

"I said, who is your mother with?"

Thumb back in the mouth.

"I asked you a question."

Fast as a piglet, Leah was out the door.

"This family," Mother said, shaking her head and stamping her foot. "Heat madness. Adah, you get the girl before she talks with anyone else. Zillah, you come with me. We've got to straighten this out before any of the men find out. No room for revenge with us cooped up like this."

They were gone without a word to me. I scarcely understood the situation. Idly I looked over the tapestry.

Suddenly, like a flash of heat, I noticed something I hadn't allowed myself to consider before. Lamech *was* more hateful looking than before; that cloak *had* changed from purple to black; and that *was* a plump baby under his foot. It was not my faulty memory; it was their tinkering.

And Enoch—he *had* been made taller. Why? None of us could remember him; but his magnification had made Methuselah smaller by comparison. Poor old Methuselah!

Unsteady as that great ship was on the undulating sea, the vertigo I felt was caused by this new understanding: While men did their best to preserve the past and to fix it in our minds like the unchanging stars in the night sky, the women were adjusting and amending it thread by thread and had been doing so for generations.

XII

PROTEST

SAPPHIRA continued to be distant and formal. I had hoped that our splash in the soup would have rekindled her affection, but she could not seem to relax after seeing me that time with my father. Perhaps she imagined some kind of family resemblance.

So I continued working in those steaming kitchens. I thought of myself as a self-indentured servant, taking on my fair share of the work. True, I was called up from time to time as a threader or for meals, and at night I returned to the relative cool of my family's deck. But surely these minor differences would not be noticed and I would be accepted; surely a few more days of this and she would join me where we belonged, down in our private garden, the hay of the Unclean Deck.

At night I was often too tired to sleep. I would lie on my mat sweating and musing with wonder at the strata which seemed to surround me. How did it all start? All those men and women sleeping in the rude quarters below me—they had no choice. The fact that they were assigned to that deck and we to ours seemed as arbitrary as the distinction between clean and unclean animals. There must have been good reasons. A world without reasons would surely fall apart.

In the dark of one such sleepless night it struck me that perhaps these hierarchies did indeed have reasons but bad ones. A frightening notion! If this were so, wasn't I obliged to make changes? I wasn't running the ship but I was close to the one who was. Well, closer than those on the deck below. I must have some kind of influence.

I had, after all, been a dutiful son. Hadn't I? Jump, he said, and I jumped. No more than a flicker of doubt. Sweep, he said, and I swept. Work, he said, and I cleaned up after a multitude of defecating beasts with no more than an occasional rumble of protest—and that from an unruly stomach with a mind of its own.

I never played the sluggard like my brother Japheth, never stole wine, never talked back or asked for favors; surely I had earned credit. Ah, the illusion of familial justice!

It was a mistake, I suppose, to let someone as impressionable as me spend time on the lower decks. It was different for my mother when she descended on occasion to plan the meals with Hephzibah. Mother never questioned her rank and no doubt assumed that living down there was no more taxing than her visits were for her. As for my father, he had his own notion of justice and I'm sure he didn't lie awake brooding about the cabin assignments.

For me, though, the scene down there was all too vivid. How incredibly long that workday must seem, hour dragging after hour with no sense of accomplishment. No satisfaction but in endurance. At the end of their labors, a meager evening meal—males separated from females as if sharing food would result in mass coupling. No time for conversation. A few complaints, a joke or two, then off to their dormitories much like the beasts below them.

How could I sleep with thoughts like these churning in my mind? As I lay there I began to practice lines which I might deliver to my father: Throw open the door, Father, let the air circulate; rotate the sleeping assignments so that we all take turns on the lower level; distribute the work evenly, each according to his ability.

XII Protest

Over and over the phrases ran until at last I fell asleep dreaming of that perfect garden in which lions allow lambs to frolic and the fruit is too green to be tempting.

My brother Japheth had taken to spending much of his time with our Uncle Jubal. This struck me as odd at first, there being such a gulf in age. They differed too in their views on wine. Jubal, the storyteller, and all his side of the family drank nothing except when required to do so for rituals. Japheth's love of the grape, on the other hand, ran deep. Still, the two shared a value even more basic: They each had a great respect, even a holy reverence, for free and open time. To them, any work was a tyranny.

It must have been a strain for them, surrounded by a family who thrived on effort. My parents, for example, simmered with energy and filled each portion of the day with tasks. Even kindly old Tubal-cain was restless without his forge. To Japheth, all this was incomprehensible. In desperation, he turned to Uncle Jubal, the musical member of the family, the one who could tootle the day away on his pipe or, when the fancy moved, spin out fantasies for the ear on the lyre.

I met them on the stairway which led down to the Servants' Deck. They often loitered there after the morning meal, chatting and catching whatever leftovers the servants were returning to the kitchen. Japheth had his first cup of wine—he must have hidden a keg in his room; and Uncle Jubal was indulging in his own addiction, the lyre. I didn't recognize the melody. Not until later did I discover that he knew no songs at all—neither sacred nor profane. Everything he played was, like his life, improvisation. I knew of no one who had a higher regard for the spontaneous and the natural. To him, any artistic expression which was rooted in effort was an affectation. Japheth considered him a genius.

I asked them where my father had gone. It was the morning after I had wrestled with my conscience, and I was determined to instruct my father in the notion of fairness.

Thanks to my lack of sleep I had arrived at the morning meal late. My father, never plagued with insomnia (the blessing of a man who is never in doubt) was early as always. And so we missed. Once again.

"Your father," Uncle Jubal said, "sweeps through here like the winds. Just stand still long enough and he'll be by—whoosh!"

He and Japheth both found that comic.

"If he were near here," Japheth said, smiling at me over his mug, "I would not be." Pause for more appreciative laughter, each the audience for the other. "What's the matter with you, looking for work?"

I had no choice; I had to share my feelings with them. I described the condition of those working below us, their need for air, and my plan for rotating the use of the decks. Oh, I should never have started, but once begun I had to finish. There was, surely, a logic to fairness. How could anyone ignore it? All I had to do was to present the facts.

"I had no idea," Japheth said when I was through.

"A tragic tale," Uncle Jubal said.

"Terrible injustice," Japheth said.

"Shocking," Uncle Jubal said.

I was encouraged. If I could make an impression on these two, perhaps there was a chance with my father.

A servant boy came by us with a tray of dirty dishes from the morning meal. Japheth reached out and caught him by the ankle. The tray tottered, but the boy caught it in time.

"Hey there," Japheth said, "we're told that conditions are terrible on your deck and the lot of you are discontent." The boy looked down at Japheth with alarm but said nothing. "Well, is that true? Is it true you're all discontent?"

The boy shook his head.

"Speak up! We want to know if conditions are terrible down there. Are you not happy with your lot?"

"We're happy," the boy said miserably.

"Really happy?"

"Really happy."

"Grateful?"

"Grateful."

"Really deeply grateful?"

"Really deeply grateful."

"Off then—and enjoy yourself."

He gave the boy a friendly slap on the thigh which almost sent the tray flying down the stairs.

"Well, Brother," Japheth said to me, "who are we to argue with that?"

For all my noble intentions, I still made my rounds on the lower level. There, that very morning, I made the discovery: two ruffled mounds in the corner of the aviary, an osprey and a pelican, both quite dead.

I turned them over in disbelief. No doubt about their state: They were stiff. What right had they to give up?

These were rare birds even before the floods. We'd gone out of our way to include them. Sea birds are not obliging; they don't lend themselves to being caught. They don't readily walk into a baited trap like the greedy vultures and they don't spend their days sleeping like bats and owls. No, they were trouble in the getting and trouble in the keeping. And now dead.

Of the heat, I assumed. Now, speaking as a fellow exile, I wonder if they had been weakened by being cut off from their homeland miles from where we held them, a homeland where fish swam and winds cleared the air. It is true, looking back on it now, that they had sulked even before that terrible heat. Wouldn't eat dead fish we gave them; let their feathers molt. Stared at me, red-eyed and resentful, lacking gratitude. But they didn't actually give up until the heat had reached its zenith. Thanks to the heat, all our work was to no avail. They were of no value now, not even for eating since they were prohibited. And there would be no more of them in the world ever again.

No more? A flurry of hope in that. Perhaps this was just the sort of catastrophe which could touch my father's heart. Not the suffering of humans; not even the agony of beasts and birds. What he faced was the violating of his Divine Instruction.

With a new confidence I took them up by the feet, one great bird in each hand, necks dragging the floors, and set out to find my father.

One deck up I found my brother Japheth again. He was

through with his loitering for a while and was making an appearance at his assigned task—tending to the clean animals. Not that he did the work himself. He had three young men under his command. That is, Japheth sat on a bale of hay while three servants did their work.

My cargo did seem to startle him. Without rising, he tipped his head way over on one side to see what manner of creatures hung from my two hands.

"Pelicans?"

"One pelican, one osprey. Dead with the heat."

"Get them off this deck."

"Where's our father?"

"You shouldn't be dragging them across this deck."

"We only had two of each. I've got to find our father."

"Get rid of them. Not here."

"Get rid of them? Down there? You want me to bore a hole and chuck them out?"

"They're unclean."

True, they were unclean. But he had missed the seriousness of their deaths. Even I knew that it takes two to perpetuate the breed and there was no reviving these. Unless conditions down there were changed, where would it stop? It was too much for Japheth's misty mind, but my father would be stricken.

I headed for the kitchens thinking he might be conducting the

daily slaughter, but he wasn't. I was greeted with consternation there. A great shouting and shooing me out, even Hephzibah waving her arms as if I had come in with the plague.

"Not here, for the love of God, not here. You realize what you have there? Don't let them touch the floor; we've enough scrubbing to do without them dragged on the floor."

It did seem a bit strange at the time—such a calm acceptance of chicken guts and heads and feet creating a great slime underfoot, but let a beautiful osprey so much as touch the floor with his poor dead head, and out came the scrub brushes and the sand and pumice stone. Still, it wasn't the occasion for a discussion of values.

On up to our own deck where I put the sewing group to rout with my two helpless birds.

"What's this?" Grandmother Zillah shouting, though it was clear enough what I had. "You want to poison us?"

She and the others left in a flurry without telling me what I wanted to know. In their place, Uncle Tubal-cain came in. I had no time for him. I would have fled except that he stood squarely in the door.

"What have you there?" he asked.

"Have you seen my father?"

"There in your hands—what have you there?"

"Here?"

"I asked you, what have you there in your hands?"

There was a certain persistence in Tubal-cain, a certain slow-moving resemblance to my father. There would be no escaping him, yet I was in no mood for a plodding conversation. I had never seen him at work—his forge and home were in a neighboring town; but I could imagine that great arm rising and falling with the weight of the hammer, a pace he so tediously echoed in conversation.

"Here in my hands? Two dead birds, Uncle Tubal. Just two dead birds."

He paused, tilting his great head to one side for a better view. Although unbearded, he looked older than my father, more weathered. Perhaps it was only his ponderous manner. "Not chickens," he said to himself, working it out. "Not cocks. No.

Not game birds." Then he looked at me, some form of recognition forming. "Those must be sea birds. That there looks like a pelican." Nod. "And the other an osprey." Nod, nod. "We no longer have a pair. Not of either of them."

He came over to me and went down on one knee, smoothing the feathers. "No more of these?" he said. "No more of these ever again on the face of the earth? Never again? This the last? Even the memory to fade?"

I looked down, astonished. I had underestimated him.

"It's the heat," I said. "The lack of air."

"Dead for all time," he said.

"Dead birds?" My father was suddenly in the room. Tubal stood. I stared. Whatever speech I had planned now left me. "What's this about dead birds?"

"The heat," I said. "The air." The words stumbled out in bunches. All wrong. The one time I had a perfect argument and I couldn't put it together in sequence. "They need air. They'll be dying down there. It's not right. Trapped there like animals."

"Animals? They *are* animals." He laughed. More of a snort. How should he know that I was talking about servants?

I was being clumsier than my Uncle Tubal who, just when I needed him, left, shaking his head. Anger at my own bumbling and at his departure gave me new courage—a crazed sort of courage.

"Look," I said, "these are dead. These two. No more of these for rest of time. Your fault. Nothing can live for long down there. The servants will be dying too. It's not human to keep us cooped up here. Not human."

A shocked hush. Had I really said that? Out loud? Right to his face? He must have been as startled as I.

Dead silence. The weight of those two birds pulled me down into the bowels of the ship. Awful lull.

Finally he spoke, his voice taking on the rumble of an approaching storm. "Who is this that gives me advice? Who is this that knows more than I do?" No answer. Louder now: "Where were you when I received the plans for this ship? Who laid out the measurements, planned the hull, the decks, the fittings? Who gave orders and kept men busy when scoffers laughed?

XII Protest

"Who made up lists and had animals gathered? Who decided to place *you* on that list? Who pulled you on board when the waters were rising?

"Can you live in the sea like the shark? Can you walk on the surface? Can you fly in the clouds for months without eating and without landing? At whose word are you dry and alive?

"Can you build another ship? Can you cause the waters to roll back? Can you raise dry land and cause the sun to shine? Can you found a new city, fill it with just people, build a new tribe without my blessing? Can you take a single step without me? A single step?

"Who are you to tell me to open the doors? Where would you be if I had decided not to grant you life? From whom did you learn the word 'justice'? Who taught you the word 'human'?

"Who are you to be teaching me values? Who are you to tell me policy? Well? Just who *are* you? Who *are* you? Well . . . ?"

"Nothing," I whispered, dropping those two dead birds.

XIII

AN OPEN WINDOW

IT was simpler for Adam. Only one prohibition. Do what you want, he was told, but don't sample that one tree. With a whole garden to choose from, he probably wouldn't have even noticed the special one without all the fuss, would have lived out his life dumb and content.

For me there were three prohibitions. First, the one against opening doors and windows. No sense to it, but there it was. The air growing heavier, tempers shorter. We kept dousing the surviving sea birds and reptiles with water each day, but they were close to death, eyes blinking, bloodshot in the twilight, staring at us as if we were their captors rather than saviors.

It was an absurd regulation, pointless as the one protecting the tree of knowledge. Even Grandmother Zillah could see the similarity. "It's bad enough to be ordered about like a second Eve," she said, spitting the words, "but look who's giving the commands: my own son, the creature of my own womb, the product of my own agony. I gave him my milk for this?"

I shared their discontent, but I had an additional concern: the instruction not to do any "rutting about" except on the lowest level. That was easy enough when we were both at home down there among the unclean animals. We were happy to give pigs and birds their first view of what it is to be human. But she was no longer willing to see me on that level. As a fellow worker in the kitchen she adopted the air of the simplest scullery girl, mumbling and not looking me in the eye. It was as if my father's conversation had cast a spell on her.

The third prohibition was also directed against me alone. Strange that I should be singled out. I never thought of myself as rebellious, in need of restraints. True, I was the one who asked questions in Sabbath School when the others lay low. But surely that was no sin—not now with the priests left to nurture the fish. There must be some holy logic to the fact that I was afloat and they were not. So why had these special ordinances been leveled at me? Why particularly was I forbidden to converse with the Ancient?

It was the forbidden tree all over again. Washing that old body had been no great pleasure, but now that I'd been ordered not to return, I felt tempted to disobey just for the sport of it. Besides, there was something inviting about the old man himself. An old tree can offer good fruit, and at my age the prospect of a strange taste only added to the adventure of it all.

Of the three *shalt-not* ordinances, this was the one which tempted me the most. After all, until I convinced Sapphira that I was my own man, she would not readily open herself to me—not on any level. As for the doors, they were bolted as securely as my father's mind. I was not going to pry open *that* issue for a while. But it was important to assure myself and Sapphira too that I, like the rebel Adam, could take a risk or two. So I set out to make a social call on old Methuselah.

This time I was moderately clean but not dressed for a holy day. After all, it was hardly a sacred act. I was merely going to chat with an old man. Cheer him up in his declining years. Brighten his day. And just maybe he would say something in passing which would explain why everyone seemed so determined to keep me from him.

Nahum the manservant was in the outer chamber. If he recognized me, he gave no sign. Perhaps the muscles on his face had turned to stone. He merely gestured for me to enter the inner room, his hand beckoning with so slight a movement that it would not have startled a gnat.

Noiselessly I slid into the patriarchal room and eased the door shut behind me, wincing at the click of the latch.

With cautious tread I headed for that built-in crib and then stopped short. It was empty. The lattice side had been let down. I turned and saw him in a chair, a simple throne seat of oleander wood. Beside him was a table with scrolls, medicine jars, quills, ink pot, a goat's skull holding dried flowers, and a beautiful oil lamp. All this I hardly noticed on my last visit; but then I'd been in no mood to take a careful inventory.

"I knew you would return," he said when I was close enough to hear. "Sit there." He gestured to a stool with just the slightest nod. "Tell this old man what has been happening below."

"Happening?"

"What they're doing. And saying. How they're getting along."

Was it possible that no one else had visited? Wasn't he our patriarch? "Everything's fine," I mumbled.

"Really fine?" he asked. "Everything?"

"Well, not really. I mean, things are terrible. The heat . . ." I paused, realizing that here the air was relatively clear, the temperature almost normal. "Not like here. You can't imagine. The heat. Birds are dying. And the kitchens are like the Underworld."

"The doors shut?"

"Bolted, locked. We're not to open them. You have no idea what it's like down there."

"I imagine," he said, his voice like a puff of wind in reeds. I took this to be the casual response of an uninterested man. I know him better now that he is long since dead, and I know what he meant when he said, "I imagine." He had a gift for that. All I felt then, though, was a hot flash of indignation and frustration. I'd tried to tell my father what it was like and I was struck down for my troubles. Now I'd tried again and the response was even more disheartening—a shrug and a yawn.

"It's cool here," I said. "Not like down there. It gets worse and worse the lower you get."

"Of course," he said, inclining his head in a kind of nod.

"Your father intended this spot for himself. Notice the vent."

With difficulty the old man raised one hand, one long finger extended as if in the act of benediction. Actually he was pointing to the small grill in the ceiling. I had almost forgotten. His window on the side was bolted shut like the doors on the decks below, but the viewless vent was keeping the place bearable. How could he possibly imagine what it was like on the deck below, much less the Servants' Deck?

"You should visit me more often," he said. "And breathe."

"They're against it."

"They?"

"My father mostly. But the others too. I'm not supposed to be up here. Not supposed to talk with you."

There was a moment of silence. As I looked at him for a response it seemed to me that the muscles on his cracked face pulled a bit on either side of the mouth. I thought I could see what that smile might have been hundreds of years ago, but it was partly my imagination. If I had not been looking so intently, I would have missed the muscular contraction entirely. Even then I wasn't sure whether he was truly amused or whether he was grimacing at some gastric discomfort.

"I don't understand," I said.

"Don't understand?" He'd lost the thread. Why on earth was I trying to learn something from him?

"Don't understand why they tell me not to see you."

"Ah, not to see me."

"My father, he told me not to see you."

"You're repeating yourself."

"Sorry."

"Now, what were you asking?"

I closed my eyes. Anything to be out of there. "Why they don't want me to see you."

"Now *that's* a good question." He leaned forward slightly and tapped me on the knee with his finger, the weight of it no more than a dried leaf.

"Because you are the third son," he said.

"The youngest? The youngest is the least important." I said this with a shrug. I had been raised to believe it, to be invisible much of the time. And much of the time I had no objection. It struck me as no blessing to take on the burdens of a first-born, shaping oneself to match one's paternal creator. Being the third was my license for independence.

"The third," he muttered. "The third." He was drifting off again. I considered leaving but that dried hand was still resting on my knee, holding me. "Sun, moon, and . . ."

"Stars."

"Stars, of course. Birth, procreation, and . . . ?"

"Death."

"Death, of course. Heaven, earth, and . . . ?"

"The Underworld."

"The Underworld, of course. All threes. All triangles. The face is defined by two eyes and . . . ?"

"A mouth?"

"A mouth. Of course. A woman disrobed is defined by two breasts and . . . ?"

How could I tell an old man? "Ah . . ."

"The nest, the nest. You think I'm innocent? A man of my years? You think I've forgotten?"

I shook my head, blushing. Of course I thought of him as innocent—just as young men think of me today.

"Triangles. Think of all the stories you have heard—both sacred and the profane. All the same. The parable of the three priests. They taught you that one? The first who thought of nothing but Heaven, the second who thought of nothing but his fellow men, and the third . . . ?"

"Thought of men and Heaven in one vision."

"And the three dybbuks, one who plagued only the sinners, one who plagued only the righteous, and the third . . . ?"

"Tormented the rest of us."

"The rest of us. Of course. And the three maidens in the field with a goat?" A goat story? At his age? "The fair maiden tried to play the lyre for him . . ."

"But the goat had no ear for music."

"No ear for music. Then the strawberry maiden tried dancing with him."

"But his hoofs had no talent for dance."

"No talent. So the third maiden, the dark one, paid no attention to him. She was on her hands and knees, looking for her lute in the grass."

"She never found it, but . . ." Delicious pause. "Took up the horn instead."

I laughed. Had to. And watched the old man's face muscles draw that lipless mouth into a semblance of grin, head vibrating as if shaken by some distant tremor.

The tale was nothing new, you understand. It was one we told and retold as soon as our dreams turned to rutting goats and rams, the comic versions of manhood coming along with the serious discovery of it all, the first preparing the way for the second. This particular one was for young boys. I thought I had outgrown it. He was teaching me that I never would.

Once again he reached out that fleshless arm and placed his hand on my knee.

"Three," he said. "Third is always vital. It is the third son who strikes out on his own. This is the pattern of tales and always will be. First is the anchor to the past; second is the filler, uncertain; the third is the pull to the future."

"And when there are more sons?" I thought literally in those days.

"There is always a third son. In the retelling we neglect the others. The third son is always the hero."

"But if there are, say, eight sons and perhaps daughters?"

"There is always a third son."

There was no arguing the point. In the pause, I started to ask one of the questions I had come to ask and then lost courage. It was not easy to chat casually with a man for whom history was personal memory.

"Come here with questions?" he asked. "Of course you have questions. Ask."

It was not the first time I suspected him of seeing thoughts take shape in the dark hole of my eye.

"Why don't they want me to see you?"

"They want control."

"Of whom? Me? You?"

"Nothing so simple as you and me."

"What then?" What could be more complicated than me?

"The past."

I looked at him, waiting for more. When he didn't continue, I nodded as one does with old men who make no sense, nodded as one does with idiots and small children. He must have known then that I did not understand. What extraordinary faith, though, to assume that I would recall that idiotic remark, worry it as the sea oyster worries a grain of sand, turning it over and over, polishing it, coating it, converting it from an irritation to a small but prized possession, something of value.

"You have another question," he said. "I have the strength for one more today. Just one. Ask."

"The doors," I said. "The hatches. The windows. All the time they are closed. Locked. My father's orders. If anything is to be thrown out, he must do it himself. No one else has even smelled the air outside. The heat down there is terrible. Birds and animals are dying. Still he forbids us even to look out. Why?"

"Control."

So here we were, back to an old man's riddle-talk. I had less patience this time. It wasn't right for him to sink into foolishness, speaking like those wandering prophets who drift into town making pronouncements no one can understand, receiving alms against the possibility that they might really be holy or have powers, and then drift on again, preaching to rocks and trees. This was no way for my great-grandfather to behave.

"Control?" I asked. A simple nod. "Control of the past? What does that mean?"

"Inventing what happened."

"We're afloat, you know. Adrift. That's no invention."

"There's plenty left to invent."

He was getting more like those sun-crazed prophets every minute. I was learning nothing. "I know what happened. I'm only asking why we can't open the doors and windows."

"Tell me what's out there."

"Out there? Water. The earth is covered with water. Nothing out there but water."

"If that were so, why would he forbid you to look out?"

Another soothsayer's technique for you—answer a question

with another question. No answer at all. Still, one question striking the other did produce a spark of sorts.

He began fumbling in his robes for something. Maddening to
watch crippled hands attempting to perform a simple task. Yet I
could not help without being asked.

"I too am not to open windows. Imagine . . . An old man
ordered around by his son . . . No, grandson. Held captive. As
I once held him. The wheel turns and there is no stopping it.
Turns again. Again . . ."

Those parchment fingers tangled with the fabric, got lost,
faltered, and with them his words. I had no patience to string
together those broken phrases; it took all my strength not to ask
him straight out what he was looking for.

Finally the fingers brought forth a thong from around his
neck. Where had that been when I bathed him? No time for
questions. With a slight nod he now allowed me to help him
raise the cord over his head. I was sure that the slightest wrong
move would snap those neck bones, would send the head rolling,
that wisp of a beard trailing like the tail of some old shooting star.

There, it was off. The thong, that is. At the end was a bronze
key. He pointed to it and then to the shuttered window at the
side of his cabin. It was the only one on that uppermost deck and
can be seen on some of the more accurate drawings.

"Not to open," he muttered. "Orders. But what he doesn't
know . . . Old Nahum's no fool. Moves like a shadow in the
dark. Eyes of a bat. Slid this from your father's collection. So
now . . ." He struggled with what I had come to know was a
chuckle. "Now I've got . . . the key."

Again he pointed to the heavy shutters which barred that single
opening. I was to open it! I could feel the blood in my temples.
Back before the Deluge it meant nothing to look out. The sun
shone, the sun hid, men went out to the fields and returned at end
of day, women took their wash to the river and returned, traders
came to the square and later rode off again—all this we saw without seeing. We never thought to give thanks for open doors,
open windows. Sight was as common as air.

Since the beginning of troubled times, however, we were
trapped by the fortress which protected us. We knew the outside

only by the moan of the winds, the slap of occasional waves. The world out there was further from us than are stars from shepherds. The prospect of seeing the expanse of it for myself was like being promised a vision.

I thrust the key in the lock—made by a dedicated craftsman who was no longer with us—raised the oaken planking which was hinged at the top. I hooked it open even before I allowed myself a view of what I knew was going to be a mighty expanse of water, a world's whole surface turned to sea with us the chosen of the chosen, sole inheritors of the Word, of Life, of the future of the race.

No, not so. Shock. Disbelief. Water, yes. More water than I had ever seen. But sole inheritors, no.

There to my left was a tree to which clung five shaggy forms. Humans? Yes, but looking more like ragged apes. All about them the rubble of any great flood—planks, crates, branches, bloated corpses. Two small children huddled in a tub; a bearded man had tied himself and his wife to a wagon shaft. Further out a section of a roof with a cluster of human forms, a few chickens, four or five children. Some sitting, some sprawled; all motionless.

To the right a boat. Not mighty like ours, but a boat nonetheless. Something which had perhaps been used on rivers. No rivers now, but there it was—for a while, at least. Open to the continuing rains, clearly sinking, it was overloaded with huddled forms. A few looked in our direction, faces dark with hatred. Not one raised his hand. They were drained of all hope.

Why hadn't I expected this? How had I imagined that the rest of mankind would take to drowning with a shrug, would remove itself as an embarrassment and an eyesore? How had I, the compassionate one, failed to see that even in the absence of an Ark, even in the absence of hope, they would cling like animals to each hour of life?

Had I assumed that the Creator whose extraordinary mind had planned and executed this deluge would for some reason prefer quick deaths to slow ones? Had I assumed that when at last He decided to clear the scene, He would do it neatly and cleanly? Did some portion of me believe that because we had been selected for survival we should with the same benevolence be protected from seeing those who were not?

XIII An Open Window

And now that it had been revealed—the vision of it all, the Divine Truth of it all—was it possible for any human being to stand there without calling to them, inviting them all, lowering lines, helping them up the sides, accepting every fellow man and woman and child until we too . . . ?

"Close the shutters now," Methuselah said softly. "At your age, take your fresh air in small doses."

XIV

FRESH WINDS

W E got our fresh air. But not as expected. Nothing ever comes just as expected. Not even age.

I knew something had changed even before I was fully awake. A shifting under me, a strange instability. The lamp which hung over me in that barren little cell of mine was swinging. Timbers were creaking. Earthquake? No, there was no earth. Waves? Was that possible?

We'd been raised miles from any shore, but we had come to know the sea from the songs and chanteys Uncle Jubal sang. There was no reason not to assume that he had once been a sailor, so vividly did he describe the winds, the waves, the storms, the wrecks. But of course they were all lies. We knew the sea just as we came to know from him every path and shrub in Eden without having been there. It bothered me when I first learned —all these landscapes and seascapes coming from his mind, visions set to the tunes of his lyre, melodies varying each time for the pleasure of it. Such deception!

In the years since then I have heard reports presented as the true record, histories and personal accounts, and I have come to

see in them all kinds of error. No doubt they are necessary—
giving learned men a sense of worth. But what I treasure most I
have learned from men who, like Jubal, played with fancy.

From him I knew we were heading into a storm just as surely
as if I had spent years at sea. It was a blessing to identify the
strange motion, to tame it with a name. Still, it is never easy to
have one's whole world rocked.

I slipped on my clothes, hands trembling with a mix of a young
man's excitement in novelty and a grown man's fear.

Out in the corridor, a clutter of family: cries of protest,
bellows of indignation, whimpering, calls for calm. They were
all there.

"Where's Noah?" someone asked and then a chorus in echo:
"Where's Grandfather?" "Where's that son of mine?" "I saw
him minutes ago." "Someone find him."

What could he do about a storm? What could anyone do?
Still, he had predicted everything else and prediction gives a man
authority. Right then we wanted authority. Not something on
high; someone there among us. We turned to him as our guide
without for a moment considering the possibility that he might
be as confused and fearful as the rest of us.

No, as I look back I must strike out *fearful*. Confused, perhaps. Probably. But not fearful. In all the years which have
passed I have not met anyone who was so sure that he was the
chosen of chosen. That gave him a certain strength. Not wisdom.
Not humanity. But strength.

All that is after the fact. At the moment, I was as anxious to
see our father as anyone. For all my mixed feelings, I preferred
his tyranny to collective uncertainty.

What a relief to see him appear! What a desperate trust we
had in him. He stood in the doorway, his hair and beard awry,
windblown. He told us to stop milling about, to stop babbling
like a pack of gibbons, to follow him into the main room.

We obeyed. The ship steadied itself. Surprising. More surprising still, he was wet. He had been outside!

"A wind at sea. Perfectly natural. Common. Jubal here can tell
you."

"Oh I've seen waves that—"

"Not now, jackass. A wind, I was saying. We'll be unsteady for a while. Rolling and pitching. But not a bad turn of events. No, it's cleared the air. Cleared the air nicely. You wanted a view? Fresh air? We'll have it now. Shem, Japheth, open the door out to the deck. Here's the key."

They rushed to do it, but it was *my* heart that was pounding at the prospect. They'd all see it now: the rafts, the trees with men clinging there, the river boats, the gaunt children, the rubble of the world we had so successfully ignored. They'd see it all.

I felt nothing but anxiety. For a full week I had been working on him to open the doors and windows to the outside, and now I felt sick in my gut at the prospect. Somehow the secret which Methuselah and I shared seemed too terrible to pass on to the others.

Top bar removed, bottom bar, and then key turned and bolt slid back. The door swung open on its three iron hinges.

There, the gray daylight. The family squeezed into the door frame as much to breathe fresh air as to see. The opening was entirely blocked with heads and shoulders. I waited for exclamations of horror. But all I heard were cries of delight.

"Ah, that air."

"A sea wind."

"At last!"

And from Shem's children, "Let me see!" "Boost me up!"

"Ham," my father said, "undo the window on the opposite side. Let the winds blow through here."

Gladly. I'd see for myself. The bolts were at the bottom here, the hinges at the top like the one in Methuselah's cabin. I swung it up and hooked it.

A different sea! Gray, fog-bound, turbulent. Waves rising and falling. I could see no farther than the length of the ship at best. If there were rafts, boats, survivors on planks out there, they were hidden. More likely, they had been swallowed in the rough night.

So that was what my father meant by "It's cleared the air." Not clear in the usual sense. Fog, rain, wind. Not clear in any gentle way. Cleared of humanity.

"That's not . . ." I shouted the words, drew attention, but

lost the end of the sentence in the mists. Something about its not being the way it was, or perhaps not being what was important —all this talk of fresh air.

"Not *what?*" My father's voice. The shape of a question, yet not really a question either. Had the Ancient told him that I had seen, that I was aware? No, more likely he guessed. A certain lack of trust there. The third son and all. His question hung in the air, the vibrations sounding to me more like a threat.

"What I expected." A weak ending. But how could I find the words?

I saw then on a wave, rising and falling, a piece of fabric—a coat, perhaps, or a tunic. Small. Perhaps a child's. "Look!" I said, thinking that somehow that would reveal to them everything I had seen previously, would unfold the feelings I had, would communicate them. Surely they would see from this one article that we were not alone on this sea, that there were others either on the surface, clinging to junk, or under us. "Look!" I said.

"What's that?" my father said, coming over to my side with Shem, the two of them adopting a rolling gate, sure-footed already, shaggy mountain goats. "What do you think you see?" Not trusting even my eyes to report correctly.

"A rag," Shem said. "Just a rag."

"This sea wind," my father said to the rest of them, "should clear the air in here. Leave these hatches open."

He smiled as if he himself had just created the winds as well as the waters.

Fresh air. Fresh energy. Even Sapphira felt it. She did her best to keep her distance, giving in only when I pressed her hard. But the change was there, clear to anyone who knew her as well as I. Those enormous eyes would come alive when I entered the room, and they would turn from solemnity to lightness when we spoke.

Her duties had been shifted and revised. From the start, you remember, she belonged to Shem and Athaliah and spent her time caring for their two children. For a while she was made a serving girl and then assigned to me as the pig girl. Her move to the kitchens was informal and not fully authorized.

Normally a servant didn't slide from one position to another. But the world's oldest bias worked in her favor: She was beautiful. Were she bucktoothed, walleyed, fat, crippled, pockmarked or merely put together in ill-proportion—one shoulder down, rounded back, arms too short—any of these and she would never have received special treatment. As it was, I happily did her pen work, Athaliah shared the child care, and Shem made no real effort to enforce her assignments. She was becoming almost a member of the family. Almost.

Close as we were, there was a wall. We could touch each other but not cross to the other's side. When I cleaned those pens and swept the floors of the kitchens I felt like a servant and no doubt looked like one. But I was only an actor. I was no more transformed than was the student in our Sabbath School performance who took the role of the cursed Cain. We were enthralled but we never forgot that it was pretense. When his lines were finished, he was our classmate once again. No curse hung over him for playing the life of a cursed man.

As for Sapphira, no matter how kind my family might appear, no matter how many duties were amended in her favor, she was still the pig girl. And if she forgot, if she approached too close to that dividing wall, my father's words, even his tone, would serve as well as any brick or stone.

All this I was only beginning to see. I was doing my best not to. My main concern was recapturing what we once had. With this in mind, I managed to persuade her that my work on the lowest deck was too much for one person. She rejoined me reluctantly, part my Sapphira and part that solemn-eyed servant girl I first met.

Now that the contact with the outside world had been re-established, we were able to dump our accumulated dung on it bucket by bucket. It was hard work, but it gave me pleasure to have my Sapphira up on Our Deck just as if she belonged there. Almost.

I continued to work with her in the kitchens, serving my time, winning the approval of Hephzibah, treating her as if she were a prospective parent-in-law, thinking she would accept me as an equal. Almost.

I would do just about anything to be with Sapphira, but for some reason I could not join her when she worked as a servant to Athaliah. Perhaps it was a matter of words. What language should I use—the phrases designed for addressing servants or those which link lovers? Surely there was a difference.

It was the same when she was serving Shem, whose property she was. Oh he would have accepted the notion of rutting about, would have echoed my father's approval. But that too, it seemed, had a special language. I'd heard Shem talk that way with town girls and occasionally with servants. It was a kind of roughly mocking, taunting voice one uses with willful ewes.

So I stayed clear of my brother's cabin even when I knew Sapphira was there cleaning up or caring for the children. Stayed clear, that is, until the first Sabbath after the fresh winds.

It was to be a long service, we were told, because we were to give thanks for our deliverance and for the fresh air which had been sent as a sign of approval from on high.

Before the inclement weather, the priests had given a form to our services. They spoke, sang, and had us chant on cue. I assumed the pattern was ordained during the Creation. But no space had been provided for them in my father's grand design and the authority they held sank with them in the rising tide. The only rituals we had at sea were those of my father's making.

This time he told us to do penance and give thanks and we were to do it lustily. So we bellowed our individual prayers loud enough for him—if not Him—to hear. No doubt the babel gave him pleasure. In our disunity, he alone held the reins.

We were free to come and go as the spirit moved. Only our father stayed for the length of it—he and Shem. Their arrival signaled the beginning and their departure the end. A simple logic there. My father could have done it alone, but Shem as always took his role as the first son with high seriousness.

When Sapphira said she was going to care for Shem's two children, Amaziah and Hushai, during the length of that service, it was with a little invitational smile I hadn't seen for some time. I said I would attend the opening, would make sure I was heard, and would join her all glowing with holy phrases. She said she wouldn't recognize me garbed in holiness. I said maybe those garments would slip off without too much difficulty; she said maybe she could help.

And the children? We didn't give them much thought. We assumed that solutions would be found, trusted in chance giving us favors, trusted in divine whimsey.

If the Great Yahweh ever bothered to listen to all that self-chastisement and self-debasement, He must have detected other vibrations from one member of His chosen congregation. Even with great effort I found it difficult to demean myself sincerely when I knew that in moments I would be entering another lovely, holy shrine. Oh I've heard prophets who could sully the softest dell of Eden just out of spite, and doubtless there will be more of that sort; but the only sin I could imagine that day was remaining there in the midst of all that chest-beating.

Besides, wasn't He the very Creator who in His infinite Wisdom designed males and females to fit together so ingeniously and so pleasurably? If He hadn't liked the idea, He could have had us encased in spiny shells for discomfort's sake or had Eve and her followers deposit eggs under rocks for us males to fondle in privacy. No, clearly He put some thought into the ways of man, had reasoned it out with an open heart, and then spent his leisure hours observing the fruits of his labor. Hadn't He said that it, like all His inventions, was Good? How could He possibly want us to abstain?

I sidled by Grandmother Adah, flanked by her sons, Jabal and Jubal, the three of them begging mercy for imagined sins and pouring out love and gratitude: ". . . and thankful for our deliverance, thankful that we were not born with them, in their line, in their tribe, in their shoes, thankful for your loyalty to us, for dividing us from them, thankful for not confusing us with them . . ."

Of the three, Jubal the singer had the finest voice. It was not until I passed directly in front of him, though, that I made out the actual phrasing: "Praise, praise, highest, highest, lowest, lowest, toady-est, mightiest, hightiest, we servants, we creatures, wee creatures, we below, toe, toe, abject, abject, high, high, my-oh-my, low, low, down, down down, grovel, grovel, all fall down . . ." All this with a splendid, rolling cadence.

Edging by Athaliah I paused just a moment to hear, "May their wine turn rancid, may their drinking songs swell their tongues, may their heads throb and their teeth rot for the sin of keeping You awake all last night." I didn't remember *that* prayer.

Quickly out, I hurried down the deserted corridor. But with a jolt I remembered the two children. How had I forgotten? That was the whole point, of course; Sapphira was to care for them while their parents performed their holier duties. What I had imagined in my prayers was my Sapphira as Eve on my brother's wide bed. Desire bends one's vision of the future.

Amaziah was a bundle of cheer, lively eyes, a mass of tight curls. Her younger brother, Hushai, was quieter but he had avoided his father's dour sense of duty, his mother's taste for scorn. They seemed surprisingly undamaged by their parents.

Perhaps this was due to the fact that they had seen more of Sapphira than anyone else. And she did give of herself.

She was too young to serve them as wet nurse, but she allowed them to suckle when out of sorts, soothing them in a way their own mother would not. It was for them a continuing lesson in generosity.

As I entered, there was a flurry of barking, cackling and quacking. I thought for a moment the animals had been released. But no, it was their game of Barnyard.

All three of them were on the great bed on their hands and knees. Amaziah and Hushai were the dogs; Sapphira the harried prey. First she would quack and they would lunge at her, yipping and growling—not hunting dogs after a kill but, appropriately, puppies lunging and nipping and falling back in disarray. Just as the duck was getting the worst of it, she let out the yowl and hiss of a wily cat, a quick thrust of claws; *yip, yip* and a falling back.

Like prayer, certain games should not be interrupted. I was on all fours in a moment, and being in a nippy mood, joined the puppies. They were pleased to have an ally.

Ee-yow, the cat fell back and then, grinning with a feline delight, lunged forward with a slash of claws. Back and forth, back and forth, until the dog, no longer pup, went for her throat with such vigor that she fell over on her back, exposing her jugular in defeat and a portion of breast for spice.

Screams of delight. And then we were all monkeys, tickling and nipping in a great pile, chattering in a clutter of sounds such as did those in the pens two decks down. The children were excellent mimics, and of course under Sapphira's care, they had spent more time on those lower decks than had any of the adults. They knew first hand what monkeys, sheep, ducks, goats, deer, and all the rest do with each other to while away the empty hours.

In the tussle, robes became undone. Perhaps all those monkey hands burrowing for lice helped. Natural enough for the children to see Sapphira half undressed, but they had never seen a man in heat—a subtle transformation we had no time to discuss. A quick fling of the blanket and I was modest. But in the rolling tumult, tossing like the waves outside, somehow Sapphira was there with me; and then, miraculously—perhaps by a lurch of the ship—under me.

Too much speed in all this for contemplation. Blame it on the Creator, if you will, for making such merry gophers and such inviting burrows.

Plunging in, I let loose a stallion's whinney and those two children, bless them, knew what this game was. Up on my back in a flash, no time to saddle, and away we went, trot, trot, then cantering over the undulating fields; now galloping, led on by our two riders shrieking, digging their heels in, shouting us on, hill and dale, up crags, up the mountainside, then down until we spilled, all laughing, on a great green meadow never touched by storm or floods.

X V

PROPERTY

I woke to the sound of breathing. Not one but two rhythms. Piglets? No, we were all curled in a blanket, not straw, tangled like a litter of mice. Had I been transformed? Ah, children. Yes, the two children intertwined with me.

My head cleared slowly. Where was Sapphira? An uneasy sense of being where I should not be. The children slept on. They felt none of my anxiety. They slept as soundly as if not yet born.

Indeed, this was their state. For them the rising and falling, the trembling when we were struck by waves, the shuddering, the creaking and moaning were all soothing reminders, echoes of that earlier voyage in which they slept in the moist hold of their expectant mother.

True, not all children are this secure in their dreams. The plump Leah, Japheth's daughter, found her new home dark and unfriendly. But she was older. And she had not been warmed since infancy by the glow of Sapphira's sunlight. In this, Amaziah and Hushai were especially blessed.

Those two children are bent and wrinkled today. As their years unfolded, they were battered by adventure, disappointment, sorrow, pride, terror, betrayal, boredom—all of it. How can one escape? But no doubt they are even now drawing on the strengths provided by that special childhood.

I looked on them sleeping there and it occurred to me that their enveloping trust was a little ark within the Ark, shutters still closed against the brutal, the unjust, the terrible. It never occurred to them as it did to me that perhaps those creaking timbers would not hold, that perhaps we were already sinking.

My reflections—light and dark—were wiped away by voices. Voices! Of course. This was not my cabin. It wasn't even Sapphira's. I should never have lingered. I was too old to be so trusting, so careless.

I froze under the blanket, a rabbit in the thicket.

"You took the children to Japheth's?" Shem's voice, almost a whisper.

"No, I forgot."

"You forgot? They're here?"

"Under that blanket."

"Why?"

"They were tired."

"But I told you . . ." All this time he kept his voice low, almost inaudible, no doubt for the children's sake. "The women are at the tapestry again." He was going to invite *her?* Impossible. Shem of all people would not break social barriers like that. "A perfect chance for us, and you forgot. You forgot."

A long pause. I was puzzled at first, then baffled. I kept expecting to hear the sound of retreating steps, the opening and closing of a door. I heard nothing. Nothing but the sighing and groaning of the ship.

Sighing and groaning? No ship had ever sounded just like that! Alarmed, I raised one corner of the blanket like a tent flap and was swept with relief. He was not kissing her.

I wouldn't have known how to react if he had been. As my oldest brother, rigid with his sense of duty, he'd been more like a father to me. Surely he was beyond reproach from the likes of me. I cursed myself for my suspicions.

Her back was against the wall and I could see her face behind his left shoulder, eyes shut but unmistakably not kissing. Listening, no doubt.

As usual, he was doing most of the talking and addressing her almost directly in her ear. They rocked as everything did with the great surges of our craft, but it seemed to be a slightly different rhythm, responding to some other storm. Could he be reciting verse? It didn't seem like him.

She opened her mouth and muttered something. To me? No, her eyes were still shut. It must have been in response to him. I ducked under again and did not come out until I heard her respond with an "Aahh," which I took to be a final comprehension on her part of some long and complex tale.

Would he tell her the kinds of coarse stories men tell each other? Merely because she was a servant? It was one thing to be pressing her to the wall and taking her time with whispered nothings, but to force on her some tale like the three maidens and the billy goat . . .

"What is this?" I said, flinging back my blanket.

It was as if I had tossed a hunting knife into the small of my brother's back. A jolt, straight up; a shudder; a quick adjustment of robes, and he spun around to confront me.

"You!" Utter astonishment. Then wonder turned slowly to a smile, smile to laughter, laughter to a spasm of hilarity which doubled him up. Sapphira, still against the wall, stared with that round-eyed look, her long face stricken with something between lament and horror. I was as perplexed by her reaction as I was by his. "What is this?" he kept saying, still caught up with his laughing. "You ask, 'What is this?' . . ." More laughter. Then abruptly he was serious. "All right for what's past, brother, but no more. This one's mine."

"This what?"

"This." He gestured to Sapphira with a jerk of his head.

"Yours?"

"Mine."

I looked at Sapphira but she would not meet my eyes. They were cast down, servant-style. And then one of the children stirred, so she went to them, pulled back the blanket, straightened their clothes, brushed their hair, behaved as if neither of us were there.

"She and I . . ." Where should I go from there?

"Obviously." He grinned, wiped his lips with the back of his hand as if he had just finished a feast. "But no more. Because she belongs to me, as you know. My servant, my property, my enjoyment."

He sat down and gestured for me to do the same. There were skins stuffed with straw which served as back rests and of course there were the usual assortment of rugs. Simple but elegant.

Seeing that Amaziah was awake and combed, he snapped his fingers and she went to him, curled up beside him. He stroked her curls in a friendly but absent way, concentrating on his words.

"We have survived," he said, "by drawing together as a clan. This is always the way of survival. Those that don't, die. But living this closely, there are certain strains. We come to know each other perhaps too well. We have no choice in this. But we can respect property. Can and must. I should be careful not to borrow your shoes even if yours look newer than mine and you have left them unguarded at night. And you, too, should not slip into what is mine even if I should leave it unguarded from time to time."

"But even a servant is—"

"Is like a shoe, like a daughter . . ." He stroked her chin. "Oh, in different ways. Of course. But if a man took my daughter away, it would be a blood dispute."

"But eventually . . . I mean, when she is of age . . ."

"Then *I* will select a man for her. A new master. That's the law."

"I don't remember where it is written."

"Written? It doesn't have to be written. Like most rules, it just *is*."

That sounded familiar. It put me in a sparring mood. "But you have a wife," I said.

"So? If a man has one pair of shoes, is there a law that says he can't have a second? Look at our grandfather. We don't *marry* two any more, but no one says we must limit our appetite. Where did you get these ideas?"

I shrugged. I honestly didn't know. He had all the experience and all the arguments. This was getting too much like those oppressive Sabbath classes, my questions groping around for air space. "Sir, tell me please where did the light come from before He created the Sun?" And "Who did Cain and Abel and Seth marry? Are we all incestuous? Are we?"

Somehow those were easier questions. Safer. What is the dispute about divine light compared with the wonder of one's love? What is the possibility of ancestral incest compared with the sting of infidelity? Infidelity? How could I claim that? I had no hold on Sapphira. I did not own her as my brother did. No court would support my case. Still, I *felt* betrayed. I wanted to shake her, ask her what she had been doing with Shem—at that moment and back over the months. I wanted her to stop playing servant, to share her feelings and make decisions, to select me or him. To be a *person.*

But all these were only feelings. There was no law, no custom to support them. How could one even put them into words? All the logic was on Shem's side, Shem the owner of the property under discussion.

There I was, right back in school. Walking into an argument with my brother or those priests was like trying to rewrite the rules in Eden. The odds were impossible. So why hadn't I learned?

I wanted to convince him that the heart had a logic too, but he would find this strange indeed. How could I put that in words? All those long hours discussing ethics with priests and classmates had not prepared me for such fluid concerns.

Or for the rage. It rose in me like a great curling wave. What training is there for that?

"So," my brother said, "we have an understanding?"

"Curse on that!" I stormed out, slamming the door, half terrified at my own murderous fury, half astonished. My own brother! Was this the blood-trace of Cain within me?

XVI

PITCHING

T H E winds, yes, there is a mention of them in the Official
Report. Something about winds drying up the waters.
Hardly.

You never know for sure why chroniclers of history decide
to include this or delete that, exaggerate one moment and mute
another. But you can be sure of this: Whenever great men are
gathered to record a crucial event, there is far more concern
for the artistry of invention than for the facts as they occurred.

In my 900 years I have seen commissions come and go. And
to be fair, that particular one was working under duress. But then,
so do most. It is marvelous to observe the exercise of human
imagination when dealing with matters of fact. There are good
reasons for this. When men agree as to what happened, they do
not call for a report. Why investigate common knowledge? No,
commissions are formed only when there is bitter disagreement
as to what happened or a widespread wish that it hadn't. Defeats
are made triumphs or at least moral victories; idiots are made
wise, cowards are called prudent; madmen are called prophetic
and opposing prophets are condemned as mad; unwanted details

are burned and scattered like ashes to the winds; gaps are bridged with the artistry of spiders. All in the name of Truth.

The fact is that these commissions, these boards of inquiry and official reports spin their own fictions. For truths, one does better with the accounts of those who can tell you what they saw and felt, helping you to share the moment. Oh the memory may have its lapses or play tricks from time to time, but at least there is no pretense of presenting the Truth like a monument.

To my mind, truths are more apt to slip up on us obliquely so that we see them from the corners of our eyes, almost beyond vision. When we catch a glimpse, we stop to tell others: There! There it is! And it is gone, quick as a flicker of lightning. A chancy business. One can only say as I do now, Come, watch with me along the horizon there. Keep looking. You'll see. Perhaps not the same flash as I see; but you'll see.

The winds, as I was saying, were not about to dry up those waters. An absurd notion. They did, however, build mountainous waves. The reason this period was demoted to a single phrase in the celebrated Official Report was that no one wanted to recall the details.

We had been at sea for two months, remember. Two months in which heat and stale air were our concerns. Now we had air but were thrust into something for which we were not prepared in mind or body.

We found ourselves raised on high and then plunged downward in most radical fashion. Our bodies tried to cooperate; our stomachs, being conservative, tended to remain fixed. From time to time the two parted company. With luck there was a container nearby. In two days of this we had every pot and kettle we could spare arranged around the common room, along the corridors, on the stairways. Most held contributions.

Dear Hephzibah did her best with herbal teas spiced with such strange roots that sleep washed over us like mists; but even half drugged, our stomachs were shifting cargoes. Those not confined to their quarters walked about with dreamlike caution as if condemned to carry jugs filled to the very brim with scalding bile.

XVI Pitching

It is one thing for servants to turn the color of dying moss and cling to doorways; and it is not either surprising or entirely unusual to see a lover of wine like Japheth stagger about in the middle of the day. But it is alarming to see someone like proud Athaliah turn gray as a corpse and lurch toward some half-filled jug, emptying her guts spasm by spasm. It is not easy to maintain beauty, grace, and dignity under those circumstances.

There is another scene which remains with me and which I know will never be included even as an addendum to any report but mine. My father loved his wine. It never kept him from work, never weakened his resolve in building this vessel or managing his clan, but when the cares of the day were over, he allowed his mind to go slack with the best of our vintage stock.

At the beginning of the storm, there was much for him to do, so he kept his head clear. But by the third heaving day he had everything tied down which needed tying, the lower hatches closed again, and ropes tied overhead along the corridors for us to guide ourselves, moving hand over hand like a tribe of apes. He had completed all the preparations. There was nothing left but to weather it out. At that point he allowed himself a few drinks. A well-deserved libation and a sampling of Hephzibah's steadying herbs. The combination buckled his knees and toppled him into a deep sleep right there in the common room.

I would have averted my eyes, moved on, left him to his slumbers. After all, what had he done against me? He deserved his privacy. It was Jubal the poet, however, who happened by and caught my sleeve.

"Look at that," he said, not with scorn but with wonder.

"Let him be," I said. But it was hard not to stare. There was my father slumped in a low chair, eyes shut, head back, mouth open, snoring, beard tangled and fouled, his two enormous hands holding on his stomach a pot into which he had earlier deposited a frothy mix of wine, herbs, and sea-gray bile.

I stood transfixed, not because this was the first time I had seen my father incapacitated after a spate of work, but because of that bronze, hemispherical pan resting uneasily on his stomach, rising and falling with each breath.

"Let me tell you something," Jubal said, clutching my elbow.

I tried to pull away. "I couldn't tell this to the others. They like the old stories, the safe ones. I don't take chances with those who feed me. But let me tell you about that little sea."

"Little sea?"

"There in the pot. See it?" He was right. In that container there was a little briny sea, waves rolling in response to the larger storm outside, sloshing first one way and then the other, a tempest as seen from on high.

"Now there's a world worth considering," he said, speaking directly into my ear. "The rest of the family don't take to speculation—except Japheth. But you'll understand. Look now, look at your father. He's the sleeping Yahweh, exhausted from the cares of His world, a trifle sick of it all; and look, he holds in His hands a flood He created but has now forgotten. Down there in the slop, Ham, are minute creatures in a vessel they made with great effort. They're raising their wee voices praising the Divine Provider on high and begging for intercession, for deliverance. They're beating their chests and tearing their hair. They're wailing, confessing their tiny sins. They're offering tribute, calling Him the One and Only, the Highest, the Creator of all, even of that tiny turgid sea. But can you hear them? No? How can they ever make their prayers heard? Even if their singers are trained by experts, their verses beautifully composed and metered in accordance with ancient tradition, their hymns set to cymbal and horn, to what avail? How will they wake the Creator in whose very mess they now float? And if they sink, gagging in the holy sea, will even their dying cries disturb His sleep? Will He even miss them? Will you, Ham? Even you?"

My own stomach was in good condition. So was Sapphira's. It was not easy to deal with the slop of others, but somehow we managed. I thought at the time it was evidence of the fact that we had been born under the same constellations; but as I grow older I am less impressed with the influence of stars and more with the stages of life. Each age has its special gift and ours at that time was a set of tight muscles—stomachs, wombs, breasts, and sphincters.

XVI Pitching

We were, I'm afraid, essentially blind to our good fortune. We took much of it for granted. But we could no longer do so with our relationship. I knew *something* had gone on between Sapphira and my brother and she knew that something had been broken between us. A natural bond had been shattered. Though we were determined to mend it, what we had left was fragile.

"Please," she said softly to me when next we met, "no more on your family's deck."

"But you have to—"

"No, I mean you and me. No more seeing each other up here. I have to do what I'm told, but let me keep it separate from you. Is that possible?"

Keep what separate from me? Her status as a servant? I hoped that was what she meant. In any case I agreed.

"But will you work with me down with the animals?"

She nodded, but there was something like fear in her face. "Don't tell anyone," she said.

I reached out to assure her that I could keep this a secret, but she pulled back. We were on the stairs and she apparently wasn't going to take the chance of being seen. I wished at the time that we had been ordered to remain on the lowest level day and night like those piglets. Life would have been simpler.

But I was content that she agreed to join me. During the next few days of stormy weather the rest of the clan turned their eyes upward with petitions to the Great Provider; we, on the other hand, cast our lot in the straw with less spiritual and more spirited members of His creation.

No, we were not continually involved in copulation. Were that the only bond, I probably would have accepted my brother's advice. He was right that there were other young women working in the kitchen and I'd heard that some of them had been adopted by certain members of my family—the reward of rank, I was told.

But the bonds which were being built between Sapphira and me were many and varied. We were learning, for one thing, to save lives. We were teaching ourselves a kind of animal husbandry never practiced before: We were caring for beasts and birds which were considered unclean and so inedible and, except for camels, useless. Most were at best ornamental. Some not even that. For the first time in history they were being given some value just for existing.

It had started with my father's divine calling, but down there amongst the beasts we didn't think about that any more than they did. In the early stages, the creatures were our companions; now with the storm raging they were our dependents.

They were in bad shape. Especially the big ones. The camels had been knocked this way and that until they slumped to a kneeling position the way some men pray, whites of their eyes showing. Ships of the desert they once were and wonderfully adapted to periods of drought, but we humans certainly had the edge in these fluid times.

We ministered unto them without expecting gratitude—indeed, their inclination to bite and spit was not weakened. Because of our skills, we were occasionally called up to the deck above to help tend the sheep, the civets, the goats, the poor fallow deer who had been cut by her mate's antlers. We tempted the chamois back from starvation with bowls of barley mush.

But our first loyalty was with our own kind, the outcasts. The largest of these needed our attention; the others fared relatively well. It made me wonder whether some day perhaps the very small will inherit the earth.

The two grown pigs, for example, were off their feed and needed coaxing. Sapphira nuzzled and I spoon-fed. But the piglets with whom we had shared our nuptial bed were like children to us, all lively and happy. After our work with the larger creatures, these little ones were our playmates. We gave them names, encouraged the runt to demand his full share, taught them all to dance on their hind legs for treats.

And how lovely were the rabbits! How absurd to call them "unclean"! Soft, gray, silent, and immaculate, they discreetly left their pellets at the far end of the cage and astonished us with their ability to keep their hair perfectly combed. They made us humans look unkempt and bestial.

Adult rabbits have a certain fondness for each other, an enthusiasm for bodily contact which we found appealing. They and the white mice and the desert gopher all managed to turn out litters with total disregard for the instability of the world about them. If anything, the perilous times seemed to enhance their natural appetites.

Fond as we were of all living things, we did have to serve baby rabbits and mice to the serpents who would eat nothing which did not panic and run. Just as man had a need for spices, snakes require a certain measure of squeaking. This bothered me at first. I tended to confuse a reverence for life with an abhorrence of death. But Sapphira was country bred before she was sold into servitude and like most of her kind could ring the neck of a chicken or watch a pop-eyed rabbit slide down the neck of a snake with calm detachment.

I asked her once why it didn't bother her—knowing how much pleasure she took in their care and in allowing their soft and furry bodies to scamper over her.

"You want to kill the snake for the sake of rabbits?" She smiled and shrugged. "A needless death."

She was not much for ethical debate—not having had the benefits of Sabbath School either in her own tribe or ours, but what she believed held together. Death for a cause was reasonable; other types were repulsive. She killed rats by throwing a cedar mallet at them, a device used by her own tribe. And she took pleasure in the sport, tossing the corpses to the leopards.

All this because rats ate grain we needed for our own survival. But mice were too small to do serious damage. Some of them she had trained to come to her hand and occasionally to follow a string of seeds up into her lap.

On this occasion she was having unusual success. We were lying moist, spent, and disrobed in the straw of the aviary, our heads propped up against sacks of grain. She had idly coaxed two little brown mice up to her stomach where she was feeding them with grains of wheat dropped into her navel as we talked. Somehow we had returned to the subject of death.

"Like the chicken," she was saying. "We feed it and then it feeds us. Simple . . ."

Her voice trailed off as she began to lure the bravest of the two mice up across the flat plain of her stomach, through the little valley, and finally around to the smooth and lovely rise of her left breast. There she induced it to sit on its haunches, nibbling a kernel at the very pinnacle. Never has any creature been so blind to his good fortune.

The thought of feasting at such a table stirred some vital part of me, but my mind was still tangled with her notion of justified death. "And when old Methuselah dies," I asked, "will that be 'necessary' or "needless'?"

She looked at me with surprise, startled that I would ask such a childish question, the ripple of her muscles sending the explorer down from the mountain top and, with his companion, across the plains, down the lower valley and into the underbrush. "Necessary, of course," she said. "He has to make room for the rest of us. Just as we will for the next. He's lingered more than most."

"And the Flood? Is that why we have the Flood?"

"Ptuh!" A perfect imitation of her mistress—startling in its accuracy, bitter scorn from the mouth of someone who was normally the child of sunlight. "If this is your Yahweh at work . . ." She could not finish. Perhaps she imagined that such thoughts would endanger our bond. And perhaps it would have except for the scurrying of those two furry friends who thought they had discovered a cozy den and had begun burrowing as is their wont, sending Sapphira into a cascade of laughter before she kicked them out of Eden.

They scampered in the wilderness of straw for only a moment before the stork spotted them, scooped them up, first one and then the other, sliding them down his throat with rude grunts.

"Yahweh?" I said. "Never mind Yahweh." I spoke softly. I didn't want His presence around there. We could deal with His creatures, large and small, but the Creator was too heavy a presence. Bringing Him into our conversation would be like having my father about. "Never mind Yahweh," I whispered, my fingers tiptoeing like the ghosts of departed mice up the plain toward the gentle hills.

"Never mind?" she said. "I try not to. But in your family it isn't easy. That god is all around them."

"Not really. They left the priests behind, you know. Left them floating there. Didn't pick up a single one."

"I noticed that."

"Not by accident. He planned that."

"Why?"

"Because they were corrupt. That's what my father says."

"What did they do?"

"What we do."

"That's corrupt?"

"For priests it is. Or was. Well, more than that, they lived too well. You know, like princes. With servants. Too much power."

"Power?"

"Running things."

"Like your father?"

"Well, yes, but different."

Long pause. Then, "Different . . . like they built a new temple and he built a floating island?"

"That's one difference."

"That's a big difference." Pause. Smile. "I'd rather be here."

There was something so sunlike about that smile—a treasured dawn—that I felt compelled to roll over on her and kiss her long and hard like drawing juices from an orange.

A shadow. How can a shadow fall in a torchlit aviary? It can and did. We looked up. My brother Shem.

He shook the woven gate, not seeing the latch in his rage. It was his silence which was frightening. I had never seen him pushed beyond profanity, beyond curses. The hinges gave way and he charged us, a bull enraged. I pulled together my robes—nakedness makes one vulnerable; but he lunged for Sapphira. Yanked her to her feet, naked and cowering.

"I told you, I told you," he said, voice low. He was shaking her, but strangely she would not defend herself.

My hand seized his shoulder. I wanted him to deal with me, not her.

I succeeded. He drove his fist like a rock into my stomach. As I doubled up, he raised his knee against my face, a camel's kick. Yet not as hard as he could have. It would have been easy for him to have broken my jaw. He didn't.

"You're an ass," he said. "But a brother. She's a bitch of a servant."

He turned back to her, but she was gone. Took her robe and fled. Not a word. Just gone. Out the door, soft on bare feet, gone as if she had flown on the back of a heron.

He started after her, but again I caught his shoulder. This time I held him at arm's length as one does a snapping dog. "Don't beat her," I said.

He stopped dead. It must have startled him to hear his youngest brother give orders. Brother? I kept my groin turned at right angles to him.

"I won't beat her."

"What then?"

"The chicken cleaver." He raised his hand and in pantomime sliced off the littlest finger. "One for today. Next time, one more. Then one more. Until she learns."

He was off, feet pounding on the planks like hoofs.

XVII

APPEALS

IT was, of course, an old custom. Time-honored. There was a woman in town who was down to two thumbs.

I never used to think much about it. Like circumcision, I assumed. Just a part of normal life. But that initiation on the deck our first day left me sensitive to joints.

Before that voyage I might have shrugged it off. I recall how as students we used to snicker at wives who were so maimed. Servants with missing digits were considered an easy mark. "Easier," we used to say in the swagger of our adolescence, "than a legless ewe." But the prospect of Sapphira facing the same fate was entirely different. I felt the weight of it in my stomach.

Was it only my status as member of the clan which kept me from receiving the same punishment? Or worse?

Never mind the moral speculation, it was time for some kind of action. I went directly to my father. I must have been out of my mind.

"So what do you want of me?" he said. I had found him in the kitchens, recovered from his illness and back at work slaughtering chickens. It was a job only heads of families could do.

Although the priests had started taking over the task, they were not with us now and we were back to where the tradition started. He listened to my story without interrupting his work and also, thank God, without interrupting me, not making sly comments about servant girls, just listening, all the while continuing his work, seizing the next bird from the slatted cage, cutting its windpipe with the ritual knife, draining the blood into a pot, opening its belly, cleaning out certain parts with a flick of his red hands, studying the exposed flesh for blemishes, then severing the head with the chicken cleaver, quick and sure strokes that left my knees weak. "So why have you come to me?"

"Losing a finger for what *I* did to her? Is that fair?"

"Fair? You'd rather lose your own?"

He turned to look at me almost for the first time, pausing before the next bird, his hand and cleaver dripping. There was a gentle smile—a smile yet!—in his eyes as if he had told a joke. But from the eyes down he looked entirely capable. Just give the word and chop, chop. Examine the stump for blemishes.

"No . . . I mean, why should *any*body be cut up?"

"No punishments? None?" He was playing with me, pretending that the question was worth taking seriously. "We should take whatever we want from each other? Do whatever we want with each other? A clan of Cains?"

"Take? What did I take?"

"Borrow, then. She belongs to your brother. So you could not *take* her, true. But you did *use* her." A smile of approval. God forgive me, but I grinned back. How could I help it? I can count on one hand (and I still have five digits) the smiles that man sent my way, so there was no ignoring it. He lay his bloody hand on my shoulder. "Not that I blame you. Tender as a fawn, that one. Long-limbed. I like them that way myself. Had one once whose skin was dark as olive, hair like a night sky; aroused, she moaned like a mourning dove, and trilled in the climax. Most beautiful thing I've ever known." He paused, looked off into the dark corridor as if he could see her. "And another with the stomach muscles of a cat. She could raise you up, lower you down, draw you in or force you out just lying there. Ah, the wonder of it. Ham, I'd sacrifice half the family to have one week of your age." In the pause I noticed that my shoulder was stained red where he had been gripping it.

"Of course," he said, clearing his throat, back to practical concerns, "you don't *marry* that kind. And we can't encourage them to go about serving everyone they wish, can we?" Pause. Rephrase, three notes lower: "I'm saying, we *cannot*."

In desperation I shifted tactics, nudged it closer to his way of thinking.

"She'll be no good to any of us when she's recovering. It might even kill her."

"Never lost one yet. Cauterize it. Bind it off. She'll hardly miss it. Besides, they don't feel pain the way we do. She's foreign, a servant, and a woman. Nerve endings of a crayfish."

"Nonsense!" No, not my utterance. My thought, yes, but the spoken word came from my mother, cutting in. I flinched, sure he would hit me, though my lips hadn't moved.

"They feel the way we feel." She gestured to a scullery girl to come over and start the plucking. Mother worked with them on this, insisting that the girls would not be clean about it if she were not on hand. "They cry. I've seen them. They have stomach aches, backaches, Eve's curse—everything. But . . . ," eyes staring up at me, fixing me to the spot, "they're as different from us as the donkey from the horse."

"Ha!" My father really liked that one. "So don't breed with them if you want a decent image of yourself." Zip!—Another chicken throat with a flourish, blood spurting.

I turned to my mother: "Would *you* chop a woman's finger off because she lay with the wrong man?"

Pause. Just the briefest pause. But long enough for me to see a look of infinite revulsion. Then it passed. She recited the answer as if it had been taught to her eons ago. "Me? It's not woman's work to slaughter."

I left. It was as if they were speaking another language. I hadn't even learned the syntax.

I thought of dealing with Shem directly. By force. A ritual knife, perhaps. But the story of Cain was too heavy on me. Besides, is a finger worth more than a blood brother?

I had lingered in the corridor, caught by indecision, when my mother joined me. She seized both my arms and looked up at me. What she lacked in height she made up with the intensity of that gaze. Frog eyes, Japheth used to say; well, they could make an insect out of me.

"At your age," she said, "you think you can change everything overnight. Get that out of your head. People don't like change, clans don't like change, nations don't like change. Most of all, men don't want change. Even when new leaders take over and make promises and everything looks different, it turns out to be much the same. Right now with ruination out there and the clan trapped in here with no foundation under us, everything is much the same. Men want it that way. You want a new order? Try. I'll bless you for trying. But keep your eyes open. A nudge here, a nudge there—that's the best you can do."

"But a *finger*. For what?"

"Men! Aagh!" Derision and resentment in her tone. "When you *are* one, remember what you feel right now. Until then . . ." She shrugged.

Such layers of bitterness! I had never suspected. I should have been grateful, I suppose, for her confidences. But she wouldn't back me and I felt betrayed. Besides, it was unsettling to see this other side of her. I didn't like to have my image of her change.

So I went to Athaliah. She was closer to my age and would be, I thought, closer to my thinking. True, she had no rights over her husband, but there was a certain intensity to her feelings. I could never appeal to her sense of sympathy. Somehow she had been born with that portion of her soul missing. But perhaps the situation justified the use of jealousy. Surely a damaged marriage was less terrible than a disfigured Sapphira.

She was still in the common room, working on the family tapestry. Good. She would be in a civil mood. But she was working along with my other sister-in-law, Ophir, and Grandmother Zillah. Well, that couldn't be helped. I couldn't split them up like some nipping sheep dog. There was nothing which wove the women of this family together like the mending of that tapestry.

"Look who's come to help us," Ophir said, a cheerful smile as always.

"Better put out the torches," Athaliah said.

"Not fair," I said. "*I* didn't fling that torch."

"You got him in the mood for it," Athaliah said.

"Men," old Zillah said. "Always in the way. Always stumbling into things. Always arguing and setting things awry. Men!"

A fine start.

"I've been looking for Shem," I said.

"You'll have to run," Ophir said. She giggled. "He's off on some search."

"Came in here," Zillah said, "like a dog after a bitch. Looked under the table and behind the draperies and in the storage closets and then out again without a civil word to his grandmother."

"Or his wife," Athaliah said, cool as dew. She saved her indignation for greater stuff. I hoped to provide it.

"He's looking for someone," I said.

"Really?" Athaliah said. "I thought maybe another pig got loose."

"No," I said.

An awkward pause. There was nothing to hold me there unless they were going to ask me who.

"One of the children?" Ophir asked.

"Children?" Athaliah laughed—more of a bark. "Shem look for a lost child? Does a stallion nurse his colts?"

"My Japheth often—"

"Besides, we have a girl to . . ." Pause. Connections were being made in her head quick as moneychangers sorting coins. "The girl." And to me directly. "The girl?"

"What girl?"

"You know perfectly well what girl. Sapphira, that's who. Is it she? The one he's after?" I nodded. Her eyes narrowed. I was into a fertile field here. "Why? What's she done?"

"She did something wrong."

"So the sun rises and sets. What else is new?" I was losing her. I would have to be more direct. "She was unfaithful to him."

"To *him?*" Ophir said, astonished. "Sapphira?"

"Shut up, Sister." And to me, "With whom?" Then her eyes opened from that narrow, questioning look, relaxed, widened into a smile—just a touch of bitterness—and she filled in the rest of the story. "You! Little brother found his way. And took Shem's plaything. Now the brothers are at each other. Oh, and the girl—I suppose he'll . . ." In pantomime she sliced off her little finger with the edge of her other hand." A laugh. Then serious again. "Oh God, she'll be all thumbs for a month."

"Athaliah! Do *not* use the name of the Yahweh as a curse. Have respect for your grandmother."

"Respect? I'd like a little respect from that husband of mine. The law may be on his side—taking his pleasure with a servant who belongs to us—but it's not right and it's insulting. I've half a mind to have her given to Ham here—let him keep her from wandering. Except I'd be without help."

"I have it," Ophir said brightly. "You can share our girl."

"Zilpah? Thanks, but she was born with a turtle's brain."

"She's not got a turtle brain. As a matter of fact, Japheth finds her very attractive. Too attractive."

"Japheth?" This struck Athaliah as comic. She had an odd sense of humor. "Japheth and turtle-brain?"

"Well, only in my forbidden week. And once in-between. Once or twice. He has an abundance."

"Now just a moment!" Old Zillah was red-faced. "This is too much."

"It's just that we're closed-in here," Ophir said.

"Being closed-in," Zillah said, "has nothing to do with it. This family has always been closed-in. A tight clan. It's just that you talk too much. All of you. What you do after dark is your own business, but this endless talking . . . Don't you know it's a sin to talk about it like that? You think spirits don't hear? You think that won't bring us black fates? Take it from me. I've lived three times longer than any of you. Talking is what rouses the spirits against you. Starts them muttering. I've heard them. Do what you want with your men and your servants, but don't sit about and chat about it as if we were at market."

"Chat!" I said. "This isn't chatting."

"Of course it is," Grandmother Zillah said, "and I won't

have any more of it." She stood up and so did Athaliah, the two of them staring down at me as if *I* had committed some indiscretion. Then they swept out.

"Don't you worry," Ophir said, patting me on the knee. She smiled as if she were going to offer me bayberry tea and fresh-baked bread. "If Athaliah can't get her servant girl given over to you, I'll lend you ours. I know how it is. Everyone wants to be caressed and held from time to time. Even me."

"You have someone . . . ?"

"Poor Japheth's often married to his wine. You know that. So . . . Well, it's true that our Zilpah can't do letters or numbers, but she's loving and always willing."

XVIII

HUNTERS

J U S T tell me this," Sapphira said, looking up at me in the grain bin where she had been hiding. "Why on earth did your Great and Wise Yahweh choose this family to save?"

The ship creaked, the winds outside moaned, the waves struck at the hull, rebounded, but no answer came from me.

Sapphira seemed calm when I found her, but her hand was cold as death and her muscles hard. She was white with grain dust—and perhaps also from the tension of the day.

"The priests would have said—"

"Never mind the priests. They guessed wrong."

"Well, my father claims—"

"Him? How can you even mention him?"

"Well, don't ask me questions like that. Look, you're safe here."

"Here?" She looked around as if she heard footsteps. "I'm not safe anywhere on this ship."

I sat beside her and put my arm around her. "I meant you're afloat and dry. You weren't left to drown with the others. I mean, things could be a lot worse."

"I used to think that."

"Before what?"

"Before I met you. I could take just about anything. I could take what came. That's the way I was raised. Staying alive was enough. No complaints. Of course I didn't smile much either."

"And then?"

"Everything changed. I smile a lot more. But I frown more too. And scared—Ham, I'm really scared."

I tried to rest her head on my shoulder but she was rigid. She pushed me back. "When we first met," I said softly, "I told you I'd protect you. Remember?"

"You call this protection? It all started when I touched you. I should have stayed where I was meant to stay. I never used to get into trouble, but now I don't know where I am. I do what I'm told to do and still I'm in trouble. I don't understand you people at all and most of all I don't understand what makes you special."

"Neither do I, but I'll get you out of this. Just be patient."

"Patient? There's no way to be patient about this. I mean, when a finger's gone, it's gone forever. Try to imagine!"

I tried. Really tried. It wasn't easy because this was a different world, a world in which pain and even dismemberment were real and immediate threats. For an instant I considered leaving her, going back to the protection of my own deck. How had I gotten into this? She had become my Eve and it was clear even then that if I followed her lead there was going to be hell to pay.

But there was no time for reflection. Feet pounding down the corridor. The drumming of vengeance. I stood up and heaped grain over her in a flurry, leaving only a breathing hole as if she were some wily rodent. I finished just as the door exploded open.

"Not here," I said to Shem.

"Sure?"

"Nowhere in sight." Incredible, as I look back, that I should have struggled so to avoid an outright lie. Shem hardly heard. He was kicking the grain in fury. "I've already looked," I said. "Really."

"Where could that bitch be?"

He was casting all the blame on her, she the violator of his orders. Me, I was a clan brother, a blood brother. He was trusting me, assuming that I would act on his behalf, would help round up the transgressor. A strange twist of logic there, but a stranger one in my own heart: I was torn apart with this deception. Imagine, there I was, deceiving my own brother!

A shrill little voice deep inside me urged that I take my brother's side and pull the girl out, winning praise, that I take her to my father, holding her hand on the block while he sharpened his cleaver, telling her to be quiet, that this was the law, that there was nothing any of us could do, that we couldn't play favorites, that it would be over in a quick flash of an instant, that with luck she would pass out, that they would bind it and cauterize it for her, would look out for her health.

All my training called for just this sort of response. Parents, priests, elders, even older classmates—the whole community teaching me and each other in words, in games, in jokes, in myriad little ways to obey the unwritten laws, to be loyal to one's own people. Aren't these the verities? Aren't these the sinews which bind our society, which keep us from becoming a scattered horde of beasts?

"The servants' quarters," I said. "That's where she'd run to. Back to the burrow. That's the way they think."

I thought I saw the grain quiver. A terrible thing for me to have said, but it was to save her from mutilation. I didn't really think of her that way. Did I?

We were off in a lumbering gallop, the two of us, brothers, off to the kitchens and the pantries. A liberation for me, threat averted. And a relief to be free from the wrench of loyalties. Running instead of thinking.

Shem was just ahead, bursting into the kitchen, sending the door hard against the wall, startling the workers there. All faces toward us, a hand paused in the stirring, a rolling dowel stopped midway in the crust; even Hephzibah in the act of reaching down a copper kettle from its hook froze, staring at us back over her shoulder, both hands up, the whole room like an artist's rendering, a scene of a tapestry. No smiles, not even from Hephzibah. Nothing like a door slammed back against the wall to suggest tension in the air.

"Where's the girl?" Shem said.

"Sapphira," I added.

"Sapphira," he said. "She's here somewhere. Give her up."

Not a word from any one of them. Frozen like rabbits—barely a flicker of an eyelash. I'd never seen them like this. In the days when I had joined them to win over my Sapphira's confidence, I came to know the special banter, the teasing, the wry irony of those in servitude. It was a view no other member of my family had. But now my brother was showing me a different aspect—one which he knew well and I was only just discovering. From him, the sound of absolute power; from them, the look of absolute defenselessness. The predator and the hunted, they living in his garden at his pleasure; indeed, *for* his pleasure.

And mine.

A chill passed over me. Until then I hadn't been able to take the threat against Sapphira with full seriousness. Punishments like that were not performed in front of children. Like hangings and stonings, they were the business of mature men. It never occurred to me that such measures would be taken against someone I actually knew. I had the notion that somehow a sense of proportion would creep up on my brother from behind, would rest a gentle and restraining hand on his shoulder.

But no, I could see now that he would have that finger just as a wolf will take the life of a rabbit which has crossed his path. Not hunger, necessarily, not pleasure; just keeping the lines clear, reminding the world and himself who rules and who is ruled.

Had he been calmer, he might have talked to me as my father had—how you can't let the little transgressions go without inviting greater ones. But he wasn't in a mood to instruct. He wasn't my father. His anger was directed against his servant. Her sin was not so much in having intercourse with another man, it was in disobeying an order he had given her. My family always took that seriously. Look where we'd be if only Adam had followed instructions.

"Stay exactly where you are," he said to them. And to me in almost the same tone, "Start searching."

Imagine a room full of cooks, assistants, scullery maids, scrub girls all frozen as if by divine order while two men moved relentlessly around the room, peering under tables, examining the depths of vats, opening cupboard doors which could not have hidden more than a ring-tailed monkey. Somehow he got it in his head that she was submerged somewhere, so he seized a spit used to roast lamb and plunged it into barrels of flour, sugar, barley. The swordplay seemed to give him great pleasure; but it made me sweat to think of what it would have been like back in the grain bin.

"Don't leave this room," he said to the rest as we pounded down the hallway to their living quarers, small rooms shared by three or four, lit imperfectly with the wall torches, not lamps. Most were deserted, clothes and covers lying about and resembling, to him at least, human forms. He tugged at these, throwing them over his shoulder when he was satisfied that they were not his prey. Wherever clothes hung on hooks, he stabbed them with his spit, driving his blade deep into the wall. If the culprit were found this way, the punishment he had in mind would be painless.

We stumbled across an old crone sitting next to the doorway, trying to catch the light from the torch in the hall. She was working on some mending, though the rag she was repairing seemed beyond redemption.

He demanded her name—courtesy still ingrained—and she gummed some nonsense syllables. Her incoherence was intentional. I knew her as a kindly old grandmother of two scullery girls who had smuggled her on board at the last moment. She posed as a seamstress. Neither Shem nor our father knew that half our staff had survived by guile rather than selection.

Shem shook her, terrifying her beyond the point of reason. He asked her whether she had seen the girl, and the old woman shook her head; he asked her if anyone had passed lately, and she shook her head; he told her to shout to us if any young girl passed, and again she shook her head.

He seized her by the hair and would have run her through with the spit, but I held his arm. "She's simple," I said. "Simple in the head. She's worth nothing."

A terrible thing to say of anyone's grandmother. But then, it saved her life and convinced Shem that I was indeed a brother. He cast her aside like a bundle of rags.

In the next room there were forms sleeping. These were the bakery girls who made up the bread during the night. Like graybacked field mice, they were nocturnal. The place smelled faintly of sour dough.

Shem lunged at the first one as if he had found his prey. He ripped down the covers and the girl was lying there entirely naked. Night clothes are too great a luxury for servants on that level. Doubtless he knew that, but he wasn't prepared for this total revelation. Nor was the girl. Up on one elbow, she stared at the intruder wide-eyed and blank-faced. At the time, I thought it was total lack of modesty on her part, a dreamlike memory of life in the original Garden. Not so, Sapphira told me later; most bakery girls have no notion of Eden and are guided by conventional modesty just like the rest of us. But because they are the youngest and the least protected creatures under our roof, and because they are habitually prone when others are erect, they are subject to frequent visitations from men—both fellow servants and members of my upright family.

At the time, I did not know that. Truth is unfolded slowly for the young, like pulling back one solid blanket after another. It is a process which is at the same moment both distasteful and fascinating. I still find it so, though there is a general feeling that men of my age should renounce all they have seen and return to innocence in action and in word. At 900, I don't have my choice when it comes to action; but they can't take from me the word. Not quite yet.

In any case, this young bakery girl was a delight to behold and for an instant my brother seemed to forget just what we had come to do. His hand went out and I thought it was to caress her, but then his sense of moral duty returned and he merely raised her face, his fingers gently lifting under the chin, just enough to check her identity.

"Not her," he said.

"No, not her."

We lingered for just a moment, and then noticed the others, dark forms in a tangle of covers, dark eyes staring at us, a little nest of them.

Each one had to be inspected. It would have been enough, I thought, to check faces. Surely the light-haired one was not Sapphira nor the one with teeth like a desert gopher. But no, Shem was a thorough one and each cover had to be pulled back, each one had to give her name. A painstaking process for one in such a great hurry. I thought for a moment that the tasks of inspection and identification would give rise to a change of plans. But I had no such luck. My brother's sense of mission was like a winter's wind.

He stood, cleared his throat, arranged his robes like a man returning to serious business, and said, "All right, Brother, you said she was here. So where is she?"

I had to think of something fast. Perhaps it was still possible to recapture the mood of that inspection. Surely my brother had teetered on the edge, caught between duty and the need for recreation.

"Never mind her," I said, voice low in conscious imitation of older brothers, older schoolmates, even uncles, "how about taking on some of these."

I was astonished at how adult I sounded. The very ring of manhood. Remember that before we set out on this voyage I assumed that women were assigned to men by family agreement and were joined by ritual for the purpose of having offspring. Now I was finding out just what free agents we really were. Some of us, that is.

"Later," he said, not disputing the principle, only the timing. "First Sapphira."

That snapped the momentary bond I had felt with Shem. He really was after blood, Sapphira's, and Sapphira was not just any woman.

"Why?" I asked.

"Can't let her get away with it."

"With what?"

"Disobeying."

There it was again. Nothing very spiritual about it. No love for her. Just the demand for obedience. To him. *My* Sapphira!

"Give it up," I said, words tumbling ahead of thought. "You've got what you want here. Leave her alone."

He squinted at me, lips tightened. I had stepped over the line, violated my brotherhood.

"So that's it," he said. "You want to keep what you found? Is that it?" Before I could answer, a new thought came to him. "The grain bin. What were you doing in there?"

No time for an answer. He knew what it was. Quick at putting pieces together. And ripping them apart. He was off at a gallop with that terrible spit in his hand and me after him, shouting, alternately begging and threatening. What sense can you make when running?

We left the bakery girls as if they didn't exist, tore back through the kitchen, down the stairs to the clean animal deck, across to the grain bin, our steps pounding, my voice echoing through that great ship.

By the time I entered, he was already at it, plunging that blade again. He was after her life now. Out for blood.

And blood he got. It welled up through the grain like a dark spring. It seeped out on the floor, spreading toward us. I sprang at him, on him, hands on his throat, toppling him, both of us crashing to the floor, rolling in the reddened grain.

XIX

BROTHERS

Cain. How many times had I studied his story? The priests had us discuss it, recite it, weigh its lessons, analyze the motives (sibling rivalry? rage against divine favoritism?), act it out (taking turns as aggressor, victim, divine voice), render its scenes in paint. Sometimes Cain's story seemed as important as Adam's.

For all our teachers' efforts, though, we were working only with shadows of the real story, flickerings of words arranged to give us some notion of events and feelings locked within us. The words did not touch us deeply. "It would be terrible," we said, "to be crossed by a brother"; yet we felt no terror. "How awful to feel betrayed by the Great Yahweh"; this with no sense of awe. How could we imagine it?

It was all word play and I was good at it. I won praise in spite of a tendency for irreverence which was as natural to me as the laughter of songbirds. I read the text closely—closer than many of my more orthodox classmates. I noted that Yahweh said sin might be lurking at Cain's door even before a sinful thought had entered his heart: Could Cain really be considered a free agent? I pointed out that the man was a fruit grower: Was raising apples an echo of the original theft, setting the Yahweh against him from the start? And Cain's flight—how similar to that of his parents' when they were his age, both couples heading east under a cloud: Was fratricide just a darker, more acrid fruit? Was murder or the dream of it just another stage of growing up, becoming adult?

All those questions were games to enliven the tedium of class. What I didn't suspect until later was that beneath the story we read and analyzed and satirized after class was a real story. Beneath the word *Cain*, which was used so carelessly when we "raised Cain," lay a knowledge, not words on scrolls but episodes deep within us seen only in the flicker of dreams.

I knew as I blocked the air from my brother's throat that I had been this way before without knowing it. And when in the long succession of years since then I have reread Cain's story, I return once more with fresh alarm.

All this in retrospect. At the time there was no reflection, only struggle. A tempest roaring in my ears, a red glare blinding my eyes, this was far from noble combat—brutish grunting, gasping, farting with effort. Out to maim; out to kill.

No recollection but fragments—a clutter of pictures, a rubble of memory. Bulging eyes look up at me, astonished. My own? His? Mine reflected in his? Shouting. How can he shout?—his face turning to plum, mouth a mere bruise. No breath to speak. No air for a whisper. Yet a gale of shouting. I am lifted and fall again, lifted and fall. My brother's neck rises in my clenched hands, snapping the head up and smashing it back against the grain-strewn floor. I recall doing this with a gourd. It broke open. Seeds and pulp everywhere. A glorious mess. Lift and fall again. Bellowing. How long before it breaks open?

Someone is dragging a form from the grain. Fur. A long snout. A *snout?*

I stare, let go for an instant. The whole scene flashes orange, fire across my face, spins. I am on my back, my brother over me, kneeling, gasping like one pulled from a well. His hands, clenched, rise and fall. Prayer? Surely this isn't the occasion. The clenched hands are plunging down on me—left face, right face. Aiming for nose or for jaw. Blessedly, I have risen above pain. The scene is flashing red, blurred by white sparks which explode and drift by me. My brother kneeling above me—is this impassioned prayer or homicide?

Homicide? It's he who should be punished. Up go two locked hands, high above me, fists joined like a gory mallet. Down, right at my skull. I twist quick as an eel, hear a shriek. He is cradling one hand with the other, cherishing it with astonishment as if his fingers had fused into the finest gold.

For the first time I notice feet about us. We are in a forest of legs. And arms. Hands pull at us both, wrenching, twisting, pulling us apart. Between the forms I see a bellowing, bearded figure—my father—holding a dripping body. He is making a terrible din, beating his chest, blood everywhere.

"Who? Who?" he is roaring. "Who dared do this?" His face is bruised plum like my brother's. I am struck by the family resemblance.

The weight of my brother is off me. Life-giving relief. He is thrown back in a heap, limp. He is still treasuring one hand with the other. It is red. I can see only from one eye. I try to rise, pulling myself up the clutter of legs, but fall back.

There is a stirring in the branches. A figure is knocking them aside, this way and that, a beast through saplings. It is my father again.

"You did this?" I think he is accusing me; but no, he is addressing Shem.

My father is holding a sack of fur from which blood drips at every seam. Where did it come from? Shem does not reply. He doesn't even see it yet.

"Sent from abroad," my father roars. "Last one on earth. Not an unclean bird. No, a rare creature. Rare. Gone!"

He shakes it, spattering blood; I see that it is the giant sloth. The most rare of our creatures. The most sluggish. The only one which would obligingly lie still in the grain, large enough to resemble the torso of a sleeping servant girl.

Suddenly a howl from Shem. He staggers to his feet. He has seen, has made the connection. He grabs the spit. For a minute I think he is after me; but no, he lunges for the sloth hanging from our father's outstretched arm. Stab. Stab. Gasps and cries of amazement, of protest. My father holding it, frozen in astonishment, watching the blood spurt anew; Shem thrusting and shouting "Bitch, bitch." And me, one-eyed, dazed, bloodied, doubled over with laughter.

And did the Great and Wise Yahweh look down and reconsider? Did He thrust a finger in the seams of that Ark and finish off the whole absurd mistake? He did not.

No, something even stranger. Something caught our father's eye and he lowered the corpse, staring across the room. Shem turned and, seeing, lowered his spit. The shouting died. I caught sight of my mother looking toward the door, mouth open with astonishment. All attention was fixed on the door, sloth and Seth forgotten. Passions forgotten.

As for me, all I could see was legs and bodies. But the sudden quiet chilled me more than the sight of gore.

I finally struggled to my knees and saw a figure standing by the door. It was old Nahum, Methuselah's voiceless servant, bent as always, standing there in silence.

There had been no shout to catch our attention, to bring all that action to a halt. Not a word. Not even a gesture. It was only his presence. We had never seen him outside his master's chambers. A recluse's recluse. Marvelous as it is to see a grown man vent his rage on a dead sloth, the greatest wonder of all is to see some fixed part of this universe out of its appointed place.

XIX Brothers

So it was when we saw the waters rise to the eves of the temple: the impossible made possible. And when we saw the landscape turn to seascape, mountains to islands, order confounded, all assurances swept aside. Now Nahum had altered his fixed and narrow orbit. His presence among us was a portent of change in the universe of our clan. Methuselah, our Patriarch, must be dying.

X X

MOTHERS

THEY all left, struggling to make their way through the door like sheep at the gate. They all left and forgot me. Me and the sloth.

I was on my knees. When I tried to stand, the effort was too much and I fell back, sitting with a "thunk," a child not ready to take his first step. I was in worse shape than I had thought.

I looked over at that oozing corpse and grinned. Try as I might, I couldn't share my father's sense of outrage. The world might never see a sloth again, but I would have my Sapphira. When it came to endangered species, my loyalties were with the one who shared my bed and my language.

True, I'd been shocked at our first losses—the pelican and the osprey, deaths which our father had shrugged off because the creatures were unclean, useless as pigs. To him the sloth was on a higher order. A greater loss. But how could I grieve when its death gave life to my Sapphira?

What a crafty ingenuity she had, what a knack for survival! Sly as a ferret. It seemed altogether right that the Great Yahweh in His wisdom should honor her bid for survival over the hapless sloth.

But should the same logic be applied to the rest of us, to this boatload which had remained afloat while others sank? We liked to think of ourselves as both ingenious and resourceful. But was it His intention to make sure that only the crafty should inherit the earth?

Still dazed, still unable to stand, I surveyed the trampled grain, the blood, the punctured body—all that violence. For what? Merely because a servant girl had turned her attention to her master's brother? No, it must have been because she had acted on her own, had made her own choice, declared herself a free agent. That's what bothers people like my brother.

"Sapphira," I said, speaking to no one, though in my mind to her. "Sapphira, are you all right? Let's go."

I had a notion of leaving that place, going with her to some quiet spot where tigers feed on flowers and people treasure one another. I'd forgotten that the gate to that garden had long since been locked.

My ears hummed with a sound like summer insects and the room turned slowly about me. I vaguely remembered being knocked about by an enraged brother, but there had been some kind of inner assault too: One moment she was dead and then she was not, agony enough for a lifetime had been transformed into a gory joke. Unsettling at best.

Steps approaching. Sapphira? Perhaps we could get out of there after all. I staggered to my feet, knees weak as green stems. I was not going to look like some casualty for her. I was determined, will pitted against my sagging muscles. But what is will without bodily support? I slid to the floor, limp as that sloth—though slightly better off.

It was Hephzibah. With a cook's good instincts, she had come back with a meat hook, the type used to drag the carcasses of sheep to the cutting table, and went right for the punctured corpse. This had not been exactly a ritual slaughter, but she was more attuned to the demands of the stomach than to those of dogma. No glance at me, crumpled there in the twilight like someone's abandoned coat. She went about her business: rolled the beast over, swung that great hook into its throat, started to drag it away, its bulk no match for hers.

"Hephzibah."

She dropped the handle with a gasp and bent over the corpse, touching it with a new respect, even awe.

"No, over here," I said. "It's me. Ham."

Another gasp, though perhaps of relief. Then she was at my side, wiping blood from my eyes and feeling for wounds.

"My God, my God," she kept muttering. "Left you for dead."

This was not quite fair, of course; they had merely forgotten me, concerned with someone closer to the abyss. Besides, what is a youngest son compared with the patriarch of the family? But I hadn't the strength or desire to set her straight. Her great softness, her closeness, her concern. I could feel my bruises healing.

"This is no place for you," she said. "Can you walk if I help?"

I lurched to my feet and clung to her broad, padded shoulder. She led me back through the kitchen and into a room beside the sultry soup pantry. Another storage area? No, there was a sleeping pallet in the corner and clothes hanging on the wall pegs. It was her own chamber located just off the kitchens, handy to her work the way grooms live next to their stalls.

"Where have they hurt you?" she asked, starting to undress me. "We must find out." I was in no condition to object. The drama of that fight was such that I imagined half my bones broken. None were, in fact, but this did not keep me from enjoying the just rewards of an innocent victim.

Her hands were marvelous. Strong and sure, broad and knowing. They probed each bone, testing for breaks, stroked each muscle in search of sprains. I imagined myself a mound of dough being kneaded. The room itelf was warm as a bakery, the air heavy with the scents of herbs and grains. The only sounds were our breathing and the creaking of that great ship. It was not me but the yeast wafting about us that caused my rising. It was all natural and appropriate in the hands of this master baker.

"My God, my God," she muttered when she discovered my condition. Her phrasing was profane by our standards, but there was something in her tone and in the warmth of that room which made it sound more like a prayer of thanksgiving. "You're not so damaged as I thought." Her voice low and close. "But you need massage or you'll ache tomorrow."

Slow, slow as tides, slow as seasons she rolled my muscles, pressed memory out of me. In some other life I had felt something like this in a fast tempo, but the recollection of all that was slipping behind me like tatters of an old dream.

She seemed far larger than her daily self. She was everywhere. Everything. I was losing my sense of self, disappearing with wonder into the enormity of her, sliding, sliding back, back to the start of things, to a moist darkness, a void without words, only the moan of the wind and the rising and falling of the waters. Good. Holy God, it was good.

There was a trace of a pale light from somewhere, a light without source, just enough to make out the terrain. We were a single, undulating mass, a slow energy turning in that faint glow, no up and no down, no need for directions. Arms, thighs, backs, robes, hips, bedcovers had become hills and valleys, groves and dark ravines, a marvelous domain, a burgeoning creation.

The two of us coiled and uncoiled, slithered in the primal marsh. I could smell the musk of growth—herbs, grasses, ripe fruit.

The sounds we made were not ours, they were the lowing of cattle, the snort and pawing of roebucks, the burrowing and probing of every creeping creature that creepeth upon the earth.

Joined, we rose in a glowing light, became the birds of the air, became the creatures of the earth, those that swim and those that crawl, those that are gentle and those that kill. We were all of them together, being born and reborn in a sudden blaze of life.

And then we fell back. We rested.

"Ham?"

It was scarcely to be believed. It could have been a long dream if it weren't for the bruises and the aches returning. I had thought only pairs of people did that, but all I could remember was a singularity. Was that possible?

"Ham."

Surely I deserved a day of rest. It was in the tradition.

"Ham."

There was no telling how long I had slept. Centuries, perhaps. But still I wanted more. Either sleep or the chance to recapture it all, re-sing it like some ritual hymn, some dreamlike melody played on a horn. Or could one perhaps recreate it all in a tapestry, thread by thread, golds and reds gleaming?

"Ham!"

Stalling, hiding there in the twilight, one eye half open, seeing the silhouette there in the doorway, half hoping to cling to the experience before it faded. What did she want anyway? It was not like her to be demanding.

"Ham, wake up, answer me."

Not Hephzibah. Not her tone at all. Familiar . . . Mother!

"What?"

"Where are you?"

"Here."

"Are you hurt?"

"Hurt?"

"Hephzibah tells me—"

"Recovering."

"Can you walk?"

"I think not."

"You'll have to try."

"Why?"

"You must. Try now. Push yourself."

I felt no inner need to push myself. I'd finished with that. It was like her to insist on effort for no reason. Merely for principle. Whenever we were sick, we had to make the effort to act as if we were not. Whenever we were cold, we were punished for chattering our teeth or clasping our hands in our armpits. When tired, we had to stand straight; when sleepy, to look alert; when hungry, refuse food; when seized with affection, show respect. Why? We never knew for sure. But it must have had something to do with not going slack. Wasn't this why I was put to work on the lowest level, why Japheth was supposed to do the same on the next deck? Even Shem had his tasks directing servants, enforcing schedules. The unstated sin: going slack, turning soft. No one ever said so, but I had the impression that if I slept through the entire morning, we as a family would begin an inevitable slide downward, that we would end by becoming servants, field workers, scrofulous beggars. But wasn't today different? Didn't I deserve my private Sabbath?

"I don't think I can," I said. Then, braver, more honest, "I don't really want to."

"*Want?*" She spat the word as if it were rancid. "*Want? Want* has nothing to do with it. What if everybody did just what they *wanted?* Do you think we'd be here now? What if I hadn't wanted to go through the agony of bearing a child again, where would *you* be? And when I was nursing you, what if I didn't want to rouse myself at night and let you suckle? What if I didn't *want* to give myself to your father's passion? Where would the whole family be?"

The familiar litany. There was no interrupting.

"Why are you afloat in this sea of corpses? You don't know? Haven't considered it? I'll tell you why: Because when you were ordered to build, you built. You may not have felt like hewing the wood on those hot and dusty days, you may not have liked the ridicule, your *dreams* may have placed you down at the river swimming with your friends, but you didn't act on your wants. Your friends—where are they now? Bloated corpses, they are. They did what they *wanted*. Can you deny that they are bloated corpses? Unburied? Floating meat?"

There was no way to counter Mother's arguments. I shook my head, struck dumb not with her logic but with her images.

"I don't mean," she continued, softer now, "that you'll have to work with your hands all your life. You weren't born to be a farmhand. But you have your assigned tasks and you'll do them when you're told and don't for a moment think you can declare your own Sabbath. That's the worst blasphemy. It's not up to us to reorder the rhythm of labor."

But, I wanted to say, I'm hurt. She rolled on without a pause: "Right now you're to see the Old One. He's called for you. I don't know why. Can't imagine. But he's asked for you. No matter how strange, his word is still law. Especially since he's dying. You don't counter a dying man's request—not without risking a curse. So it doesn't matter whether you've got aches or broken bones, you have to go to him. Now. You've no choice."

No choice. There was that phrase again. One part of me had come to accept it long before we set out on this cruise. I had resigned myself to the fact that I was not free to skip my lessons, wear a torn tunic, talk like a gutter-sweep, or swim in the river with the goat girl, because I was the son of Noah, the grandson of Lamech, the great-grandson of Methuselah. And he, as everyone knew, was the son of Enoch who walked with the Lord Himself, and what would happen to the order of the universe if the great-great-grandson of the one who had walked with the Yahweh decided to take a private Sabbath?

Once again I was being told that I had no choice. What had my father offered me on that rainy day by the gangplank? Wasn't that a real choice? Or was it uttered in some kind of irony? In any case, I had no choice at this moment. Not even the illusion.

I struggled to my feet, suddenly aware of my physical state. The bruises and dried blood were easily accounted for—an unseemly but manly and natural dispute with my brother. But how was I going to explain the smell, the unmistakable musk of womanhood?

She led me into the lighted kitchen. In spite of her lack of height she was strong. She half supported and half directed me. With her, it was never easy to distinguish one from the other.

There she straightened my clothes as best she could, combed my hair with her fingers, called for wet sheeting from Hephzi-bah, cleaned the blood from my face and arms.

"The smell," she said, cocking her head to one side, trying to place it.

"It's them cats," Hephzibah said. "He's been cleaning the slop from the big cats."

Her smile turned on me and the memory of our recent union washed back as if from the beginning of time. My legs almost melted again. But my mother never noticed. Her mind had seized on a higher concern, the use of language. "*Leopards,* you mean. Not cats, Hephzibah, *leop-ards.*"

"That's it," Hephzibah said, nodding her head, "the big cats."

My mother, brushing grain from my clothes, caught my eye and smiled for the first time, shaking her head in wonder at the persistence of ignorance.

XXI

FATHERS

THEY were all there, all clustered in Methuselah's ante-chamber, standing, sitting, leaning against the walls, children squatting. Every one of them. Even Japheth, face solemn and sweating but somehow taller and tougher than usual, hardened in sobriety. Beside him, his obedient Ophir and little Leah, round and mournful. All of them mournful. I began to hear little phrases which were repeated earnestly and in hushed tones as if each were a fresh insight: "There's hope while the Ancient breathes"; "The end is surely near"; "His hours are numbered"; "It's out of our hands"; "Nothing to do but pray."

Lament hung in the air heavy as incense. This puzzled me since I had not heard them express affection for him in the past. Yet I heard Zillah say, eyes brimming, "If only he could linger long enough to see the dry land again" and Japheth mutter, "Surely the leader of us all." And from Athaliah, "We'll never see one like him again." They passed these phrases back and forth, nodding, treasuring each one as if examining a collection of lustrous pearls.

As for me, dazed by recent events, I was caught in a tangle
of feelings. It seemed terrible that he was really dying. There
was so much left which I wanted to ask him. Yet Sapphira had
taught me to accept the cycles, and certainly his was overdue.
In any case, I couldn't share in the muttered laments. It was as
if my family had learned a chant which was new to me. Pray for
him? With what in mind? An extension of hours after all those
years? Surely he wouldn't be asking for that. In any case, I
couldn't speak for him.

My silence was considered unseemly, even surly. Women,
ignoring my bruises, nudged me with questions. "How will we
get along without him?" Ophir wanted to know. Much the
same, I imagined; but unwise to say it. "Was there ever such
a leader?" Mother asked. Since I had no way of knowing, I
shrugged. An honest response, I thought, but she almost hit me.

Worse, my father overheard her question, saw my response.
His glower transfixed me. No, something else is going on. Some
little drama. It appears to involve me. He turns to Shem and
gestures in my direction, a quick flip of his head silently in-
dicating "There he is"; then the same to Japheth who nods,
understanding, in on it. "Let's go," again without words, the
three of them coming toward me. What have *I* done?

There is tension in the air when three men approach a fourth
without words, without expression. The ominous mask of the
blank face. And silence. Not one but three forbidding fathers.
No way to judge the degree of anger. Much easier to bear a
man's shouted insults, profanities, curses—inner storms made
outer and visible. I'm used to that. But today is different. Perhaps it is death in the air. Nothing is simple or direct. Much is
held back, kept hidden.

They approach, all three, and I have a dreamlike notion that
they are about to perform Sapphira's punishment on me. Without thinking, I put my hands behind my back. I'll deny everything. Except for a brotherly tussle, I've done nothing. Haven't
touched a woman in weeks. The smell? I've been cleaning cat
cages, cavorting with goats, buggering sheep—good, healthy
boys' play. No, I'd never touch someone else's property. My
God, the three of them look serious.

Flip of the head. I'm to follow. Down to the kitchens? To the meat counter? The cleaver? No, back down to Our Deck, to the very rear, back to the shafts. The door closes behind us, is locked. This is the men's side. We have privacy here. A horrid place, though, stinking; the worst end of humans. Here the bitterness of urine soaked into black boards, the lingering fumes of feces, the sound of dark waters below us, sucking up and down in those two stained shafts.

Silence. Facing three faces. Shem's still bruised and puffy. Behind them the open squat-holes, our daily reminder of the liquid nether world below us where we would now be were we not sons of Noah. My mind slips, stumbles, and for an instant I imagine that they are going to give me a grim choice: Behave in an upright manner or leave—headfirst. But no, the holes are too small for more than small portions of me at a time.

I need to hear words to set me straight, to wake me from this dream. Oh for a reprimand, a curse, a fatherly blow to the head!

When the words come at last they are worse than I imagined.

"Dear son of mine," he begins, two loving hands on my shoulders. I can scarcely stand the threat of such affection. "Your great-grandfather is dying."

Pause. Our castle heaves, the waters rise in the shafts and then flush down again with a rush. I say nothing. What words can the rabbit utter while held in loving talons?

"He wishes to see you."

Nod.

"You, the youngest."

Nod, nod.

"We don't know why."

He doesn't know? Only a hint of uncertainty but good to hear. This man who one breath earlier knew everything, con-trolled everything, has just lost that perfect hold. The talons have released their grip. Free flight is not fun, but for a bruised rabbit it's the next best thing to soaring.

"Wants to see me?" I ask, wide-eyed. Phrased like a question but not really asking. It's more of a statement, a reminder: Wants to see *me*. But not put that bluntly. Rabbits don't taunt hawks.

"Or so he thinks," Shem says, his voice cutting in for the first time. "He's old."

Another good sign—trying to pass the Ancient off as crippled in mind as well as in body. But if they truly believe this, if they really see Methuselah's requests as pointless wanderings, what are we doing in the shafts, secluded in the men's section, talking in tones which would suggest that the future of man is at stake?

"He's been saying things," Shem says and pauses.

"He, the Ancient, that is," my father says.

"Muttering, actually . . ." Japheth.

"Yes, muttering," my father says, "almost incoherent . . ."

"About third sons," Shem.

"Third sons," Japheth says. "As if there were something . . ."

"Special," my father says. A pause. And then in a rush like waters flushing, "He wants to see you and God only knows what he'll say or promise you or say about the family, and you watch out for the way his mind works because after a point an old man's words should not be trusted. Do you know what I mean? A man's mind keeps growing, you know. Has to, storing up all those experiences, like a chest into which you keep putting layer after layer of clothes, it builds up. All those memories. All those ideas and notions. But the skull cannot grow. Am I right? The skull remains the same. If anything, it contracts like a raisin. Meanwhile, layer after layer of children and grandchildren and great-grandchildren and on and on, each of them with names that have to be remembered and nicknames and each with special peculiarities, one with a bad stomach, another fond of sacred singing, another clever with sums, another with doubtful parentage. Oh, it's not enough to remember names—all these oddities about them must be remembered and remarked upon. And their ages change. Every year. And soon as you have them placed, they're married and have more of their own. More information to store. On and on it goes. Can you see what it is to be truly ancient?"

I nod. Understanding nothing, I nod.

"All this in the same old skull. Do you understand what I'm saying? The same size. All these pieces of information added layer by layer in the same container. What happens when you keep adding coats to the same old chest?"

"It won't close?"

He gives me a glancing blow on the shoulder. "Japheth, what happens when you keep adding coats and robes to the same old chest?"

"Splits open."

"Aaag!" He sprays spittle in disgust. "You're not following. Shem, do you see what I'm getting at?"

Wise Shem nods wisely but says nothing. "What?" I ask Shem, calling his bluff. But the old man will have none of that. He cuts in before Shem can make a fool of himself.

"They get rumpled," he roars, shaking me by both shoulders. "Creased, rumpled. Almost beyond recognition. That's what. Do you understand now?" What is there to understand? "About his mind? Do you understand that his *ideas*, his *ideas* . . ."

"His ideas?"

"Exactly. Now you have it. Even you. You have it. His *ideas* are all twisted up. He's *crazy*."

Awful silence. The unutterable has been uttered. The Ancient, our Patriarch. Crazy? An insult to the whole tribe.

"Well, I don't mean *crazy* crazy. You understand? Just crazy jumbled up. Frayed at the ends. Addled. Scrambled. Unhinged. Sprung at the seams. Batty. You understand?"

Understand! Does he? In trying to reverse himself he has just stated the unutterable seven different ways right there in the shafts, a room steeped in honesty, a room where men speak candidly with fellow men in the natural brotherhood of bodily needs. We have to take his pronouncement at face value. Yet what terrible implications! If we cannot revere age, to whom should we turn? Whom should we trust?

"It doesn't seem possible," Shem mutters, also shaken. "A patriarch!"

"A patriarch but not a leader. *I* had this ship built. *I* gathered the clan and the beasts together. *I* kept my mind on matters at hand while he spun out theories which could sink us all."

"Theories?" Japheth asks.

"You wait. He'll use his last hour to discredit us all. And you . . ." he turns to me, ". . . are the most vulnerable. Being youngest. He is a seducer and a corrupter of youth. Just keep this in mind, Ham: He'll give you some astonishing ideas all right because that's all he's got left to give; but *I* was the one who gave you a berth. Never forget where you are."

In the silence we feel the floor shudder and fall away under us; a creaking of timbers, a heave of stomachs, a lurch as we slam into the trough, and the two squat-holes vomit geysers of filthy water from below.

XXII

GREAT-
GRANDFATHER

B Y the time we returned, old Nahum had finished the medications, had washed his master, had propped him up, had opened the door to the family. They were all in there.

It seemed to me that a man might be given the same privacy on his dying day as he is normally granted on his wedding night. After all, there must be tensions on each occasion, a good chance of making a fool of oneself, a chasm between intentions and abilities. One is relatively inexperienced at each and who wants to be on display as a novice?

Most are in fact granted privacy but for other reasons. Only dear and close friends are willing to sit close by, watch the descent, listen to fears, share the agony. It is a service I have given many times and it is rarely a pleasant experience. I'm not surprised that most would prefer to avoid it. But this was no ordinary dying.

It seemed as if Methuselah was suddenly overburdened with dear friends. I wondered at first how much adoration was directed at the man and how much at this figure as a lingering link with the past. Perhaps they were seeing him as damaged threads in the family tapestry.

But no, surely this was heartfelt compassion. I watched as they shoved old Nahum aside and took possession. Wipe the brow, arrange the covers, smooth the hair, clean spittle from the chin, hold the withered hand, massage the arm, the neck, the shoulder. They groomed him like gibbons, muttering in low tones, referring to him for some reason in the third person.

"He needs air."

"No, the dampness will clot his lungs."

"Raise his head. That pillow there . . ."

"Lemon oil—there on the cabinet—for his chest. Ease his breathing."

"Here, let me."

"I'll do it."

"Careful!"

"Oop!"

"There you've done it! Quick, towels. Last lemon oil on earth. Soaked him you did. Damn clever."

"Shut up, Sister, and hand me those towels."

"You're leaning on his chest."

"I am not. Watch it—catch the drool from the corner of his mouth. God's-sake don't smother him."

They must have been aware even then that this was a historic moment. Years later I would hear them say to one another: I ministered unto him at the very end, I was there, yes, that's right, the great Methuselah himself, I served him at the very end.

And will they serve me the same way? Will I feel ministering fingers like mice running over my body and hear their hushed directives to one another? I have no right to compare myself to him. I am not as ancient as Methuselah was nor will I ever be, yet there has been a bond over the years, a warm link which has jumped two generations of coldly willful men. And now, here in this Babylonian tower, a part of and yet also apart from the tumult outside, I am in many ways closer to him than to that awestruck boy who stood at his bedside. If I should look up and see some young descendant standing at my bedside, tears welling up along his lower lids like minute springs, I too would try to reach out, try to touch him, try to give him warmth to sustain him in this dynamic but heartless land.

"There is my inheritor," Methuselah said, voice like leaves

rustling, hand rising, fingers circling my arm, holding me. *Me!*

"No," my father said. "This is only Ham."

"My inheritor."

"This is Ham, my *third* born. Your youngest great-grandson."

My face was prickling with the heat of it. I had not asked to be his inheritor—whatever that meant. I had not ever said anything to him against my eldest brother or against my father. What could the Ancient know about my secret thoughts? If there were a rebellious level to my nature, it was hidden down there on the lowest level. I had decided to come aboard, hadn't I? Who was I to speak out against the holy ordinance of primogeniture?

"The eldest and the youngest," the Ancient said. Was that a smile or a grimace?

"The youngest?" my father, feigning miscomprehension, fooling no one, "over here. Your great-*great*-grandchildren."

He parted the crowd roughly, seized Shem's two children, dragged them like sacks of grain to the bedside. He held them up there by their collars, toes barely touching the floor. "Here," he said, his wine merchant's voice, "Amaziah and Hushai, first and second born of my son, Shem."

"Put them down," the Ancient said. My father dropped them. They fell in a heap then scuttled on hands and knees, disappearing between legs like a couple of crabs into the reeds. "I know perfectly well who they are," the Ancient said. His voice was sharp-edged, a reprimand. "I was speaking of adults. The oldest and the youngest of adults. The end of knowledge and the new beginning."

There was silence now. All that subdued chattering had stopped. When a dying man talks, who is to tell which sentence will be the final one? We place great weight on terminations. Besides, in this case he had just reprimanded his grandson, my father. He could do the same to anyone present. If a simple chastisement becomes a man's dying words, it takes on the force of a curse. It can warp an entire life.

"Rest now," my mother said.

"There'll be time enough for that. I'm telling you that the third son sees with the eyes of a sage. Consider that. A sage."

I was mortified. I would have preferred a curse. Setting me up as a sage! At my age! I would never live this down. But there was no stopping him.

"In all our folk tales, it is the third son who strikes out. In all our parables. In the stories we men tell over wine. Remember the three horny brothers who called on the well-digger's daughter . . . ?" This again!

"Grandfather!" My mother daring to interrupt. The courage of a lioness. "Wine did you say? Can we get you a mug?"

"The three rampant young men knock on the door. The maiden is in bed. Naked as the day she was born. 'What do you want?' she calls—" He was interrupted by a terrible coughing spasm, an intervention later declared divine. "The first—" More coughing. "The first . . ."

"The first? Here he is." My father shoved Shem forward, deflecting the story. "My first-born."

"The first . . ." The Ancient looked puzzled, lost the thread, then focused on Shem. "Ah yes, the first-born . . ."

"Right here. Shem, my eldest."

"Right," Shem murmured. "I'm the oldest."

"The first is always an echo of his father. All duty. Cold duty. You built the ship. Thanks for that. And you'll build the cities. Take pleasure in that. High values in some ways, but cold. Cold values. You deserve the best land, I suppose. Take the best land. Now the second . . ."

My father yanked on Japheth's arm, sent him stumbling into the bed, spilling jars and bottles. The Ancient continued, not noticing. It was as if he were talking principle, already beyond the particulars. "The second has no place, is lost but does not know it. Leave him your songs and a keg of wine. But the third . . . warm, uneasy . . ."

His voice failed. His face lit up as if with some vision, staring into empty space. The great ship heaved, and my great-grandfather's arm fell to his side, his lids closed.

From someone near came the first hesitant, high wail of mourning, "Eeeee." Then another. A third. Soon they were all at it, baying, moaning, sobbing in a great chorus of lament, an outpouring of grief.

"Oh for God's-sake shut up." His eyes wide-open again.

Utter silence. Shocked silence. The blasphemy of it. And the chicanery! Playing a trick with his own life. And making them look like chattering apes. His own descendants. Even I felt at the time that it was in bad taste—though I well may play the same game myself in time. No doubt a man needs one last taste of power.

"My testament," he said. That shut us up. If there had been a roach on the wall, we would have heard its heartbeat. As it was, we heard only the hiss of rain and the sigh of wind on the outside, chilling reminders from which we were protected on the deck below. "My testament," he said again. I think half of us had stopped breathing. "To you," he said, grasping my arm again. *My* arm! I could hear a gasp close to me—my father? mother? brothers? It could have been any of them. Or all. This was a time for the blessing of the eldest son, my father, and no time for tricks. This attention given to me was like a sentence of exile. I prayed—forgive me—but I prayed for quick termination. I stared at those red and watery eyes, willing them to shut, willing his mouth to close again. Until now, his words could be written off as the ramblings of a crazed man. But this was a fresh gathering of energy, a final effort at coherence. I was in for it.

"They've told you," he said, voice soft but calm, rational, clear, "of my lineage—of my father, Enoch, of Jared, Mahalalel, Kenan, Enosh, back to Seth? You know that line well?" I nodded. I'd been taught to recite that before I could scratch my own name on parchment. "You've studied the tapestry?" Nod. "Memorized it?" Nod, nod. "Well, it's a lie."

Pricking heat ran through my scalp, down my neck, across my back, under my arms. Lie? Everything?

"Stop him," someone whispered, but only a whisper. Who dared to stop a dying man?—A dying patriarch, yet.

"Here is my true lineage: I was born Methushael, my father was Mehujael, his was Irad, his Enoch, and his . . ." Pause. "His was not Seth but Cain."

That is what he said. The very words. Everyone there heard them clearly. I am the last alive of my generation, but there was not a member of my family that did not hear it. And we could not fail to believe it. A man does not lie on his deathday. Cain! Our link to Adam through Cain, not Seth. The rest a terrible coverup, woven into tapestries, chiseled into our memories since our first day of schooling, memorized, recited. Believed. And now taken away. Cain: the murderer. Worse than Adam, his crime was against his brother. My skin crawled.

"My testament," he said. I think he was beginning to smile, working toward it. "My testament; your inheritance. Just that. But think . . ." Was this the end? No, his mouth was forming more. When he found the breath, the words came forth clearly, with resonance. "But think how marvelous it would be . . ." Pause. Breath. "Marvelous it would be if, knowing that, living with it, you could . . . still, Ham, still achieve . . . warm values. Harmony . . . Grace."

The smile finally broke through. That old leather cracked like parched earth. Smile achieved, it settled on him in death, became a part of him. Even as the body cooled, even through the final washing, even after their efforts to turn the mouth down for the final viewing, to hide the crinkles each side of the eyes, even then his gentle smile prevailed. His words were a confusion, but the smile remained with me as his most treasured gift.

XXIII

GUSHER

I found her in the pigpen. She was hunched up in the corner, hair a tangle, listlessly fondling piglets. She'd gone back to that solemn face. It didn't even light up when she saw me.

"How long have you been here?"

Shrug.

"I've been looking all over for you."

Shrug.

I sat down, clearing a little space in the damp straw just opposite, and tried to put my arm around her. She slid away from me, wedging herself closer to the wall as if she would shove right through it into the water if she could.

"What's wrong? Are you hurt?"

She shrugged again, avoiding my eyes. I'd seen that look before but not in her. I was slowly learning to identify it—the face of those who have given up hope of escape. It is resignation. It is the last, deadened retreat of prisoners of all sorts, of those whose lives are owned by others. Their safest response is no response, their safest emotion no emotion, their safest pose is stupidity. I didn't know it then, but there are more humans in that state than in mine. I, my clan, and you who have the leisure and the ability to read this account are the exceptions.

I reached out and put my hand on her knee. She shivered. She didn't withdraw it, didn't welcome it; her spasm was that of the lamb at slaughter. I could feel her fear in the depth of my stomach. I removed my hand.

"I'm not Shem," I said softly.

"You're his brother."

"So?"

"Your clan is his clan."

"I'm *me*." A pointless observation, perhaps, but it seemed highly important at the time.

It must have meant something to her because she slowly shook her head, disagreeing. How was that possible? A moment of perplexed silence. Then I tried again.

"What's different now from before?" Pause. "Say something!"

She looked up at me with alarm. I'd adopted the voice of authority—at my age! It just slipped out.

"I dream," she said in a whisper.

"Of what?"

"Men coming after me. To punish me."

"Who?"

"My master." She meant Shem, but I hadn't heard her use this servants' term before. "My master and his father. Or his brothers. Sometimes one, sometimes another."

"They're all the same?"

A piglet nuzzled her leg and she fondled it. Still at the suckling

age, it seized her longest finger, taking it for a teat. She seemed not to notice, but some of the darkness lifted from her expression. "When you've lived as I have lived, it seems so."

"Even me?"

She looked at me directly for the first time. "There's two of you," she said softly. "There's Ham and then there's his father's son."

An accusation, somehow. Yet it was hardly one I could deny. Where would I be if I were not my father's son? Another time I might have explored that; instead, I put my arm around her and my head on her shoulder. This time she did not pull away.

"Things used to be simpler," she said. She spoke softly, almost to herself, or perhaps to the piglet who continued to work on her fingers, moving from one to the next, looking for his midday meal. "I did what I was told. Never thought not to. Some of it was pleasant enough. Some was nasty. But I never expected it *not* to be nasty. D'you know what I mean?"

I nodded, but of course I didn't. Not really. "I get ordered around too," I said. She was not impressed. Being at the bottom in a family like ours had its irritations, but it was not the same as being at the bottom of the world's order. And that's where she had been. A bonded servant since birth and a woman as well. Bottom of the bottom. What did I know about that? There are limits to imagination.

"It didn't pay to think about the future. Or the past. My parents were servants but I barely remember them. Traded off for camels, I heard. Who knows? I was raised in kitchens and slept in storage bins. There were always those that were worse off. Fieldworkers, for example. Out there digging and weeding. And those that are born ugly. The ugly always get it. Maybe it's because they don't look like their masters. It's easier to hit them. Anyway, they're worse off. And then there's those that get killed. They're worse off. I guess. 'You're lucky to be alive' Hephzibah is always saying. And most of the time I believe her. When we got nailed into this crazy boat, I wasn't so sure. But all that water sort of convinced me. I don't like the idea of drowning."

"Neither do I." Treasured, these intercultural areas of agreement, these universal values.

"But then this thing with you."

"Thing?"

"Loving you," she said so simply, so straightforward that I didn't have a chance to respond before she went on. "It's stirred everything up. Your brother after me. And me getting a picture of . . . well, what it must be like for those who can do just what they want. Get up when they want, drink when they want, get meals by clapping their hands. I never really thought about that before, never could see myself living that way. It's not fair showing that to someone and then hiding it again."

"Showing it?"

"When you share with me, you're showing me how it might be. Shem never did that. When he forces me, I'm still his servant girl. You see the difference?"

I was just beginning to, a slow learner. "So how am I hiding it again?"

"Not you alone. You as a clan."

"How?"

"See these?" She held up her fingers, all wet and glistening from that adoring piglet. "You know what it would feel like to have them chopped? There's a scullery girl who went through it. You pass out at the time. If you're lucky. But then it goes on hurting for months. Even now she can't put her hands in hot water without feeling it right up to her elbow. Wakes up at night screaming." She shook her head, gave a wry smile. "I'd rather swim than go through that."

"You won't have to." I had no assurance. Not in my family. Moral convictions run deep with them. "I don't think you'll have to."

"That's what the Ancient said."

"What Ancient?"

"*Your* Ancient. Oh . . ." She looked at me, wondering, I suppose, whether she had said the wrong thing, wondering whether to trust me.

"Methuselah? You saw him? You spoke to him?"

She pulled back from me as if I had hit her. Then nodded. "After I got out of that grain bin. I thought maybe I could appeal to him. I mean, I *did* appeal to him."

"Old Nahum let you see him?"

"Of course not. I sneaked in."

"And you spoke to him?"

I was astonished. True, I thought of myself willing to defend her to the death, but what a brazen thing for her to do, going right to the top without being invited!

"Just walked right in? What on earth did you say?"

"I said 'hello.'" And then she grinned—either at the absurdity of it or at the brazenness of that piglet who had returned to his passionate finger-kissing. "It was just a bit embarrassing for us both."

"You knew who he was?"

"Of course. Everyone does."

"And he had seen you around?"

"I don't think so. Except that one time with you. But he *thought* he'd seen me ages ago. Back when he was young. He couldn't have, of course, but he thought he had. 'A vision,' he kept saying. He was looking right up at me, but I think maybe he was seeing someone else."

"What did you say?"

"I tried to tell him about you and about us and about your brother and the punishment he has in mind for me and how it was unfair and all—it all came out in a jumble. I didn't know how much time I had. I told him everything."

"And he understood?"

"I don't know. He just made me stand very close to the bed. Explored me with his hand."

"You let him?"

"Well, I wanted to get my story out. All of it. And he couldn't hear very well. But he could do a lot of things with that hand. Like a spider it was."

"Awful."

"Only at first. Anyway, I kept talking and he kept exploring and when I finally got to the end of my story he let out a kind of whoop—"

"A *whoop?* Methuselah? What kind of whoop?"

"A happy whoop. Astonished-like. And then a kind of wheezing laugh. I hadn't said anything to make him laugh. Really I hadn't. But he sounded so happy that I got to giggling. And then he doubled up, knees up to his chest, and he rolled over on his side, curled up like he was in pain. I was sure he was dying.

"I bent over to listen to his breath and he said it was better. He thanked me in a whisper and put his hand right on my heart."

She took my hand and slipped it under her robe onto her left breast to show me exactly where the Ancient had touched her. "And he blessed me," she said with astonishment. "Blessed me."

Blessed her! If only we had witnesses, this would have freed her from bondage. But who would believe a servant girl?

One part of my mind worked like a member of the court, presenting arguments to my brothers, my father, to the whole lot of them. Here was a girl who had been blessed in the final holy hour of the Ancient's life. A sanctified moment, a priestly laying on of hands, a holy act. Who were we to counter our Patriarch's dying gesture? Surely the girl had been freed.

Another part of me was conscious of the fact that my hand remained on the very spot that had been blessed by our Patriarch in his final hour. Perhaps it was my imagination, but it seemed as if the nipple was still warm and roused from that ceremony.

I would have discussed the significance of her new state, the impact of a blessing like that, her elevation, as it were, except that our attention was drawn to the piglet. He had settled on to her middle finger and with a kind of orgiastic wriggling had convinced himself that he was receiving the sweetest nutriment known to pigdom. With her free hand she massaged its lower belly, sending it into spasms of delight.

There must have been some signal in his asthmatic breathing, or perhaps a more subtle message spread from his tiny musk glands, because his siblings ran to join him, tumbling and squealing in a party mood. Pink and merry, there's nothing quite so naked as a piglet. I took the liveliest and slid it under her skirt, sending it up the corridor between her lovely legs. There are those, I imagine, who would find that less than pleasant, would jump to their feet. But not my Sapphira. Giggles turned to ripples of laughter. I moved quickly, seizing the moment, kissing her eyes, her mouth, her neck, swinging her gently from sitting to a supine position, lying crosswise over her, tongue grazing, nibbling from neck, down across the throat, down to where chest turns to breast, she writhing and unresisting, knees raised, welcoming Ham above and pig below, each in his own territory, each so dedicated that it was clear we would continue like this right through to the peak, my body against the straw but mouth against her bare flesh, feasting as was my friend until we all peaked in a great squealing and laughter.

Exhaustion. My head at rest, lying ear-down against her bare stomach, my own body lying groin-down in the wet straw, I had the distinct feeling of having flooded the lower deck. She had gently ejected her other lover, closing the entryway. I could hear the inner working of her body—the gastric rumblings, the heightened heartbeat, and ripples of silent laughter. Her wonder and delight at what had happened, her sheer astonishment at the variety of experience within God's creation was surely no less than Eve's.

As for me, I was overwhelmed at my own potency. I was awash. Was this what I had given her in our earlier, more conventional times together? Surely neither of my brothers nor my father himself had ever given anyone such an oceanic gift.

"Incredible," she said, finally finding the strength for words. She couldn't have meant my potency—that being remote from her—but that was how I took it. I was not being logical. I was awash with self-adulation, flooded with my sense of manhood.

Even the piglets were impressed by my powers. They backed off, clustering on the other side of the pen, making plaintive noises which I took to be piglet hymns of awe and praise. I was God of the pigpen.

"Ham," she said, serious all of a sudden, "this straw is wet."

"I've noticed," I said, smiling modestly.

"Soaked."

"Can't help it. My nature—"

She sprang up to a sitting position. My head flipped into the straw and splashed. Splashed!

My sense of self rose on the crest of a wave, dreamlike, and then crashed. The piglets and the sow were squeezed into the only dry corner of the pen.

"My God," I cried, "we're sinking!"

XXIV

SINKING

WHILE Sapphira and I were exploring personal relationships down on the lower level, our elders on the upper deck were involved in a religious dispute. Although I missed it, I was later able to piece it together from reports. The issues were new, but the method of debate was so familiar I felt as if I had been present.

Like many religious debates, this one focused on ritual. On the one hand were the traditionalists who insisted that the word *burial* suggests, even requires earth. Dry earth. Death meant shovels. As vintners we were used to them. Our stock in trade.

No earth, the argument went, no burial. How could we manage the symbolic shovelful? How could we close the grave and mark the spot? There was no way in those shifting waters. Not a single member of our family from the time of Adam—yea, not even Cain—had been dumped in the waters like refuse. Surely we were in no position to start tinkering with holy tradition! The Patriarch would just have to wait.

The opponents argued that these were radical times and that only a radical departure from our old practice would serve.

Weather reports were not good. The dream of settling some-where in a couple of days had long since been swept out of our minds. Predictions about the length of this trip were being ex-panded daily. Some had wondered aloud whether we would ever land. After all, if the entire world were covered with water as our father insisted, where on earth would it drain? Perhaps we were doomed to spend the rest of our natural lives in this floating menagerie, revising our notions of what was edible according to the logic of our stomachs!

In any case, it was clear that we were to remain afloat longer than it takes meat to decay. No matter how revered, our Pa-triarch was unquestionably made of flesh. Those who had doubts would be convinced soon enough.

Dramatic debate was an art well practiced in our family. New issues merely added fresh vigor. As in the past, my father chose the conservative position but did his best to sound tough as any radical. "Don't try preaching to your betters," he thundered at Shem. "The man is dead. He won't mind waiting for a dry home. Meanwhile, all we have is a culinary problem. Treat the body like mutton—smoked or spiced, take your pick."

"Verily, verily, the earth is the ordained place for a burial," Shem said, raising his hands Heavenward, sounding like some ancient priest. To cover his radicalism, he did his best to shroud his argument in piety. "But it was the Great Yahweh Himself who turned the whole Earth into water. This is no mere trick of nature. This is no ordinary water. The Flood was a Benev-olent Act on the part of the Creator to rid the world of pet-tiness and sin."

"Yes, yes, get on with it."

"I'm saying that this is water in appearance but land in essence. With that in mind, we must use it as land is used. Con-sider it proper for burial. Anything less would be impious."

"Impious? Don't talk impiety to me! I knew what piety was when you were nothing but a grub in your mother's womb. As for that water, try planting vines out there. Just walk on it for a start. Show us how. Go on, now, show us how solid your argument is. Well? How about it?" Each question driven home with a fearful shove.

Such jolts would render a lesser man speechless, but Shem had been raised to argue by his father. He dodged, danced free, returned with a pummeling of logic not seen since the demise of the priesthood: "It is the nature of water to consume whatever it is fed, right? It is the nature of water to swirl about and interchange in continual movement, right? Thus, in a year's time the remains of our Patriarch will be represented on every shore. We can gather on any beach and perform our memorial ritual. Indeed, if we place a drop of these holy waters on our tongues at that time, we will take within ourselves the flesh and blood of our Patriarch, share in his spirit. Come, let us raise our arms in thanks to the Great Yahweh for such a benevolent gift!"

And the hands went up. Even Father's. Chests were struck, praises were given. Shem had made a beachhead in the long campaign for eventual leadership.

Or so we all thought. Not until much later did I learn that our wily father had wanted to get rid of the body as quickly as possible all along. Already thinking of history, he was clearing himself even in the midst of the cruise, making sure that the charge of impiety would not be stuck on him, alive or dead. As sure as he had been that there would be a Deluge, he was apparently just as sure that there would be an end to it one day and that the survivors would be judged.

When Sapphira and I raced up to Our Deck we found everyone crowded out there in the open between the cabin wall and the railing—family and servants too. The service was already in progress. I had almost missed it! Me, Methuselah's friend, down there sporting with piglets and my love while up here important rituals were being conducted. Still, if it were not for my delinquency, we never would have discovered that we were sinking. Perhaps we had been led to the hay by divine intent!

Standing on tiptoes, I could see my father in his finest robes delivering an oration, arms Heavenward. The weather was windy, gray, and spitting rain, but it was certainly an improvement over the atmosphere inside. The rumble of his voice reached me through the moaning of the wind, the muttering of the congregation, the sneezing, the coughing, the crying of children. Always the crying of children.

As best I could hear, he was praising the Creator's powers, His loyalty to His chosen tribe, His fairness and kindness, His discernment in picking this particular family to carry out His word. We'd heard it before.

More dramatic was the sight of the Ancient Methuselah in his finest attire, laid out on a plank, raised high above the railing, his arms crossed on his chest as if he were napping through the oration, enjoying the airs at some lakeside resort. I had an uneasy feeling that he was not dead, that he would sit up at any moment and say something irreverent, something which would scandalize the congregation.

Sapphira and I tried to work our way through the crowd, but it was not easy. Those who had come early for a good position assumed that we were trying to take their places. My clothes were in bad shape and some of the servants took me for one of them. Having Sapphira at my side didn't help.

Shem would never have put up with it. He would have made himself known, made his rank known, and they would have fallen back. But I had mixed feelings about demanding privilege— especially with Sapphira next to me.

I longed to give them our news, to tell them we were sinking. It would have opened a path quickly enough. But some might have become excited. I had to reach my father so he could handle the situation with a calm and steady hand.

"Let us through, please let us through," I kept saying. But their attention was fixed on my father's oratory, his voice rolling on, commending the Great Yahweh for His sagacity, His wisdom, His discernment in culling the pure at heart for this Divine Mission.

By the time I reached my family, Sapphira was lost behind me in the crowd. There was still the fear of Shem. I worked my way forward, right to the rail, right to my father.

"Father," I said.

"We Your humble serfs and slaves—"

"Father, a moment."

"Humbly thank You for Your Infinite Wisdom and Kindness . . ." one raised hand swept down in an apparent gesture of emphasis and caught me right across the mouth. ". . . Your Benevolent Understanding of us, Your sons . . . ."

"Father, we're *sinking*."

"And Your holy Trust in us, Your children. Your Love and Patience."

"*Sinking*. The boat. Water."

"So we return to You, to Your Holy Waters, this our Patriarch, this man of piety, of honor, of wisdom—" Suddenly looking me in the eye for the first time. In a growl, "We're *what?*" And to the others in his oratory voice, "Wisdom, honor, piety, our Patriarch, we deliver—"

"Sinking. Going under."

"To the waters, to sink—to these holy waters—" He was off course, struggling for syntactical direction.

Shem suddenly broke through the crowd and charged me like a bull.

"What are you *doing?*" Shaking me. Seeing *me* as the cause of this disruption.

"Let go. It's—"

"We gather to pay homage to our Ancient and revered Patriarch," my father bellowed to the congregation while Shem, still shaking me, tried to drag me from the central position, muttering fiercely, "Are you drunk? Crazy?"

I shoved him in self-defense; he gave me a quick jab to the stomach. I toppled backward into my father, the two of us staggering into the platform. A great howl arose. A sudden squall? No, a human chorus. I followed their pointing fingers, turned to the platform. No Methuselah!

Risen in body? Taken to the Lord by a covey of angels? Anything was possible.

But no, everyone was at the railing. A great moaning and wailing as if the entire shipload had been stricken with gastric upheaval at the same instant. I fought my way to the edge and looked down at the dark and oily swell. There midst branches, boards, crates, and our own garbage was our revered Patriarch. He was half disrobed, half submerged, scarcely distinguishable from debris. Premature in his flight, he was neither wrapped nor weighted. He would have to be retrieved.

But how to reach him? Our ship had no sail and was far too large for oars. We were in stasis out there, victim of currents. As was he.

"What? What?" my father shouted at me, though his face was inches from mine, hands gripping my robes, shaking me back and forth. "What's this?"

"Sinking," I said, my head waving like a fig on a branch.

"Not sinking," Shem said, his head over the side. "Just bobbing there."

"Sinking," I said.

"Look for yourself," Shem said. "We weren't ready for the burial. He'll never sink without weights." And to my father, "We've got to get him up."

"Get him up?" my father shouted. "Of course. Don't just stand there, get him up. Look at him—like a dead dog in the cistern!"

"Father! Shem! We're sinking."

"Get him up and put weights on him," my father said. "Then sink him right."

"Grapnels!" Shem shouted and clapped his hands for prompt action. Back home there were always grapnels handy. They were used to draw down fig and olive branches at harvest time. They were also used to fish children, dogs, and drunks from the wells. But who would think you'd need a grapnel on a ship? So perhaps we should have known, but remember this was our first time at sea.

"Grapnels," others were shouting, clapping their hands, sounding officious, trying to share in the business of giving orders. But they might as well have called for a grand staircase down to the sea. We had none and there was no going back for forgotten gear.

It was essential for everyone to look as if they were solving the problem. Cries of "Grapnels!" and "Ladders!" and "Quick— some ropes!" A great shoving and pushing, some wanting to get to the rail and see the problem first-hand, others fighting to go back in, determined to find what we obviously didn't have. Those in the lower ranks who had been in the doorway all along had no clear idea of what was going on but they did their very best to help by shouting phrases deemed fitting for such occasions: "Man overboard!" "Women and children first!" "Give him air!" "Camel down the well!"

It seemed to me that we could do with some calm assurances from our captain, but he chose instead to berate his bobbing grandfather who was scarcely in a position to reply.

"Vulture! Lapwing! Blood-sucking bat!" he roared, leaning so far over I feared he would join his ancestor prematurely. "Nine hundred and sixty-nine years not enough? Irreverent, impious old cuckoo with your crazy stories about our family line, linking us with that brother-killer. Six hundred years I've put up with your sly talk, your fox-ways. Long enough! Easier dealing with my brute of a father than with you, Old Man. Say what they will of Lamech, he was a two-fisted fighter who talked straight. Not like you and your cat-ways, your little smile, your joking and questioning, making me doubt my own decisions. You and your soft talk and your raven's chuckle; you and your blasphemies and your filthy jokes. Get off my back, Old One, get out of my dreams. You laughing dog, you jackal, it's my turn now. You hear? Let go! Sink, Old Man. Sink, damn you, *sink*."

There was no moving him from the rail. The best we could do was to busy ourselves as if we could not hear the monologue. We located lengths of rope, sections of harness, belts, even strips of bedding. We attempted a hangman's loop at the end but none of us was quite sure how to tie it properly.

When the device was ready, Tubal-cain was ordered to do the snagging. He was selected, I suppose, for his blacksmith's strength—assuming that the hauling-in would be the greatest problem. But he was slow by nature and his eyes were clouded. As it turned out, he had to be directed every step of the way by our father.

"Left, left, this way," our father intoned. "Now farther out. Farther out. Not so far. To the right. There, let it coil around the leg there. Wait. Don't pull. *Don't*, I said. Aah, missed again, you adder-brained idiot."

With each failure a chorus of women onlookers uttered cries of lament—"Oooooh!"

Sapphira joined me, keeping her face hidden from Shem. She watched with solemn astonishment. "Is this the way you people usually do it?" she asked.

My father's litany continued with Uncle Tubal-cain dutifully responding to each command.

"Now to the right," my father said.

"To the right," Tubal-cain murmured.

"Let it sink again."

"Sink."

"Give it time. Don't be so impatient."

"Patient."

"Ah, almost over the neck."

"Neck."

"Snare him like a dead dog."

"Dead dog."

And from the scandalized chorus: "Aaaaeeee!"

Shem, with the instinct of a leader, stepped to the rail and placed his hand on his father's shoulder, steadying him, calming him. Or at least that was the intent.

I knew it was a mistake. Knew it from experience. He hated to be touched when concentrating. Sure enough, the old man spun, caught Shem a glancing blow, and bellowed "Let go!"

"Let go," Tubal muttered.

"Not the rope!" I shouted, but it was too late. The whole length slithered into the undulating sea and coiled itself over the corpse below us in a great tangle.

"Fucking *toad!*" Father rained blows on his brother's head and shoulders.

Shem tried to separate them and received a fist in his stomach.

"OOOOOeeeeeaaaaa!" went the chorus, wailing and tearing their hair.

Father wheeled on them. "Harpies! Stinking ravens. Ring-necked vultures. Out of here!" He lunged for them, scattering them, sending them inside with shrieks of lamentation and indignation.

There was no one left to hit—no one within range. He stood there, mouth open as if in mid-shout, yet soundless, hands pressed on either side of his temple, eyes wild.

We'd seen that pose before. An effective way of dramatizing a point. But this time he held it too long. He could not let go. This was no performance. I could see him frozen there in that very pose, lifeless, embalmed, a rigid statue, the family figurehead.

Shem was never incapacitated by imagination. He went to his father and threw his arms around the old man, held him in a bear's embrace. For an unguarded instant, the strength left our father and his arms lowered, clutching his son.

It was all so fast, I wasn't sure it had happened. But it must have because when he recovered he was calm and sure. Chillingly sure. Indeed, that slack moment seemed to have brought back the tight control we all remembered, the absolute assurance he had on the day he first announced that we would build a boat on the dry fields.

"All right then," he said, his voice slow, etched on tablets, "the sea is his grave. The whole sea is his grave. He'll have his privacy. Every dead man deserves his privacy. Close the doors. Lock the shutters. And nail them."

A moment of hesitation. Nail them? Sapphira's grip on my arm tightened. My father continued:

XXIV *Sinking*

"Let his soul go where it will and let his body return to . . ." Dust? "Return to the elements. I'll not have members of this family, servants, everyone, looking out and watching an old man . . ." His voice snagged on something, then recovered. ". . . an old man decay."

It was up to us to attend to the details. I took my turn with the hammer, Sapphira handing me the spikes. It didn't seem right, but I worked as hard as everyone else. I didn't want to think about our Patriarch's humiliation out there, turning naked in the waves. We had failed him. And behind that failure there was a greater one which had settled on us, had become an unuttered part of us. With every blow of the hammers we were barricading ourselves against a sea of reproachful corpses.

X X V

SHARING

WHEN the sound of hammering died there was a strange hush. Looking around, I realized that almost everyone had gone—all but Sapphira and my brothers. So much effort had gone into closing ourselves in that I had forgotten about Sapphira and Shem. And perhaps she had too for she gave a startled cry and stood there, rooted.

"Never mind," Shem said gruffly. "Things have changed. Father says I've got no rights over the girl and he doesn't want her punished. I think Athaliah got to him."

"I'm not owned?" Sapphira stared in open-mouthed astonishment.

"That's what he said. But forget that. We've got to fix the leak. He's in no condition to deal with it. Come on, show me where it's coming in."

We started off, first walking and then running, Sapphira and I in the lead, Shem and Japheth following. I felt a great elation welling up in me. Sapphira had been freed partly to meet the demands of an outraged wife but perhaps more to avoid discord in the face of a larger emergency. Shem too was preoccupied by

XXV Sharing

the growing crisis; he had spoken to her almost as an equal.

As we headed down the stairs my sense of elation turned to thanksgiving, a rush of gratitude to . . . No, not to the Yahweh, but to the magnificent leak. My apologies in retrospect, but remember that it was our Creator who devised the hierarchies from the very outset: those rigid divisions between man and the beasts of the earth and every creeping thing which creepeth, declaring who shall have dominion over whom, each in his place, each on his own appointed level.

Yes, He was a great one for classifications. Adam as the first lord of the manor with dominion over the earth, the beasts, and woman; Eve placed under him in a number of ways. And in succeeding generations, the divisions between the highborn and the low, the owners and the owned, the residents of palaces and the palace workers, the habitually overfed and the perpetually overworked, those who plan wars and those who bleed. Then too, those who float and those who are left to drown. A divine predilection for strata.

But the Leak, that splendid Leak, my new ally, came as the great leveler. True, disaster faced us; but I was blind to that, seeing only the release from that social order which until then seemed unassailable.

Halfway down that final flight of stairs we stopped dead. For just a moment our exuberance was drowned in reality. The dark and putrid waters had risen to the third step; pigs were swimming about, making plaintive squeals. From the other end there was a clamor from the aviary. Even the waterfowl knew this was no ordinary tidal rise.

A number of servants, hearing our footsteps and sensing our alarm, had followed us down and now gathered behind us on the stairs. They shoved us knee-deep into the waters. A rude shock. The bridal bower I once shared with Sapphira was now a dark and undulating sea, chill and layered with pigshit and bird droppings, a reminder of the fate we thought we had escaped.

Then a voice—not mine or Brother Shem's. A voice from someone whose life had been closer to this aspect of reality than any member of my family. "To the kitchens," Sapphira said.

"Pails, pans, jars. Anything that will hold water. Hurry up now. What are you waiting for?"

Waiting? Yes, those of us who had been educated by the priesthood were still thinking of implications, still stringing out metaphors like pearls on a thong, still tangling with the mysteries of divine intent, still coiling ourselves with the prospects of death like snake dancers, letting the cold scales of Truth slither over our bodies, making us sweat and tremble with the implications. Even as I do now.

Not so Sapphira. Unburdened by metaphysics, she moved without delay to the strategies of survival. We followed her orders, obeying like willing servants, relieved to have duties.

We occupied the kitchens like ants, seizing every utensil available. When we stripped the main room, we moved on to the milchik section, then to the bakery, mixing the containers in brazen disregard for ritual and tradition. I felt a flurry of guilt, but it was swept away by necessity. As for Sapphira, she never had understood the subtleties of our faith. She supplied her willing workers with containers, insisting only on speed.

In all this shared activity we recaptured our high spirits, joking about the containers, wondering if we would ever separate meat bowls from milk pans or either of them from slop pots, wondering brazenly whether it would make any real difference, suggesting that Hephzibah add bilge to her soup for spice—childish stuff but all a part of our liberated mood. And it allowed us to speak to each other in the same tongue.

In a rush and a flurry we formed a human chain, tallest men standing in the waters, filling the pots, others along the stairways, passing the putrid stuff up, hand to hand, on up past the Clean-beasts Deck, to the Servants' Deck. There, they were tediously poured down the shafts, a slow process made necessary by our newly shuttered state. From the outside it must have looked as if our Ark were suffering from dire intestinal disorder.

Sapphira remained our leader. It was as if we had elected her without a show of hands or even a vote by voice. Once she had her troops organized, she turned her attention to the animals. She voluntarily waded waist deep through the stinking waters to rescue the remaining pigs and set them on the stairs. The young ones bounded up the stairs to explore the rest of the ship, seeing how their betters lived, frolicking in the dry grains reserved for sheep and goats. Even the old sow made her lumbering way up to the higher levels, neither reviled nor ridiculed. Old taboos had been suspended for the present by our new concern for mutual survival. To see even a pig go under would be a sharp reminder of what we ourselves faced.

The camels were more disruptive, of course. It is not easy to pass buckets and make room for a surly beast of that size. But man and beast were on good behavior. Lord only knows how animals perceive the world about them, but clearly the camels had discovered that up was good.

It was a marvelous sight to behold my Sapphira appearing out of the darkness, an angel of the night, carrying eagles, osprey, kites, and vultures, one on each trip, wings held under her arm and one hand securely on their necks to keep her charges from snapping. You might think that these creatures should manage on their own, but there was little room for them to fly and no motive. If they had seen open sky, they might have headed for that. But as far as they were concerned, this was a flooded cave, one section as terrible as another. It was only human vision, seeing beyond what the eye could behold, that saved them. Once on the stairway and aimed in the right direction they, like the camels, caught the notion of elevating themselves and with great flapping and smashing against walls they managed to make their way upward.

All this time I had been working alongside my brother Japheth. He was slinging buckets and pots with the rest of us, keeping up without complaint. He did not slacken, did not claim the excuse of a backache or diarrhea as was his wont in times of manual labor. Indeed, I don't believe he had even taken his morning wine.

It occurred to me that we as a family had slighted him over the years. We cast him in the role of Fat Japheth and the family sot, but who could say for sure whether these titles were descriptive or prophetic? The very simplicity of his needs seemed to put him out of step with this family.

Poor Japheth! A gentle soul who loved his sturdy wife, took occasional pleasures with her versatile servant girl, adored his daughter, and went on to have more. He wanted no trouble with the world, protecting himself against its strident clamor with fermented grape.

We who dealt with wine by tradition and predilection had seen all types of excess—both within the family and out. Grandfather Lamech whose repeated bragging about how he killed a man for shoving him never included the fact that he was too drunk to recall the victim's name; Noah who once burned the plans for the great barge in mid-construction, boasting in his manic wine-dream that the Yahweh would provide copies by morning. Ah, the wonder of his impervious pride when he had to spend the next week painfully redrafting from memory.

Even Shem, tight-reined Shem, cut loose on the full of the moon, the wine going straight to his groin, sending him through town like a crazed goat. He was not brutal in his quest, but insistent and, from what I kept hearing, persuasive. Four, perhaps five in an evening. And when finally all doors were locked and barred against him, he turned to the sheepfold, performing for an audience of men and rams, speechless in admiration.

Such is wine for those who feed on their own power and enjoy the very taste of it. Not so poor Japheth. For him the wine was like a soft mist, a gentle veil between him and the world. He moved his girth almost with grace, slipping by the obstacles of life, skillfully managing to avoid the sordid, the brutal, and the difficult.

XXV Sharing

So in a sense it was he whose performance was the most remarkable down there on the lower deck. The urgency of the moment had reached him and he was raised from his lot as fool just as those born to slavery are freed by war or natural disaster.

My turn for rest came with Japheth's, slightly before our oldest and strongest brother. Sapphira was told to take a break to counter the chill from wading in that terrible water. We joined a group of others in the corridor and slid to the floor, leaning our backs against the wall, closing our eyes, giving in to exhaustion.

Occasionally one would rise and voluntarily return to the bucket line, relieving another. These transfers were made with a minimum of talk but with a certain grace. We were all joined in a harmony which is not created by orders and laws.

One of those who came to rest turned out to be Shem. He nodded and slid down beside us with a sigh, one arm over my shoulder and his head against Japheth's shoulder. In that dim light we were indistinguishable from the servants.

"Are the animals out?" someone asked.

"All out," Shem said.

"And are we gaining or losing against the water?"

"Holding our own."

There were grunts of satisfaction. Our real communication was in work, not words.

And how was all this effort managed? It occurred to me that men I had never known—slop-boys and stewards—had taken on new authority and were giving what few directions were needed. They did so not with arrogance but with an ease of natural authority. Astonishing, I thought, that I should glimpse a Golden Age there in that darkened hold of a sinking ship.

XXVI

SOUNDS OF ANARCHY

TH A T long night was exhausting but wondrous in its harmonies. The only missing element was our father himself. So it seemed natural and right to invite him down to where the effort of survival was going on.

He'd been soured by the events of the previous day and had slept badly. He seemed to have the notion that leaks were something the lower orders could handle on their own. Perhaps he had a lingering faith that our workmanship should have made that hull perfect.

Japheth and I did our best to describe the special aura of voluntary effort and cooperation, the ease with which old distinctions had been erased to deal with the emergency.

"No good will come of it," he muttered, but he headed down with us.

It had been my idea to urge him to go down and take part. There was some logic to it: He was our leader, after all. But behind that was a dream which came to me during one of our breaks. In my mind I had returned to my place among the bucket-passers but was revitalized by the presence of our father.

There he was, joining our ranks, entering into an easy camaraderie, sharing the natural rhythm of the work.

I can see it now, vivid as life itself: this dream father serving as the very model of a happy worker, spending hours on the line while others drop and are replaced.

"Marvelous," they mutter, "and him all of 600."

And as more time passes, they urge him to take a break. "Every man has his limit," they tell him.

"I'm good for a while longer."

"I'll spell you."

"I'm doing fine." A fleeting smile. "A bit more."

Continuing until he drops from fatigue. Just drops without a word. Cries of sympathy and admiration.

"I *told* him he should have taken a rest."

"Just doesn't know when to stop."

We drag him to one side with tender reverence. He sleeps there on the stairs, buckets passing overhead, until he wakes—a mere catnap—insisting that he be put back to work.

Back in the line he leads the group in a rhythmic song, a work-chant known to sailors or perhaps fieldworkers from time immemorial, the deep sound ringing through the corridors, causing donkeys to bray and pigeons to take to the air. At the end of seven verses sung seven times over with spirit, our father calls for redoubled efforts and the toilers respond with cries of "On, on!" and "Praise be to the Ark!"

That was dream. Reality was something else.

As we passed through the kitchen, through to the stern of the ship where the bucket line was still at work, I half-expected to hear singing. But there never had been singing. The only ones who knew the lyrics were the field hands and they had been left at home. Besides, the surge of spirit which accompanies any emergency had passed. These workers had been at it all night and no doubt their task was beginning to resemble the worst of their daily lives.

No, no singing. All I heard were grunts of effort, the clatter of buckets, the slop of water as it spilled on the stairway. All I saw were dulled house servants, men and women, mindless as those aging camels whose dreamlike, endless circling draws water from deep wells.

Had I really expected a cheer for our father, our leader? They barely looked at us.

They pressed themselves to the wall to let us pass without so much as a mumbled greeting. Slowly, awkwardly, we began our descent to the animal decks. Occasionally we would hear a muttered "Watch it," or "Coming by," but there was no way to tell whether these were directed at each other or at us.

It was a great disappointment for me. I had hoped to show my father something he hadn't expected, something ennobling in the human spirit. Yet all he saw here was a repetition of what he had witnessed all his life: blank-faced workers toiling like mules.

We finally reached the lowest deck and stood there at the water's edge. Dark, dank, echoing with the sounds of brute labor. You'd think he might feel some gratitude, some need to commend this effort. But no, he was in a black mood. The leak was clearly an affront to his craftsmanship.

I saw then still another reason for their depressed spirits. For all their work, the water level was the same as it had been when we started. Just up to the third step. No higher and no lower.

Had it been gaining on us, perhaps we would have been charged with a sense of dire emergency, energized by fear. Or had we been gaining on it, doubtless we would be drawn forward by the prospect of victory. We would become a team and our labors would become a sport. But as it was, we were locked into a long, dull effort. A routine as unsatisfying as weeding vineyards or hoisting buckets into irrigation ditches.

As we headed up again I began to hear mutterings and grumblings on the line, phrases which I had missed on our way down. They didn't seem to be directed at us but, rather, to the steps, the walls, to the buckets which they swung.

"Devil's work," I heard and "Nailed in," and "No air down here." Others seemed worried about the future—"Slow drowning," one muttered, and "Working to death" from another.

If there was ever a time for my father to join in, that was it. But it never occurred to him. He had not been raised that way. He was tireless with his own tasks, but working shoulder to shoulder with members of the lower orders was another thing.

"Don't spill so much," was what he said.

It was a relief to get up out of the dank lower decks, but as we passed through the kitchens it occurred to me that they had changed for the worse as well. With all the help putting time in on the bucket lines, the stoves had been allowed to die. Gone were the smells of bread and cooking meat, gone was the cheerful chatter of kitchen staff and the clatter of pans. There remained only a few reclining forms, men and women lying on sacks of grain and one on the cutting table, taking time off from the bucket lines.

From the sleeping quarters I heard a grumbling argument between two or three. Their voices rose and fell and their words were slurred. I gathered that they had broken into the wine supply to ease the pain of their labors.

In the murky light I could see that the pigs had rooted out supplies of figs and onions. It shocked me to see such disorder in that kitchen, but how could I blame the pigs? Having lived with them I could sympathize—their lives too had been disrupted.

"What's this?" my father said, voice low and rumbling in disapproval, kicking at a covey of molting ravens who flew up, raucous, flapping about us in the gloom like bats, settling on the tables and stools behind us.

"We had to set them free," I said.

"Why?"

"They would have drowned in their cages."

"Will of the Lord," he muttered. "Filthy, unclean animals."

"But . . . I thought we were to protect them."

"Two. Just two. And in cages. In their proper cages. Let them out and look what happens. There'll be no end to it." He flung a cooking pot at one of them with deadly aim and knocked it flat. "No end to it."

Without another word he headed up the stairs with my brothers. Sapphira and I remained there, too astonished to move.

"You thought he was a lover of animals?" It was Hephzibah. She had been standing behind us, just up from a turn on the bucket line.

"Why then . . . ?" Sapphira gestured to the birds and mice all about us, to the animals still caged below us.

"It's not for me to guess," she said, mopping sweat from her brow. "But I've heard of kings in foreign parts that take everything with them when they die—pets, cattle, servants, and even family. Right to the grave. That's what I've heard."

We were interrupted by a great ruckus from the next room—squawking, squealing, and high-pitched human cries. We looked to the door which led to the servants' quarters and for a moment there was nothing—just that extraordinary clutter of sound.

Then like a flash flood came a cascade of small animals—pigs, gophers, hares, rats. The air was filled with swooping forms which I took to be ravens, bats, and other winged creatures. Behind them a covey of disheveled bakery girls clutching bedclothes, looking anxiously over their shoulders. Next came grooms and stewards, not pursuers but themselves pursued by some still-unseen enemy.

We stood there speechless with astonishment as the creatures swirled about our feet, the girls racing past us, some of them leaping to tables, chattering like magpies, all eyes on the door.

That's when I heard it. Over all the commotion, over the babble of frightened humans: the rasping cry of a camel pushed beyond endurance.

At first, only his head and shoulders were clear at the door. I could see him desperately trying to bend his front legs as they do when about to lie down, wedging himself left and right to get through. I couldn't imagine what for. What but the scent of a female in heat could drive one of those beasts to charge? Surely none of us were ripe enough to meet his standard. Not until he had rammed his way halfway through did I realize that he was not charging. He was fleeing.

At his haunches was a pack of snarling, leaping desert dogs, hyenas, jackals. They'd been set free and were wild for action. One had his jaws sunk in the hind leg of the bellowing camel, others were harrying, snapping, yelping.

Once out into the kitchen, the camel was an even match for the pack. He had a mean kick and a vicious bite. He used both. Neither dogs nor men were safe.

Back home in more normal times, such a conflict properly managed often served as entertainment for workers. On festive and holy days they deserved some simple, manly sport. Many is the time I watched them pit dogs against a tethered boar or ram for the blood-pleasure of it. But here at close quarters it was different. There was no room to stand back and enjoy

the art of it. We were right in the arena. It had begun in the bakery girls' dormitory, the camel tearing up their sleeping pallets, looking for fresh straw, and being set upon first by humans and then by wandering dogs. Camels are not known for docility and this one was no exception. He crapped in rage, splattered a jackal against the wall, kicked a bakery girl in the thigh. The affair had overstepped the bounds of our traditional blood sports.

Besides, the servants were not really in the mood for entertainment. I had never seen them in quite so surly a state. The crisis had drawn us together, but as with most crises the energy and harmony it produced was short-lived. Puzzling, though, to have it drain so quickly. We had worked like an army of ants for our father when building that ship. And I had heard of times when the threat of plague or war had drawn family and servants together under the skillful management of our father or the flinty Lamech before him.

All I knew was that the mood had certainly changed. The men cursed camel and dogs alike and the stools they used to beat the beasts into submission hit fellow men just as frequently. The servant girls were less violent but their shouts bothered me. When they snarled "Get out of here" and "Go back where you belong," I had the uneasy feeling that perhaps they meant me as much as the beasts.

Brutality does reap results, though. It was not long before they achieved a kind of stalemate. Two of the dogs had been killed and the other driven, snarling, into the next room. One steward had been knocked flat by a fellow worker's backward swing with a chair and another dumbly searched the littered floor for lost teeth. As for the camel, he was backed up against the wall, haunches high and front legs kneeling in a kind of prayerful stance, dazed and baffled by the turn of events.

"My kitchen!" Hephzibah gasped. "Look at it!"

"The bunk room's worse," a bakery girl whimpered.

"Disgusting," someone else said. "How can we live like this?"

"It's not right."

They all joined in now, heaving complaints at one another as if they were stones. "Crap all over the place." "Not fit for humans in here." "Found a bat in my bedcovers." "Wart hog drowned in the soup." "Vulture's got his eye on me." "Stinking beasts—send them back where they belong."

Since none of them had any control over the situation, I assumed they were talking indirectly to me. I couldn't remain silent.

"Look," I said, shouting above the din, "I know what it's like." Sudden silence. "I mean I've been working with you. I know what it's like. But there's—"

"Know what it's like?" one of them said. "What are you talking about?"

"I've worked on the bucket line and—"

A harpy shook her fist. "Don't give a damn about that. It's the filthy creatures from down there we're talking about. They've got no right to come up here." A chorus of agreement.

"But it's flooded down—"

"We don't give a damn about that either. That's their worry." She came up to me and grabbed my robe with spidery fingers, her garlic breath in my face. "You don't know nothing. So I'll tell you one thing to fill your head: This place may not look like much to you, but it's *our deck*. Not theirs, *ours*. And we're not going to share it with no stinking horde of furry, feathered, flea-bitten crappers from down there nohow!"

XXVII

MOVING UP

IT would be unfair to call my family unadaptable. As the land turned to water, we managed to shift from terrestrial living to aquatic. And now, as meals turned from elegant to sparse, from hot to cold, and from prompt to tardy, we merely prolonged the time of conversation and libation.

Oh there were complaints. They drifted into the conversation as frequently as the weather used to, back when we could see it. And formal protests were made at almost every meal. When the serving girls finally came to clear the dishes, they were burdened with hostile messages for the staff.

"Tell Hephzibah," my mother would say, "that she must get meals up here on time."

But there was no heat in the complaint. Clearly the bucket lines had to be maintained if we were to stay afloat and if bad meals were the cost we had to pay we should, Mother reminded us, do so with fortitude.

For me those days of privation had a private blessing. My Sapphira was given, she told me, a simple choice of remaining in the kitchens working with Hephzibah or returning to her

duties on Our Deck. I wasn't sure who had given her this choice
or why, but she led me to believe that the mood of the ship had
hardened and that she was no longer free to move back and
forth as she once did. All that was important to me at the time
was the simple fact that she chose Our Deck.

Although she had her duties, they were not as demanding
as they once had been. There was a certain laxness everywhere.
It was as if the stiffening had gone out of the family. Shem's
hostility receded as if it belonged to an earlier, cruder era. If my
father objected to his son seeing so much of a servant girl right
there on Our Deck, he no longer made an issue of it. His attention had turned to having the uppermost cabin refurbished for
his own use.

So Sapphira and I were free to walk the corridors together
without criticism from the family, free to spend nights together
in my little cabin. The only restriction was meals. For her to
have sat down to eat with the family would have suggested
something altogether different. There were still limits.

To my mind, this was an ideal state. What more could a
young man want? My only complaint was what I then saw as
a certain moodiness in Sapphira. Later I came to understand that
her needs were more complex than mine, her perceptions broader
and deeper.

There were days—inexplicable to me—when she seemed to
feel she had made the wrong choice. There was nothing I could
say which would pull her up from these dark haunts. When
I suggested that she go back down for a visit with her old friends
she shook her head.

"They're down on me now."

"Down? For what?"

"For taking up with you."

"That's nothing new."

"You joining me down there was one thing. Me spending
time up here is another. Very different."

"Us being together is the main thing."

"Not to them it isn't. There's no bottom deck any more and
I'm not working in the kitchen, so to them I'm moved out. Up.
That's the main thing to them."

How could I argue with her? These were her people. Still, it seemed strange to me that we who had so successfully walled ourselves off from the rage of nature should still suffer so much ill wind.

Mealtimes were increasingly marked with expressions of indignation. I was glad that Sapphira was not allowed to attend and was kept busy instead feeding the children in the next room. It would not have been easy to stand between my family's view of social justice and that held by those on the deck below and shared at least in part by Sapphira.

"Where would they all be if they were not protected by my efforts, my handiwork?" My father's words, naturally. Who else could so easily confuse the first person singular with the first person plural? We had been waiting even longer than usual for our evening meal and he was pacing, addressing us all.

"I'm sure they understand," Adah said.

"All *I* understand is that they are deliberately starving us to death. The gratitude of beasts!"

"And how is the work on your new chambers?" Adah said, tirelessly the conciliator.

"Work? You call that work?"

The job had gone slowly, he said, due to the natural ineptitude of laborers. It hadn't occurred to him that perhaps refurbishing the captain's suite on a sinking ship might strike the crew as something less than the first priority. In any case, they tended to lose tools, forget schedules, suffer from mysterious ailments. "There's not a good carpenter in the lot."

"It's not carpenters we need," Athaliah said archly, "it's a good cook and a couple of willing servers. What's happened to them?"

"*Our* husband," Zillah said, "would never have put up with it."

"He had a way," Adah said, nodding. "Oh yes, he had a way with the servant problem."

"When his soup wasn't hot enough," Zillah said, "it went right in the face of the one who brought it."

"They did learn quickly."

"Those that didn't work out—well, we'd never see them again."

"No reason for a meal to be late," Athaliah said. "All you have to do is start earlier. Right?"

I glanced at Sapphira, waiting there at the doorway for the food to arrive, maintaining that blank face of all servants. When our eyes met, she raised hers Heavenward.

"If it were up to me," Grandmother Zillah said, "I'd fire the lot of them and start fresh."

The conversation rumbled on without a moment's pause. I wondered if her desire for a clean sweep might have echoed that of the Creator when He thought up the Flood, but they were already talking about bats in the bedrooms, leaving the servant problem far behind.

I longed to tell them what it was like down there, but how could I place them on that lower deck by mere words? Even a tour might not have changed their views. Our father, after all, had been down to the nether region and back and still he could talk about maintaining standards of service.

I had been down twice but my father discouraged me from volunteering more time on the bucket lines. I would never, he told me, win love and I would most certainly lose respect.

But what little I did see gave me a perspective the rest of my family did not have. Torches were going out; the ovens and soup cauldron were left untended, making the place chilly for the first time. The bakery girls had to put up with not only the resident camel but also a number of other intruders including male servants now blessed with leisure time. The new freedom seemed to leave the girls more overworked than ever and strangely did not cheer the men.

There were no extra cages for the animals and birds released from the lowest deck and no materials to build new ones. Who could have foreseen the need? What was once a spotless kitchen had become a barnyard. All those lowly creatures were now free but they didn't look very happy either. They were too scattered for regular feeding and had to forage on their own, guarding against enemies. Desert dogs snapped at piglets, ravens stole bread and stained the kitchen tables, doves nested among the pots and had their work smashed by servant girls, camels continued to eat straw bedding, defending themselves against men and predators. This was no peaceable kingdom, this was a jungle pressed within four unyielding walls.

"It's terrible down there," I said suddenly. "No one can live like that."

"No?" my father asked, his voice deceptively calm. "Then perhaps you can suggest a solution. They should live elsewhere? Walk home, perhaps?"

"What's terrible for you," Adah said, patting my arm, "can't be terrible for them."

I struggled for words which would bring a picture to their minds. It seemed to me that whatever sentences I could construct would be refashioned by them, altered as they did their tapestry, made into whatever image they found agreeable.

My efforts were interrupted and not by words. Not, indeed, a single syllable. The door opened and we all turned, expecting the meal. Instead of servant girls with platters, there were men —stewards and stable boys. Dirty. Some of them wet from bucket-passing. Unshaven.

My first reaction was embarrassment. They were good men making fools of themselves, appearing like that. And, too, it would be awkward responding to them. There was no real precedent for such an audience.

It may be that they felt as ill-at-ease as we. They looked about, blinking in what to them must have seemed like a squandering of torches. If they had planned to make demands to our father, they forgot their purpose. They merely flooded into the room. Behind them, some of the women servants.

We had bread on the table from the previous meal, and some of them sampled pieces. They couldn't have imagined that it tasted better than what they themselves ate since it all came from the same kitchen, but still they munched, dropping bits and crumbs.

Some felt the draperies. Others picked up plates, tested the weight. One examined a lamp which had been in the family for generations and spilled oil on the table.

Not a word all this time. We stood there, astonished. It was not as if we had been attacked. We were being treated as if we didn't exist. It was a humiliation we individually and collectively had never experienced, an affront for which we had no ready response.

Two of the men sat down, one in our father's seat, and looked about as if waiting for the meal to be served. Another was impressed by our mother's robe and fingered the fabric. In doing so, he stepped over the line. Our father's arm rose and like the prow of a ship fell on the man's wrist.

Not a word. Surely the bone must have cracked; our father's hand must have felt like fire. But neither man uttered a word. Just looked at each other. No doubt it astonished our captain to learn how deeply he was disliked.

"All right," he said at last, "you've looked around. Now go."

"No," the servant said, voice even. "We've come to stay."

"You've no right," our father said.

What did the steward know about rights? He'd never been given any to examine. He wisely chose not to answer. Words

were not his forte. He merely looked around at the growing crowd of sullen workers, noting in the sweep of his gaze that there were more of them than there were of us. Without as much as a spoken word his glance presented an abundance of evidence and a logical conclusion, a straightforward assertion about the rights of man.

I think that would have done it, would have forced our retreat right then, if Hephzibah had not stepped in with a different appeal. The situation didn't call for it, but something in her did —some notion of fairness, perhaps.

"You don't know what it's like down there," she said, voice low but resonant with feeling. "There's nowhere to put those filthy creatures and they're into everything leaving their messes everywhere and we can't kill them because they're here by the Lord's will and we can't cage them for lack of wood and we can't sleep for the stink and the pawing and the grunting and the God-awful cackling and cawing and we're alive with vermin. The Lord didn't mean for us to live with beasts."

"He didn't, did He?" It was just the opening our father wanted. My heart took an extra beat, knowing the deluge which would surely follow. Threatening our father with words was like brandishing a spear at an army of archers. "The Great Yahweh made promises to the unwashed of the world, did He? A private Covenant, perhaps. A secret parchment? Yea, That the Unwashed of the World Shall Never Suffer Contact with the Brute and Birds? Is that the Sacred Wording, perhaps? And where does this document lie? Written in pictures, perhaps, for those who have not mastered letters? Drawn out on the sands of the desert? Carved on some hillside? Well, listen to this: If such a Covenant ever existed, it's been washed away in the Flood. Erased.

"And a good thing, too. You know why? Because if a Secret Covenant between the Great Yahweh and the unwashed of the world were still about—yea, if it had even been seen before being washed out by the Divine Flood—who would tend to our flocks? Who would cut wool from the sheep? Who would milk our goats? Who would slaughter our calves?

"There is no line between your lives and those of beasts,

no natural boundary, no division. Never was. Accept, accept. Those creatures are your brothers. You are all children of the Yahweh."

Pause. Then the big steward belched. "Like I was saying, we're staying."

Incredible! Was he deaf? Dazed? He'd been cut to the gut with words and did not even wince.

We stared at him in astonishment. None of us could respond, not even Shem. The steward remained sitting in our father's chair, one foot on the table, peeling one of our last and treasured apples with a breadknife. We waited for him to give reasons for his decision to stay, to defend his position as Hephzibah had; but none came. He seemed content with the statement itself. Even pleased with it. When he was through with his peeling he looked up at our father and smiled. Smiled!

My face prickled with humiliation. If he had only entered into some reasonable discussion, I might have summoned the courage to join him, to turn the weapons of debate against my father, to prove conclusively the ponderous errors in my father's argument. But how can you make a defense for a man whose only point is the tip of a breadknife? It was indeed a test for my rosy liberalism.

A test for our father as well. With superhuman effort he held back further words, froze his face, presented a mask. But I could see the blood redden his neck, then his ears. I expected gore to burst from his eyes.

His listeners were no more impressed than a team of work-weary camels. Yet he couldn't handle the crowd like animals either. There were too many of them. Disdain was the response he chose. And of course he chose for us as well.

"Come," he said to us, turning his back on the insurgents as if they did not exist. "Come."

And so we went. All the family, me included, and Sapphira at my side. All of us. Up to the Top Deck.

Oh it was a fine gesture, walking out like that. Dramatic. Intended to humiliate them, I suppose. Shame them for their impertinence.

But how would we ever know whether they felt such shame?

Or what else they felt? We had barred the doors against them just as solidly as we had earlier closed off the outside world. A strange way to achieve our Patriarch's dream of harmony and grace!

X X V I I I

S I E G E

THERE we were at the very top. Just where our father had always wanted to be. But it was hardly as any of us had imagined. We were packed into those two rooms, sleeping cheek by jowl like fieldworkers without so much as a straw pallet, privacy denied, door locked and barred, windows still nailed shut against the sea, our only contact with the outside being that little air vent in the ceiling high overhead from which we could not see but could, with difficulty, pour our slop jars, coating the outside of our great vessel the way gulls soil the rocks they inhabit.

We would have starved, of course, except for the food which mysteriously appeared outside our door. There was no human contact involved—that would have hurt our pride. But when the light from that vent turned dark and told us that night had passed over the waters, the women would quietly remove the bars from the door which led from their antechamber to the hall, turn the great lock, and peer out. There on the floor were the various pots, our evening's ration.

It was hardly elegant fare. Stewed things. Mostly gone cold.

Sometimes a jelly of yellow fat on the surface. Lord knows what forbidden creatures they were slaughtering. But a day of fasting turns slop into a holy feast.

In spite of the vent, the air was not good. Those two rooms were never meant for a crowd. Chamber pots stood around for hours before someone—usually me—stood at the foot of what was now our father's bunk and with great care raised them overhead and poured the contents out that little vent. For all our elevation, our bodies continued to work like those of any beast.

The old longing for a view crept back. But our father would have none of it, calling the sea an open grave, fearing the vision of his unburied patriarch. Or could it be that he was haunted by the others too, that great lost multitude? He who had once taken such satisfaction in the rising waters. In any case, he would not let us discuss the need for open windows.

Japheth tried to counter this, having me stand guard between the two rooms, making sure our father stayed steady in his nap. I could hear poor Japheth using elbows and feet to pound at those shutters, but to no avail.

It was Uncle Jabal who had him stop. "Won't do any good," he muttered. "You'll only bloody your fists."

Uncle Jabal, you recall, was my father's half brother and a true brother to Jubal the lyre player. I had known the tight-lipped Jabal only by sight, remembering him as the tent dweller. I learned later that he was no simple shepherd; he owned the greatest flocks in the area and had others tend them. He had been a rich man until the waters swept away his wealth.

"Help me, then," Japheth said, whispering to keep from waking my father. "We'll put our shoulders to it."

"It'll break your bone."

"The two of us—"

"It'll break your shoulder bone and you'll be whimpering all night and keep us awake." He spoke between tight lips like one long-accustomed to solitude. "Listen to me: Your father had them spiked shut. There's no way to release them until we have hammers, and there's no way to get hammers until your father meets with those below. As long as we're on his ship, we bow to his whims."

An undercurrent of bad feeling there. Surprising to hear it from someone I assumed had no opinions whatever. Still, he was trapped as we all were, and like all of us could hardly complain to the one who had saved our lives.

Our attention was turned from the windows by a gentle moaning. It was Grandmother Zillah. She was sitting against the wall, draped with shawls, eyes shut, rocking slightly and sounding as if she was in pain.

"Don't touch her," Adah said. "One of her spells."

Routine, perhaps, for one who lived with her; but unnerving for those of us who were for the first time sharing her more private life. When she began muttering Adah said "Pay no attention," so of course we all strained to listen.

"Ah, Bildad . . . Joppa, little Koa. How gaunt you look." Zillah's eyes were open now; with a shiver I realized they were not focused on us but on people of her imagining. "And your clothes . . . still wet? But what could we do? What on earth could we do? So many of you . . ."

"Never mind them," Adah said.

"Was it so terrible? Did you linger? You were given a plank? Then He must have cared. Surely one more hour of life was a blessing. Wasn't it? Bildad, Joppa, wasn't it a blessing of sorts? Why such silence? I had nothing to do with it. Nothing. I went where I was told. Like the deer and the sheep. I had no more choice than you. Really. And you . . . can't you be grateful for your gift of an extra hour? Can't you? Please speak. I want to know. I do care. Please . . . ?"

"Hush now," Adah said. "Enough of that."

Zillah blinked and turned on Adah: " 'Hush,' you say? You've no rights over me, Sister. Just because you're older—Careful, children!"

Hushai had been chasing his cousin Leah and had almost slid into his great-grandmother. It was strange that while confinement turned the adults in on themselves, exposing their inner selves, it had the reverse result on the children. They needed their exercise and in that small space they were as restless as wild hares in a cage. Even underfed they had to burn off excess energy. The older women there had all raised children, had all known the needs of the young, but now they seemed to be more concerned with the decline of standards.

"I never would have put up with it," Zillah said, shaking her head. "Those children need the switch."

"No kindness," Adah said, "letting them run wild."

"They let them do anything these days," my mother said, shaking her head.

"It's the motion of the ship," Zillah said.

"More likely the parents," Mother said.

"Has to be the motion of the ship. I've never seen little ones so wild. This rocking—must have addled their little minds. All that chattering and leaping about. Never saw children like that. A pack of jittery apes. Next, they'll be growing tails. Mark my words."

My father also had difficulty dealing with the young. He was into his 600th year, remember, and not showing signs of mellowing. The genius it takes to build a ship and organize adults does not necessarily extend itself to the understanding of children. No doubt he'd rather have kept them in pens until, like colts, they were ready for breaking to the harness.

They gave him a wide berth, darting this way and that, quick as mice. Most of the time they could stay clear of him, but with the games they played this was not always possible. From time to time he would catch one by an arm or a leg and give the child a frightful swat. And then the howling. Lord, what howling!

Ophir was good at entertaining the young ones. Her status shifted from the ignored wife of Japheth to a valued peacemaker in her own right. "Ophir," Shem would shout, "*do* something with them." Usually the *them* were his own two. Athaliah was not born to deal with domestic problems directly. All her life she had worked through an array of servants. Her solution to unruly children was to stand in a dark corner with her hands over her ears, cursing her fate.

Sapphira blossomed in much the same way as Ophir. She helped out as a kind of sister. When the children were calm enough to respond, Sapphira taught them simple lessons. Those were treasured moments hearing her low, melodious voice go through the tables: four digits to a palm, three palms to a span, two spans to a cubit, six cubits to a reed. Or animal families: the dog with its pack, fish in its school, the desert hen in its covey, the lion with its pride. She'd picked up more education than I had realized.

Everyone was so grateful for her efforts that they no longer addressed her as a servant. In fact, Athaliah frequently held her hand or stroked her face by way of thanks.

No matter how resourceful Ophir and Sapphira were, however, the children had to spend much of the time working off energy. They made full use of a few uncaged animals and birds which had been living there when we moved in. The game which the children liked the most and the elders liked the least was called Catch-the-Piggy. First they would coat one of the livelier creatures with grease from the evening's stew; then they would form a circle around him, shrieking and stomping, driving him to hysteria. Released, he became the frenzied target for recapture.

Back and forth the two rooms, under tables, around cabinets, ricocheting off walls, the race went on for hours.

Our father retreated to Methuselah's bunk, blanket over shoulder, and studied sacred texts. He tried several times to outlaw the game, calling on the ancient unwritten law prohibiting any contact with pigs, but there was no way to cap that bubbling energy. Athaliah was no help there in the corner mumbling what some thought were prayers but what in fact were bitter protestations against the Yahweh Himself for sentencing her to so terrible a fate. "What have I done?" she kept muttering. "What have I done to deserve this?" It didn't soothe her to see Sapphira and me applauding and cheering as if at a sporting event.

When the pig tired, he simply flopped down in a corner and slept. Just like that. Enviable talent. The children then turned their attention to the raven who was also in the chambers before we moved in and locked the door against further immigration. A raven, as you may know, is one of the more intelligent birds. Whether you can educate it or merely encourage what it finds amusing is an open question, but the children imagined themselves trainers. They tamed it with dried strips of meat and vegetables saved from the daily stews. Then they induced it to sit on their shoulders, probing their ears for food. Next, on their heads, raking their filthy hair for tidbits secreted there. Never mind that their grandfather bellowed at them not to put garbage in their hair, never mind that Ophir reprimanded them, giving them as much of a slap as she could manage without subjecting us all to the agony of howling. The prohibition itself—like the one given to Adam and his mate—lured them into transgression.

Trivial stuff? Perhaps, yet aspects of these games worked their way into the Final Report. Not accurately, of course, but in fragments. No mention of the children or the siege or even of the servants' existence; but that absurd little raven made it, immortalized through no special effort of his own.

It started, actually, with pig play. They'd been at it some time. Even Sapphira and I had long since tired of it all—the shrieking, the dashing back and forth, the squeals of that slimy pig who by this time had begun to turn rancid.

Our father had retreated once again to his bunk, holding some sacred scroll before his eyes. I have no idea whether he was reading it or merely using it as a screen between him and the barbarous children, grinding his teeth in smoldering rage.

The game had become livelier than normal, and even the raven joined, swooping back and forth, landing here and there, giving raucous cries. Now pigs are not generally known for their jumping ability, but this one was driven to new heights merely out of enthusiasm. Streaking across the length of the room, he leapt up on the bunk, landing in a clutter of sacred parchment and the old man's tangled beard.

The poor creature was caught up in a whirlwind of thrashing arms, kicking feet, shredded parchment, and the roaring of a gored bull.

From the raven's point of view, gesticulating arms were an invitation to a game, luring him to find the bits of meat; he flew down into the fray and clung tenaciously to the tangled locks, pecking with his accustomed enthusiasm.

You'd think a man was being murdered. Bellows turned to howls, punches became wilder, shredded parchment went fly-

ing, and the three children, with the best intent, threw themselves into the bunk, shrieking at their pets, struggling to catch
the pig, save the bird, protect their grandfather. One could not
tell pig from child, man from beast in that great churning, bellowing, squealing, and cawing.

And then it stopped. Somehow in all that random action, the
old man had caught hold of the bird by the neck and the pig
by a rear leg. He was up on his feet with a lurch, standing
on the bunk, one creature in each hand, the only sound a muffled
blend of squeal and whimper.

Directly over his head was the vent through which I dumped
the chamber pots. He swung the bird up and forced it, wings
flapping, through the opening. And then the pig.

Cries of "No, no," from the children, but there was nothing
which could be done. Besides, it was probably a kinder fate than
what he could so easily have chosen for them. Remember that
he was accustomed to performing the ritual slaughter. Only
their status as unclean animals had saved them from having their
necks twisted.

It was a long time before we quieted the children. You can be
sure the old man did not help. He returned to his studies as if
nothing had happened. He chose not to hear the sobbing.

We assured them that their pets were better off outside, but
there was something unnerving about the sound of that poor
pig scuttling back and forth overhead. As for the raven, we
assured them that he could withstand whatever winds and rains
might arise and might even then be posed as a figurehead of our
tired, stinking old Ark.

There was only one remaining creature among us and that
was a dove. No one had paid it much attention since it preferred
to sit up in the rafters, cooing on occasion. It is a tribute to the
resiliency of children that they finally dried their tears and turned
their attention to that elusive bird. They made no fuss. They
merely called to it, cooed, and offered it the late raven's tidbits.
No harm at all—yet even that was too much for our father.

"One more bird?" he asked, putting down new scrolls. "A
dove, is it? At least it has a function. Nothing better than a
dove pie. I'll take care of it in the morning."

How he was going to cook it was one of those little details he chose to ignore. All the children knew was that he would slaughter it. The howling rose anew, reaching new heights and this set our mother to chastising her husband for stirring up trouble once again, driving them all mad, her own voice adding to the general hubbub.

At long last it was time for the children to retire for the night with the women. I took them aside and heard myself promise that I would catch the dove before dawn and release it through the same hatch. Catch it? In the dark? I'd promised that? They were delighted, of course, but their peace had been won at the cost of my own anxiety.

I take my pledges seriously. I woke up repeatedly, heart pounding, ready for the job, but always there was someone else awake. Once it was the tight-mouthed Jabal with a coughing spell; next, Shem was pacing with insomnia, muttering curses in the darkness. Longing for his father's patriarchal bunk? As a family we were not used to sleeping on the bare floor. There was scarcely an hour which was not punctuated by someone's wakefulness. I considered sharing my scheme with whoever was up— some might have served as my ally. But how to keep my father from waking to all that whispering? He was getting sensitive to plots. And once on to mine, he'd stay awake for the rest of the night. He was a determined man.

The next time I woke, there was a patch of gray through that little vent. Almost too late! I snapped out of my sleeping position, imagining our father, knife in hand, slicing the windpipe of that poor bird right before the children's eyes. Bad enough for them to be introduced to death that way; it was far too soon for them to learn that promises are not always kept.

Up in my bare feet for silence's sake, I moved a chair to where I knew the bird was nesting. With difficulty I reached up to that cross-beam. There she was! I managed to get my hands about her before she truly woke, holding her wings to her sides. Unlike the raven, this gentle bird is not raucous in her alarm. Her utterance is a low trill. I hoped this would be indistinguishable from the sighing, moaning, and whimpering with which we uneasy humans punctuate our sleep.

The capture was actually easier than I had expected. I stood there in the middle of the room, dove in hand, pleased with myself.

But then I realized that to reach the vent I would have to stand on the bunk and that this time it was not empty. Indeed, I would have to plant my feet on each side of my father's sleeping face.

It was a help having that faint gray patch of light to work by, but it was also a threat. Our father always woke with the sun. This was only a pre-dawn glimmer, but it was getting late for such an exploit. I got my right foot up on the bunk, resting on the coarse blanket just one side of his face. My muscles, responding to the cold and the tension of the moment, began trembling. Still, there was no turning back.

I swung myself up, placing the other foot on the other side of his sleeping face; I had made it! Now it was just a matter of lifting the bird to the narrow opening.

At that precise moment a number of events occurred so

rapidly that there is no way for my narration to keep pace. First, the dove's patience ran out and she began struggling. If I released her in that opening above my head, could I be sure she would fly out? What if she took our prison for her own Eden? How could I persuade her that unlike Eve she was being evicted for her own good?

In that moment of hesitation there was a great pounding on the hallway door. The women woke with cries of alarm and beneath me there was an upheaval, my father struggling to rise. But my foot was planted on his luxuriant beard. Nothing so infuriating for a natural leader than to find himself pinioned to a mattress. He roared, heaved; the dove convulsed, slipped from my grasp. I caught her by one wing and she spun in erratic circles.

"The door," someone shouted. Men charged from our room into the antechamber, trampling the women, stumbling about, some trying to unbolt the door and others attempting to barricade it against the attackers.

"Murderers!" my father bellowed from between my legs, convinced that we were already invaded. "Kill them!"

"Open the door," someone shouted.

"Bar the door!"

"Arms!" my father yelled. "Knives, clubs, picks!" Never mind that we had none. "Defend yourselves! Kill!" The poor dove was in a panic.

With that last cry I lifted my foot from his beard as if it were a scorpion, but he caught hold of my ankle. I turned and twisted just as the bird circled with its one wing, each of us spinning in panic.

In the other room someone must have unbolted the door in spite of protests; even from where we were we could see the glare. A gang of former servants holding torches. A vision from the underworld.

If they were about to attack us, there was no defense. They had the weapons, the numbers, the sense of purpose. We had nothing. We were lost.

I threw the dove high in the air and watched as she circled once and then swooped through the opening. I would have joined her if I could. Why, I wondered, oh why had the Great Yahweh chosen to give wings to this simple creature and not to His finest, noblest creation?

XXIX

VIEW FROM THE
DECK

T H E Y did not come to kill us. Indeed, they came with astonishment and even fear. They had discovered that the water in our lowest deck had mysteriously disappeared. My reaction was relief and then joy. But our father was less trusting by nature. He told them he would not fall for their tricks and sent them off with a flood of curses.

When he slammed the door again there was a gasp of dismay from the family. We had completed seven days in those two rooms and we were not growing accustomed to it. I think we would have accepted any trick if it meant avoiding an eighth day facing each other in such close confines. Besides, they did not seem deceitful. They were too awed, too baffled not to be trusted.

Perhaps under calmer circumstances our father would have agreed, but remember that he had waked to find his head pinned to his bunk like a staked bear. Rage and panic do not lend themselves to clear thinking. By the time his spirit cooled and he could see the situation in perspective, he had already made his statement, established his policy. Like a camel who will not on principle take a step back, he now had to find a way of circling without so much as a hint that he was reversing directions.

We were all thoroughly awake now. We began arguing how we should interpret the servants' claim. Some held that the bucket line had simply become more efficient, had drained the water faster than it was leaking in. But who could believe that? The last we had seen, the attempts to keep that effort going were at a low ebb. Besides, those who had come to us did so with astonishment, not with any sense of pride in what they had done. Clearly some other factor was at work.

Adah announced that it was the work of the Great Yahweh, that He had been testing us and found us true and had sucked up the water from the ship and that we should give thanks. Zillah agreed and the two of them started chanting a hymn of eternal gratitude in their high, dry, quavering voices. Our father told them to shut the hell up.

Shem argued that the leak had been dried up by evaporation. The theory at least had the sound of logic, but none of us could believe that such a cistern of water would dry in a week's time—especially in dank weather.

"It's perfectly obvious," my Sapphira said suddenly. I shut my eyes. Even if she had been given some eternal truth by divine annunciation it would not have been considered good form for her as an outsider to take over the conversation like that. I could see the older members of the family stiffen. She moved right ahead without noticing: "We're aground and the waters are going down. All this time we've just been draining like a cracked melon."

An unfortunate metaphor. And an unflattering picture of us, so blind to the world about us that we had no way of knowing the crisis had passed. Still, it was true that we felt no rocking. I was suddenly aware of this. Yes, she could be right. And if she were, my father would never forgive her.

"We would have been given a sign," he said. He might have added, And not from a woman. No need. The matter was settled. Or at least rendered unarguable.

We all retreated in small groups, Sapphira and I separated from the others, sitting in the corner like bad children.

"What did I say wrong?" she said, whispering in my ear.

"There'll be hell to pay if you're *not* wrong."

She shook her head in wonder. "Some family."

We waited. Even the children were hushed. The longer I sat there the more acutely I became aware of the fact that the motion we had felt weeks ago had indeed been missing for some time. Gone too was the sound of rain, the rumble of ocean swell, the creak of timbers. The possibility that she might be right became increasingly apparent. I stopped worrying how our father was going to admit that Sapphira was right. His problem, not mine. For the first time I allowed myself the notion that this voyage might indeed have an end.

My fledgling hopes were dimmed when that poor, mistreated dove came winging her way back through the upper vent and circled the room. The children were delighted at first, but when our father made a dive for her, they started screaming. The commotion drove her out again. Again I wished I could have joined her or at least stuck my head through that vent, but it was too high and too small. Our only view would have to be from the side windows. Opening them would mean negotiating with rebellious servants, asking them for hammers and axes. My father's pride was swollen as tight as those ironwood shutters.

We spent the following night in silence, but I suspect that Sapphira's explanation was winning converts without a word being said. It was like our father's first prediction of rain back during the drought. None of us really believed him at first. But when the clouds began to build, so did our faith in him. New notions often come to us not in a flash but drop by drop, building slowly through the night.

The next morning we heard that cooing again. There was the dove, back once more. And this time—was it possible?—she had a twig in her bill. A *live* twig. We started in silent astonishment. Then of her own free will she flew off again for the last time.

We were surely aground. Indeed, we must have been so for some time. Astonishing that our leader and patriarch had missed such a simple truth. And as we were about to discover, even that was far from the whole truth.

"Time to take a look," our father said. No admission that he had been wrong, of course. No nod of appreciation in Sapphira's direction. No grin, no shrug. The camel had reversed direction without taking a single step back.

Out that door he walked as if there had been no revolt, down the stairs as if he were the unchallenged leader, through our old common room as if it had never left his control. The rest of us followed with less assurance. The scene was a horror: chairs broken, tables chewed by goats, garbage and feces everywhere, wild dogs snarling over pieces of piglets. The landscape of anarchy.

"Axes," he said to the motley gang of servants. "Picks, sledges. Whatever you can find. Get these damn doors open."

Not a simple task. Spikes are far easier to drive in than to pull out. Swollen wood holds as if barbed. It seemed like months ago that we were doing the very opposite for him, turning the sea into an open grave for Methuselah, fastening those doors like coffin lids, hiding the dead.

But now the crisis was over and behind us like a war died down, a plague burnt out. The land out there was for us, the living. Confined for so long, we now felt like exploding outward. We worked like prisoners longing for open space.

At last we broke free. Splintered planks flew in all directions. We poured through the jagged hole and spilled out onto the deck, our father first; then eldest members of the family; next, my generation; behind us the children; and finally the servants. All of us in order once again.

And not a word. Not a gasp. Not a murmured prayer of thanksgiving. We simply stared.

To one side was land ruined by floods. No surprise there. Deep gulleys, topsoil swept away. Gravel, rock, and mud-dark, bloated forms which might once have been men or beasts. That much we'd expected.

But to the other side, up the hill, trees. Living trees. They could not possibly have been under water. Why hadn't we guessed by the dove's green branch?

This by itself would have been a shock, believing as we had that the entire world had been covered. But the rest was what took our words away, knocked the breath out of us.

People. Hundreds of them. Ragged, gaunt. Some leaning on crude staffs. The men bearded, unkempt. The children hollow-eyed. Stomachs extended. They had come down from tents and crude huts high on the hillside. They stood there looking up in sullen disbelief as if we had descended from a distant star. No, more hatred than that. As if we had devised the whole catastrophe, had watched their agony from our castle walls.

"How can that be?" I whispered to my father at my side.

"Dark soil," he muttered. "Good vineyard country."

X X X

A BIRTH

ONLY a true leader could be proved so wrong and not admit it, not be flustered, not give the satisfaction of even an involuntary gasp.

Remember that he had promised from the outset that we would be the sole survivors. We alone would float on the waters, we the miraculous clan, the chosen family, we the elect. Our craft would be a single dot on a vast and unbroken sea. The picture was clear in his mind and he'd taught it to us in every detail, gathering us each evening during the building. Even before we believed it all, we could see what it would be like. After a time, the repeated words became reality for us. Once actually afloat, we assumed we were alone on the sea—we and our goods and our chattel. With the windows and doors barred, all views blocked off, what other opinions could we hold? Who could blame us for behaving as if we were the center of the universe? That was, I suppose, the true reason behind his closing our eyes to the world.

Perhaps I should have had greater understanding after that glimpse Methuselah gave me, but somehow I managed to con-

vince myself that those poor lingering creatures had only prolonged their agony by another week. Besides, hadn't they been
chosen for destruction? It was nothing we had done, this water
play. What but Divine Intent could have arranged it? And who
are we to question the mysterious ways of the Creator? Some are
born sickly, some poor, some in servitude; some die even before
birth, some after only a day in this world. As long as I accepted
His hand as the only one behind those seemingly random events
which punctuate every day and night, it was natural to see His
will behind the largest disaster. Surely His deluge was different
only in scope from our own efforts each spring to clear our
house of ants. We used to stomp, crush, sweep, yes even flood
them with buckets of water, offering hardly a word of apology
or explanation to those humble and baffled creatures.

With such perfect logic to protect me, why was my sleep
plagued with the faces I had seen through Methuselah's window?
Surely the part of me which was my father's son was equipped
to wipe my mind clean just as my Creator had apparently wiped
clear the surface of his world. Or almost clear. Was it only that
I was still too young, too imperfectly raised? Would I in turn
learn to deal with practical matters in a forthright way as all
leaders must?

There was some indication that I was growing up, maturing,
drawing on the model of my father, for when the windows were
officially opened after those first storms and we were all allowed
to look out, I certainly felt relief sweep through me like a sea
breeze, a gratitude that we would not have to look once more
on those gaunt faces. But unlike my father I continued to see
them in my mind's eye. And still do.

At the time I wondered what earthly good the old Methuselah
had done showing a young and impressionable great-grandson
the tattered remnants of humanity. Is there any virtue in haunt-
ing a boy's sleep? Even if I had voiced my uneasy conscience,
would I have saved as much as a single person? I wondered if
perhaps it was my father who was the kinder, more understanding of the two, closing the shutters between us on board and
those who were beyond help out there. They would have sunk
us had they come on board in body; would anything be gained

by allowing them to invade in spirit, inhabiting our dreams for years to come like unruly beasts in the kitchen? Who would gain? Was it possible that my bullish father could have such subtle motives, such tender concern for our sensibilities?

I was sure it was possible. After what we'd been through, anything was possible. And remember that my mind had been trained by agile teachers to leap from point to point, to jump through hoops, to perform all sorts of tricks. I told myself my father had not lied. When he said we would be the sole *survivors* he was indulging in a figure of speech. Sole *inheritors* was what he must have meant. Surely those tattered creatures down there below us were not survivors except in the crudest physical sense. They had lost their property, belongings, burial grounds, temples; worse, they had lost their customs, their sense of worth. They had lived through the chill of dusk; they were undone.

Still, in retrospect I must admit that my father was no more accurate than the sages who put together the Official Report. The slaughter was not a clean sweep, the destruction less than

total. There were certainly dry hills and mountains all about. No denying them. And on each there were refugees, displaced tribes. Their history of physical survival was brutish, fragmented, filled with confusion, disorder, disease, factionalism, but marked on occasion by sacrifice, even heroism. Unwritten tales. Not even dignified by verse. I did not know it then, but their sagas would become the last of the many losses from the flood. Those little epics, barred from the Official Report, forbidden from the classroom, were finally buried forever along with the rubble of towns, of farms, and the bones of forgotten families.

None of this concerned our father. He noted the condition of the land, the potential for new vineyards, the plenitude of docile labor. He was at that moment as inexplicable as the Yahweh Himself.

And as decisive. As soon as we had had our look, he shooed us back in like a flock of fowls.

"In seven days you'll be on solid ground," he said to us all. Seven days? That favorite number again. It sprang to his lips as quickly and naturally as if landing a ship on a flood-wracked mountainside were an annual ritual. "Six days to put this place in order. Really in order. I want it fit for a celebration. Dazzle them. Strike them dumb with the elegance of it all."

Elegance? Some task in that stinking menagerie we called our home. How were we to make gold from dung? But remember that we were a family who had somehow made a ship from a man's dream.

When the servants were off, driving animals back down to their natural station, taking up mops and brooms, my father ordered the family to clear up their own quarters. Then he revealed his plans to Shem. It is always a fascination for me, prone as I am to speculation and query, to see how men of action plunge into a project without hesitation.

"They are without a leader," he said. "Our task is to organize them, give them something to work for. Keep the family inside. The two of us will deal with the horde."

As for me, all I could see was envy and hatred down there below us, all I could sense was the threat of violence, all I could imagine doing was speaking to them in gentle tones, telling them that we were not responsible for their plight, that we had only followed orders, had arranged for our own survival, had suffered ridicule in our labors and sickness on the high seas, that no one was as well off as he looked to others, that we had done no less than they would have with our means, that we really meant well. That's what I would have said. And they would have butchered me in mid-sentence.

I was ordered to stand out there on deck, serving as scribe, while my father and Shem spent the day shouting down to the survivors, having them identify themselves by tribe, clan, and family. Those who were strays were assigned. Each man who claimed to have some authority was noted, his tribe recorded and sanctioned. It was a demanding job for me to keep all those names straight—my first assignment as recorder of history. Or was I a creator?

There was, I remember, one Hadad, which is to say *joy*, though you could not see a trace of it in his visage. He was a metalworker. His wares were known to us through trade. He and his wife and surviving relatives were named a tribe. And Magbish, a breeder of sheep known by reputation to my Uncle Jabal. His fellow survivors had long since devoured the last of his flock, but he was a familiar name to us and was given authority over all who were related to him. So also Hadar—which is to say *greatness*. None of us knew him or his kin, but his name was the same as an upright family in our town and by this chance connection he was given status.

Hardly fair. But the notion of fairness had been clouded of late. My father and Shem were not reflective men; they were set on creating order. So desperate were these beaten refugees and so in awe that they accepted our labeling without complaint.

It was a sorry, tattered remnant of the human race down there and our father was careful not to join it. He remained with us on deck, bellowing down like a voice from Heaven, creating order simply by naming them all. It was no doubt a racial memory of his primal ancestor who, we are told, took time to name the beasts, the birds of the air, the fish of the sea, and all the creeping things which creepeth upon the earth and so, in the naming, won dominion over them.

Evening came, and that was the close of the first day. In the morning of the second day, the newly named tribal leaders gathered together their followers into work gangs and began the task of constructing a walkway from the ground to our unloading door. No, not even the littlest animals were released, nor were we—though we could have helped them with our energy and our talents. They were to build the bridge by themselves; this was a part of our father's plan. By their labors, they were building a society, and all the time they were looking up to our deck as if it were a castle wall, up to that bearded figure who was teaching them what was up and what was down. He knew what he was about.

All this took days, of course, and while the strangers worked outside, family and servants worked inside. Floors were scrubbed, furniture repaired, pens patched. Merely separating men from beasts went a long way to recreating the order of the past. So also the division between masters and servants.

Sapphira and I barely saw each other during this period. She worked inside with the women and I spent much of my time on deck keeping records, inscribing my father's edicts and documenting the divisions of the new society below us.

My work gave me an overview of what life had been like for the survivors. They had lived on the shores of death itself, heard its current every day and in their sleep. Without shelters, without so much as a rat's burrow, they had withstood more than a month of continual rain and another five of dark, dank, raw days and nights. They had lived in mud, surrounded by the sick and the dying, had endured the numbing sense of despair and the fear of discord. The laws of nature had failed them; no less the laws of man. Anarchy of the heavens matched the anarchy among themselves. They had become beasts—uprooted beasts at that.

Imagine our Ark as seen through their eyes: not a ship but a fortress sprung fully formed from the mists, a palace inhabited by a tribe whose fortunes must be directed by the stars. How else could one explain such cosmic favoritism?

They sweated to build that ramp. No doubt they dreamed of

seeing how we lived, learning whether we were men or gods. Neither they nor I realized then that only a few would ever step inside. The tour, I learned, would be one of the rewards for the chosen leaders. For the rest, words would suffice: stories told in wonder, retold with embellishments, elegance growing with each version.

At the end of the third day I was released to supervise the refurbishing of the lower deck. The brute work had already been completed. The stable boys had scrubbed off the slime, aired the dank stalls, repacked them with straw which had been hoisted from our new allies on the outside. Wondrously, the rebellion of our servants had receded with the waters and vanished totally with the appearance of the outsiders.

We rounded up the stray birds and some remaining pigs and returned them to their proper places. Indeed, everything on board was being put back in place—men and beasts alike. Beyond this, the new cleanliness, the new torches, the fresh air, the fresh spirit all combined to wash away old hostilities. It was hard to believe that Hephzibah had been surly, that doors had been locked between us and our staff. We were beginning to forget that it had ever happened. Just as, apparently, did those at the inquest.

I do not mean to be unkind about the boards and the committees and the subcommittees which tried to put the story together. They were at it for years. It was hardly their fault that after all the compromises they ended up with such a cluttered patchwork of contradictions and omissions.

But on two matters they closed ranks, agreed without a murmur of dissent: There was no rebellion on board and there were no survivors on land.

I've heard impious souls question the benevolence of the Yahweh in drowning scores of thousands, including all those cattle, merely to tidy up His creation; yet it was men—decent scholars— who doubled the carnage by wiping out even the survivors! And why? For neatness, I suppose, for clarity, for narrative impact.

At the end of the fourth day we were ahead of schedule. Or perhaps it was that those laborers on the outside were behind the schedule which had been set for them. It is easy enough for a healthy, well-fed, confident tribe to reorder its own domain; far more difficult for men and women overlooking the valley of despair to find strength to act. True, they had the raw materials. The olive trees from which that dove had plucked its twig were nearby and ready for cutting, juicy with such abundance of moisture. But organizing a society, teaching men to work in groups, persuading them that the effort was worth it—all this took time. Our father stood on that deck and exhorted his new-found lieutenants, chastised them, instructed them, flattered them, cursed them, raised them step by step from beasts to manageable humans.

Our own assignment was easier. After an initial period of intense, spirited work, Sapphira and I found ourselves with the treasured luxury of the fortunate: free time. We looked at each other with astonishment, with wonder, and with reawakened needs.

"Done with the scrubbing," she said.

"Last of the wet straw cleaned out."

"Pens rebuilt."

"Fresh straw throughout."

"Fresh straw . . . Hummmmm," she said.

"Fresh, soft straw. Hummmmm," I said.

We were off, down the flight of stairs from our deck, down to the kitchens which once again smelled of baking bread, down to the clean animal deck, down to our own deck, through the length of it, and to the end, down once again into the fresh straw, into the company of pigs.

We grappled at clothing, rolling and sneezing in the old tradition. But we were interrupted by an urgency of grunting which was surely not our own. There beside us, that grand old sow was on her side and seized with spasms.

Involved as we were with each other, our concern lurched from ourselves to that splendid creature who clearly was in need of help.

"Birthing," Sapphira said. "And not going well. Keep her from biting."

Indeed, the sow was half out of her mind and snapping at her older offspring and even doing damage to herself. I held that great head, muttering as if she were human—"There, there, easy now, gentle, gentle now . . ."

Sapphira went right to work at the other end. Something was blocked. She reached in and now there was blood everywhere while the sow turned from squealing and grunting to what was closer to human screaming. And incredibly she tried to heave herself up on her feet as if to run from the scene.

"Hold her down!" Sapphira ordered. I did my best, fixing my eyes on her snout, her ears, her neck—anything to avoid the look of slaughter at the other end.

"There!" she said and laid something awful in the straw. Not until the next one did I realize that these were alive. In all that mess, Sapphira had somehow separated the living from the gore.

Four of them. Sapphira freed them, wiped their eyes, and nestled them against the sow's belly.

We stood and then held each other, still trembling with the exhaustion of it. Strangely the bond of that intensely shared effort was similar, even greater, than what we would have drawn if left to our own thrashing. And when we pulled back, resting our arms on the other's shoulders, smiling at the satisfaction and the absurdity of it, she dark stained with blood, hair and robes a tangle, she never looked more beautiful to me. Like the Ark itself, we were at a new stage.

XXXI

NEW ROBES

Is it possible for a great people, a chosen tribe, to be stricken with an ailment so common and so vile as to be scarcely mentionable? Yes it is.

And perhaps we should have foreseen it. Six months and seventeen days at sea, remember, with scarcely as much as an orange or a lemon after the first few weeks. Last of the apples gone at the time of the revolt. Not for months had we seen a ripe squash, a juicy plum, a succulent pear. Fruits and vegetables had been rare even before our departure, due to the drought; the rains which did come were too abrupt—better for boating than growing.

Now it appeared that these miserable people were rich in nothing but wild fruits. Their vegetables had done poorly, seeds rotting in the ground, and meat toward the end consisted of a few rodents divided among many; but there existed on those highland slopes the remnants of orchards—fig, olive, and plum. In addition there grew naturally a number of crab apple trees, field berries, and wild roses laden with hips. All these had responded to the Deluge as if it were a divine gift.

XXXI New Robes

Over the months, the rabble had understandably grown tired of that diet. They almost broke into riot dividing a single goat which we gave them. We, on the other hand, welcomed their excess fruit, which they readily provided. We hauled up sack after sack by rope and gorged ourselves, devouring both the green and the overly ripe with abandon.

The body does not react kindly to such a violent shift in diet. And it is not true that humans by instinct eat only what they need. Men, women, and beasts behave with equal excess; and on the seventh day, the very day on which we were to celebrate the completion of the ramp and give their leaders a tour, our bowels rebelled with a ferocity we had not thought possible. We were stricken with inner floods as damaging to our guts as the Lord's had been to the world.

We staggered about, wordless in our agony, lining up at the shafts with utter shamelessness. What a leveler that is—the queue of necessity.

I was not without symptoms, but they were mild, thanks to my Sapphira. Her humble background had given her better knowledge of the body than we who had been trained in logic and rhetoric.

"That fruit will turn you to mud if you overdo like the rest of them," she told me. "Take it with cheese or not at all." I didn't have faith in folk remedies, but I used restraint to please her. She managed to stay healthy and I was only touched. It was not the only time I was to be reminded that not all knowledge comes from on high.

When I saw for myself the powers of restraint and cheese, I went with her to tell my father. We didn't have to go far. He had been on his way back from the shafts, heading for his chambers which the rest of us had vacated, but he had not made it up the stairs. There he was crouched on the first step, knees drawn up as if his gut had turned to snakes. It was a sight which filled me with shock, pity, and distasteful satisfaction. It wouldn't be the last time I would be stricken with a turn of mind worse than any disease of the gut, a momentary urge to say, Look here, everyone, the Great Man revealed, the Great Man exposed!

"Can I help you to your room?" was what I said.

He would not lower himself to speak, but a subtle motion of his two arms—a slight rising as if in some great wounded bird—suggested that we were to support him.

Sapphira and I lifted gently, easing him to his feet, and we began the ascent up the stairs.

He is old, I thought. He is frail. He is as others are, subject to illness, decline. Even death.

Never had I felt terror and joy yoked so close, take hold of me so strongly. Step by step those strangely disparate sensations led me just as Sapphira and I led the dazed old man.

On the upper deck we helped him through the antechamber and into that empty inner room, into that vacated bunk bed, a spot still haunted by my revered great-grandfather. We could not both share the awkward business at the bedside, but as he eased back he flung both arms around my Sapphira and let her take his weight until he was flat down on the straw mattress.

Strange, startling how the touch between the two of them struck me then as wrong. I wanted to wrench them apart, to separate the two. But of course by the time those unnatural dream-thoughts sent out the alarm, the moment was over, the figure there was old again, my woman had stepped back, and I was chagrined.

"I'll leave you two," she said, withdrawing, almost as if I had asked her.

"Leave us," the old man said, holding her hand for an instant before dismissing her in gesture as well as in word. Once she was gone, I felt nothing but concern for my poor, aging father.

"You should get rest," I said.

"Rest? On the day they are to enter the ship? The tribal leaders. They're waiting out there. Until the sun is high. That's the signal. Rest you say?" He raised his fist, looking not at me but past my shoulder to some higher point. "This is my reward? This is Your pleasure? Your notion of a joke, is it? Make Heaven laugh?"

"Never mind now."

"Never mind? It is mid-morning and you say 'Never mind'? With them coming?"

"We'll put them off. Until tomorrow."

"*Tomorrow?*" It was as if I suggested another flood. "Put them off? Admit we're sick? Vulnerable? They'd be at our throats by sundown. Is that what you want?" He was up on one elbow.

"No, of course not."

"Of course not," he said softly, lying back on the straw mattress again. Pain crossed his face like a sudden squall and he turned on his side, drawing up his legs. There were droplets of sweat on his brow. How could I have allowed a single moment of gratification at his condition? I would have felt better if he had struck me. But he hadn't the strength. Besides, could he have sensed that flurry of rebellion in me?

Yes, of course he could. And did. Now that I am older than he was then, I can see it. Now that I am alone in this tower, dependent on my own offspring, I know that he knew. Knew a son's flirtation with revolt; knew that it was not yet a serious threat.

"That woman," he said, looking up at me from under tufts of thick eyebrows, "she's yours now?"

I couldn't tell whether he was thinking of her as an indentured servant given to me by my brother or as my intended bride, but in those days there was no great distinction.

"Yes."

"I can see why. All my men have good eyesight." He managed to smile, I think. "An eye for height, good lines, spirit. All of that. All my sons—except Japheth, who settled for a heifer. Never mind that. You have your eldest brother's standards. The oldest and the youngest. First and third. But . . ." He drew his knees up in another contraction, curling like a hedgehog, then uncurling again, moving on with disdain. "But, she's in rags like a kitchen maid. Get some clothes on her before the leaders come on board."

"Clothes before noon?"

"From Athaliah. Same height. That peacock woman has enough to dress the survivors of the world. Tell her to give up her best. Have her show the girl how to wear them. Tell Athaliah I said so."

He gestured me out with his hand. The audience was over. Normally his word was law and even Athaliah knew it. Still, our father lay sick in his bunk, curling and uncurling on the straw, and the law has a way of going soft when the speaker's voice no longer resounds. I had no assurance that Athaliah would comply, especially through an agent as young as myself.

I had Sapphira wait in the corridor and rapped with some trepidation on Athaliah's door. I had heard her tirades often enough and I was in no mood to deal with them.

But there she was, struck down as badly as our father, more molting sparrow than peacock. I started by offering sympathy, planning to approach the matter of clothing with care. I was cut off after a single sentence.

"Sick? *Sick* is not the word. I've never been like this in my life." She reached out her hand from her pallet and I took it as one might a dying friend's. "There's nothing left in me. Drained. It hit me harder than the rest. I'm not built like men. Or even most women. All my bodily organs are gone—liver, spleen, everything. Empty. It's the end of me."

"Look, tomorrow you'll—"

"Tomorrow? I'll never see it."

"You'll be—"

"I know." She rolled her eyes terribly. "Oh you don't have to tell me. The terrible irony—enduring months of the worst food I have ever known and then to be struck down like this. Still young . . ."

I noticed with astonishment that her eyes were filled with tears.

"Look, just another day of this—"

"Oh, I know. By this time tomorrow . . . I'll never last the night. But you won't hear me cry or make a fool of myself. A dignified end, a release. Just that. You won't hear me complain. Not a word. If the Great Yahweh wishes to dispose of me, cast me off like a husk, a mere woman worth nothing to Him, an afterthought in His creation, who am I to complain? Besides, I'm luckier than some. At least they won't throw me to the waves. I couldn't bear being abandoned, left to float like a dead fish. No, I'll have a proper burial. Won't I? Ham, have them pick a grove. A fig grove. Or olive. Not vineyards. I'll not be food for those damn vines. Maybe a mountain hillside, a meadow filled with flowers with a view for miles. No great shrine, please. Just a simple temple with a statue and graceful columns . . ."

"Athaliah, look . . ."

"Don't worry about me. I can face truth. You don't have to tell tales to keep me from making a fool of myself. I've always faced the truth, looked it right in the eye. Don't worry, Ham, I'll not whimper. You won't see me whimper or complain. Right to the end. There's nothing now but selecting the right garment . . ." She trailed off, fingering the robe she wore. "This? Or do you think . . . ?" She pointed to another she had draped over her wardrobe. "Hold it up for me? Please? My Shem has deserted me. I've been abandoned. You've come in answer to my prayers. I've been cheated out of life—at least I won't be buried in something vile. The Lord has sent you to save me from that."

I held up the dress for her. "Actually, I've come about Sapphira."

She raised her hands to her mouth and stifled a cry. "Sapphira? Gone? Our little Sapphira?"

I explained as patiently as I could that Sapphira was not gone, that indeed she was waiting in the corridor, that she was to be dressed for the occasion, that this was our Patriarch's explicit desire.

"Oh but of course. What need have I for all this? Poor little Sapphira should be laid out as beautifully as possible. Oh Ham, what a terrible end for us all!"

I found myself caught up in the mood. By the time I opened the door for Sapphira, my face was wet with tears.

She stood there in astonishment, looking first at me and then at Athaliah. There was no chance for her to utter a word.

"Ah, my little princess," Athaliah said, reaching out her arms. "Your time has come too?"

"My time? Not for a fortnight."

"Athaliah," I said, "is convinced that—"

"Never mind," Athaliah said. "We must find you the perfect dress."

Sapphira and I looked at each other, exchanging a shrug, raised eyebrows.

"Nothing," Athaliah said, "would give me more pleasure. My last act. Tell Shem . . . tell the others that my last act was to dress my little Sapphira like a princess."

She reached out a hand and Sapphira went to her, kneeling at the edge of the pallet. "All I ask," Athaliah said softly, "is some simple memory to take with me to the nether region."

"The nether region?" Sapphira asked.

But she received no clear answer. Athaliah had drawn her down and was kissing her on the lips. Something deep inside me suggested that I should leave, but something else suggested just as strongly that I should not. It was one of those choices they don't prepare you for in Sabbath School.

"You may go," Athaliah said to me, releasing herself for a moment. I glanced at Sapphira and she shook her head very slightly. No alarm; merely the suggestion that it would be best for me to stay.

I sat there, legs crossed like a prophet in meditation, my action serving as my answer. Athaliah seemed hardly to notice.

"Quickly now, while there's still time," she said, her voice low and throaty, almost convincing me that she was dying—"off with your clothes."

Sapphira stood and clothing slipped from her as naturally as it once did for me. And why not? Sapphira had been "in the family" for some time. Still, there was something marvelous in seeing her sort through the various robes, picking up first one and then the next, oblivious to the fact that she wore nothing whatever.

She tried on something blue and the two women decided it was the wrong shade. Next, something the color of desert sands. Then raiments so light and airy that they could only be of use in the privacy of one's bedroom. I could not see the sense of them since they would not serve either to welcome tribal leaders or as burial shrouds. Yet Sapphira continued to model, and her little audience made no move to stop her.

All this took time, but Sapphira showed no sign of tiring. Perhaps she was spellbound by the luxuriant variety of choices, or perhaps her senses were bedazzled by the feel of fabric, I could not tell. In any case, she was thorough, moving gracefully, smiling at us from time to time. She tried on formal pieces, daily wear, and silken robes the likes of which I had never seen. Some were unbelted and unfastened, leaving a long, vertical vista from throat to calf which opened and shut as she turned.

Athaliah seemed to be recovering. Her face was taking on better color, her breathing was deeper. With great patience she began teaching Sapphira womanly arts such as how to stand, how to move her arms gracefully, how to turn, how to arrange her robes to the best advantage. It seemed to me that I was watching a slightly awkward, slightly boyish servant girl emerge into a new being, unfolding like a butterfly, not quite sure what to do with her wings, but delighted.

Which was not to say that she was wholly dependent on training. She had a natural grace which I had not fully appreciated when we were content to be children. There is no need for elegance when gamboling in the pigpen. But all that was behind us. Sapphira under her newfound sister's guiding hands had put away childish things.

She stood with her back to us, clutching three or four robes to her, unable to decide and unwilling to let go. Her slender form was from behind as naive as Eve's before she tasted the flesh of new fruit.

Then, decision made, she let all but one fall to the floor. She turned and held it to one shoulder. It was a purple fabric, royal in its richness, adorned with gold stitching. The collar was finished with a band of white fur and this she pressed against her cheek.

As she stood there one half of her was as elegant as any princess, a young version of Athaliah herself; the other was open and unadorned, as naked as she had been in our times together—shoulder down to toe.

"My mirror," Athaliah muttered. "My sister-image lingering after I'm gone."

XXXII

NEW ROLES

S HEM, they're out there waiting."

"We're not ready. Tell them to come back tomorrow."

"He said not to. I was just with him. We're not to put them off."

"Have to."

"Said not to, and besides—"

"Then we've got to get him out of bed."

"He can't stand."

"Prop him up."

"He won't be touched."

"Then the three of us will have to do it. Japheth, my God! Have you—"

"Not more than a whiff. Touch of the grape to ease the pain."

"A touch? More like a keg. Wish you'd drowned in it."

"Don't lay a curse on me, I'm your own sweet brother."

"Someone get Ophir. Tell her to get him out of here. Where is she?"

"My poor Ophir's sick unto dying. She's being ministered to

by that servant girl of mine and they've locked the door on me."

"Enough! Athaliah, take him out of here. Get him out of sight."

"Addle-brained men. Ptuh!"

"Hold your tongue. If our father were here—"

"Your father's turned to jelly. And you don't look far from it."

"This morning you were dying."

"I was cured by a miracle. It'll take more than that to put this family together. Sisters, it's up to us. We'll save—"

She doubles up and groans, is supported by the widows Adah and Zillah, is led off to the shafts. Japheth laughs, then turns to the wall, brow against the planking, and heaves up his own gastric deluge, the sound of a village pump gushing forth, then working dry, *Uu-ak, uu-ak, uu-ak.*

"For the love of God mop it up," Shem says, clapping his hands for instant action, but there are no servants present, only family. He shakes his fists at us for not jumping at his command and then clutches his gut with both hands and runs for the shafts.

So it came to pass that at noon of that glorious day the tribal fathers came up the ramp in order of rank and greeted the leaders of the new order, a young nobleman named Ham and his recent bride, Princess Sapphira.

The couple filled the visitors with awe. For more than five months—some were sure it had been ten—they had not seen a shaven face, combed hair, had not seen clean, unpatched robes, had not seen that calm, sure look of absolute self-possession.

In hushed silence they followed their guides, marveling at this floating castle which had appeared from nowhere and so clearly was here to stay. After those months of mud floors and dripping boughs for roofs, they were astonished to be walking on dry wood planking. They stopped to touch the dining chairs (recently mended), run their hands over the surface of the table (newly sanded), point out the mighty roof timbers.

They proceeded down to the kitchens and were warmed by the great ovens. Each was given a slice of fresh bread. Not one dared ask for a second piece, though each could have eaten a loaf. The servants, lined up along the walls, were better dressed than the visitors.

Then down to the Clean-beasts Deck. In the early weeks of their exile, the refugees had slaughtered all the animals they had managed to take with them. Who could imagine a flood lasting more than a week? Besides, it was safer to eat what they had than to risk having it stolen. In the absence of law, no one was safe from theft and violence.

From then on they learned to stomach rodents and beetles. So now they beheld with the wonder of Adam such sights as the well-fed cow, the roebuck, the fallow deer, the ox, the goat heavy with milk. They ran their hands through the wool of a ewe as if they were blind, uttering little cries of astonishment. We saved the bears, the lions, and those dreadful leopards until the last. They evoked terror. For our guests, this was indeed a new world.

What leader can resist the temptation to lay down new rules in a new world? This surely was our father's dream, with Shem as his aid. Correct the errors. Create perfection. Natural enough for those who were born to lead. But tempting also even for me, the youngest son, the one who was once happy to work in these very kitchens, the one who volunteered to clean the pens of unclean pigs, the one who felt at home in the straw and found joy sharing his life with a servant girl. Even I felt the aura of new robes, me in raiments borrowed from my oldest brother, she in the purple fabric trimmed with white fur, the two of us gliding as if gently levitated three digits from the floor.

There was no need to spoil the mood by taking the guests down that final flight, no need to revisit old haunts. It was enough to point out the stairway with a sweep of the hand, saying that of course there were more decks below them, decks hardly worth considering.

Did this new Ham imagine that if he and his princess descended once again all those piglets would recognize their former playmates, would pick up the scent of the groin, would leap up, squealing in delight, and pull them down once again in the straw, tossing and rolling and wriggling, to the utter astonishment of the assembled guests? Or did he fear not so much the memory of pigs but the memories of humans who were once at home in the hay? It is hard to recall. At 900, the fabric of memory is threadbare in places, frayed with ceaseless thumbing.

"More decks below," I said, gesturing to the stairway not taken. That much I remember. It sticks in my mind because it was the first distinct lie. More decks implied a multiplicity. Were I nimble as a priest, I could now clear myself by describing the exaggeration as a metaphor, as hyperbole used for effect, a poetic extension devised for instruction. Surely it was *as if* there were unlimited decks below, each containing creatures more taboo than the last, each revealing further depths to which humans may descend once they take the stairway down. A dazzling conceit there. As my Sapphira said to me years later, I should have been a priest.

Instead I am only a chronicler of events and procreator of the rulers of men—co-procreator, that is. And now, alone in this tower, my Sapphira lingering only in memory, I am the captive of the rulers we raised. A certain logic there. We trained them to take charge.

Back then, though, it was I who had taken charge. Sapphira and I. There she was beside me, maintaining a regal coolness. They must have thought she had been born to it.

For the first time I imagined her as my queen, sitting at my side, taking part in the lengthy ritual of coronation, my brothers bowing down, presenting gifts, humbling themselves at our throne. For the first time in my life I could taste the sweet honey of power.

Up we went to the main deck again. A ritual toast of wine with our tribal leaders. It was their first sip in five months but they were careful not to reveal surprise or wonder. They too were leaders. They drank each toast—to health, to future crops, to the new and harmonious society—with straight faces as if they had expected wine. We were equally formal as if we had from the outset expected them to survive, had planned on their being there, had predicted each detail. A stranger would have assumed this was what we always did at that season. Ritual, after all, is the pretense that we are in complete control of our lives

and the world about us. No, it is not quite a lie; not that coarse.
It is a conjurer's act.

There was only one flaw in our little performance. After our
toasts to their health and their abiding loyalty to us and their
toasts to our guidance, leadership, and paternal concern (me at
half their age!), little shock waves must have traveled from
each shrunken stomach, up the link of the spine to the source
of discretion. Thus released, one of those leaders asked a question for which I was not fully prepared.

"And the old, bearded one, where is he?"

"The old, bearded one?"—my tongue acted as echo while my
mind considered strategies.

"Your . . ." He paused, groping. *Leader* may have been
posed on his lips, but perhaps this would be insulting to the two
who stood before him. "Spokesman," he finally said, playing it
safe. "The one who so brilliantly arranged us into tribal groups

and put down our rivalries and organized the work and gave us hope through his leadership. Where is he?"

A precedent came winging to me like an angel. "Our Ancient," I said, "keeps to his chambers except during holy days and on special occasions. You were privileged to see him in person. He is in our eyes a most holy man."

"In ours too," the tribal leader said and the room was filled with soft mutterings of "ours-too, too, too, ours, aye, ours-too, too" like a covey of doves settling down.

That wrapped it up, concluded it. There was a general shuffling toward the door, toward the walkway which led them back to their peoples. And while there may have been some reluctance to leave our solid floors, our rain-tight roof, our supply of bread and wine, there must have been some compensating attraction to returning as leaders among their own tribes.

Where had that power come from? *They* felt it came from our father, the "holy one," the "Ancient" who kept to his chambers except on extraordinary occasions. But I have seen more since then, have seen the theater of it all. No doubt some of them also understood that while our claim of authority was no more than illusion, it was an illusion which they themselves could employ, gathering their women, their children, and their servants in the same way, directing their lives. No doubt there are other ways to band together, but fear of disorder makes us seek the protection of the pack. How else is power retained so easily by the same families, the same tribes down through generations?

And so it was that the clan leaders went down that walkway both empowered by and indebted to our family. It was my father's doing, but I with my princess beside me had taken part. And what a heady sense of accomplishment!

We shut the door and turned to each other, astonished at our success. No, we did not grapple like apes in heat, we did not clutch and squeeze like youngsters; instead we faced each other, holding each other's hands, staring with admiration and astonishment, allowing ourselves just the slightest hint of a smile, knowing that there was fraud involved, yet elevated with the wonder of our new stature. We had succeeded as makers of law, as directors of human events—both singly and together as a ruling couple. We stood there in the sunlight of the open door with nothing whatever to fear.

Nothing, that is, until my father appeared. He was hollow-eyed but recovered, almost his old self. I imagined, somehow, that he would be pleased. Hadn't we saved the day? Yet as I opened my mouth, I knew he would not see it that way.

"Where is your brother Shem?"

"Shem?" An unexpected tack. "I've no idea. Look, I'm not my brother's keeper."

"Usurper," he said, voice rumbling.

"All I did—"

"Was to strike out on your own."

In the instant before he stormed off, he stared at me as if I were a murderer.

XXXIII

THE SENTENCE

IN two month's time you would have hardly recognized the place. Reeds and saplings had grown up around our edifice making it look settled, substantial. What was once hull became our palace walls. Strangers assumed it had all been there since Adam's day. Who could imagine that this structure had once been adrift in troubled seas and even now rested on nothing more substantial than muck?

My father encouraged the illusion of permanence. He had towers built at either end for ventilation and for the view. Flags flew above them. They could be seen for miles.

Outside the main door we established a marketplace which flourished and grew, rows of booths with roofs of hide and thatch. We attracted trade and managed to take a reasonable percentage of each transaction in return for space and protection. There were few arguments. Those who were uncooperative were given land to till beyond the eastern horizon—a venerable tradition.

We cut new doors from the lower decks directly out to paddocks and pens, expanding our domain. What had once been the

bow was now a welter of new constructions—stables, quarters
for our growing number of field hands, a tannery, the smokehouse, cooperage, and Uncle Tubal's forge.

As the valley below us drained to bog, then dried to meadows,
we divided up sections marking the boundaries and designating
the fields for various grains, vegetables, and of course vineyards.
Yes, our extraordinary father had packed root samples of every
grape known to civilized man and had kept them moist.

The lots were turned over to the tribal leaders who in turn,
out of gratitude, pledged loyalty to us and a tithe of the produce.
Willingly they agreed to meet certain quotas, accepting the
terms for late payment—a severed hand. These arrangements
were formalized in colorful rituals attended by all, culminating
with bonfires, dancing, and chanting as the new owners placed
their drop of blood on the parchment. We were great ones with
the pageantry.

We? *We* slips out naturally. The community saw us as a
working unit—the famous father and his three sons. We did our
best not to disillusion them. But the unity was only an illusion,
a performance.

During all this time I lived under the threat of dire punishment. I had acted in my brother's place who himself was about
to act in his father's stead. We were both in disgrace in his eyes,
but my sin was apparently the greater. I was furthest from the
seat of power and had acted as if my brother did not exist. Those
who create order seem dead-set determined to maintain it at all
cost.

None of this I heard directly. My father wasn't speaking to
me. It was Uncle Jabal who was willing to give me some details.

"He sees it like murder," the old tent-dweller said, shaking
his head. "Sees the youngest doing away with his brother and
taking over. Curses you and old Methuselah for giving you bad
notions."

"But what was I to do?"

"Your father doesn't fill in details."

Apparently Sapphira was under the same sword. Oddly, she
was not sent to the lower levels but was kept in seclusion by
the older women. It was as if our father was waiting to consider

the right punishment.

I had been assigned to Uncle Jabal as an apprentice. I worked with him every day as he in his dour, tight-lipped way went about building his flocks. He wandered far and wide to find surviving sheep and sent others out as well. I kept his records, paying his workers in notes of credit. While others worked alone in a dispirited manner, he gathered followers and paid them with promise. It was clear that he would reestablish within the year the position he held before we came on bad times.

What none of us knew was that he was even then planning to move out from under his half-brother's rule, out of our settlement to open land where he could dwell in tents as he once had. Already he had drawn together a few faithful followers, including old Nahum, Methuselah's ancient and silent servant.

Jabal was not known for talk. Or for kindness. I suspect that I was assigned to him as a preliminary punishment—to keep me working hard and in line. And work I did.

His first move was to a tent near the family residence. I spent the days and most of the evenings there, though I was expected to return each night. After the sun set and I completed recording the trades and promises of the day, we would sip hot goat's milk and talk. He was a different man from the one who with mixed feelings had joined the family during the flood.

"You came close to exile," he said late one evening. I lay down my quill and parchment. "He was that angry." I felt a shiver. How could someone my age survive in the wilderness? "But he is not as sure of his power as he appears. He doesn't dare reveal dissension between you two. Besides, there's bad feeling between him and Shem too. He can't go scattering his family like fat on hot coals."

Down on Shem? How could that be? Yet I had to believe Jabal. He was no inventor of tales like his brother Jubal.

"What have I done? Tell me, what does *he* think I've done? Is it all because I'm the youngest?"

"It's all because *you* did what *he* wanted to do, what he thought he was destined to do. Besides, that first-son business is overdone. Look, both my soft-headed brother Jubal and I are older than he is."

Astonishing revelation! It was as if someone had ripped that family tapestry before my eyes. But his eyes were on the flickering lamp between us and there was no bitterness. "Jubal prefers the life of a child and I like open space. Noah's welcome to what he's taken. And part of the price he has to pay is amending the record."

Then he looked directly at me. "As for exile, it's in your future. The day will come."

A memorable night, that. And recorded more sharply by the fact that the next day he moved off with his small band, leaving me only the lamp which we used to share on those evenings. Jabal means one-who-glides-away and he was true to his name. A strange bond. Like Methuselah, he became important to me just before the bond was broken. Was nothing on a firm foundation?

The call from my father came the day after Jabal left. I half-expected it. No doubt my father looked on his half-brother's departure as a disturbing sign. Family unity meant a lot to him. Besides, I would have to be given a new taskmaster until I was of age and in those days being of age was determined not by the seasons but by my father's word.

"You're to find Sapphira," Shem said to me, "and go to Father at once."

"He's in a bad mood?"

"Who can tell?"

"Is there bad feeling between you and him?"

"Where did you hear that? Well, if there is, it's not your concern." So much for brotherly love. I started to go when he reached out and held me by the shoulder. "Ham," he said, "whatever he has in mind for you two, watch out. He's no longer to be trusted. Not since we've landed. Just watch out."

With this warning I went to Sapphira. True, the sword had hung over us ever since we took over the welcoming, but there had been times for me when I could forget it. Now I could think of nothing else.

I found her in her new room, a freshly decorated chamber from which a door had been cut leading out to one of the many new balconies. She had a broad view down the length of the valley in sharp contrast with mine which, like those of my brothers, was on the other side, the commercial side, overlooking the noisy market place.

It was hard to connect this woman with the one I had known. She was seated by the window, sunlight on her hair, on her yellow robe, on the little practice tapestry in her lap, on her hands, on the bone needle which drew threads through from one side of the fabric to the other. Athaliah must have taught her stitches intended only for decoration. She had also taught her not to squat but to sit gracefully on a chair with knees together, shoulders turned slightly one way and the head the other in counterpoise.

"You've changed," I said.

She shook her head. "Just some things Athaliah gave me."

Athaliah, it seemed, had given her more than things. But I had other matters on my mind. "We're to go to him now," I said.

"Him? Noah?"

"Right."

"He's still angry? What did we do that was so wrong?"

"He'll tell us."

"I used to wonder what it would be like to be a free person."

"How does it feel?"

"Much the same. Except the rules are strange."

I took her hand and led her to the door. "Most of the time I don't understand it either."

It was a bond of sorts, this shared confusion. We climbed in silence to the uppermost floor with each other as solace. There we were directed to the stairs which led to our father's lookout roof between the two towers.

He was at the edge of the parapet, muttering to himself, pacing, frowning, clasping and unclasping those great hands behind his back, the eagle overlooking his domain.

We stood there, waiting for our presence to be recognized. There was a slight breeze and the air seemed thinner. Or perhaps it was anxiety which made the blood pump so.

He finally turned and looked at me without a word. Why does the tiger take time to stare at his trembling victim? There can't be a practical reason. Prolonged anticipation must rouse the appetite. Strange how the rituals of death resemble those of love.

"Still breathing hard?" he asked at last.

"It's a long climb."

"At your age?" Then, looking out, talking to the horizon. "There's no limit at your age. Run, leap, plunge deep. Start again." He turned back at me, scowling as if *I* had said something wrong. "You think I'm not capable? Who.designed this palace? Who had it built? I could mount those stairs and anything else that comes my way and still not puff and wheeze." He turned to Sapphira. "Each generation is a weakened echo of the one before it."

He stopped talking to us, paced a bit, mumbling. He was not the kind of man who put you at your ease.

"You think we've landed?" he said to me, voice loud with fury.

"Well, I thought—"

"*Wrong*. Still at sea. Still pitching and heaving. Still turning in the gales. In need of a captain. More than ever. Can't have people wandering off on their own. Can't have youths dressing up like their betters, pretending to be what they're not.

"Look down there," he said, suddenly shifting his gaze from me to the scene beyond the parapet, the clutter of tents and rooftops on the commerce side. "All that was wilderness two months ago. Nothing until we came. Water-swept. Desolate. Brutish creatures in hovels. I've created men out of savages. My creation."

We surveyed the scene with him. Yes, we could see it was good. But a voice within me protested, pointed out that it had not been his work alone, that I had done my part, that those men and women out there had made efforts too. An honest voice, mine, but too faint to be heard.

"Women," he said to me, "create infants one by one, one by one. Men create the society. It's men who weave the whole fabric."

If there were some small protesting voice within Sapphira, it was no more audible than mine. Rhetoric does not come easily to the rabbit in the grip of talons.

"Look out there," he said again. We kept looking, eyes watering with concentration, yet relieved that we did not have to stare him in the eye. "A masterful design. Right? Right?"

"Masterful," I murmured.

"Masterful. And who is master? Who? Well?"

"You."

"Me, of course. Where would you be if it weren't for me?"

Lord, would I ever get out from under that question? "Nowhere," I said.

"Either dead or like those brutes. You think saving our skins is the peak of my life? Those savages saved their lives too. Even rats and roaches are good at surviving. No, what I'm salvaging right now is all that out there."

He gestured with a sweep of his hand at the entire settlement, those market streets radiating from what had once been our loading door, cross streets intersecting like a spider's web, the dwellings beyond, then the fields and vineyards and pasturage where the sheep and goats were grazing, a green and sunlit scene. Such an intricate interlacing of human effort.

"All this," he said, clearly struck with the wonder of it. "All this harmony from my labors." Another sweep of his arm as if he were gathering it all in, drawing it to him; and with the other hand he steadied himself on one of the twenty barrels filled with spears and arrows. He was by nature a man who planned for a rainy day.

"Like a spider's web," I muttered.

"What? What's that? Spider's web? Well, yes. A poetic image. A spider's web. All right, tell me this: Ever see two spiders arguing about how to build a web?" A joke of sorts, but he wasn't smiling. "And this too: A web can be swept away at any moment. Storms, floods, unruly offspring. Terrible dangers. Always. No time to relax." He paused for a moment.

"So much there," he said, voice lowered now, musing, astonished at his own powers. "So much from nothing. And more to be done. More building and more planning." Again he paused, more drawn to the scene than to us. "And you know why? Not just for personal pleasure. No, more than anything because it is our nature to do so. Like spiders and their webs. If we're not spinning, we're dreaming of spinning." He turned and looked at me. "You too."

XXXIII *The Sentence*

"Me?"

"You. And you," he said, nodding at Sapphira. "Spinners." And then in a sudden wave of fury, "But I'll not have anyone taking over my work. No one."

Here it was. The sword trembled before it fell. "You took your liberty; took it prematurely. So now you lose it. Both of you." Long pause. Would a father execute his own son? "In two weeks," he said, "you two will take your marriage vows."

The proclamation hit us like a sledge. What a week before would have been received with the greatest joy now struck us as some terrible trick, a hidden punishment. Better to have heard the sentence straight. But he was not through. In a voice from dark clouds: "And you will have a son. His name shall be Canaan. He shall rule over the tribe of Shem and Japheth. His brothers shall be his servants. Rejoice!" Over what? "Come here."

I went to him stiff-legged, a tethered lamb. Any moment now the knife would gouge my throat. But no, his bristly face was being pressed to mine, first one side and then the other. My muscles had given up, but he held me with the grip of an Abyssinian bear. When he set me back again, a jerk of his arms willed me to stand where I was told. Now it was Sapphira's turn.

She went to him without prompting, knelt before him without hesitation, and kissed the hem of his raiment. Now where had she learned that?

No time for speculation. In that fraction of a moment I saw his fingers slither out from the fabric of his sleeve and slide across the flesh of her cheek. Just that. No more.

"In two weeks," he said with priestly assurance. "Two weeks from now. A major celebration. The storm is over. We've won. We owe ourselves a celebration. You'll be our cause for festivity." He raised Sapphira with a snap of his fingers and spoke directly to her almost forgetting my presence. "You will reside in our house and through your son, Canaan, establish the line, *my* line, down through unbroken time."

He stared at her in silence, face close to hers as if studying, I assumed, future generations of the family—history itself—in the dark recesses of her eyes.

XXXIV

CARNIVAL

I must have been there. My wedding, after all. But in the tapestry of my mind I see the altar with two bearded priests and a couple, she with head covered, face completely hidden in heavy shawls, he robed, and between them a screen; the room filled with people.

But it could not have been a room. It must have been a tent. It was later that they built their temple of brick. I have been in so many since then that they blur—hides, timber, brick. They blend. As do the priests. One of them that day must have been my father, but all I recall is the ebb and flow of ritual garments; no way to identify which was my procreator. Metaphoric father, perhaps; mystic father. Not a father of the flesh. The beard and black robe which hid the man are indistinguishable from the beards and black robes in our genealogical tapestry. They blend with the procession of beards and black robes which have officiated at the Sabbaths of my life—no sharp line between the artistry of weavers and that of dramatists. Even during the short period of my early manhood when I had the authority to appoint them, creating them from nothing, knowing them by name and seeing them frequently, testing the strength of their loyalty to the Creator and to me, even during that heady paternal period, I could not tell one from the other as soon as they mounted the altar.

Was this what happened to the nuptial couple as well? It is not entirely an old man's weakening hold on the past. The events which followed the service are vivid and personal. Right then, however, there was a suspension of individuality. A bride, a groom, a priest, an assisting priest, an altar, an audience as witness and chorus. No room for individuals.

There is a point in our rites at which the screen dividing the couple is removed and the fabric is lifted from the bride layer by layer, and finally the two are instructed to behold each other for the first time. There are those who say *as if* for the first time, but they are wrong. For the bridal couple that day it *was* the first view of each other. Some other couple had explored the lower depths together, had turned night to musky day, had probed every orifice, had cavorted with piglets and performed before birds; for the couple at the altar, however, this was the first and moving view, each of the other.

And in recollection, it remains so. None of the events which followed so closely on that ritual quite managed to sully it.

From that point on it was celebration. Our first in what seemed like years. Oh it was nothing on the scale of what my son, Canaan, and his sons have brought to the cities of Gomorrah, Gaza, and Sodom. And it didn't have the elegance of what we put on here in Babylon, the city of my declining years. But for a fledgling society we did very well.

How marvelous it was to hear music! Of course the horns were water-soaked and moldy, long in disuse, and the lutes newly made by amateurs, improvised with rabbit gut, the drums from hides not yet properly cured and attracting flies. Still, rabbits and cows never sang so sweetly.

We began with the public portion of the reception, lying there on cushions, watching the dances with the townspeople, listening to the music, drinking their vile fermented honey, picking out the ants, smiling to assure the populace that it was as good as vintage wine.

Earlier I had protested as best I could about our not sharing the family wine with the townspeople. I was told that they would be content to receive whatever we concocted and that no matter what *I* thought of that honey mess it was far better than what they were accustomed to. Besides, our wine was all antediluvian vintage and although the supply looked large enough to entertain the world, it clearly wasn't. "Start giving it to everyone," my father growled, "it would be gone before sundown. And then what? They'd be at our throats for not giving them more."

Sapphira and I could not relax completely. We were on exhibit, putting on a performance of sorts. Yet from the start there was something heady about being the focal point, the cause for the celebration. We had not felt quite this way since we served in our father's place, welcoming the tribal leaders on board. In the loosened mood, we no longer asked ourselves why the punishment we had expected had turned into this. We should have.

All kinds of musicians and performers came forward to entertain us. None were refused. Some were terrible. Midst all this tooting, drumming, dancing, singing there was gift-giving. One by one the townspeople came forward with their offerings—not jewels and gold but common items just as precious in those simple times. There were lambs with legs tied, bars of soap recently made for the occasion, leather jerkins and hunting boots, crude bracelets carved from bone, baskets of fruit which we were careful not to sample.

For me, this homage was a pleasant amusement. For Sapphira it was a waking dream, a winged flight into a new world, a transformation of her clay life into gold. Others might have asked, Why me? But not my Sapphira. Still pagan at heart, she did not expect justice, did not look for logic from the heavens. In her view all this had come to her not as a reward for piety or good works but simply from a divine capriciousness. There is a certain appeal to such notions, but one is never free from the fear that what one has received by the whim of amoral gods can just as easily be taken away.

At first she acted regally, still solemnized by the ritual we had enacted, still dazed by the wonder of it all. She picked up each piece of jewelry or costume and displayed it for the rest of us, nodded graciously to the donor, maintaining a kind of elegance in her silence. It was impressive, though it was hardly the Sapphira I remembered.

We drank and listened, drank and watched, drank and accepted gifts. The sweet-sour honey melted her stiffness, liberated her tongue. She began to thank donors in warmer, more rounded tones. Once when an old man gave her an anklet carved from the thigh bone of his favorite mule drowned in the flood, tears came to her eyes and she kissed him.

The next I recall, we were back in the family section of the tent. The children and most of the women must have gone home because Japheth was singing obscene songs. My uncles were there, my brothers, my father. She seemed to be at ease, lying back in the cushions, laughing and clapping in appreciation. That seemed to please my father who—was it possible?—was smiling. Perhaps he had never seen a woman of his tribe take to droll lyrics. Actually the songs weren't that funny; but then, I had heard them all before.

Japheth sang the old favorite about the woman who lived with a serpent. The lines have left me, but the story lingers: The snake was old, wily, and bothered by the harshness of sunlight. He persuaded her to allow him to enter one orifice after another, seeking the dark and the pleasure of it all. Each was better than the last. There were, as I remember it, three verses.

It didn't seem right, having my bride listen to lyrics like that so soon after such a solemn ceremony. Weren't we now adults? Weren't we supposed to take on a new dignity? But who was I to protest when he sang so well and made my father snort with delight, banging his mug of wine, joining in the chorus? How could I complain when my brother's singing made my bride laugh in ripples I had not heard in weeks? I alone was left uneasy but I held my tongue.

Uncle Jubal took a turn with a ballad entitled "The Bull in the Wood." I first heard that when I knew more about the activities of cattle than about men and their women. A young married couple become lost in the wood at the close of day. Years before, those introductory verses struck me as tedious, but as soon I knew the story, they were charged with anticipation. The couple are terrified of having to remain there through the night. But they meet a talking bull who knows every trail. We always laughed at that—his knowing every trail—even when we were too young to explain just where the humor lay.

Naturally the couple asks him to show them the route out of the forest and naturally there is a price to pay. There always is. The bull explains that he has performed in wondrous ways with his own kind, but he had never seen nor imagined just how men and women entertain themselves. Will the couple describe it? Ah, the hoots and hollering we innocents used to give at that!

The couple, naturally, are too shy to describe any such thing. So the bull sends the young husband off to a particular glade where he will find saplings which can be broken easily. He is to select one, return, and sketch the ways of men and women in the forest floor.

When the young man finally returns—the climactic verse—he finds the bull blissfully asleep and the wife lying in the ferns, smiling dreamily, disrobed, and too tired to rise. "Never mind your sapling," she says, "never mind your sapling ever again."

That refrain has remained like a thorn in this aging mind. I can hear it as we used to sing it when we boys were young and again that wedding night in the fellowship of mature men, the repeated lines sung in cheerful disharmony and laughter. My laughter too. Blame it on the mood and the libation.

It was cozy there in the inner chamber with my family—more hides on the floor to protect us from the damp, more pallets and pillows. Less caution now that the rituals were over and done with, the public dismissed. Best of all, we had shifted from that cloying honey syrup to good, vintage wine. I was grateful to my father for his generosity and drank a toast to him. He raised his mug to me. We downed the liquid in warmth. It landed well, but mixed poorly with a bellyfull of that people's drink. The mess curdled in my gut.

"You look unfit," my father said, "for the night ahead. Step out and clear your head. And your stomach. That's the only cure."

A kindly, paternal suggestion, I thought. He even sent my brothers along to support me. Next I remember I was outside emptying my stomach in the alleyway. I was well rid of the stuff, though it left my throat burning and my head spinning. At sea once again.

That was when they made the sacrifices. Then or later. I recall standing with my brothers, leaning against one of the booths, staring at a tower of flame in the central square, watching celebrants fling on live lambs and goats. The bleating melded in a collective wail, a high note over the roar of the inferno. The writhing creatures did not seem to be consoled by the fact that they were celebrating our survival.

It was an old-fashioned practice even then and, I thought, wasteful under the circumstances. But then, I have never fully appreciated the hunger for violence. In this I am closer to my great-grandfather, Methuselah. My own sons and grandsons, builders and doers of great things, are the true inheritors of my father. They are at home with all kinds of excess.

Still, how can I fault them, my seed, militant leaders of men and creators of new worlds, the dazzle of Gaza, Sodom, Admah, Gomorrah. The vitality of Babylon. These are the centers which produce the art, architecture, philosophy, and poetry; is it their fault that they generate an equal passion for rape, murder, and mayhem? The city which attracts thinkers from all over the known world is also the city in which no man walks unarmed. No doubt it is better to throw a helpless lamb on the fire to celebrate gods than to throw oneself on a helpless girl, impaling her to celebrate manhood. But both bring us down a notch. Far better to thrust the same energy into the building of a temple or an epic poem. I am forever astonished, however, that one cannot point to a city which has attained true heights without also stooping to the lowest depths.

Sensing my lack of enthusiasm for the show, Shem reminded me that the revered Abel was praised for burning flesh, the first-lings of his flock. Surely, he argued, the stink we were raising in my name would smell sevenfold as sweet to the Yahweh. A matter of taste, no doubt. As for me, I kept getting the dry heaves.

I would have returned to the tent but for my brothers. They walked me to settle my stomach, told me jokes, urged me to enjoy myself, reminded me that all this celebration was in my honor. Later I could enjoy myself in a different way, I was told with guffaws and punches; right now I was to share a portion of the evening with my brothers. My obligation to fraternal friendship, Japheth told me with a thundering belch.

A juggler. Where had he come from? We were watching him perform on a barrel. How long had we been standing there? He was a strange sight, his swaying form lit by firelight. Normally I take to jugglers—simple people performing simple entertainment. But this one was different. There was something about him being above us on that hogshead, or perhaps it was the way he was lit with the sacrificial flames, his gyrations set to their music. He was no simple artist. More like one of Sapphira's capricious gods—the kind she had abandoned. When we renounce deities, is there any assurance that they renounce us?

"Higher!" the crowd was shouting, he tossing the colored balls higher, his body undulating in the smoky-red light. "More!" they were shouting and he, blank-faced but hearing, drew more from his pockets, adding them to the pattern, each in its own orbit.

Impossible to make out these little spheres clearly, but in the dreamlight they looked to me like suns, moons, stars, like little lives, like us. The crowd hooting, cheering, shouting catcalls, whistling. I kept silent lest he lose his rhythm. It seemed important to me, but he was losing interest, growing careless. One slipped from his catch and he shrugged, letting them all drop. The crowd roared laughter.

Jolly Japheth had somehow become our leader, determining our unsteady course. It was his kind of evening. We were with a band of singers, adding verses of our own, and found ourselves watching a bloody fistfight, cheering the loser to keep the performance going. The shouting became bidding and we were at a cock auction, birds being touted, held aloft, a great din, Japheth adding his share, ending up with a lively rooster of many colors, paying a price which would have bought a bull on a sober morning. He carried the bird under his arm, letting it peck a path through the crowd, delighted in its spirit as if it were our talisman, we the elect of this group, the chosen of God's creation.

Wherever there were three or four gathered together as spectators, we joined. When the crowd was dense, Japheth forced his way to the center, joking, shoving, letting his cock peck a route, dragging us behind him. At some point we were in a central circle staring down at two savage little animals snapping and tearing at each other in the dust. They were a blur, but I finally made out what appeared to be a ferret pitted against a lean, hairless dog. The creatures were bloodied but evenly matched and active. The betting was still going on. I was struggling with another wave of dry heaves, but my brothers bet for me, putting up my leather jerkin, a wedding gift, against a keg of donkey dung for which I had no great need. I tried to enter the spirit of the sport, but I wasn't sure which animal I was supporting. It didn't seem like the right time to ask.

The ferret won, I think, working its way into the throat of the lifeless dog, tearing at the flesh. Or was it the other way round? In either case, the victor had lost a leg, and the last of its life's blood was sinking into the dust.

All this, of course, was in celebration, in joy. Everyone else was laughing, paying debts and receiving payment, retelling the details, slapping one another on the back. And why not? All of us there had survived—some of us more successfully than others. And we had completed the first wedding in the new age. Surely we had a right to mark the occasion in some memorable way. Stupidly I kept staring at the two twitching forms in the dust.

The smell of burning fur and flesh wafted over me and I realized that they were still at the sacrificing business. Such tireless attention to the Yahweh's appetite! But in my dazed condition I wondered if perhaps it were His creatures here below who were taking pleasure in the slaughtering; for if we did not, wouldn't we have declared our Maker a vegetarian?

Such thoughts weighed me down when everyone else was buoyed up with cheer and comradeship. Why couldn't I join in? I assured myself that *I* had not set dog against ferret or tossed live lambs and kids on the flames. I should stop this dark analyzing and take pleasure in the celebration. After all, hadn't I just won a keg of dung?

The scene tipped, slid, and we were watching two girls dancing in the street. I washed the blood from my mind and clapped in tune with the others. The music was an untutored, sincere, wailing performed by some self-taught horn blower; but the girls had practiced. They had a natural grace and moved in unison, apparently sisters, one the mirror of the other. I saw no coin pot and was not approached by the usual collector, so I could only assume that they were performing for the love of it, smiling from pleasure and not from artistry.

They finished with their climactic whirling and were greeted with clapping and cries of approval and stomping on the ground in the manner of country people. The girls spotted us and smiled at Japheth, still clutching his lively cock. It served as a natural introduction. He and Shem moved in on them, sweeping me along too, engaging in that old, familiar banter of men hot on the trail.

Oddly, I felt the need to protect the sisters. They were only children.

"Let's go," I said to Japheth. "Perhaps the dogs are still goring the bull."

I had no deep need for more blood, but it was the only attraction I could think of to call off my brothers, who were already joking, flattering, fondling, their hands moving everywhere— holding the girls' hands, sliding up their arms, holding their shoulders, slithering down, carelessly cupping a breast, slipping discreetly under the fabric. It was a practiced sport for them, but they were moving a bit faster than usual, lubricated by the spirit of the evening and led on by the innocent delight of the girls who seemed ready to laugh at anything. It was funny when Japheth let his bird peck at their robes, tugging at the fabric, making them squeal; it was funny when he offered the creature to the crowd and tossed it heavenward only to have it torn to bloody pieces by the throng; it was funny when Shem pretended that there was only one girl standing there, his eyes seeing double from drink; it was funny when Japheth claimed to have the power to see through clothes and described each portion of their anatomy in devious but sensual figures of speech; it was funny when one of the girls said we'd talked long enough and their place was nearby and the three of us men would have to decide right now who was willing to wait for slippery seconds because otherwise there were apt to be arguments at just the wrong moment.

"Don't worry about him," Shem said, "he's got a willing bride back in the tent."

"Unless she's been carried off by now," Japheth said with a snort of a laugh and a clap on his brother's back.

But no one else laughed. "Carried off," one of the women said. The phrase must have broken through to something in her past, some nightmare from their lawless period in the wilderness. I saw that she was older than I, more battered by experience. There was fear in her eyes and it flashed to me. *Carried off? My Sapphira?*

At the same instant I saw or thought I saw Shem slap his brother across the mouth, the motion of a man silencing an unruly dog. I backed off from them both and they reached out to restrain me, to keep me with them. There was something more determined in their gesture than the love of companionship. It made no sense; I felt only a wild alarm. I wrenched myself from them, turned and ran, knocking my way out of that circle of celebrants, striking a path before me. I didn't even pause to apologize.

XXXV

ANIMALS

THREE young men blocked my way, grinning, darting first to the right and then left as I tried to pass. Others laughed, joined the game. I had to charge them, a bull through reeds. They stopped laughing and fell back.

I was an affront to everyone. While the crowd had happily rid itself of time and purpose, here was someone who was in a great hurry and knew where he was going. Virtues like these had become vices and I, the transgressor, fair game.

An older woman caught me by the arm, swinging me to a stop, holding me close, grinning, reeking of garlic and fermented honey, asking me whether I was always this fast, telling me how she could teach me to take my time, to take my pleasure right there. I hardly listened, struggling to escape, her words not making sense but the tone and the leer clear enough. I had to box her on the ear to get free. I heard her howl of protest behind me. I was being pursued by a pack of her male friends. I'd sullied her honor, they shouted; I'd insulted her good name. But they were hardly in shape for the race. Last I saw, they were doubled up with laughter in the roadway, paralyzed by their parody of outraged manhood.

I should never have looked back. A foot extended from nowhere and I flew into a fruit cart, produce flying, crowds howling like hyenas. I looked up and saw the juggler, face lit by the sacrificial fires. Cool and steady, he moved as if to help me, then flipped me when I least expected it. The crowd roared its delight, but he did not even smile, content in his mastery. Once again I tried to rise and again I was tossed in a most unexpected way, landing upside down in mashed fruit. I almost despaired of escaping when I saw him turn and walk away with a shrug. He'd grown tired of me; on to other tricks.

Free at last, I left the crowds, left the firelight, found my way back to the tent in which I had been married. A great silence here, the place deserted except for a sleeping beggar and an old dog. I crossed to the family tent. All but one of the torches was out.

There in the gloom was my father. His face, at least. The beard, the heavy brows over closed eyes, the weathered skin. Oh it was our father, all right.

But the rest of him was a stranger: a great, heavy, muscular, naked body. A body I had never seen.

Yes, the face was still sacred in my eyes. Even with all the resentments, even with the hostilities, the jealousies, I looked on that as holy. I tried to fix my eyes on that priestly face, the patriarchal beard, but my gaze shifted of its own volition, down across a foreign, fish-white expanse—the massive chest, rounded belly, down to the limp instrument of my creation. Above the neck, *our father*, leader, patriarch; below, *my* father in the flesh, producer of hot seed, the impregnator, the bull himself. Was it possible that the holy spirit and the gonads were in fact part of the same creature? If so, nothing was made of it in Sabbath School.

The notion washed over me like a new flood, leaving me gasping for air. And with it, another wave: The bull in the forest is not satisfied with his own mate. He is forever on the prowl.

Something in me cried out at this, a kind of whimper. No, the sound was outside my head. It came from a pile of pallets and pillows. It came from another form. It came from a woman. From my Sapphira! Or the one who was once my Sapphira.

Half dressed, half exposed, she had raised her head just enough to see me. There was no hope in that face, no appeal for understanding. Frozen in despair—hers and mine too.

Locked. Mind and muscles straining but unable to move. Unable to speak.

I heard muffled hoofbeats out in the larger tent. The flap flew open and there were my two brothers, panting.

And did they look at my disrobed father? Of course they looked. At him and my Sapphira as well. Took it all in. Never mind reports to the contrary. How else would they have grasped the situation? This was no common occurrence.

It was Shem who spoke, Shem the inheritor of the line. "All of you listen," he said. "It was the bridegroom who did this. Took his pleasure early. No one is to tell a different story. Is that clear?"

"*Story!*" I said. "Is that all you care about? That's not what happened."

"It's what happened because we say so."

"Look what he's done!"

"It's not up to us to judge our father."

"Who then?"

"For your own good—it happened the way I say."

Then, having taken care of the record, he turned to the sleeping man. He took Japheth's robe and the two of them went forward to cover their sleeping father. Yes, at this stage their faces were turned aside. In respect? Perhaps. Or was it more the way we avert our eyes from one struck down in a sudden and bloody accident?

The old beast slept like a baby. Not even bad dreams. I tried to look at Sapphira, to say something, but I couldn't bring myself to touch her—not even with a glance. We'd all been corrupted by this—beyond redemption.

Shem, his back to me, arranging the robe over his father, bent in a way which revealed the dagger which he always kept at his waist. Without plan I jumped forward and wrenched it from its sheath.

Both brothers whirled and then froze. Sapphira gave a cry. I held the weapon, held them at attention.

"Wait," Japheth said, his voice high. "We didn't—" I gestured toward him and the glimmer of the blade stopped him in mid-sentence.

"Drop it," Shem said, but there was no authority left in his voice. I raised the blade, swung it down, plunged it into a pillow. Then again and again. Feathers flew. Another pillow. The air was filled. Pallets, couch covers, table cloths. All in shreds. Then the tent itself—fabric stabbed, sliced open, feathers and streamers wafting up. Blindly I cut tent lines and heaved myself against the central pole. Down it came. We were smothered in a sea of fabric. Cutting my way to the surface I saw forms rising and falling in the darkness, heard muffled cries like those of drowning swimmers. Breaking free, I turned and ran for high ground.

XXXVI

IN OR OUT?

Away. That's the only possible direction. Just out of there and away. Into the night and up the rough terrain away from lights and the sounds of people, toward silence, toward blackness.

Blot out that woman, that man, the whole tribe. They have no right to survive. Wipe the slate clean, leave the page blank. Escape and head for the blackness.

Stony trail; perhaps no trail. Feet stinging with cuts, knees bleeding from falls. Stomach in bad shape. Just keep going toward silence, toward blackness.

No preparation for this. No time. No need. No heavy cloak, no blanket, no flint for fire. Mind set on getting out, getting away without words with anyone, without seeing a soul, moving toward silence and blackness.

Wild animals, perhaps. Beasts saved from drowning for no good reason and now free. Lions, leopards—rip, tear, a flash of red and pain and then nothing but silence and blackness.

Fear of death? Not a flicker. It will be as peaceful as the void before birth. No violence back then. No betrayal. Not as much as a thorn's prick of pain. Not a whisper of jealousy. In the beginning—the very beginning—there was perfect peace. From the moment of creation, agony began. Effort began. The dark cloud of futility was born. From that point, we drag through each pointless day. All the other fears pale before the fear of more sunrises, more days, more living, more effort. Dragging oneself like a broken insect through the length of days until released.

On and on, step by step through the night for no good reason. Too dark and too tired to know why. No words to make sense of it. Pictures float before me but are flushed out as quickly as possible, too much to stand. Keep heading for that pit of tar, that final silence and blackness.

Some boulders here, imperfect protection against the wind. Legs go limp with fatigue. I settle only because I cannot go on. I am somewhere up that mountain—not the top but far from sound or sight of the settlement. Eyes try to close, falling shut, but blink open again, more frightened of the inner scene than the one about me. Not the time for thought, but nothing else to fill the mind and keep the pictures from taking shape.

I am waiting in darkness. Waiting for what? Waiting for light. But I want no light. When it is light I will wait for the darkness again.

Back before the upheaval the priests from time to time wiped out a day to set the calendar in line with the heavens. Please make the day on which I was born one of these!

Did I say that?

Yes, wipe out the day I was born. Obliterate the night I was conceived. Scrub it clean. Leave no trace. Turn it to total darkness. Let no one look for it. Remove it from the tapestry of days and nights. Not a starlit night but total black. Dreamless. Nothingness. Void.

And so it was that I touched bottom. Were I unhesitantly pious I would look back and give praise to the Yahweh for the fact that He had not given me courage. Surely I would have taken three lives that night—the two transgressors and my own. He saved me from that. But if He cared for details, why hadn't He provided me with at least some of the comforts offered to wandering prophets? Those privileged men have a way of find-

ing caves. Dry caves. Usually with a view of the valley below. Occasionally with a supply of manna. None of that came my way.

No cave. No grand view. I was not nurtured by a lioness. No spring gushed forth to assuage my thirst. No throaty voice rolled down from on high, no message for mankind. That's what comes of asking the wrong questions in Sabbath School.

Light did appear at last but it was without warmth. It brought no great insight. Indeed, the wine had shrunk the tubes of my mind so that the simplest thought threatened to break through the front of my skull. I was in no condition for revelation.

No real shelter up there. Just those gray boulders as protection against a world not to be trusted ever again. Worst of all, I didn't even seem to be dying. I studied the pattern of blood on my knees. It had stopped flowing, had clotted. Little deltas of rich brown remained like fertile valleys after a flood.

I was safe as long as I could exist alone like this. Just beyond those boulders there were flickering images of men and beasts, indistinguishable, scuttling creatures to be kept at bay. Sometimes I could hear voices, grunts, dry coughing, whispering, but as long as the drone in my head continued, the outsiders would not intrude.

When the light faded, so did my consciousness. I passed from one day to the next without more than a whisper of dark thoughts, a flicker of memory.

I was into the third or fourth day. Time had moved and stopped, moved and stopped like a grazing animal. My body passed beyond complaint. My mind remained like that of a simpleton, too dazed to touch the past or fear the future.

I was not surprised to see a hooded figure appear over the edge of the rock. Surely visions were in order. It ducked down, popped up again, then disappeared. Later—hours or perhaps only a moment, it returned. It took the form of Japheth, but of course it was only a spirit, a shadow in my mind. Still, it was good to see him.

He brought what appeared to be pears, bread, a slab of cheese, and a small cask of wine. I knew they would disappear if I touched them, but this did not trouble me. I had no need of such things.

He squatted there, gestured to the gifts of food, smiled and gestured again as if I were from some foreign tribe and did not speak his tongue. Which was, of course, the case.

"It's all over now," he said at last. "The tents are put away. Everyone back at work. It's all behind us now."

He spoke softly. Did he think I was ill? And what was it that had drifted behind? If life itself were "all over now," then peace and darkness were not far off.

"What's all behind us now?" My voice sounded strange, from another body.

"All that. Here, have some cheese."

"All what?"

"With Father. Anyway, nothing happened. Look, no one knows anything about it. The townspeople don't even know you're up here. They've been told you're sick. There's those who say you've exhausted yourself on your wedding night. So nothing's happened. You can come back and everything will be the same."

"As what?"

"As what? As . . . Well, as it was."

"I thought that's what you meant."

Poor Japheth ran out of words. He sat there cross-legged in the dirt, his great paunch hidden in robes, staring at the ground. Without looking, he broke off a hunk of bread, added some cheese and began munching in a slow, bovine manner.

"You're making too much of it," he said at last, taking a pear with his other hand. "It's all up to us whether to take a thing seriously or not. I mean, if it's not real pain or hunger, we *decide* whether to take a thing seriously. All you have to do is to *decide* not to take this seriously."

He looked at me, smiling at the wonder of his logic. And should I have smiled too? The muscles of my face had withered. I watched him as he washed down a mouthful with wine.

"I could decide not to take myself seriously?" I asked.

He shrugged and took more bread with cheese. "Until you got hungry. Then you'd decide to take your stomach seriously. Say, what *have* you been eating up here?"

I had almost decided that this was not a spirit, that this was my true brother. Surely no shadow would take such good care of its stomach.

The moment I accepted him as real, the events of my wedding night came flooding back, also real. I closed my eyes against the weight of it all, but the faces I saw there were not ones I wanted to see.

When I opened them again, I caught Japheth's shrug, his lifting of the keg to his mouth, liquid spilling from the bunghole, cascading down both sides of his mouth. Then he set it down before me and belched.

"On your empty stomach," he said, wiping his face, "you wouldn't want too much of that anyway."

I nodded. He heaved himself to a kneeling position and awkwardly seized me by both shoulders, pressing his face to mine, left side and right. He smelled of sour grape and ripe cheese but the very familiarity of it brought tears brimming to my eyes. "Don't worry," he said.

He staggered off. His uneven course suggested that he would have a long time of it down the trails.

I was wondering what it would be like to remain on the surface of things for an entire lifetime when a second form appeared. My father? Here? No, it was a spirit resembling Shem. It must have been waiting for my brother to leave.

"Never mind him," the spirit said. "I told him not to come, but he stole up here before me. I've got some serious things to say to you."

"Serious?" Had Japheth and I been joking?

"For one thing, this is a dark day for the family, thanks to you."

"The family?"

"I don't suppose you thought of that. If anyone saw you, you'd be the laughingstock of the town."

"You're not laughing."

"Of course I'm not. Look at you!"

Not easy to do, me with no mirror, no knife blade for reflection.

"What's wrong?" I asked.

"Wrong? You look like one of the cursed, not like one of the chosen. You look as if you were washed up here, one of the damned."

"That's the way I feel."

"Your choice."

This again. Had they met on the trail and agreed to say the same? No, Shem would be off on a different route. His own.

"What choice?" I asked. "The damage has been done."

"If you think of it that way."

"But it did happen. There's no way to undo what they did."

"It happened whatever way we say it happened. All you have to do is support the story they now believe. They say in the marketplace that the groom was over-zealous, over-lusty, and made himself ill. And the bride's worn out. You're a hero for the men. And a beast for the women. The women shake their heads and cluck. They can picture the whole affair."

"Where did they get that story?"

"It was worded about. Look, Ham, that's the story they be-lieve because they *want* to believe it. After all, we're the elect. People expect us to set standards. You want to undermine their faith?"

I was undermining *their* faith? I tried to think like Shem, to share his values. He did have them. But they were cold as blocks of stone. I tried to put them together the way he did but my mind just wasn't up to it.

I made one last effort to get at the heart of it, to make him understand.

"All my life," I said slowly as if each word might drag me under, "I had a father. Now I have none. He is no more. And for a while I had a bride. Now I have none. Everything has been taken away. Everything. There's nothing left for me."

"They haven't been taken away. You've abandoned them."

"Me? How?"

"By coming up here. Look, if you really wanted them you'd support the story we've . . . The story which is widely held—that the groom and bride were excessive in their joy."

"Joy? How can you even use the word?"

He drew himself up, clenching his fists in exasperation. For a moment I had the impression that he would strike me with his heel. But instead, he shrugged. He'd decided the serpent had no fangs.

"In that case, stay. The spirit's gone out of you. No sense in sustaining the body. Not much left of that either. Don't worry, you'll be remembered for your passion. So go ahead, renounce God and die."

He was off in a fury. Odd that *he* should have the fury.

I lay down and was washed over with sleep. All those words and nothing had changed. I expected no other visitors. It was a jolt, therefore, to open my eyes the next midmorning and see a large form sitting next to me. A woman. Waiting for me to wake. I squinted to focus my eyes, but the sun was behind her.

"About time you woke up," she said, "Lie still like that and the vultures will land. Not that you'd give them much of a meal."

I'd heard that voice before. Kindly derisive. Had I been her student?

"Hephzibah!" Astonishing to see her up there, up out of the kitchens. The real Hephzibah or a spirit? I reached out for her but she simply stared at me, shaking her head.

"What are you?" she said. "There's no animal on earth that would stay up here dying of hunger. He'd be down where the food is. Food and his mate. No animal as stupid as you."

Mate? Wife? Sapphira. I'd just been explaining to someone that I'd lost her. My father . . . How could I explain things like that to a woman?

"You don't know," I whispered, more of a raven's croak.

"Don't know? Of course I know. She was taken by your father. I know that. Taken just like he tried to take your brothers' wives."

"My brothers . . . ?"

"They didn't tell you? I'm not surprised."

"Tell me what?"

"How the old man—*the goat* we in the kitchen call him—wants one more son. Your mother's past the age. And she'd never put up with a second wife. Not her. So he goes to each of your brothers and demands to take on the wife for a week, tells them the child will be theirs to raise, will be named Canaan, will be blessed. All of that. But it will be his seed. His holy seed! Men! Always jealous of the Creator. Your father more than any. Imagine, him at 600!"

"And they refused?"

"Not for the sake of the wives. You can count on that. They refused because they couldn't stand the notion of another man doing their job. A thundering storm over that. Shouting and bellowing. Everyone in the kitchen heard it even if you didn't. So that's when he told you to marry Sapphira. Your two brothers out of favor. Of course they did their best to make up to him. Kept you busy that night, didn't they? Some brothers! Let the old cuckoo lay his egg in *your* nest. Kept their own clean—in a manner of speaking. And it worked. Not so much as a squawk from you."

It was true: I couldn't utter a squawk. I answered her only

with the twist of my face, the feeble effort to rise. She took no pity; continued to thrash me with words.

"You thought you could stay clear of it all did you? Thought you'd stay pure up here. Make them feel sorry for you and repent? Thought things would right themselves? Well, look what's come of it—your bones sticking out, skin raw, eyes bulging. You stink like a dying ass. You know what'll happen when your father sees the vultures swoop down on your remains? He'll breath easy. That's what. You're the only one that might tell the story. The other two will keep quiet. When your bones are stripped by the birds and polished by the ants, he'll rewrite the story, he will. Noah and his *two* sons. Oh yes, they'll include the fat one. Better a drunkard than a talker. The story will be rewritten, that tapestry restitched, and no one will remember the slave girl. If there's a child and he's a boy he'll be Canaan and he'll be known as Shem's child. But no Ham. Like he was never born."

Erased? Forgotten? What right had they? I'd done nothing. No, that was a part of it—doing nothing. Doing nothing was making it easier for them. Doing nothing was helping them rewrite the story with my name gone, Sapphira gone, vanished.

"I should kill them both," I said.

"Ha! There's a fine solution. He'd probably get you first. And if he didn't, Shem would get you in return. More blood than at pig-slaughtering time. Wipe out the family. Might as well have drowned—the whole pack of you."

"I can't ever go back to her."

"Why not? What could she have done against that goat of a man? What have *you* done?"

"She may even be carrying his child."

"You give him a lot of credit. Not even your cock-sure father can be that certain. Besides, if you act like a husband within the week, who could say you weren't the father?"

"I couldn't live there. All that plotting and hatred. But if I take her away, he'll curse me and our child."

"Curses, curses—members of your clan are forever being cursed. Cursed for eating the wrong fruit, cursed for losing your temper, cursed for talking back. What's in a curse anyhow? So

it smarts a little. Did you ever see someone curl up and die from
a curse? Not even Cain."

"Is it true about Cain? About us coming from Cain?"

She raised both hands in exasperation. "You've got a woman
down there in trouble and you're asking me questions about
Cain? You know how long he's been dead?"

"But did we? Or is the line through Seth?"

"You want an answer? Both. You've been told both, right?
Well, believe both. You're cursed and blessed at the same time.
Don't ask me to make sense of it. Just believe it. That's the
way it is. And right now you've got a decision to make. Are
you going to start putting your life together or turn it over to
vultures? Looks to me like you haven't got much time."

I looked up at her, that great dispenser of foods, of nourish-
ment, and recalled the kitchens—the smell of bread baking, of
soup simmering. All that warmth. What was I doing up here?

I looked up and saw in Hephzibah an image of my mother
looming larger than in real life, and now she seemed to become
Sapphira. We reached out for each other, this woman-figure and
I, two halves drawing together.

All that survival work—the hewing of wood, the fitting of
planks, the gathering of animals, the rejection of neighbors and
friends—all that had been done by men of action. Harsh work
it was. Cold decisions. A cold set of values. The mortar of tribes
and new nations. Of kingdoms. The stuff we read about in
history.

Now once again I was being asked "In or out?"—this time by
a woman. There were differences. For one thing, the vessel was
larger. Life itself. And for another, the tone was warmer. Was
this what Methuselah had meant by "warm values"? In any
case, this woman was telling me that, yes, *in* is better than *out*,
dry is better than *wet*, *upright* is better than *crouched*, and even
crouching is better than being laid out.

But what of the others? I knew I could never forget them—
me the sweeper of decks. How much easier it would be if I too
could keep the windows barred, the doors locked, my gaze
averted, pretending that no one out there is drowning. But my
eyes even shut would retain their image for a lifetime. I would
be their witness.

XXXVI In or Out?

Would we ever build an Ark with room enough for everyone? Not easy, but that was surely the goal. No doubt there were more floods to come.

But before I could do anything about that, there was the matter of keeping myself afloat. Myself and Sapphira. Had I already lingered too long? The fear that I had lost her through my own inaction gave me the needed jolt of strength.

XXXVII

THE NEXT VOYAGE

T H E last I saw of the Ark, the settlement, the fertile valley was from the back of a covered oxcart. It was a hot, muggy day, threatening rain. The overcast was luminescent, the scene strangely luxuriant, ripe with growth.

It is not easy to leave a well-planted garden. But the harvest had been poisoned for us and we had no choice. In the tradition of dissidents we'd been royally cursed and sent to a rocky waste-land beyond the mountains.

I sympathized with Adam. Cain too. Both of them baffled by the turn of events. What warnings had any of us that our crimes were so heinous? But perhaps we would have moved without being shown the way. I was, after all, the third son.

I had my Sapphira—at least in body. She would not speak, would not look at me, lying on the far side of the cart on top of grain sacks and supplies, sheltered, as I was, from the elements by a curved roof of hides. She was alive and with me, but her spirit was not.

I had a following of sorts in that strange caravan. Hephzibah, for one. Several of the kitchen staff. A few fieldworkers and their wives, adventurers. A number of malcontents with petty grievances against my father. What did they know about grievances? Still, I needed workers.

Five oxen, as I remember it; two camels, consumptive from long confinement; two mules; two donkeys. Those and a supply of grain, seed, and garden implements. My mother, with tears but with no protest, had given us linen and coarse blankets. And I had the lamp Jabal left me, the light which recalled my apprenticeship with him, my introduction to a life apart.

The family's contribution was larger than I had expected due to the general sense of embarrassment. The old man's curse had been excessive.

Never mind whether he was drunk or sober that evening when I came down from the mountain. Never mind whether he was speaking as Patriarch, preserving the clan, protecting the reputation of his lineage and himself, or reacting to baser emotions. Never mind whether he did or did not have tears in his eyes as he stood there in the market square saying those things about me and my descendants, yea even unto the third generation, turning me to rage, causing me to shake my fist. The fact is that he said them. In public. On record.

It is action, not motive, that counts. It is action, not motive, that nudges history this way and that. It was my return which set him off; it was his raised arms and flood of words that placed me in an oxcart, rocking as if on the high seas once again.

I was the black son that day, all right. Tarred with a father's misplaced rage. I heard my mother had plunged herself into mourning—but who was to say whether it was for my leaving or for what my father had done to himself?

I had no way of knowing what went on in the mind of my battered bride. I knew only that she was speechless. There had been a time when I thought she had been taken from me, that she no longer existed. Perhaps she had come to think the same of herself.

As for me, I was rendered dumb with uncertainty. Like lightning which hangs in the clouds, I hovered, dark and brooding.

Should I have lashed back at him as he cursed me? After all, he had stolen my bride just to counter his horror of growing old; he'd laid his baser self bare before us all. And now he was withdrawing my birthright to protect his reputation.

I had not flung these charges at him. Probably just as well. Aside from the fact that he would have killed me, no one would have listened to my accusations. After all, everyone in that town had a vested interest in keeping their leader unsullied. They had been through hard times, remember. They were ready for reconstruction. They wanted no scandal, no unnecessary rocking of the boat. The ejection of an erratic, younger son was enough drama for that season.

Would it have helped if I had known that every line of his curse would be borne out? Would it have buoyed me up to know that the crushing weight of those dire predictions would be balanced by a disproportion of blessings? I would not have believed it then.

Yes, Canaan was our first born. I have entered him in the record as the last born merely to reassert my paternity. I wasn't the first to tidy up the record by juggling lineage.

My Canaan was indeed cursed by various corruptions—visible and invisible—as are all those who exercise power. He and his brothers, founders of cities, drew far more from my father than from me or Methuselah. They were doers, not much for reflection. And it was true that Canaan was a "servant of servants," the son of a slave girl and a man who once worked in the kitchens to win her trust, her love.

And the Yahweh certainly did "enlarge" Japheth just as He was requested to in my father's famous diatribe. Lord what an enlargement!

But to Canaan, the curse was faded stuff. The grumblings of an older generation. He devised new traditions, new laws; his eyes were set on the future. He and his brothers, Cush, Mizraim, and Put, built some dazzling cities. Oh I know what they say about Sodom, and there are some who have harsh words for Gomorrah and my adopted home, Babylon, but these cities are impressive. They have energy. They will be remembered.

That curse on Canaan turned out to be more of a prod than a burden. Like the one laid on Adam. But knowing that at the time would not have helped my mood. I was not concerned with history. Not then. All that mattered right then was the storm building within me, dark and charged. In my self-centered mood it never occured to me that a similar climate was building within my silent bride.

Those wooden wheels creaked and groaned, the cart rocked, the air grew heavy with moisture. It was worse than on the Ark. Time gnawed at us until we were raw.

"I won't go!" Her voice as a clap of thunder. She sat up and so did I.

"You'll stay with me."

"I feel filthy," she said. "And you're disgusting."

"The marriage—"

She interrupted with a shriek of laughter. A witch's sound. "The *what?*"

"The ceremony. You believed in it."

"Then. *Then.* Before the rest of it." She started scrambling to get out of the cart, shouting something about there being nothing left. Or nothing left of her. Or of me. I had hold of her ankle and she tried to bite me. I was disgusting, she was telling me. All men were pigs, apes, rutting goats. Outside, the rain let go and was beating on our frail cover.

She was half outside the cart and I yanked her back in, robes ripping in the process, and she suddenly shifted tactics, flung herself on me, pressing my back to sacks of grain, speaking to me in snarls.

"The lot of you," she said. "Acting so great. But always in heat. All the same. You think in the dark I could tell your prick from Shem's, your hand from Athaliah's, your panting from your father's? You think there was any difference between one deck and the other on that ship? A bunch of jibbering, grunting, farting, howling animals you are."

"You too. You just as much as anyone. In heat day and night." I wrenched myself from under her. "A bitch in heat."

A long silence. We lay on our sides, eye to eye, chest to breasts, groin to groin, breathing heavily. "And," I said at last, "wondrous."

"Can't be both."

"Why not?"

"Both?"

"At the same time."

Still on our sides, we held each other and the cart continued to rock us. Rage against each other transformed itself into desire as if two forms of the same passion. The motion which moments ago had been an irritant now roused us and we drew together, tears of astonishment in our eyes.

Gently, very gently—like handling the injured—we entered each other, still on our sides, and softly slid into a world with its own rhythm. We undulated in perfect equality. The cart rocked us; we rocked the cart. The tempo rose and with it we rose up from those sacks, levitating without losing the beat, just an arm's length at first, tentatively, not sure of our ability. Then higher, the two of us still joined, rising up through the roof of skins, up through the cool of the rain, up through deck after deck, up above the gray of clouds, through purple mists, into the blue firmament with gold above us, up where it never rains, sun hot on our skin, simmering our blood, bringing it to a boil, building the pressure, exploding. . . .

Then drifting down, gentle as two dove feathers, cleansed, circling, spinning, landing at last on those sacks of grain. We peeled back from each other, still joined below the waist like a single sapling half split.

We laughed for the first time since before . . . since before the bad times. We laughed, naked and smelling like any two animals after the act, lying there on those same dusty grain sacks, back in the same old cart, yet knowing that somehow we had transformed everything.

Disengaging ourselves, we looked out. The storm had almost passed. A light misting persisted as the sun reappeared.

And there, incredibly, an enormous rainbow. Every color the world has known, every shade the eye can behold. It rose from behind the hill we had rounded, from the hidden Ark, and the settlement we had left. The arch passed directly over us, descending far ahead, beyond the horizon, warming the spot where we would begin again.

It led us from old to new pastures, it was not ours alone. Years later I saw it lead my sons and daughters out—each cursed and blessed in various proportions, each spending a term at sea, most but not all finding solid ground, a place to build and grow. Would that everyone could survive the storms, share that bow, that vision of harmony and grace. It is the covenant with life.

Stephen Minot

Stephen Minot is the author of two previous novels, *Chill of Dusk* and *Ghost Images*. His short stories have appeared in the *Atlantic, Harper's, Playboy, The North American Review, The Sewanee Review, Kenyon Review* and others. A collection of them is available under the title of *Crossings*. He and his wife live in Connecticut and Maine.